AF250221

The Immeasurable Corpse of Nature

Christopher Slatsky

Trade Paperback

Cover art by Vergvoktre

Illustrations by Käthe Kollwitz

Cover and book design by Anna Trueman

Edited by Jon Padgett

Grimscribe Press, New Orleans 70118

© 2020 Grimscribe Press

Printed in the United States of America

1st Edition

vastarien-journal.com

CONTENTS

It is not easy to describe the propulsive, unsettling dread stirred up by Christopher Slatsky's second book, *The Immeasurable Corpse of Nature*, but it is easy to describe what it isn't. It is not hewn from what is trendy. It just does not feel contrived, does not impart the forgettable parting shot of having sequestered the weird horror in a ramshackle state of in-your-face inevitability. An elusive quality makes slippery—and dreamy—the stories' grasp of the robust, nihilistic dark. So, whenever we negotiate their meanings on the page, we come away suffused with the memory and sense of ensnarement, an ensnarement we are made to believe is *there*—but, in fact, isn't.

The dark lore of the Capiznon in the Western Visayas region of the Philippines talks of the *amalanhig*, a risen member of the undead that is said to follow a person around, imitating what that person does and says. One variation of the amalanhig urban legend has it performing its duplication of a person's motions and utterances in reverse—timewise, to further emphasize its perversion. I don't exactly understand how this version of the myth works, but I take it to mean literally like this: if the person that the amalanhig is mimicking crosses the street at noon, then that person's amalanhig-tormentor would take the exact same path to cross that exact same street at midnight.

For those privileged with a decent purchase of the world's culture-spanning pantheon of supernatural horrors, the amalanhig's touted physical manifestation could seem downright boring, even resembling a basic B-movie monster. It is said to exude the sickly-sweet stench of rotting flesh. It also cannot bend its legs, though this does not prevent it from moving so fast that outrunning it is impossible. When doused with water, the amalanhig is said to turn into a heap of maggots, its vulnerable form. Many other mythical creatures present a far more frightening construction than the amalanhig.

But what truly sets it apart for me is this: the cruel, menacing machinery of torment that anchors the amalanhig myth represents one of the most unsettling iterations of dread because there is no defining purpose of its replication of human acts, which seems absolutely pointless, needless. There is, of course, an element of calculation behind its actions. Malign intelligence exists behind its instincts. Chaos might appear to be outfitted with a cold, perverted heart, but it is still structured from order. In the case of the amalanhig, its intent is perpetually tucked away from sight.

What does the amalanhig want from the person whose actions it is replicating when it is not even attempting to take over that person's body or that person's life? Is it hungry, but not in the same way that the Chinese *iiangshi* is hungry? Is its sadistic torture consistent with its aberrant psychology? Why does it do what it does? Nobody knows. It can be killed with water, but what is it trying to accomplish when it copies a person's actions?

Avenging nature spirits, for example, tend to do what they do to relieve the source of their perceived injustice, which makes their motivation understandable, less frightening—and, at least, one is still presented with the choice of whether or not to mess with them. Urban legends based on the depiction of the amalanhig as a vengeful creature are probably urged on by this desperate finding of a way to see, this trying to come to terms with the nagging unanswerable whys, which can't be extinguished by squashing the life out of the heap of maggots that an amalanhig ultimately becomes in the presence of water.

This fulfillment of the checklist of whys, even when couched in a ludicrously rudimentary manner, assists in an integration with primal order, a way out of the chaos. What used to be scary ceases in part to be scary once we are able to see through the whys. In Hideo Nakata's *Ring,* for example, when we finally learn that Sadako is just a stereotypical yūrei coming out of the television screen hell-bent on revenge, the whole horrific ordeal is no longer that terrifying. In the terrorizing fabric of chaos, we find a semblance of order. We find the wrinkle and know where to press the flat surface of the smoothing iron. We notice the snagged part of an otherwise neat line of running stitches that secure the hem; it can then be tightened at the end of the day. We expose the mortality of mythical monsters, the disgruntled forms and crude stand-ins for the generational anxieties of civilization, each time we try to read them through our lens of moral principle as well as the social conditions that create them. Except when we can't.

The Immeasurable Corpse of Nature proposes that we can't. We can only mediate and navigate what it terms as "illusion of purpose." We can also learn the language to enable mediation but not necessarily dictate the terms of our escape.

Christopher Slatsky's prodigious knowledge and diabolical imagination will have us reeling in an abandoned airfield where we follow through a shocking conclusion of what has become of a father searching for his abducted son. In "Engines of the Ocean," we become the character Cordelia breathing the brine-smelling air in the pulsing interior of her childhood house, where her trauma was conceived. We inhale with her the acrid reek of ghoulish nostalgia, the haze through which we collect the hideous bits and pieces of our blasted id in an attempt to reconstruct them into shapes we pretend to recognize.

Then, from this house of childhood nostalgia, we move to see part of what dwells inside a pit in the woods in "The Carcass of the Lion," easily my contender for the most emotionally resonant story in this book. In that story, a terminal-disease-stricken character finds comfort in her backyard beekeeping colony where "[t]he bees must have brought something wrong back with them." Meanwhile, in "The World Is Waiting for the Sunrise," the séance of American Prohibition-era stock characters, slogging around with their anxieties written in a blisteringly compelling way, lulls the reader into a refreshing illusion of order and safety.

Taken together, the stories, as well as the one-act play and the academic essays, are vast, robust in their terrifying implications. This book pursues unlikely and complex lines of inquiries, paths where the

Anthropocene compulsively carves out spaces for its unacknowledged phantoms.

Slatsky specializes in the attentive, obsessive reinterpretation of places that evoke our shadowy despairs and fears, our degraded edges. The unused airfield. The rest stop. The basement study where a "frustrated engineer, relegated to a field service technician position for the city's water department," sketches plans for his "weird machines." The derelict lookout tower and its forested environs in "Palladium at Night," an extraordinary literary formation of visceral terror, as setting for the time-bending ramifications of the government's dabbling with dark esoteric practices. The ventriloquist's country house where there is a constant dissolution of what distinguishes dolls from their doll maker. The circus magician's house where enchantment is its own special curse. The psychotherapist's office where the harrowing Anthroparian Integration treatment commences to heal a patient's built-in seraphim—*seraphim*, not soul—from depression and self-mutilation. The newly discovered trapdoor to an attic in a house of irreparably broken people, an attic that had not existed before. The cluttered house of a man, who is valiantly resisting the symptoms of age-related cognitive decline, as staging area for encroachment by two people claiming to be the man's children and exhorting him to sign away his end-of-life decisions. The third floor of the Cal State Fullerton library, where astonishing truths about the Split-Mouth woman of Japanese lore are revealed.

Then finally, the sprawling compound where members of an antinatalist cult, The Ones Who Walk Away, performed their mass suicide. The compound in question is Omelas Farm in the title story "The Immeasurable Corpse of Nature." The reference to the iconic Ursula K. LeGuin short story is not coincidental, since The Ones Who Walk Away cult operates as a self-sustaining model-unit with utopian goals, with their utopia premised on reconciliation with nature. Something had been discovered buried under the scarecrows in Omelas Farm, something unexpected, difficult to unread, and may even have something to do with one of the vegetable-headed scarecrows erupting a lateral incisor, with intact connective tissues, in its hollowed-out, vegetable-mouth.

In *The Immeasurable Corpse of Nature*, dark chaos presents itself with a sharp serrated edge. The saw pattern becomes evident each time it cuts through something. We end up inferring cues from the wounded artifact. As for those cues—it is easy to misread them.

Kristine Ong Muslim
Maguindanao, Philippines
December, 2019

Looking at
    all of them
    death, the children
    patients in waiting-rooms
    famine
    the street
    the corpse with the baby
    floating, on the dark river

—*"Käthe Kollwitz", Muriel Rukeyser*

PHANTOM AIRFIELDS

Randall still saw Jacob's face in crowds.

He sat alone in his truck's cab, absorbing vestiges of warmth seeping from the vents. He found a purity in this ritual, parking near the airfield, basking in a sorrow so profound it surpassed suicidal thoughts, circling back to attain something spiritual. Life doesn't just pass from living to non-living; there were quiet moments in between, little snatches of sleep and dream and hope along the way. Such thoughts helped him get through each day.

A fist-sized hole had rusted through the floor on the passenger side. The snow beneath the truck was gray. Randall looked out his windshield at the expanse of white ground, still pristine, icy veneer yet to be damaged by any living thing. A tall fence stretched across the field, preventing the curious from trespassing onto the abandoned Sodder Airfield.

This geography drew him in, spoke in a language that refused to be ignored. Here the ground kept luring him back, seducing him to walk among the broken buildings. There were no longer any signs of the old runway—in spring, weeds grew over any trace of what this place had once been used for; in winter, snow obscured any remaining secrets. Randall breathed mist onto the windshield, ran a finger across it.

He watched a mangy dog dart from the trailer park on the other side of the street and into the woods. The animal held a filthy diaper clamped between its jaws. The sight of the stray's muzzle slathered with excrement made Randall think of metal implants in abductee's mouths, of devices surgically imposed to intimidate, to conduct biotelemetric analyses.

The rest area was just a mile from here.

He'd stopped returning the detective's phone calls. Cooperating with the investigation meant accepting their interpretation of events. He was done sifting through photos of children's corpses. Done with everything.

He pressed his palms against his face, pads pushing against eyes, nostrils filled with the odor of gas station pink soap and grilled onions from the burger he'd eaten late last night. When he lowered his hands, the dog was gone. He remembered the day it happened. Remembered the panic and mounting grief. Running across the rest stop parking lot into the bathrooms, bellowing *little astronaut!* his voice echoing between the empty stalls, the affectionate nickname perverse in his mouth.

Hands pressed against temples, running around the rest area picnic tables screaming *stop hiding dammit, stop hiding dammit!* Blaming Jacob for wandering away. Blaming Sarah for not watching their child closely enough. Blaming himself.

His wife's voice escalating, their son's name mangled by her screams.

Stop hiding dammit!

All he saw was their car in the parking space, no other vehicles, the open road beyond empty save for a glorious silver light that filled Randall's body with a trembling wonder at the majesty of a moment so potent it ruined him.

It seemed as if it had happened yesterday. He put his Styrofoam cup of coffee into the holder and stepped out of the truck.

A raven dipped its beak into a puddle of antifreeze fluid on the pockmarked blacktop that led to the trailer park. It shook its head. Feathers rippled like fur. Randall felt a pang of remorse. This creature meant no ill will, was only obeying its basic survival needs. But the poison would finish it off soon enough.

He slammed the door shut. The doomed bird flew away. The chill of the snow penetrated his boots. He sucked frosty air into a mouth sour with black coffee.

The trailer park was starting to wake up: chatter of right-wing AM radio talk shows, wheeze of an unidentified instrument played by clumsy hands. Probably a child's recorder, borrowed from school, presumably much to their parents' dismay. The sky was bright with a post-snowfall glow. Randall's ear lobes stung. White plumes of exhaust spiraled from worn car and truck mufflers as people began their daily commute.

He didn't need to worry about going to work; the final wave of layoffs at the mortgage company saw to that. His ineffectual boss had crumbled under pressure from corporate and now a dozen employees were desperately seeking new ways to supplement their income. Nothing but time these days.

He followed a familiar path towards Sodder Airfield. Scuffed his feet through gray slush, slid down an embankment beneath a closed bridge. Concrete pylons prevented vehicles from passing over from either lane. He walked along a shallow stream. Clumps of gravelly ice on the surface made disconcerting sounds, rasping like teeth scraping against aluminum foil.

He ducked through a gap in the 12-foot high fence. Corroded wires snapped. Bureau of Land Management property, but Randall had yet to come across any security monitoring the land.

He passed over nearly a mile of level landscape before arriving at the abandoned airfield. Sodder Airfield had once managed P-40 operational overflow during WWII, but all that was left was an ILS antenna, the upper half having long fallen to the ground to sink into the soil, winter-yellow weeds covering any remaining metal. The low generator buildings had crumbled into empty squares decades ago. There was one wooden shell Randall thought may have once been a guard station. On the other side of a knee-high fence, beneath a mound of snow, a row of battered 50-gallon drums sat, the bottom of most having rusted away.

He paused to stare at the spaceman spray-painted against a slab of concrete leaning like a dislodged piece of ancient dolmen. No matter how many times he saw the graffiti, it filled him with an indefinable dread.

He studied it for the hundredth time. It reminded him of the Solway Spaceman. The puzzle of that photograph, the menacing figure looming behind a child—did they mean to abduct her or merely observe? It all promised a life far more exciting than what was available here. Of better worlds where mysteries were benign, and parents couldn't be destroyed in one brief moment.

The graffitied figure's helmet was a perfect circle, the artist utilizing cracks and pits in the concrete to add a decayed effect. The crooked jaw was sloppy, a spattered application that captured an otherworldly appearance. A hint of a human skull lurked behind the visor, teeth faintly visible.

Randall noticed a slight decline in the landscape, a subtle depression deepening further away. The ground had been flat every time he'd roamed previously, but now sloped into a shallow crater about the circumference of the water fountain in the center of town.

When had this occurred? Had the weight of the snow collapsed an underground bunker or storage area?

He pondered this new mystery for several hours before heading back to the truck.

"I don't think Chloe and I can stay in the house, Randall. I don't like coming home anymore." Sarah nestled their baby daughter securely under her arm, deftly twisted the cap tighter on a sippy cup. The diner was filling up fast. A movie must have just let out at the theater next door.

Randall saw Jacob's mannerisms in Sarah's gestures, in her black, tightly curled hair, the tapered shape of her hands. She was so much like Jacob in so many ways. He reached across the Formica table for his daughter.

"You need to stop going there," Sarah said.

"Where?" Randall paused, hands frozen in position to take Chloe.

"Don't play dumb. You know what I mean. The airfield."

Randall lowered his empty hands, picked up a glass of soda, held it tightly, the cool surface firm under his grip. All he had to do was let go and the glass would shatter on the diner's chipped linoleum floor. Or squeeze it as hard as he could until it fractured into slivers. Create one pristine simple moment.

"Wide open space. Helps me think."

"Isn't that what your therapist is for?" Sarah shifted their daughter to the crook of her other arm. Chloe began to wriggle.

Randall slid his glass away. "I can hold her, you know. You don't have to do everything."

Sarah looked up abruptly, surprised by his offer.

Chloe rejected the sippy cup. Her fussing became louder.

Sarah had kicked Randall out of their house four months ago. Days later, a terse text message confirmed she'd initiated divorce proceedings. Randall knew she needed time and distance. They'd never be the same again, but a respite might help. They'd done their best to remain cordial. Sarah had even agreed to meet him once a week, usually at their favorite greasy spoon, to spend time with his baby daughter.

Chloe was whining now. A piercing wail that all babies acquire to announce their distress, to force parents to drop what they're doing and come running because everything revolves around children. This is what's expected of them; nothing left to do but obey the commands of an infant, even if it meant your life was effectively over.

Randall took a sip from his soda. He could bite down and break the glass against his teeth, lacerate his gums, express his helplessness with howls and drooled blood foam, a stupid pointless tantrum of violence. Fantasizing about hurting himself was the only semblance of control he had these days.

Chloe was screaming. A shrill-voiced creature reminding Randall of his inability to protect his family. A terrible thought ran through his head—what if their daughter had devices implanted inside her, something that influenced her behavior? Something to control Chloe, and in turn her parents, manipulating them to react in ways they wouldn't normally react?

Keeping them from learning the truth about what happened to Jacob.

Randall tamped down an atavistic urge to break the glass over his child's skull. To shut her up so he could gather his thoughts, have a normal adult conversation with his soon-to-be ex-wife. A few moments of peace and tranquility. Stifle the acidic panic that filled his gut, spilled from pores like sharp vinegar.

One terrible moment. He loathed himself for even thinking of hurting his daughter.

Sarah bobbed Chloe in the air. Made cooing sounds to calm her down. A young couple at the booth next to them looked over, frowned in annoyance at this intrusion on their date night.

"Stop going to that airfield. There's nothing there. You disappear for days sometimes, and I can't get ahold of you. What if detective Curtis needs us to identify something?"

Randall heard a car alarm in the distance. He imagined himself bobbing in the air, through space so cold it snagged his skin like hooks. He could see the curve of the planet in the distance.

Sarah changed tack, "I can't go into Jacob's room anymore."

Her voice pulled Randall to attention. "Why's that?" His mouth felt dry despite the pool of sweet cola on his tongue.

"I thought I saw..." Sarah gave a weak smile, not trusting herself to explain what she may have encountered. Chloe made deep gulping sounds, gagging on her own phlegm and frustration.

"You saw Jacob?" Randall asked.

Sarah's eyes burned. She hesitated.

"What did you see?" Randall persisted.

"I don't know. It was, someone, someone in his room. I thought it was him at first. But that can't be." She lowered her head to look at the untouched mound of Eggs Benedict on her plate. Breakfast dinner had always been Jacob's favorite. She pushed a fork through the thin hollandaise sauce.

"A shadow, a car drove by and its headlights made it look like something silvery was moving in the bedroom. A silver light. Just a car."

She seemed to grow older in that moment. A filter of time applied over the lens of how Randall remembered his wife. He thought she'd grown more lovely as time progressed. The haunted were capable of depths of compassion most were not capable of expressing. Those who'd suffered tragedy were less likely to trivialize the tragic.

"Just a light, Randall."

Sarah touched the dry, coarse knuckle of his right thumb. She looked at him with a trace of resolution. She'd always care, though they'd never share lives again, their tremendous loss a chasm that kept them apart. Her eyes were bright. Pupils wide.

Randall couldn't stop thinking about broken glass and Chloe's head dangling limply. He heard himself before he knew what he was going to ask.

"You saw an astronaut in Jacob's room, didn't you?"

Sarah began to cry.

Randall returned to Sodder Airfield the next morning. The sun had just risen, soft-edged shadows and clumps of snow melting away under its glare. It was too early for people to start waking up. He liked these calm moments when he could look to the sun and it wouldn't harm his eyes.

He began walking towards the airfield.

Sarah left a voice message saying she and Chloe would be out of town at her sister's place, so Randall couldn't see his daughter until next weekend. He knew this may or may not be true; she'd prevented him from visiting before. He didn't care anymore.

His Survivors of Child Abduction support meetings offered sixty-minute increments of gray mouths opening and rarely closing, smacking teeth against tongues, against palates, forming words into sentences of self-help platitudes. They talked at great lengths about how Randall must never give up hope.

He couldn't argue the point. Hope helped snag a few hours of sleep before the sobbing woke him up. Hope meant that Jacob might actually be safe and sound, and the slim possibility this stubborn insistence wasn't a phantom in a distressed brain to ameliorate the shock of it all.

Little else had come of therapy save for a steady prescription of Paxil that made Randall feel as if his head was as empty as outer space.

He'd once confided to his therapist about his theory regarding Jacob's fate. But she'd countered with bizarre scenarios: a cabal of child abusers had tricked Randall with magician's props, deceived a grieving father's susceptible mind. She spoke of a conspiracy of kidnappers, of military technologies, sonic machines that scrambled minds, intravenously administered drugs to distort perceptions—all manner of trickery utilized to concoct artificial memories concerning stolen children. Pseudo-memories to protect him from accepting that his son had been led from a rest area bathroom to a stranger's vehicle.

Randall found her allegations far more outrageous than his own hypothesis. As time passed, however, nothing seemed real. The depths of grief assailing him at every turn held a false aspect. Mind controlling machines implanted by a conspiracy of pedophiles was just as incomprehensible as a child being whisked away by a stranger.

Tragedy was absurd in all its manifestations. Jacob hadn't wandered over to the vending machine near the bathrooms, fascinated by the soda can lighting up every time he pressed the button while his parents argued over whose turn it was to change Chloe's diaper, oblivious to their son's whereabouts. This could not be how lives were crippled.

The sky was enormous this morning, so clear and pale he could still see last night's stars. The airfield's crater was a dark oval from this distance. As he drew closer, a chartreuse glow caught his eye. He moved towards the source.

The glow was emanating from something on top of the snow in the center of the crater. He slid down the shallow embankment. There were no footprints, the snow was undisturbed. A translucent spaceman. An action figure, articulated better than those he'd played with as a kid. Glow-in-the-dark plastic casing, magnetic ball and joint limbs. Jacob had been obsessed with astronauts and rocket ships—he'd been playing with something like this when they'd parked at the rest stop. Randall put the toy into his jacket pocket.

It had to be Jacob's. No parent should ever have to be submerged beneath the vast reach of hopelessness.

As Randall began the trek back to his truck, he saw a silvery orb float behind one of the concrete structures. He explored the area but found nothing unusual. He looked up into the sky, then around the rubble to see if a Mylar balloon had been caught or deflated at ground level.

He didn't find anything.

❇

Randall wandered the house like a phantom the first few days after Jacob disappeared, not sure how to proceed with the day-to-day routines. Lifting a toothbrush to his mouth had become an effort. He'd quit shaving, neglected to brush his hair. Even today, eight months on, he still felt like a ghost buffeted about by gentle gusts, pushed through darkness from room to room on gusts his weak soul was unable to resist.

Tonight, he crawled through the unlocked window of Sarah's house. The divorce proceedings forbade him from coming onto the property—this was no longer his home, but Chloe and Sarah were still at her sister's place and Randall couldn't resist. The lure to return to his old home was second only to the call of the airfield.

He stepped into Jacob's bedroom. Sarah had kept the room exactly as it was the day he was taken. Bed perfectly made, toys in their place. Even the dirty clothes hamper remained untouched.

He reverentially touched the dresser, the bed, bookshelves. Opened the closet. Rows of shirts, never to be worn ever again. He ran his fingers across the fabric, luxuriating in the memory of his son—the smells, the tactile warmth of the cloth. He was touching the garb of someone holy and they were going to step out of the closet any moment now, lay a hand on his brow, tell him everything was going to be alright.

There was a piety in forcing himself to experience this heartache again and again. Scrolling through baby photos on the computer. Hearing his son's laughter in videos of their trip to Yellowstone Park. Breakfast dinners. He was a pilgrim seeking penance, the thought of his son's absence a whip across his skin. He wanted to die.

If only they hadn't let him out of their sight. If only they hadn't dropped their guard to allow the monstrous to intrude.

Randall had a recurring dream shortly after Jacob's abduction. In the vision, an astronaut opened his bedroom door, peeked in with its bulbous shiny head moving ever so slightly as it watched him. It shut the door.

Then opened it again.

Closed.

Opened.

The helmet glistened like wet skin. Its smooth gray face reflected a cartoon frog nightlight near the bed, like star shine on the surface of a placid lake. The head jiggled as if it was going to fall off. The spaceman floated into the bedroom.

It was the size of a child.

The intruder tilted its head from side to side, surveying the room. The front of its helmet, where Randall assumed its eyes were located, turned to him.

The eyelid of its face slid open.

Randall wasn't sure if he remembered the dream accurately, or if he'd borrowed it from his son. His memories felt loaned, passed back and forth between those he loved, slightly distorted each time like a psychic game of telephone. He felt as if he were recalling an event that had occurred in some other time, on another path he'd neglected to follow.

He no longer remembered when or why he'd given his son the *little astronaut* nickname.

He allowed the memory of his dream to recede, like a tide pulling strange life back into its depths. He walked into the kitchen. Weeks after the tragedy, he'd been standing in front of the refrigerator, wondering whether to box away their son's art or leave it tacked to the door with magnets. He'd moved a magnet aside to expose Jacob's scrawled signature. The paper had fallen, slipped beneath the fridge.

That day came back all over again. He collapsed on the floor, shook with great heaving breaths, feeling as if he'd betrayed his boy once again. Destroyed a fragile piece of history.

The day of the incident, when Randall, Sarah and a sleeping Chloe had returned home after hours at the police station, the couple just sat quietly on the living room couch and didn't speak until Sarah said she was going to check on Chloe then go to bed early. Randall drank in a failed attempt to forget everything. He woke in the morning to find a deep gouge out of his left thumb, a dish rag collecting most of the crusty blood. He didn't know how he'd hurt himself. Never found anything in the house broken.

He'd never retrieved Jacob's drawing from beneath the refrigerator. As far as he knew, it was still under there.

It seemed like yesterday. He wriggled his fingers into the gap beneath the fridge. There was nothing.

He found himself in the living room. He turned the TV on, the volume muted. An anthropomorphic train smiled, rolled its eyes crazily as it sped down a track. Jacob's favorite show.

The engine's face was human. The gray metal organic, as if it could sweat. If Randall placed his palm against the surface, he'd feel warmth instead of cold steel, pulse of vital liquids pumping inside, hot exhalations from between the train's pouty, full lips.

This was deeply unsettling.

He turned the TV off, went back to Jacob's room. He placed the glow-in-the-dark astronaut toy on a shelf, then exited back through the window.

Randall listened to Sarah's voice message. Detective Curtis had found a new piece of evidence. Randall hadn't bothered to check his phone in days, much less return any calls, so Sarah had gone to the station to identify it by herself.

When he heard the abject devastation in Sarah's voice, he knew that the pants found buried in the woods near the trailer park were the ones Jacob had been wearing that day. He knew they'd still be cuffed just the way Jacob liked them.

Randall didn't need to listen to the rest of the message.

The cab of his truck spun. He pressed his palms against his face, drooling hot saliva onto clammy skin. He thought of tracking devices sliced into muscle tissue, machines injected into blood, sewn beneath skin, sending electrochemical signals to the brain and nervous system. Underground bunkers filled with the soft bodies of children. Manipulations and a universe that maims and kills and abducts, all to some mysterious end.

This must be why the ghosts of Sodder Airfield called to him, the reason the past taunted Randall with its secrets. Like the Nazca lines, the Wurdi Youang in Australia, the Carnac stones. Sites visible from above.

A memory of Jacob years ago, sitting in his highchair, contentedly chewing on a mushy portion of toast.

A memory of Jacob in his perfectly cuffed pants.

A memory of Jacob.

Randall let the remaining voice messages play as he howled silently into his open hands.

He parked in front of the trailer park near Sodder Airfield. He sat in silence. The cab stank of stale coffee. The morning was clear and crisp. The snow deep, the sky bright. He held a box cutter in his hand.

He left the truck, walked towards the faded runway, to the familiar dilapidated buildings and chunks of concrete.

The box cutter's hard plastic handle was cold.

Randall planned to hurt himself, then curl up in the center of the crater and bleed out. Maybe that would force them to bring Jacob back down.

But the airfield had changed.

Antennae now sprouted from the earth like monstrous insect palp, the molted remains of something that had long departed this planet. Their tips flaunted blinking lights. Rows of these pencil-thin antennae ran through the center of the airfield. The metal was putty-colored, as if the alloy was decomposing. Their topmost points swayed in the wind hundreds of feet above, swinging back and forth with a strange metallic hum audible on the surface of the planet.

Randall approached the depression. A flash of silver caught his eye.

An astronaut stood in the center.

It turned towards him. The blue sky reflected off its featureless face.

Randall didn't know if it was a plastic helmet, or aged bone brittle from the abuse of months. Its cranium was cracked, stained a putrid yellow, as if a sickness was leaking from inside. The visor was thick as a cloudy cornea. A perfectly aligned row of gleaming teeth was visible within.

The astronaut scrambled out of the crater, shuffled towards Randall. Its skin flaked away like old crinkled aluminum foil. Silvery specks mingled with snow that had already been polluted with a lead-colored substance.

The lights on top of the antennae grew brighter.

The spaceman stumbled, its short legs and the snow preventing it from moving any faster.

Randall waited patiently. He wasn't afraid.

The astronaut's helmet began to fall away, the thin cord connecting skull to neck fraying from too much jiggling. A broken toy that had been played with too much.

Its arms and legs moved in a familiar manner, the tilt of its shoulders all too recognizable. It was so very small. Just a child.

Randall dropped the box cutter in the snow, ran to the astronaut. Fell, regained his balance, ran until he embraced the small corpse.

He said *oh my my my little astronaut* because any other words were out of reach. He held his son against his chest, cradled his wobbly head to prevent it from dislodging. Wept until his lungs burned, the sensation dissipating into the vast cold emptiness of the morning. He wasn't sure what to do, didn't know what was expected of him as a father.

He couldn't open his son's visor and view the familiar face. To look past the time and decay, to see what he'd set out to find all those months ago would confirm every fear, every desperate certainty that there was no joy to be found in a world governed by entropy. Everything rots. The world dilapidates. Everyone will vanish into nothingness.

Children are taken away from bathroom rest stops.

Little astronauts never return home.

So, he told Jacob made-up stories instead. Old ones heard many times, new tales he'd never had a chance to tell. He spoke of his boy's first steps, first words, favorite toys, told him about his little sister, how his mother missed her son so much. He recounted every maudlin parent cliché he could imagine. But Jacob never made a sound or acknowledged he understood anything at all.

Randall continued until the tiny, graceful presence of his boy lulled him into the first semblance of comfort in far too long. His face touched his son's helmeted face. His grip loosened.

He felt his son's head waver, then tumble over his shoulder onto the ground. The head gouged a shallow furrow in the snow as it rolled away towards the crater.

Randall wanted to call out, to halt its progress. Wanted his boy put back together, to be a whole child once more so they could be a family again. But his limbs ached, unwilling to move his sore body any more than was necessary to maintain a heartbeat. He stared at the dirty snow.

His life wasn't worth Sarah's life. Or Chloe's. Wasn't worth Jacob's life. Maybe things had worked out for the best. He loathed himself so intensely nothing could harm, humiliate, or affect him in any manner he hadn't already inflicted against himself.

His boy's body dissolved into silvery bone meal in his arms. The dust trickled from his lap to the ground, then dispersed on a sparkling breeze. Randall tasted sunlight.

He didn't deserve to see the dust speckle the air with resplendence. Didn't deserve to see his son's head fall into the crater, the air around the hole shimmer with a glorious fervor the color of nebulae, the diaphanous form of the reconfigured child astronaut ascend, picking up speed the higher he rose towards the exosphere.

Randall kept his gaze below, mesmerized by the patterns and pocks in the snow. He only deserved to stare at filthy ice.

Jacob waved at his father far beneath, but Randall couldn't rescue his son from oblivion. Couldn't even own up to his responsibilities as a parent and reach out. Couldn't save his family. Couldn't save himself from eternity.

Jacob kept waving, but Randall remained motionless until he became nothing more than a speck on the surface of the planet.

Then the little astronaut faded into a pinpoint of silvery light.

Then they were both nothing at all.

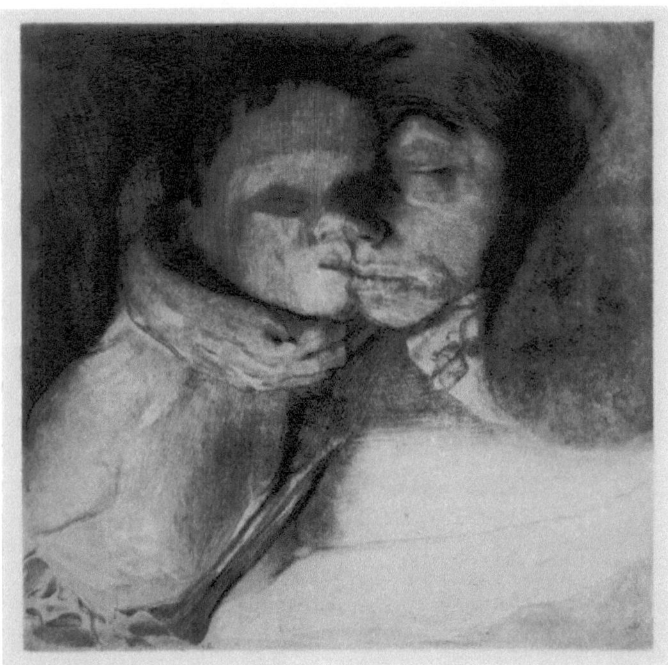

ENGINES OF THE OCEAN

ora. dearest...

❋

On first receiving the letter, Cordelia chalked it up to a simple postal error. Her father had died long ago, and the note she'd sent thanking him for the birthday present had no reason to come back to her decades later. There wasn't an explanation as to why the envelope had been opened then sealed shut again.

Whoever had resealed the flap had done so quite expertly, the intrusion nearly undetectable. Cordelia would have blamed the odd occurrence on a postal employee's curiosity, then subsequent attempt to cover their act, if she hadn't seen written in blue ink at the bottom of the paper beneath a fold-crease now loosely held together by fibers:

Cora dearest, I still have your salt in my hair.

She wasn't sure how to proceed, if at all, until recognizing the swooping curves and loops of the letters as her father's handwriting.

The forgery was perfect. Why anyone decided to make such an effort and follow through on the hoax all these years later was baffling. And how had the sender known to perfume the paper with the moist, salty scent of her father's private room?

That room in the basement. The stuff of childhood terrors. She'd never actually entered it, only glimpsed the brick-lined interior on those rare occasions the door had been left ajar. The unpleasant scent of the space was forever in her memory. A sweaty residue—or was it more like the ocean?

The room had always been off-limits. It was where her father wrote his ideas down, sketching various machine designs as a hobby. A frustrated engineer, relegated to a field service technician position for the city's water department, she'd never seen any of his finished projects actually operating. The weird machines of unknown function never made it from the page to fruition, and nothing ever led to a promotion.

While Cordelia's mother had always been the doting, familial type, her father was a loner. Always hidden behind that door in his study, working at all hours so frequently that Cordelia and her brothers made jokes about him being a serial killer. The secret room became an abattoir where he disposed of his victims. Or maybe he was a mad scientist, building underground engines to take over the world. The children's gruesome imaginations ran rampant.

But Cordelia knew better. She remembered her father spending time with her, playing tag in the yard, listening to him read her favorite books. Their frequent trips to the beach were particularly memorable. She'd been awed by the power and immensity of the ocean. The mind was an unreliable thing, all too often preserving dark moments while neglecting the joyful. There was some light in between the cracks of a dreary childhood, and most were illuminated by their adventures at the ocean.

Cordelia decided to take the long drive back to her old home to satiate her curiosity. Maybe this would quell any remaining vestiges of childhood nostalgia. She didn't expect to find anything of consequence, much less evidence of ghosts writing letters from beyond the grave. But it was as good an excuse as any to visit the neighborhood she hadn't seen in so long.

The ten-hour drive to Oak Field was uneventful. The town had been hard hit by the recession. All of the shops she drove past were empty. Blank windows with the occasional FOR LEASE sign interrupted the monotony.

She passed the Klein Theater where she'd seen her first film unaccompanied by an adult. The front of the building was boarded up, the side appeared to have collapsed due to fire damage. The small parking lot was weed covered, parking lines faded and barely distinguishable.

But she was surprised to see that the corner grocery store was still operating. The front door was open, screen door shut with a handwritten OPEN sign taped to it from the inside. Cordelia had spent many an afternoon loitering here, drinking Cherry Cokes and dropping quarters into the *Meteor Madness* video game that was obsolete even when she was a teenager.

Nobody greeted her on entering. The cash register was unattended. A curtained off area behind the counter led to the employee's break room.

The interior was a relic from a bygone age: cereal boxes with mascots retired from the company's marketing were still on the shelves. All of the magazines on the rack were dated thirty years ago. Even the old *Meteor Madness* video game was in the corner, the screen flickering with pixelated chaos. Flavors of sodas that were no longer bottled filled the refrigerator in the back. The store was immaculate, free of dust or grime. A cold bottle of Cherry Coke in hand, she headed to the front to pay.

She rang the silver bell on the counter next to a jar of pickled eggs. She didn't want to think about how long the rubbery snacks must have been soaking in there.

Minutes later, she rang again. Something made a noise in the back, but it must have been the refrigerator's fan turning on. "Hello?" Cordelia called out anyway.

Nobody answered behind the curtain. Resigned, she left the correct amount of cash on the counter, dropped the drink into her purse, and left. As she reached the car, her phone rang.

The number was from a lifetime ago. She'd called it countless times from school to let her father know she was ready to be picked up after volleyball practice. Called it more times than she could remember from Janice's house, to ask her parents if she could stay the night.

She touched IGNORE. She'd only imagined the call was from her old home. She'd transposed the numbers, shuffled them around from disparate particles of memories. A wrong number.

Walking to the house from the convenience store would have been a nice nostalgic stroll but was also out of the question—the sun was setting, and the streetlights weren't on yet. The sidewalk held too many shadows, offering the potential to hide someone. The houses didn't have any lights on either, though people had to be home since most had cars parked in front.

An unusual white crust on their hoods and wheels made Cordelia suspect the vehicles hadn't been driven in quite some time. Opening her own car door, she felt crystals scrape against fingertips. It was too gloomy to make out what it was, but the substance was granular and rough. Tentatively, she touched her tongue.

She tasted salt.

Everything was layered in a fine dusting of the mineral. Something to do with the soil salinity, flushed out by neglected sewage systems, or improper irrigation perhaps? She took a long drink of her Cherry Coke, rinsed her mouth out, spat the liquid on the asphalt. Cordelia imagined she heard a rumbling, as if great engines under the earth's salted crust were churning to life.

She drove down the darkening street to her childhood residence.

Pulling up to the curb, she noticed an unusual atmospheric phenomenon playing out in the sky. Bloated sheets of silver mist rolled overhead like a brackish spill. The house was coated in a white rime, though it was far too warm for ice to have formed.

The home still looked like a cream-colored layer cake, the crown molding a delicate filigree like piped frosting. The colors were vivid, and there was no weathering damage visible. Someone must have bought the place after her father died—she wasn't sure about the details. It looked as if nobody had lived here in the years since; while the house had been maintained, the driveway was pitted, and the weeds jutting from the cracks made her doubt anyone had parked here in quite some time. A house left vacant for decades made little sense.

The sun had lowered further, but the streetlights were still dead. Their malfunction emphasized the emptiness of the neighborhood. Cordelia couldn't hear any traffic from the main road two streets over. It used to be so loud when she'd play in the front yard as a kid.

The lawn was low dry yellow grass, speckled with tiny white bits. A rectangle of blackness caught her attention. The concrete lid covering the water meter was gone.

Those meters terrified her as far back as she could remember. The purpose of those clockwork machines eluded any rational explanation—or so six-year-old Cordelia insisted. She'd been absolutely certain the meters were buried on the lawns so they would be easier to access from *below*. Her mother's explanation that they were how the city determined water usage and billed accordingly had never been an acceptable answer.

Their subterraneous purpose was a mystery. Her father's playful claim that meters monitored the neighborhood crisscrossed with catacombs filled her with anxiety. He'd said this with a wink, but simply entertaining the possibility that devices worked their oily machinations at all hours to measure the rising waters and their mysterious tides was traumatizing.

She once lifted the concrete lid of a meter and bashed a brick against the glass cover inside. The glass shattered, the meter buzzed angrily, but the dials continued to turn, documenting their strange unfathomable course. She was certain that vandalizing the machine meant the equipment beneath would fail, allowing the oceans to rise, the gutters to overflow with water. Her neighborhood submerged in vast seas.

The lock on the side door to the garage was corroded, the wood frame soft with age. A heavy shove and it swung open and she was inside the old place. The garage was empty, but the door leading to the living room was unlocked.

Little had changed inside. The exact same wallpaper pattern that always made her think of fluttering eyelashes. The very sofa in which she'd spent many a Saturday morning watching cartoons. The ancient TV was still on the same nightstand, though the crack in its screen meant it was probably no longer working, even if the electricity were operational. The curtains were the same fabric and color, the carpet powdered with salt but recognizably original. Even the rotary dial phone was intact. The receiver was on the hook, though it wasn't possible to tell if anyone had touched it to call her. Everything was preserved.

Hadn't her mother taken the furniture with them when they'd moved? It was so long ago, and she was so little when everything happened the memories were conflicted and fragmentary. Cordelia couldn't fathom why so many of the house's old trappings remained.

A thin covering of fine salt particulates on the coffee table quivered from air currents as she moved. Flecks of pale grit on the walls, furniture, and floor sparkled. The air was soupy like brine.

Cordelia looked into each room, closet, and entryway. Of course, there was nobody here. For one brief moment she thought she'd best call her brother in case anything happened here, even though ghosts weren't real. And if there existed anything that deserved to be called such, they'd be insubstantial, composed of enough matter for light to bounce off of, but little else. A phantom wouldn't be able to touch, strangle or make a phone call. Spirits were just history projected against nostalgia.

Entering her old bedroom, she found it empty. The wallpaper near the defunct light switch was peeling at chest level. Beneath a layer of white powder was written *CORA age 6*. A dash mark showed her height at the time. She pulled away the curling flakes to reveal numbers and marks descending down the wall to the age of two. The only reminder of who she used to be.

A short flight of steps crunchy with white granules led down to the basement. She faced the door to her father's study. The door was covered in powdery splotches that may have been handprints if she wasn't certain the place was uninhabited. The knob turned freely, but the door was jammed, or something was blocking it on the other side.

She remembered her mother telling her that dad wasn't well, and prolonged care after brain death wasn't in his best interest. At the time, Cordelia was so young she didn't fully understand why her parent was essentially no longer her father. The thought bothered her so much she refused to visit him in the hospital, throwing such a fierce tantrum in the lobby a nurse said she'd watch her while the rest of the family went in. It was long ago, and any repercussions from her absence had dissipated like ripples from a single grain thrown into the ocean.

Cordelia explained away her shame over the years: he'd fallen into a coma; her visiting would have been all but meaningless even if he could have comprehended his daughter's presence. A contraption pointlessly functioning because nobody had the courage to switch it off. When he did pass away, he took any and all reasons as to why he'd decided to retreat to his private room on feeling the stirrings of a blood clot in his head.

And Cordelia was certain he'd made that choice. He may have died from a stroke, but she'd no doubts he'd felt that black-eyed dog nipping at his heels while retreating into his personal space for the last time. Returning to the scene of her father's tragedy should have been emotionally resonant, but she felt only a flake of the guilt she'd expected.

After heading back upstairs, she walked into the dining room. A pristine picture of the house formed in her mind, but long ago, when everything was bright and immaculate from her mother's persistent housekeeping. She'd always cherished talking to her parents here at the table. They'd discuss school; what she wanted for dinner; their favorite TV shows; made the same silly jokes they'd always made to each other. All while sitting at that familiar antique oak dining room table shipped from Poland at great expense.

If she closed her eyes, Cordelia could see them again. She gazed at their faces lovingly, marveled at the familiarity of their presence. The way her father moved his hands when talking, the way her mother's gray hair curled at the temples. If she concentrated, she could hear the parakeet they kept in a small blue cage in the living room, chirping and fluttering in its confines. She smelled potpourri bundled in a wooden bowl and a lavender scent blown in on a breeze through an open window.

Cordelia could picture the yard out back as it used to be; bright green behind the sliding glass doors. The pomegranate tree used to be full of fruit, the trellis built by her dad's hand covered in ivy. Roses once grew; the stone birdbath once active with aviary life.

They'd play out here, her dad chasing her around a lawn that felt enormous to a child. He'd throw her little body into the air, always catching her just before she hit the ground.

Cordelia wished she could tell her father how much she missed him. Even in her memory he seemed delicate, as if he were propped up in a chair and a touch would collapse his body into inert bits and pieces.

It was an odd recovered memory, but she remembered glimpsing something unfamiliar in the back yard. A drainage pipe poking out of the ground, the metal surface scaly with rust. A distant moaning emanated from the pipe.

There was nothing visible from where she now stood, but she distinctly recalled the dinner plate-sized opening to the pipe had been covered with mesh to prevent wildlife from entering. And it hadn't been a moan, but the sound of waves from deep down. Another thought came to her, something more aggressive than nostalgia. An old dream perhaps, or several dreams, more vision than reminiscence.

Something had once moved behind her. She'd glanced back to see the pomegranate tree fallen over. Its prodigious, leafy branches blocking the entrance back into the house. The upturned roots had gouged a deep depression in the ground. Cordelia thought she may have peered over the rim of the hole to see a large brick-lined room below with several brick-lined passages trailing off into darkness. The sound and smell of the salty sea drifted from within.

The memory gripped Cordelia with such intensity she could still hear the ocean nestled in her ears, like the moist beginnings of an earache. But she was here, in the present, the table solid beneath her hands and her parents no longer part of her life. She stood, her handprints remained behind in grainy salt particles over the wood's polished veneer.

She looked through the sliding glass doors into the backyard. The pomegranate tree was intact, but there was no hole in the ground, and the lawn was dirt. The sun had nearly fully set, the scant remaining light emphasizing the salt spread across the yard. Her memory hadn't been particularly frightening, just troubling, like hearing the tinkle of broken glass in an unoccupied room late at night. Only the crisp dome of the sun was visible now, the sky nearly sown with stars.

Turning from the sliding glass doors, she walked down a short hall into her brothers' shared bedroom. It was slightly *off*, something missing that didn't quite match what she'd once known. The rational part of her brain knew her old home never looked exactly like this—her memory must have created as close an approximation as possible, yet realized it hadn't quite managed to recreate the details perfectly. She'd fallen into the uncanny valley of sentiment, a childhood imperfectly replicated.

Her parent's room was unchanged. The bed was still here, though the blankets were missing. The shape of what Cordelia assumed was a body was stained onto the mattress, presumably in sweat. Fine crystals of salt glittered inside the outline. The figure was too thin to be either of her parents.

The hutch displaying her mother's ceramic collection remained, the little figurines unmoved in all this time. The sensation of returning home, decades after her father's death, was all rather bittersweet. But an air of distress persisted. None of this made sense.

She picked up a journal on the nightstand. The first page read,

On some distant wedding anniversary, I remembered you handing me a book made out of silk, each thin page covered with painstakingly ornate handwriting. But I wasn't sure if this had actually happened or if I'd merely wanted it to be true. I don't have any silk books in my collection.

It may have been her father's handwriting. Cordelia wasn't sure.

She heard someone moving around in the back yard.

Racing to the sliding glass doors, she saw the suggestion of a pale face fall from the pomegranate tree, then roll to the other end of the yard.

Once outside, she was convinced that what she'd seen must have been a flurry of salt tumbled on the wind. She cast her phone's light beam around. The pomegranate tree's leaves were green, but the little remaining fruit had split, oozing a resinous sap swarming with gnats. Globules of the syrup had gathered on the ground. The phone's light shone upon the piles like rubies.

The fence defining the property was mostly intact, though a few patches of weathered holes allowed a glimpse into the neighbor's back yard. Cordelia leaned down to peer through. What the phone light could reach revealed that the area around the swimming pool was a dirt lot.

The pool was filled with salt.

A sound at the stone birdbath caught her attention. Shining her light on it showed the slimy water was squirming with tadpoles gathered around a U-shaped object, like sperm around an ovum. She blew on the water to part the animals. The tadpoles moved enough for her to see they were clustered around a rusty orthodontic retainer.

Flakes of salt fell gently from the sky. She hurried back inside.

A noise, as of something crumbling apart as it moved, came from the basement. She rushed to the steps.

Whatever had been preventing the door from budging must have fallen away; this time, it opened with no difficulty.

Her father's private room was smaller than she'd expected, only furnished with an office desk and chair. One corner of the desk was piled chest high with papers. The room reeked of the ocean air. So many memories came cascading back she was momentarily breathless.

Something shuffled in the shadows at the back of the room, sounding as if it had difficulty maintaining its shape. Cordelia thought of a broken hourglass, spilling its bulk across the floor.

She poked the phone light's beam into the darker recesses. There was nothing there but a brick wall, crumbly segments on the floor here and there.

The layer of salt on the desk had been recently disturbed. She shook the paper on top of the pile, looked it over, then another. Each bore a sketch her father had been working on, with a date recorded at the bottom. She rifled through several more, increasingly reluctant, though compelled to look at each and every one of his concepts drawn over the years.

The pages had been scrawled in an amateur's hand. The clumsy drawings of an intellectually deficient child.

She noticed a sheet on the floor beneath the desk. Shaking the salty residue off revealed blue words clearly written by her father:

Salted with fire, they seem to show
How spirits lost in endless woe
May undecaying live.

The room was increasingly dank. What must have been faulty pipes in the ceiling failed to keep strands of saltwater from splashing in increments. The wet touched Cordelia's skin. Salt granules spackled her clothes and hair.

This was where her father had thought his last thoughts. Perhaps he'd retreated here to capture a perfect moment, freeze time at the only instance he'd ever been happy, in here, working on his ideas that were nothing more than scrawls of nonsense. But what moment of his life had seemed more bearable than previous moments? By himself, building useless engines in this room? Away from her?

Cordelia realized the depths of her sorrow. Too many years had gone by to make amends of any sort, but she felt the weight of grief, the burden that comes from absence.

The room was small, but she was suddenly confused by its layout. She couldn't remember where the door was. Taking a step towards a wall, she knew she'd made a mistake, so she turned to face another wall. She found herself before an endless progression of brick corridors that hadn't been there before. A pale crust glittered on the bricks and floor.

Deep down the corridors came the gentle sound of waves lapping at an unseen shore. Machinery churned within damp niches. Backing away, she bumped her calf against an obstacle. She squatted and gripped it to get her bearings.

She held a pipe poking out of the floor. Lowering her face to the grate-covered opening, she breathed deeply of the ocean air. It was increasingly difficult to see. There was too much salt on her face. A shuffling, laborious gait moved towards her.

Something ashen appeared. A crystallized thing preserved in a ghastly semblance of life. Cordelia suddenly lost sight of it, her eyelids lowering from the accumulation of salt.

Someone spoke, but Cordelia couldn't understand over the roar of the ocean. Hands gently touched her face. She tried to pull away, but they caught her with such certainty she knew she'd never hit the ground.

Gritty arms held her with waning strength. She returned the embrace so tightly pieces of the body crumbled away. There was so much salt in the air now. The engines ran faster, pumping more spray into the room, though quieter, more efficiently. Cordelia could now hear the figure whispering,

Cora dearest.

Now that they were together again, maybe they'd be able to visit the ocean once more. Maybe she'd be light enough to lift above his head and twirl until she was dizzy and exuberant like she used to be.

But Cordelia knew she was too big now, and her father was too long gone to do much more than hold her while she fought back tears with profuse apologies.

They needed to get away from this room, back to the rest of their home that had miraculously sustained itself all this time. But the gleaming lattices of salt were already too bright, and her father was far too dilapidated to sustain himself.

Who would repair the water meters when they eventually break down? The panicky thought came to Cordelia with such despair she could only accept the inevitable with quiet grace.

Her father's minerals dissolved in her blood, particles collected on her skin. The lantern of her world was shuttered, the flame within snuffed out by the pinch of an unseen hand.

The murmur of the ocean continued to flow out of the pipe from far below.

THE CARCASS OF THE LION

Sylvia couldn't tell where the bees ended and Hazel's head began.

An absurd twinge of jealousy shot through her as she watched the tiny animals brush against the older woman's cheeks and forehead, tap against her eyelids, run tickling trails across her lips. Sylvia knew that even though her friend's arms were protected by a loose cotton long sleeve shirt, she must still feel the bee's delicate yet substantial weight through the fabric. Hazel's hair was bright as hammered silver in the sunlight.

The beekeeper's veil stuck to Sylvia's sweaty forehead, fine gaps in the material blurring Hazel's body into a gauzy ghost. The flurry of insects around her now made it appear as if she had a halo of bees. The hive boxes seemed strange in this setting, like building blocks left behind by a monstrous child. Sylvia continued walking alongside a stream that originated in the forest, bubbling from below into a thin path to join a shallow pond the bees and other wildlife used as a water source.

"Hazel. Dearest. What in the world are you up to out here?" Hazel turned on hearing Sylvia's voice, startled by the sight of her in full beekeeper regalia, as if she were a bug-eyed alien from a 50s sci-fi flick just stepped from its saucer.

Hazel had become so thin in such a short time. The cancer was eroding her away in unrelenting fits and bursts. It wasn't fair; she was as mentally fit at 74 as she'd been at half that age, but corrupt cells were deteriorating her body. Sylvia was reluctant to blame God for this violation, but who else could be held responsible?

Sylvia was a child when she first met her, and they'd remained neighbors and close friends all these years. Growing up on the outskirts of Goodmanswood meant she held many fond memories of the countryside, despite her parents' vicious quarrels in the childhood home. Sylvia jumped at the opportunity to move back into the old house after her mother retired to Australia summer before last.

She'd returned only to watch Hazel grow gaunt, day by day. She'd always been there for Sylvia, with a comforting word and a glass of strawberry milk (berries gathered from the wild clumps that grew all over the property, macerated into unpasteurized milk by Hazel's own hand). She was there when Sylvia's parents' relationship became so violent, she was certain she'd come home from school one day to find her mother's battered corpse.

God was cruel. Sylvia saw no reason why such a Creator *wouldn't* cock up bodies with wisdom teeth and vestigial bits, since the bastard had also seen fit to add oncogenes to his Creation.

"I miss the girls." Bees flew between Hazel's wriggling fingers, like an act they'd practiced many times. Her voice was a thing of beauty—Scotch husky and decades of professional singing had blessed her with the bygone charisma of a movie star era glamor. Those genetics had led to a successful modeling career when she was younger, followed by commercial gigs, and Hazel had only retired after losing her husband to a stroke.

Sylvia grew up dirt poor. Struggled for everything she'd acquired. After graduating from university, she'd spent more terms than she was willing to admit teaching various biology modules to apathetic Comprehensive School students. She still had regrets over her choices. An art education had been deferred in pursuit of more financially viable options, per her parents' pressure from an early age. Despite this, she was sure her mother and father had loved her. They'd just reserved their hatred for each other.

"The bees miss you as well," Sylvia said.

"But they *chose* you." Hazel playfully wagged her finger.

Hazel had taken to beekeeping shortly after her cancer diagnosis. Sylvia understood why she'd been smitten by the mystery of the bees—their strange habits and the day to day care of the tiny beauties was compulsive. But Hazel had become too ill to care for them by herself.

Sylvia held her tongue when her friend defended the validity of apitherapy to tackle the cancer. As long as she saw her doctors regularly and took the prescribed treatments, Sylvia didn't care how much royal jelly, bee pollen, apitoxin, or honey she ingested. Every beekeeper worth their honey grew used to bee stings—if that's all it took to make Hazel happy, then Sylvia saw little harm in dabbling in pseudoscientific practices as long as it made her feel as if she'd some control over her failing body.

"I miss going through the bees." Hazel said in a wistful voice.

Sylvia loved that phrase. It simply meant an inspection of the hives, to note anything unusual. But it also held mythic connotations, of Aristaeus, of Ra's tears, of gleaming yellow beings plump with pollen.

Now that spring was here, and the change in weather meant swarming season, Sylvia was busier than ever. She'd checkerboarded the boxes (which discouraged bees from forming new colonies), discarded the old cedar hives, built replacements from scratch—from the stand to the deep brood box to the honey supers. She'd even trimmed the grasses and weeds around the twelve hives, making it easier for the bees to fly back and forth with fewer obstacles.

Latex paint applied to the boxes in bright pastel colors helped reflect the sunlight, and also reminded Hazel of her trip to Cork all those years ago. Hazel loved to reminisce about the city's rows of buildings alongside the River Lee, done up in pale blues, soft purples, and squash yellows. Talk of returning to Ireland was often mentioned, but waning health meant no time to follow through, even to someplace so near. Sylvia found it nice to hear her make plans, though they both knew the trip would never come true. Hazel turned to walk back to her house.

"Please stay. This won't take long," Sylvia said.

"I refuse to be a burden, love." Hazel looked to the forest as if anticipating someone. Sylvia instinctively glanced in the same direction, but all she could see were trees.

"You've yet to be." Sylvia said as she lit the cotton fuel in the Etna smoker. Moving slowly, she gave three quick puffs to the front of the hive, confusing the guard bees, then slid the top cover out. After ejecting some more smoke into the opening, she set the smoker on the ground.

Using a thin, flat metal tool, she pried the propolis glued wooden frames apart. The honeycomb was intact; brood apparently healthy; plenty of room for the queen to lay her eggs; sufficient pollen and honey. No signs of foulbrood.

But the wax cells were wrong. If asked to explain just why they were *off*, Sylvia wouldn't have been able to put her finger on it. The honeycombs' color and shape were somehow unfamiliar. Not broken or sagging, but slightly malformed, no longer pristine little hexagons. She couldn't quite wrap her head around what was different.

"Are you alright there?" Hazel didn't turn her attention from the woods when she spoke.

Had the bees brought back a contaminant from the forest? Sylvia could imagine an odd growth out there, a lichen or moss permeating the pollen and nectar the bees gathered from tainted flowers. In fact, she held a hazy memory of stepping barefoot on a patch of iridescent lichen when she was a child. It caused a virulent rash, and Hazel had to apply an entire bottle of calamine to Sylvia's feet. An allergic reaction brought feverish, hallucinatory nightmares that night. Sylvia never mentioned those fever dreams to Hazel, much less her parents.

Maybe the bees had picked up something similar, those foreign cells stored in their stomachs, passing the corruption from one worker bee to another till the nectar's water content was all but removed. Then the spoiled honey was secreted into the comb's cells. That was one possible explanation.

Sylvia couldn't help but think of this as an invasion, a perversion of God's natural cycle. It'd be best if she did some research among the books on beekeeping back home, or failing that, visit the library in town for clarification on what else this could possibly be.

"Girls are all good." Sylvia lied, gently replacing the frames into their proper positions. Beyond the obvious distress it would cause Hazel, she wasn't sure why she had to keep this find secret. It just felt right to keep quiet.

"Such lovely creatures. God's perfect little design." Hazel had a beatific expression.

God *designed fists perfectly shaped to punch. Designed speech to insult. Designed families to harm each other.* Sylvia wanted to say this out loud but kept quiet. The sun was bright overhead, its mild warmth soothing her face flushed with sweat. She removed her veil and gave Hazel a smile, but the older woman was facing the forest again observing something only she could see.

Sylvia woke up long before sunrise to read the previous day's edition of the *Guardian*. Devastating unemployment, police brutality that led to an uprising in Brixton, abject disparity, women and children slaughtered by the military in El Salvador. The world was chaos.

Random, vicious events splayed out across history's timeline, contrasted against humanity's calculated depravity. No rhyme or reason to anything—unless it was humanity's proclivity for barbarism. A roll of the dice by a malicious gambler.

Maybe a brisk walk beneath starlight down to the main road, past Irene Fuller's place—the only other neighbor within walking distance—to Hazel's shire would clear her head of these cynical thoughts. She put on her Wellingtons and jacket, then left the front door unlocked on parting.

At 4:50 a.m., the countryside was so quiet she could hear the stream trickling into the pond, even though it was a good ten-minute stroll away from the main road she walked on.

Hazel was her dearest friend, but Sylvia still felt uncomfortable trespassing during early morning hours. They were in the country, and people in these parts trusted each other. No crime to speak of, and no animals clever enough to break in and burgle anything—not that Sylvia was aware of anyway. She kept telling herself this, even as she felt eyes tracking her from the woods. That familiar quiver up the spine was just wildlife nervously assessing an intruder on their land, though it felt as if the forest itself was scrutinizing her every move.

Looking up the hill, past the narrow gravel driveway to Hazel's old home didn't alleviate Sylvia's spooked mood. The dim porch light illuminated the first two stairs up to the front decking and little else. The place was vulnerable, exposed. There was nothing homey or welcoming here. The dark woods beyond rose above, cresting over the house like a tsunami's shadow. Sylvia didn't want to linger outside too long.

Even on a morning so dark, the slivered moon allowed her to see the surrounding field abundant with life this time of year. Crowded with the majestic hues of Lemon Gem, cowslips, lavender, clematis, and snapdragons. She could smell patches of Russian sage, hyssop, and wild angelica. The bees had plentiful food in the clover, cat's ear, milkweed, and mint that threatened to dominate the property. A nearby low stone wall provided a windbreak for the hives. Its surface was clotted with a blue-green lichen she hadn't noticed yesterday, though there was something decidedly familiar about it. A steady stream of insect bodies exited the colorful hive boxes, their buzzing a pleasant murmur. The boxes glowed in the lambent starlight as if generating an internal energy source.

But honeybees weren't normally active this early in the day. Sylvia found this curious—they usually conducted flight activities after the sun had fully risen. The bees flew over the pond into the forest in a steady stream, but Sylvia refused to enter Goodmanswood when it was still dark.

She once saw a lion in these woods. Sylvia was eight years old, it was late in the afternoon, and she was doing her homework but couldn't focus because her parents were hitting each other again. So, she climbed out the bedroom window and rode her bike all the way up to Hazel's acreage. She approached the tree line, dusk settling in, that moment at the end of day her grandmother once referred to as "the blind man's holiday," only to apologize on seeing how much the phrase upset her granddaughter. Sylvia would never forget staring into these black woods so many years ago.

A creeping fear sneaked up on her, a sense of confronting the sylvan unknown sparking a strange sort of joy. Vast weald of unexplored timber and bosks, miles of mysterious regions, tantalizing secrets—it was overwhelming in its allure. She remembered movement beneath the sacred trees, of things frolicking to and fro, too tall and too broad to be real animals. There was no forgetting the forest's massive blinking eye, which must have only been a shuddering limb, or shadows cast by rustling bushes expertly mimicking silent gaping mouths in prelude to a roar. The restless trees had just been wind and a little girl's imagination, not the Green Man playing hide and seek with a child's innate curiosity.

Then Sylvia saw him.

A large, tawny shape moving between the trees. He walked with a casual gait, as if confident of his woodland reign. His mane was filled with twigs and dry leaves. Thin flanks and protruding ribs made him seem that much wilder, not starving and weak, but dangerous. He never even glanced in Sylvia's direction. When the lion reached the meadow, he paused, then paced along the tree line, until returning to the forest, disappearing among the growing shadows.

But she was an adult now and knew there'd never been any lion. Maybe she'd mistaken a puma for the king of the jungle—though England had no native big cats, and the recent capture of a puma in Scotland turned out to be an escaped pet. It had likely been a fox or a feral dog, amplified in her memory into something far more impressive over the years. She was an imaginative child. Whatever it was would be long dead now. Maybe she'd dreamt the whole encounter.

But it wasn't just the strange animal sighting long ago that prevented her from going into the woods—the idea that some faiths prayed to nature, and practiced their rituals deep within sacred groves, was also deeply worrisome. Communicating with vine-clad gods under leaf shade, dancing upon sidhe mounds with demi-gods below centuries old branches—the very thought filled her with a delicious fear. Hadn't she once played hide-and-seek here? The thought was a blur. She didn't recall having any companions her age to play with in the area, but the impression she'd hidden deep inside a hole out there while something tried to find her was persistent. She shuddered at the morning chill and the memory. The woods terrified, the woods exhilarated.

Something was restless in the pond. Sylvia's first thought was that it must be a hedgehog, though it was difficult to reconcile the magnitude of splashing with such a modest-sized creature. She moved quietly through the grass towards the sound.

Hazel stood at the water's edge, her bare feet slick with mud. She was only wearing a nightdress. Sylvia was relieved to see her clothes and hair weren't wet. Something else must have been responsible for the boisterous splashing, though she couldn't see or hear where it'd scampered off. A smattering of unusual tracks in the mud must have been caused by Hazel's meandering around the pond—they certainly couldn't be the paw prints of a large creature. Hazel's eyes were open, staring at the black gap where the bees flew into the forest.

"Dearest?" Sylvia gently placed her fingertips against Hazel's elbow and upper arm, to guide her back to the house. The cool air raised goose pimples on the older woman's thin mottled skin. So frail and delicate, like wet newspapers draped over a thin frame. Sylvia was surprised to find that Hazel's arm was covered with a down of velvety hairs.

Halfway across the pasture, Hazel shivered, eyes widening as she woke up. She turned to Sylvia with an apologetic smile, her skull visible beneath translucent skin. "I'm so sorry, love. Someone told me to follow where the bees were going."

❋

Later that morning, after the sun had risen to scare away any remaining pockets of shade, Sylvia explored the Goodmanswood, searching for where the bees had journeyed to earlier. The hives were active, the bees back home, but there might still be a few somewhere building a new nest. She had to satisfy her curiosity and collect any strays if necessary.

The absence of small animals rustling through the moss and lack of any motion from squirrels or insects was unsettling. The emerald stillness put her on edge. The creak of a tree bending from a gust too high to feel reached her ears. A crack reverberated through the forest, another limb groaned as if commiserating in a secret language. Leaves whispered in conspiratorial sighs.

Half an hour later, Sylvia found a large cavity in the ground. Was this an animal's den? The opening was wide enough for a bear-sized beast to lumber into, though any such mammal was long extinct here. Several rocks had been pushed aside to make room for a dozen incense censers forming a haphazard circle around the pit. Had Hazel been meditating over the pit in this serene setting? The rocks were covered with a bluish-green lichen sprouting thin sporophytes, tips dabbed with globules of tacky dew, like tiny crystal balls. She'd seen this growth before, though when and where eluded her.

A single bee lazily circled the den. When Sylvia approached, her foot brushed against a censer, the ash inside spilling onto the ground. The bee quickly flew down into the depths.

Something was dead inside. An earthy stench, marrow and hot saliva, rose from the darkness. It was too deep to see the bottom, though a cerulean hue was faintly discernible deep within. She rolled a lichen scaly rock inside but didn't hear an impact at the bottom. The ground below must be thickly carpeted with moss. She kneeled, planted her weight on her palms, and leaned forward to get a better look into the hole. The lichen left a viscid residue on her fingers.

A strange compulsion to drop down on all fours and crawl deep into the opening came over her. It was the same compulsion children contend with, that urge to squeeze into cupboards or curl up inside claustrophobic pillow forts. Safe, hidden away in their own private worlds. She entertained the notion that something was buried inside the den, twenty, maybe thirty feet down. Something the forest wanted to contain.

It was a silly whim. Sylvia stood up, wiped her palms clean on her shirt. She wasn't a child anymore, and sure as hell wasn't going to scare herself for the thrill of it. Contaminated soil and tainted lichen infecting the hives was more of a concern. A corruption thriving beneath. The bees must have brought something wrong back with them. This is what mattered. Her initial suspicion that a stronger nest in the woods was seducing residents from Hazel's colony didn't seem as plausible anymore.

She hurried out of the woods and exited near the pond, relieved to have escaped the overwhelming presence of the trees, the unusual lichen, and that peculiar hole. Their existence made her think of an intrusive species infiltrating the land, something that did not belong in these parts, roaming the flora and fauna.

Here at the border of the pasture, the vegetation had a religious quality. Grasses led up to the tree line, shuddering in an unfelt breeze, as if giving away the presence of a substantial animal skulking low to the ground. The flowers bright in the sunlight promised something mystical in their splendor.

Someone was near the pond, standing not too far from the hives. From this distance, with the sun in Sylvia's eyes, the figure appeared to be a gnarled root bending under its own weight.

She walked briskly downhill. As she neared, the root became a woman holding hand to brow, blocking the glare to better observe Sylvia's descent. She hadn't expected Hazel back so soon.

But she quickly realized that the person was too short, their hair too dark to be Hazel. She approached the trespasser, held her hand up in greeting. The figure mirrored her action.

It was Irene Fuller, their neighbor down the hill. The Fullers were recent transplants, having arrived shortly after Sylvia moved back. They ran an artisan cheese business from their small farm and bought any excess honey Hazel was willing to part with. Sylvia only ever saw the husband or wife, never both, and had yet to see their kids. Two boys, two girls? She wasn't sure.

She'd only spoken to the couple twice last year—Irene's husband (Alan? Adam?) on Boxing Day, then Easter when Irene herself dropped off a gift basket of cheeses, one of the best Simnel cakes Sylvia had ever tasted, and whatever artisanal products they'd included in their catalog that season. The Fullers advertised their faith on the packaging with a dove and New Testament verse. It was a detail that annoyed Sylvia.

"Long time no see. Hazel around?" Irene was a wiry, tough woman who could help a mare give birth at 3 a.m., then be up two hours later to milk the goats. The iron-on transfer of her Duran Duran t-shirt was peeling away at Nick Rhodes' hairline.

"Not at the moment. She drove into Brichester. Anything I may help with?"

Irene stuck her hands deep into pockets, tilted back on her heels like a teen asking a boy she fancies out on a date. She looked to the beehives, nodded as if coming to a decision she'd been struggling with all morning.

"It's about Hazel, actually."

Sylvia was attentive now. There'd been no bad blood between them, but she'd never been comfortable with the Fullers. Didn't care about their politics, or stand on social issues, but something about stamping all their products with Biblical passages felt crass. Equating faith with profit didn't sit well.

"Saw Hazel on the road few nights ago. Last Wednesday," Irene continued, "wandering like she was fit to be lost. Passed her, but by the time I turned back she was already off the soft-shoulder and gone. Headed into Goodmanswood."

So last night hadn't been Hazel's first nocturnal stroll. Sylvia gave an exasperated sigh. "Cheers, Mrs. Fuller."

"Seen her do the same near a fortnight ago as well. Old woman living all alone out here. In her condition. Things could go off in the woods."

"She's quite well, Mrs. Fuller."

"I'm certain she is, but you being her best friend and all—had to mention it."

"And so you have."

"My nan went senile. It was an ordeal; I'll tell you that and more."

"I understand. Hazel isn't my nan *nor* senile, but I appreciate your concern."

"Didn't mean to speak ill, Sylvia. Just wanted to relate what I'd seen."

"You passed it along."

"That I did."

Sylvia nodded, a curt move signifying the conversation had gone past done to well-done. Irene cleared her throat, gave a terse wave, then headed back down the hill towards the main road.

The day was warming up. Hazel wouldn't mind if Sylvia let herself into the house for a cold glass of water. She entered the kitchen, stood at the sink, looked out the large window that gave a wide view of the pasture and beehives. Apart from the receding dot of Irene Fuller, the scene was beautiful, like a framed painting. The hives were particularly lovely in the way the sun caressed their surfaces. The boxes' off-kilter geometry reminded Sylvia of Margo Price's Escher-esque paintings, every angle, every detail suggested something interesting lurking just out of sight. She turned the tap on and filled a glass.

She thought of *plein air* painting and beekeeping, how both relied on differential light, and the passing of seasons. Monet painted the same landscapes again and again, to capture subtleties over time, chronicling slight differences in countless moments. The gleam of sunlight or moonlight on water in the morning, noon, and night; the shadows in a flower's contours and folds at various times of the year.

A deep sorrow made her skull feel heavy. It was all she could do to keep her head up. Eyes burned, threatening tears, but she wouldn't allow self-pity to ruin this view. She was just an artist imagining what could've been. Dreams were all well and good, but the practical aspects of life all too often atrophied aspirations. Marriages failed. Parents weak and filled with rage. She rinsed the glass, dried it with a dish towel, and placed it back in the cupboard.

She turned the tap back on, cupped a pool of water. *Wake up, wake up, wake up,* she whispered each time she slapped her face with the cool well water.

Hazel had yet to return from her physician's appointment, so Sylvia decided to occupy her time by checking the hives. She removed the frames, down to the final square, holding it vertically by the top bar.

The honeycomb had mutated further. The cells had altered into seven-pointed stars, waxy lines intersecting the gaps. What was that geometric shape? A *heptagram*? She'd never seen anything of its kind before.

She'd read an article on how honeycombs were formed. Hexagons yield the greatest surface area to the quantity of waxy materials, utilizing the inherent geometry of nature. Tightly pack a bunch of circles together and the result is inevitably hexagonal, the shape with the lowest resistance and no gaps. Nature created glorious structures with no intent or foresight, the Giant's Causeway being one such example. *Competence without comprehension.* The illusion of purpose by the purposeless.

But she couldn't imagine how this heptagram star-shape was possible by chance alone, by unthinking bees, without a guiding hand. The colors in the comb were captivating, a nacreous sheen, though such a simple description didn't adequately convey the depths of its beauty. Sylvia felt tongue-tied, dizzy and sour-mouthed.

Hopefully Hazel hadn't been eating any of this honey. She'd let her know that something was wrong with the hives as soon as she returned.

The bees were aggressive, bumping against Sylvia with the force of hurled pebbles. Maybe hornets had trespassed recently, and an alarm pheromone had been released. That might explain the escalated sound from their wing beats, a steady vibration she felt in her sternum. Surely that was a better explanation than the thought that someone was humming so aggressively in the woods their voice carried through the ground.

Hazel's old Volkswagen van rattled up the driveway, spitting out gravel from beneath its tires. Sylvia hurriedly put the frames back into the box, careful to avoid crushing any bees, for their corpses emit an odor that agitates others, inciting them to sting. She didn't take her veil off until reaching the van.

Hazel stepped out of the Volkswagen. She was beaming.

"Please tell me your smile means the doctor had brilliant news," Sylvia said.

"The best news!" Hazel had tears in her eyes.

"So tell me!"

"No more cancer."

"No more?"

"Total remission, love."

They whooped. They hollered. They embraced. They broke into laughter at the miracle. Sylvia was so elated she didn't even think to warn her about the honey, or mention the corrupted hives, much less ask about the incense holders in the forest.

They drank cheap wine late into the night, celebrating Hazel's victory over malignant cells. They reminisced about years gone by, lost friends and family, and loved ones that remained true.

Hazel would live.

But something wasn't right. Of course, Hazel gave all the credit for her miraculous fortune to the apitherapy treatments and didn't consider the possibility that the medical procedures and medications had some bearing on the matter. Sylvia still wasn't convinced royal jelly could heal diseased cells.

None of this was of any consequence anymore. Hazel would live.

When Sylvia was a little girl, she wouldn't seek her parents' comfort after a nightmare. She'd wait to ride her bicycle over to Hazel's house and talk to her. Hazel would always prepare her special strawberry milk, and she'd ask Sylvia the same question, *Dreams too aggressive?*

That had stayed with Sylvia all these years. *Aggressive dreams.* Not nightmares, but dreams playing too rough. Her best friend calmed her anxiety by using the perfect choice of words.

Sylvia had aggressive dreams the night after Hazel announced her cancer remission.

Waking up later than usual with a slight hangover, the sun had already cast a rosy glaze across the bedroom. Sylvia's first thought was to run to Hazel's place for strawberry milk and solace, but she hadn't done that since she was twelve. Ambiguous post-dream scenes roamed in her head. An intruder had come down from the mountains, losing itself in the heart of Goodmanswood. Someone was crying from within the tree trunks. Sylvia was scrabbling down a deep hole, the lush soil walls moist with turquoise light. Hazel wasn't Hazel and Sylvia couldn't save her from what she wanted to become. This was all vague though, impressions that left smudged memories, nothing she could flesh out in any detail.

The tea kettle whistled just as the phone rang. Sylvia turned the gas off, then picked up the receiver. She heard a woman's voice on the other end, a calm, rational voice informing her that Hazel had gone into hospital earlier this morning and had written Sylvia down as the sole contact. Hazel had taken a turn for the worse, the cancer having spread to her brain.

The caller wouldn't listen to Sylvia's protests that she must be mistaken, that Hazel was healed, every trace of cancer had left her body. Royal jelly or honey or God had purged the sickness from her protector, her childhood defender.

The voice continued patiently, telling Sylvia that Hazel must have told her a white lie so she wouldn't worry, but she'd have to stay until further tests were run. Her prospects were grim, so Sylvia had best get there as soon as possible.

Sylvia thanked the voice, then returned the phone to its cradle.

But she couldn't leave yet. Couldn't go to the hospital. She hadn't been to one since that day her dad seriously hurt her mom. She wasn't able to explain why, but she was compelled to go through the bees once more. The desire was more irresistible than the compulsion a child has to peel away a scab.

By the time she arrived on Hazel's property a low fog obscured the ground, thickening the closer it approached Goodmanswood. The sun was high enough to disperse most of the shadows, but those that remained clung to the trees stubbornly. Sylvia ran across the pasture, her Wellingtons collecting damp until heavy with dew.

Hazel must have been here earlier, before she drove herself to hospital. The frames had been removed, stacked against hive boxes, or haphazardly dropped to the ground.

All of the bees were gone.

Sylvia picked up a frame. The honeycomb was beautiful with disorder. A glorious pestilence that perverted the hexagons into patterns and ultraviolet shades she'd never imagined human eyes were capable of detecting.

The comb was a subversion of design from the undesigned, patterns boiling from the patternless, exhibiting glory in such beauty. She wept at God's terrible inventions. If the world *was* intentional, it had been formed maliciously, the maker intent on antagonizing its handiwork.

She heard herself utter a strange, inarticulate noise.

She expected a beautiful light to blossom before her, but only saw an absence of luster, yet the colors still captivated, still presented a spectacle, preparing Sylvia to receive their full radiance. She didn't understand how this could be, though she was certain she wasn't hallucinating. Any thought beyond the magnificent sickness within the hive was irrelevant. A cosmic hum filled the world.

Entropic forces unfurled their random actions. She glimpsed something yawning widely in the woods. A mouth spoke.

Sylvia was compelled to obey the roaring voice from the forest, from *within* the trees. The voice insisted she travel beneath its archaic limbs, underneath its tangled roots. A part of Sylvia relented, a portion of her soul obeyed that rumbling command. She hesitantly walked into Goodmanswood.

The infected trees pressed in. An encroaching avalanche of green pushed fractured limbs and splintered wood. The earth shuddered like the flanks of a beast twitching away a fly, a trajectory of startled birds spread into the sky. The ground gave an atavistic moan, as if shrugging off any remaining pretense of disguising itself as the forest.

Sylvia was certain she was in the throes of nightmare until the twigs and brambles scratching at her exposed skin forced her to accept that she was awake. A strange musk drifted on the air, like the odor of a cage at the zoo. She was already near the mysterious den.

She found the lion.

His belly was split open. Raw viscera spread out, splashes of blood coating the moss and leaves in a wide radius. Heavy, dark blood flowed in a thick line from the animal, pushing bits of forest floor flotsam ahead, dribbling over the lip of the den into the darkness. The stench of torn bowels and ammonia stink of urine masked any other forest scents.

A mass of bees had gathered inside the open wound of the beast's stomach, crawling over each other in an agitated ritual. A strangely shaped honeycomb was already in progress, dripping golden light. The insect's buzzing reverberated from the lion's open gut with such force it appeared as if it was breathing shallowly.

The lichen on the rocks had spread across the floor, and onto the trunks of several trees. It glowed a beautiful blue green. Moisture on the filament's tips pulsated like minuscule stars.

Sylvia's palms were sticky from the lichen. She didn't remember touching them.

She stared at the mutilated lion for an undetermined duration. Time no longer seemed of any importance. She sat down on the forest floor, at the edge of the pit, to continue her vigil.

The hive continued to grow inside the lion, and Sylvia idly thought that Hazel would love to see this magnificent work of art. But this would never happen. Sylvia's protector, her childhood champion, would never experience this.

The sweet stench of blood, raw muscle, and decomposition wafted from the hole. Sylvia wanted to curl up and sleep. Her only desire to be secure once more, hidden away in a confined space. Sheltered.

The pit was unreasonably inviting, its refuge beckoning. The struggle to stave off the urge to enter was that of a child refraining from tonguing a hole in their gums after a tooth has fallen out. She leaned into the opening.

As she began her descent, a sudden memory of the last time her father was in her life came to Sylvia. He was hollering. Punching her mom. He hit her so hard the roof of her mouth split open. Then he stormed out, never to return. Sylvia called the emergency number for help. She held her mother's hand while they waited for the ambulance.

THE NUMINOUS IN GOD, NATURE, AND HORROR

Caspar David Friederich's painting, *Woman Before the Rising Sun* (alternatively titled *Woman Before the Setting Sun*) elicits a profound awe at the majesty of nature. The woman's outstretched hands convey something like prayer, or a supplication of wonder at the sight of dawn (or dusk). Friederich's paintings in general demonstrate a transcendental realm where nature reigns. His art conjures astonishment at humanity's tremulous presence on Earth.

Hiroshige's *Wind Blown Grass Across the Moon* accomplishes something similar. While it would be a chauvinistic mistake to make a one-to-one comparison, Hiroshige's portrayal of grass contrasted against a full moon is similar to *Woman Before the Rising Sun*; both evoke terror and wonder in the face of Nature.

Volumes could be written on African art alone. Take the Yoruba, for the,

> ...deft, luminous peace of Yoruba religious art blinds us therefore to the darker powers of the tragic art into which only the participant can truly enter. The grotesquerie of the terror cults misleads the unwary into equating fabricated fears with the exploration of the Yoruba mind into the mystery of his individual will and the intimations of divine suffering to which artistic man is prone.[1]

---

[1] Wole Soyinka, *Myth, Literature and the African World*, (Cambridge University Press. 2000), 155.

There's an ominous quality to these arts—in paintings, film, music, literature, the emphasis on nature occulted, yet also gloriously pious, conveys a sense of awe, of the universe's scope and our infinitesimal place in it, of God, of beauty and mystery. There are so many fascinating examples amongst various cultures I can't possibly do justice to the varieties of art that explores the connection between God, Nature, and fear.

Of course, we're dealing with Rudolf Otto's awful terror, his oft discussed *Mysterium tremendum et fascinans*. It's the numinous reverence at the heart of religious, as well as artistic and literary fervor. Rather than give my interpretation of Otto's concept, I'll let his own words clarify the idea,

> We will take to represent this [absolute overpoweringness] the term *majestas*, majesty—the more readily because anyone with a feeling for language must detect a last faint trace of the numinous still clinging to the world. The *tremendum* may then be rendered more adequately *tremenda majestas*, or "aweful majesty".
>
> ...there is the feeling of one's own submergence, of being but "dust and ashes" and nothingness. And this forms the numinous raw material for the feeling of religious humility...[2]

Regardless the art or time, there's this difficult to define liminal (as opposed to liminoid) stage where ecstatic fear and religious ecstasy in the face of one's faith, or the natural world, coincide. That groveling submission before something so beloved it intimidates and inspires, is paramount. What are its origins? Why this submissive dread, this overwhelming fascination with the ineffable that invariably informs so much art, so many religions, and horror fiction specifically? Most importantly, does the numinous reside within the believer *and* non- believer; the deist, polytheist, monotheist, atheist, and the

---

[2] Rudolph Otto, *The Idea of the Holy: An Inquiry into the Non-Rational Factor in the Idea of the Divine and its Relation to the Rational*, trans. John W. Harvey (Oxford University Press. 1958), 19.

secularist throughout human history? As philosopher Almond states, "...the numinous experience may be conceptualized in theistic, trans-theistic, and non-theistic terms."[3]

I have a distinct memory of when I was 5 and we'd just moved from Southern California to Oregon, to our new home, a house hidden away in the woods on an isolated 32-acre forest covered mountain. I remember the first night there, standing by myself outside, looking into the dark woods free of any light pollution in such a distant place. I was dumbstruck by the majesty and mystery of it all. Like Sanderson in Blackwood's "The Man Whom the Trees Loved," I too was consumed by what I can only describe as a pantheistic fervor and raw atavistic fear at what I could not comprehend lurking within the darkest depths of the forest. I experienced that pious terror in the grandeur and power where nature, religion, and horror embrace.

The vastness of the natural world may invoke reactions similar to those moved by pious revelations, and this is of great relevance to the terrifying grandeur of weird storytelling. The uncanny is omnipresent and seems to be an innate aspect of being human, of how we view the world and how the irrational, surreal, and disturbing distortion of the physical world invokes unease.

As a species we're captivated by infinite expanses—it informs our concepts of an afterlife, religions, our gods, thus inviting fear and wonder. This reaction to never-ending spaces and concepts is likely innate. Psychologists Dacher Keltner and Jonathan Haidt write in their groundbreaking study,

> ...two features form the heart of prototypical cases of awe: vastness, and accommodation. Vastness refers to anything that is experienced as being much larger than the self, or the self's ordinary level of experience or frame of reference. Vastness is often a matter of simple physical size, but it can also involve social size such as fame, authority, or prestige. Signs of vastness

---

[3] Phillip C. Almond, *Mystical Experience and Religious Doctrine: An Investigation of the Study of Mysticism in World Religions*, (Berlin: De Gruyter Mouton, 2014) 113.

such as loud sounds or shaking ground, and symbolic markers of vast size such as a lavish office can also trigger the sense that one is in the presence of something vast. In most cases vastness and power are highly correlated, so we could have chosen to focus on power, but we have chosen the more perceptually oriented term "vastness" to capture the many aesthetic cases of awe in which power does not seem to be at work.[4]

I'm reminded of the brilliant writings of R.H. Benson, whose Catholicism informed his ghost stories as sage warnings against spiritualism, a heartfelt condemnation or offense at the intrusion of the supernatural. In his novel *The Necromancers*, a "Thing" has traveled from "a spiritual distance so unthinkable and immeasurable, that the very word distance meant little."[5]

Vastness. Light years. Parsecs. Immeasurable gulfs. There's a tattoo of the numinous inked in our brains, and so this indescribable dread in the face of the supernatural or Nature's majesty is unavoidable. Few writers captured this so passionately as Benson.

John Gatta points out that the poet William Cullen Bryant makes an interesting point relevant to the numinous in Nature (referring to Bryant's poem, *The Prairies*),

> Only by looking beyond this vacancy, and beyond the current vitality of insects, birds, and 'gentle quadrupeds,' can [Bryant] imagine the prehistory of human races that once inhabited this land. He then finds the landscape haunted by ghostly powers.[6]

---

[4] Dacher Keltner and Jonathan Haidt, "Approaching awe, a moral spiritual, and aesthetic emotion," *Cognition and Emotion*, 17, no. 2, (2003), 303.

[5] R.H. Benson, *The Necromancers*, (London: Hutchinson & Co., 1909), 305.

[6] John Gatta, *Making Nature Sacred: Literature, Religion, and Environment in America from the Puritans to the Present* (Oxford University Press, 2004), 78.

Gatta goes on to refer to Thoreau with a similar observation,

> And insofar as the sacred corresponds most broadly to an experience of the numinous—that is, to an encounter with something "wholly other," beyond the usual bounds of human culture, the nonhuman world of nature is evidently allied to the numinous. Confirming nature's "wildness" has at least a potential religious value then, insofar as it helps us, in Thoreau's words, "to witness our own limits transgressed, and some life pasturing freely where we never wander."[7]

God, Nature, and horror are inexorable aspects of our being.

Our brains assume the persistence of our thoughts, emotions, personalities, and *minds* after death. Studies have proposed that children implicitly support belief in an afterlife, as it is impossible for the human brain to comprehend non-existence.[8]

There is tantalizing research on humans being "implicit" or "intuitive" theists—that is, primates programmed to interpret design in disorder, patterns in nothingness, order in ambiguity. We are set to attribute intention to natural objects.[9]

Humans are "promiscuous" teleologists, interpreting natural phenomena as being there for *us*. The world revolves around Homo sapiens, and any perceived design is surely the consequence of supernatural forces choosing to single out humanity. Horror taps into this atavistic theism in that it may fill the reader with a form of awe that allows one to contemplate whether there's

---

[7] Ibid., 129.

[8] J.M. Bering & D.F. Bjorklund, "The natural emergence of reasoning about the afterlife as a developmental regularity," *Developmental Psychology* 40, (2004), 217–233.

[9] D. Kelemen, & C. DiYanni, "Intuitions about origins: purpose and intelligence in children's reasoning about nature," *Journal of Cognition and Development*, 6, (2005),3– 31.

something *beyond* this physical world, an order, an ineffable truth that sets us to gape at the majesty of chaos. The conceit of an ineffable cosmos caring about us is a seductive thought, and even permeates secular humanist ideologies in exemplifying the virtues of our accomplishments through art, science and such, as if we've achieved some pinnacle on the Great Chain of Being.

Even if we're born with the assumption of agency, and the glories of the numinous may be part and parcel of that genetic bundle, theism *isn't* universal. Otto assumed Christianity when proposing his *mysterium, tremendum et fascinans*. The concept of the numinous is still important despite Otto's monotheistic default. Humanity's insignificance in the face of storms, the ocean and its depths, vistas, massive mountain ranges, the vastness of the cosmos, in the complexity of the infinite, of numbers, Fibonacci patterns, fractals, infinite repetitions in the natural world, doesn't require theism to inspire and thrill. Nature is awe-inspiring. Nature is terrifying. We're all the product of the same evolutionary processes; we have a numinous seed planted in our heads regardless the culture or era we were born into.

The numinous remains relevant to non-theistic expressions. There's something more, if not universal, applicable across a wide swath of humanity, thus "[t]heistic cognition is so deeply ingrained that even atheists, agnostics, and less religious people display implicit responses consistent with religious beliefs."[10]

Of course, much of this may run the risk of putting too much credence in sociobiology, or evolutionary psychology, as explanations for human behaviors. All too often the rather tenuous findings of sociobiology are cherry picked and shoehorned into specific political opinions. But when it comes to the numinous, I think an acknowledgement of its persuasive influence across cultures, among various faiths and philosophies, in wildly different artistic expressions, merits some consideration. This humbling, frightening astonishment occurs whether contemplating one's place in the universe, the nature of the gods, or peering

[10] Eric Luis Uhlman, Andrew Poehlman, and John A. Bargh, "Implicit Theism." In *Handbook of Motivation and Cognition Across Cultures*, ed. by Richard Sorrentino, Susumu Yamaguchi (Cambridge: Academic Press, 2008), 72.

into the dark recesses of a vast unexplored forest.

Nature and pious wonder are inexorably bound. The mystery and beauty of the natural world inspires a breathless admiration comparable to religious mania. This universe is awesome in its scope and impenetrable depths; this existence is awesome in the terror it invokes at our inability to fully comprehend its secrets.

All we can do is wallow in our venal imperfections. We're all gazing out upon the abandoned, dead universe with something like jealous admiration and fear, dreaming of no longer being alone. We tremble before the majestic realization that we will never know anything with certainty. We mourn our fates as primates anchored to a physical reality that denies us the seduction of anything beyond the tangible.

BIBLIOGRAPHY

Almond, Phillip C. *Mystical Experience and Religious Doctrine: An Investigation of the Study of Mysticism in World Religions.* Berlin: De Gruyter Mouton, 2014.

Benson, R.H. *The Necromancers.* London: Hutchinson & Co., 1909.

Bering, J. M., & Bjorklund, D. F. "The natural emergence of reasoning about the afterlife as a developmental regularity." *Developmental Psychology,* 2004: 40.

Gatta, John. *Making Nature Sacred: Literature, Religion, and Environment in America from the Puritans to the Present.* Oxford University Press, 2004.

Kelemen, D., & DiYanni, C. "Intuitions about origins: purpose and intelligence in children's reasoning about nature." *Journal of Cognition and Development,* 6, (2005).

Keltner, Dacher and Haidt, Jonathan. "Approaching awe, a moral spiritual, and aesthetic emotion." *Cognition and Emotion,* 17, no. 2, (2003).

Otto, Rudolph. *The Idea of the Holy: An Inquiry into the Non-Rational Factor in the Idea of the Divine and its Relation to the Rational.* Translated by John W. Harvey. Oxford University Press, 1958.

Soyinka, Wole. *Myth, Literature and the African World.* Cambridge University Press, 2000.

Uhlman, Eric Luis, Poehlman, Andrew, and Bargh, John A. "Implicit Theism." In *Handbook of Motivation and Cognition Across Cultures,* edited by Richard Sorrentino, Susumu Yamaguchi, Cambridge: Academic Press, 2008.

THE WORLD IS WAITING FOR THE SUNRISE

"The table floated *and* danced!" Alice Haraway addressed their guests, Howard and Rose Comstock.

"My wife neglected to mention that Walter also stopped all of the clocks in the house at the precise same moment," Gregory playfully interjected, splashing a slug of Canadian whiskey, vermouth, and grenadine into a cocktail shaker with practiced ease. "*Margery* the psychic wonder indeed."

"Who?" Rose asked, attempting to adjust a blue cloche hat over her hair while balancing a petite raspberry mousse cake in her other hand.

"*Walter*. Mina Crandon's deceased little brother. Quite the restless spirit." Gregory poured the cocktail into four martini glasses lined up on the bar.

"No, no. I mean you called Mina, *Margery*."

"Aha. I s'pose I did. Margery is Mina's alias. All the papers have been alluding to *Margery's* séances. Looks like Scientific American is going to investigate her. They've gathered quite the gang of Harvard and MIT men."

"I read that Houdini is to be part of the committee as well." Rose said.

"Is that so? A magician! I can't imagine what he could possibly contribute. I suppose Mina has *everyone's* attention these days." Gregory said with disdain.

"Certainly captured *your* attention, Dr. Haraway. A regular Isadora Duncan that girl." Rose laughed at the hoary joke, then turned to her husband Howard.

"Am I right, dear?"

"Hm?" Howard sighed away a haze of cigarette smoke in an exhalation of irritation, as if acknowledging the discussion was of great inconvenience.

"Linger Awhile" played low and jaunty through the Victrola's horn.

"Mina. We're speaking of Mina Crandon." Rose didn't restrain her annoyance.

"Oh! All that ectoplasmic so-and-so. Psychic cantilevers, strange flabby things. Like a fat baby's arms— that is, a curious rotary of the furniture." Howard indicated the spinning record with a tilt of his bald head. He rolled another cloud of smoke from his mouth to join the reeking fog gathered at the ceiling.

"Things got pretty thick on that fourth-floor room. So, you two've been?" Howard directed his question to Alice.

Alice smiled demurely, uncomfortable at the attention. She spoke softly, "Two séances early last year, though Gregory attended a few more before the, well, before we no longer felt welcome attending."

"Oh dear!" Rose raised a perfectly manicured eyebrow. "Due to the rumors?"

"What's that?" Howard asked.

"Dr. Crandon *has* been known to perform, eh, operations of a *delicate* nature." Rose explained.

"You mean feticide?" Howard's mouth was more smirk than smile.

Alice's gaze fell to the wood floor, a habit she'd attained to keep herself from appearing overly confrontational when responding. She ran her palms against her pearl-gray brocade gown. "Howard, please. I insist on kindness. I stopped going because I was not comfortable engaging in morally questionable religious practices."

"Dr. Crandon's Boston Brahmin, through and through. I'm not one to question his moral choices." Howard's pale, blue eyes peered over his spectacles in judgment. "Much less his medical ones."

"Howard. Rose. Alice. Here you are."

Alice was grateful for Gregory's interruption as he handed them each a drink.

"A couple years' worth of liquor has held up rather well, hasn't it?" Gregory said to no one in particular as he crouched to replace the bottles back into the well-stocked hutch.

Rose perked up at that, "Look here, Gregory is worried Volstead himself will knock down the door!"

Amused, Gregory lifted his glass, "Here's to our right to enjoy ancient whiskey—may those who use it never abuse it."

"I believe you mean 'ancient *rites* and recent *wrongs*,'" Howard said, laughing at his witticism.

Languidly sipping her drink, Alice feigned amusement as was expected of her; any risk of negatively influencing Gregory's social standing was not one worth taking. A lecturer in clinical obstetrics, her husband had recently acquired a tentative circle of acquaintances including Dr. Crandon and Howard Comstock, Assistant Professor of Philosophy at Harvard. The Comstocks were recent acquisitions to the neighborhood.

After the Haraways' falling out with the Crandons, Alice had become overly cautious when it came to gatherings. She'd play the part of the doting wife to perfection, hosting and worrying over their guest's every whim. But Howard's smug countenance and cocksure attitude incited something dangerous and barbed in her.

"What's this?" Rose placed her hand on a book next to a lacquered cigarette box on a tea-table. The title read, *The Psychic Structures at the Goligher Circle*, by a W.J. Crawford, D.Sc.

"Gregory is always reading about spooks and psychic flap-doodle." Alice said more dismissively than intended.

"*Your* Dr. Haraway? So, Dr. Crandon isn't the only Harvard man interested in Spiritualism. Your husband is quite the mystery, isn't he Alice?" Rose said coquettishly.

Alice's face flushed. "We share an interest in the same mystery."

"I don't think it's flap-doodle for a father to want to know whether the living may contact the dead," Gregory said.

Alice's expression was both morose and accusatory. "Must we speak of Noah in front of our guests?"

"I don't see why we shouldn't." Gregory emptied his glass in one tilt.

"All this talk of Mina and rites and psychics—we simply must do a séance!" Rose blurted out with such enthusiasm several drops of liquor slipped over the rim of her glass and slid down her chiffon dress like pearls from a broken necklace.

The Haraways had only known the Comstocks briefly, so they hadn't told them about their son Noah. Alice had no cause to find Rose's callousness affecting, but a growing disgust at their vile personalities poisoned her mood.

"We'll use this table. And it's an easy matter to extinguish the lights." Gregory was clearly captivated by the suggestion of a séance.

"But the windows—" Alice protested.

"The sun has set." Rose said.

"And we can tack sheets over the windows." Gregory's enthusiasm touched Alice, until she realized his demeanor was incumbent on how much he'd had to drink.

"I'm not certain we should do this, Gregory." Alice said.

"You seemed interested at Mina's séances."

"I was—" Alice hesitated, not confident enough to relay her true feelings on the matter. She chose her words carefully, "I was more willing to suspend disbelief then. I'm no longer convinced Mina truly communed with the hereafter."

"That's just my Catholic girl talking. Where's the adventurous girl I married?" Gregory didn't seem to realize he'd increased the volume of his voice. He turned to the linen closet to fetch sheets.

"It's not that so much as my hesitation to accept what I saw as anything but hooey." Alice blushed at her bluntness.

Rose butted in, "Even the Transcendentalists with their floral poetry and talk of nature believe in something. I shudder to contemplate your bleak view. To think! Of nothingness!"

Howard gave his wife a look of approval, then turned to Alice, "No Summerland? I cannot understand how one could accept a Catholic Heaven yet deny any other."

"But I haven't—"

"Alice," Gregory interrupted, "think of it as a scientific investigation. Nothing more. Leave your religious concerns behind for one evening."

"I suppose there's little harm in such a thing." Alice acquiesced.

"Nor is there in harming little things." Howard said so quietly only Alice, who was closest to him, could hear. He gave an unadulterated mocking grin as he stubbed his cigarette out in a wooden ashtray.

Alice clenched her jaw, thought of Howard's flesh torn and bloodied by her fingernails raked against his face. To calm her rage, she busied herself with helping her husband tack several sheets over the two windows in the third-floor room. Howard and Rose moved the tea-table beneath the only light source.

"We clasp hands and maintain the circle no matter what may occur. And Alice, since you're the most pious of us heathens, would you mind leading the séance in prayer?" Gregory joked with a contradictory solemnity.

"Oh, I'm not—" Alice began.

"Please, dear. It would mean much to me. And Noah."

"Gregory. I am not certain I'm ready."

"Together. We'll try. Just this once."

"May I ask who this Noah fellow is?" Rose indelicately spoke up.

"A departed loved one." Gregory spoke curtly. "Someone we would very much like to hear from again."

Alice sat down, defeated. She was surprised to see her martini glass empty, as she was a modest drinker at best. The glass sat on the tea-table's surface, a ring of liquid forming around its base. Gregory took a seat to her right, Rose to her left, and Howard across from her. Alice was relieved she didn't have to touch Howard or have him touch her.

Gregory stood abruptly, reached to the pendant light's chain above. He pulled the cord.

The room flooded with blackness. Gregory took his seat and fumblingly reached over to grip Alice's right wrist with his left hand, and Howard's left with his right. Alice felt Rose's ostentatiously ringed fingers heavy on her hand.

The circle completed, they bowed their heads as Alice led a prayer. She faltered at first, uncomfortable with the words. Summoning the dead was ungodly, but was the Communion of Saints such a vastly different thing?

Gregory had been so eager to hold a séance, Alice thought there must be some value in this. Despite her husband's medical training, he believed in the primacy of the immaterial over the empirical realm. He'd long insisted that spirits *did* return, having experienced such visitations before, their taps and frenetic cavorting about Mina Crandon's séance room making a devout believer of him over a year ago. In his view, science was all too obstinate in its reluctance to study phenomena not already well established, and philosophy remained the luxury of effete intellects—but Spiritualism was tangible proof of an afterlife, incontrovertible evidence that death wasn't the end of everything.

Alice knew he clung to this reasoning in hopes he could speak with Noah once more. But as to the question of whether or not contacting spirits afforded any redemptive possibility for humanity, well, Alice was all too skeptical. Despite her profound faith, she didn't share her husband's views on any afterlife. She wasn't convinced that anything divine dwelled within nature, or that an ideal spiritual reality was germinating within humanity's breast.

The séance proceeded with little of interest occurring. After nearly an hour of singing and prayers for Noah to make himself known, all four grew weary and decided he wasn't going to appear tonight. Alice quoted a passage that seemed relevant given the occasion:

> "For we are sojourners before You,
>
> and tenants, as all on the earth are like a shadow,
>
> and there is no hope."

Howard muttered that her piety was inappropriate, but nobody paid him any heed. Relieved the charade was over, Alice was about to break the circle when she felt Gregory move his hand away from her wrist.

It took but a moment for him to adjust his other cuff, a reprieve which allowed Alice to move her hand forward several inches towards the center of the table. When her husband gently placed his hand back to its original position, he gripped her further up the arm, allowing substantially more freedom for her to bend her wrist and wriggle her fingers undetected. Certain he'd done this unconsciously, she decided to take advantage of the situation.

"I sense a presence," Alice intoned.

Gregory stiffened, startled by her announcement.

"A young man, encompassed by aetheric light."

"Is it Noah?" Gregory's words were slurred with alcohol. He squeezed her arm with such strength Alice feared her skin might bruise.

Alice tipped her head back, released a dramatic moan. If medium she be, she'd play the part to perfection.

"Oh, it *is* our dear sweet Noah!"

Slowly waving her fingers back and forth in the darkness, she tried to contact the empty martini glass she'd set down before the light was extinguished. She stretched her fingers as far as they could extend, doing so with the utmost care, preventing the muscles and tendons in her forearm to tense and betray her intentions to Gregory or Rose.

Gregory's voice cracked as he held back tears. "Please speak to us. Your mother and father are here!"

Why was she doing this? To mislead? To confirm her own faith while disputing any pretense the dead could speak?

When her fingertips brushed against the glass, Alice restrained a celebratory gasp. Arching her wrist as far back as possible without attracting attention, she ran a finger up the side to the lip and over. The first knuckle of her index finger bent, she hooked the glass and carefully turned it on its side so as not to make any sound against the table.

"Give us a sign, son!" Gregory was no longer concerned if the others heard the rawness in his plea.

Bending her wrist away, Alice opened her hand and swatted the glass, her limb from wrist to shoulder completely relaxed. It rolled noisily across the table's surface, over the edge, and hurtled through the air.

She heard the glass strike the far wall with an emphatic thump, followed by a series of lesser impacts culminating in a shattering on the wooden floor. The effect exceeded her expectations; the pitch-black room amplified the din. She only wished she'd managed to hit Howard with the projectile.

The reaction from the sitters was immediate. The normally unflappable Howard breathed an impressed *whew-w-w!* while Rose squealed with delight.

But Gregory sat resolute, giving no indication of his thoughts on the phenomenon. Alice felt his grip loosen. She was filled with a sense of importance, a relevance that elevated her from drudgery to jubilation.

When Gregory turned the light back on, Alice's cheeks and chin were found to glisten with what Rose proclaimed to be neither tears nor perspiration, but that miraculous fluid known as *ectoplasm*. All heartily agreed that pseudopods had parted the darkness and thrown a glass.

Alice was certain it had been too dark to see anything. They'd mistaken spots in their vision as ectoplasm. A heady imagination conjured all the necessary elements for a séance.

She couldn't dissuade them of their certainty, even if she'd any interest in doing so. Let them surmise her sweaty skin as a miraculous occurrence. This was what they'd requested. This was what they'd wanted. Let them wallow in a spiritualist stupor. She understood now how believers could so easily become followers.

"We simply must do this again!" Rose insisted.

Alice looked to her husband. Gregory's forehead was flushed from a combination of the hot room and booze. His beard bristled with the humidity. Standing before her, his hands on her face, he said, "Oh you are wonderful. You are wonderful." He was openly weeping.

Despite her trickery, Gregory's adulation filled Alice with something she was wary of identifying as hope.

Everything in Alice's home took on an ominous air after that first séance—the curve of a chair's back held suggestions of empty spaces allowing unseen forces to reside. The Victrola brimmed with malicious possibilities. Something untoward could shriek from any record, from behind a window, from any shadow pooling by each and every piece of furniture.

Even Alice's strolls about the South Slope, along Mount Vernon Street past the fire station and Sunflower House, were now fraught with trepidation. Entryways yawned, the streets no longer familiar, they veered at sharper angles than remembered and led to unfamiliar cobblestone-covered blocks. The city trembled with a soft blackness about its edges.

That evening, she dreamt of a beautiful clear day long ago. The rolling hills were dotted with old masonry, a veneer of deep green moss on every stone. Shallow valleys sheltered apple trees, their branches sagged with bright fruit. It was a familiar memory of the Back Bay Fens, where her husband and Noah rode horses, near their old picnic spot where they'd enjoy cheese and bread and watch the wind shake yellow papery Sugar Maple leaves. The Virgilia blossomed so profusely that year the branches dipped, inviting Noah to clamber their length. Noah, sweet handsome Noah, would always be an integral aspect of this geographical memory.

Alice would forever picture Noah as an 8-year-old boy, not the strapping 19-year-old man he was when slaughtered in the Champagne Marne offensive, struck down among the cratered earth and jagged tree trunks. She'd seen photographs of the war, of corpses held upright in rusty wire, bodies mangled by German bullets, doughboys rotting in the mud. Of course, none of this was explained in detail on the telegram, only a terse, "Death was instantaneous. We were unable to retrieve his remains and he lies in a soldier's grave where he fell."

Eight was the age that held the most distinct memories for Alice, the moments of triumph, the age she kept coming back to again and again. That was when they'd relocated from Fall River to Boston for Gregory's work, excited at the prospect of a city with such a vibrant history. Back when she held a vestige of happiness inside.

But the vague message on the telegram didn't prevent her from envisioning her son's lower jaw dangling loosely, his mutilated mouth held together by strands of flesh, a raw absence that exposed his open throat. His fingernails splintered and clumped with earth.

Alice woke Gregory with her cries. He rushed in from his bedroom, in hopes he could smooth out her nightmare.

Embracing her, he said, "I'd do anything to have him back, Alice." His skin and hair stank of sweat and whiskey.

Bleary-eyed, not yet fully awake, Alice spoke with no restraint, "I wish you'd gone in his place."

Gregory drew back in surprise. "I would have gladly gone, but I was already too old for the draft."

Alice knew it hadn't been a possibility; it wasn't until much later that the policy had expanded to include men up to the age of 45. But she still imagined her husband stepping forward, insisting he go to Europe, draft registration card in hand, ready to fight in their son's place. Noah would have stayed behind with her and their lives would have continued with or without Gregory's safe return. The only joy Alice felt was when fantasizing about the death of the man she'd married, so the life of their only child could continue unabated.

"I would have gladly gone in my boy's stead." Gregory repeated with growing anger.

"I know. I know."

His mood soured, Gregory spoke with no expectation of disagreement, "I want us to try another séance. The Comstocks want to participate again."

Alice looked at the sheet wrapped around her body, transfixed by the folds and soft wrinkles in the Italian linen. She didn't speak.

"I have an early morning tomorrow." With that, Gregory stood, then hurriedly left her bedroom.

Alice knew he'd be late to work again, though a ready explanation to excuse his drinking and others willing to cover for him had always disguised his mistakes in the past. She wanted to refuse another séance, insist that what had been done was done. Noah was dead. God had a Plan, and they were not to interfere. Instead she stared at Gregory's silhouette as he walked away.

Gregory slapped the newspaper onto the table.

"Let those top-heavy Harvard men subject their scientific instruments to those willing to be prodded! I'd refuse to allow my wife to be subjected to such a carnival!"

Alice looked at the headline for that Tuesday's *Boston American*:

HOUDINI BRINGS $10,000 TO CHALLENGE
'MARGERY'

"A magician has the gall to question what occurs in a séance? With a cash prize? That low-minded sweatshop sheeny wouldn't know a spirit if it—"

"Kindness, Gregory," Alice said. Gregory had insisted the Comstocks join them for dinner and cocktails, and she was embarrassed by his behavior in front of their guests.

Gregory ignored her, "Anarchists. Rebels, the lot of 'em. How many new faiths have made Boston their home? Far too many in my estimation. And this! This *magician* comes to our town and—"

"Pity that King's Chapel is home to the anti-Trinitarian rabble." Rose gently teased, an aspect of distaste in the shape of her mouth.

Howard nodded in fervent agreement. "They flock here like Jews to Marxism. All of these strange new faiths. This town seethes with barbaric practices as of late."

"Kindness, Howard!" Alice protested.

"Yes, of course. Kindness," Howard murmured over the slick of scotch sliding past his lips.

"I find it charming how Spiritualists have their séances and the papists their All Souls' Day—is there really much of a difference?" Rose was clearly goading Alice, though no one else seemed to notice.

Alice knew the Comstocks had no interest in friendship; they were only here to participate in another séance. She found the prospect ghastly. Her world was growing darker, the prospect of pretending to speak to Noah again heart-wrenching. He was gone. Best to leave him in the bosom of Christ.

Séances were vulgar. An etheric force visiting this plane? This craze was ghost worship, a parlor game mistaken for a new faith, one that bore more than a whiff of blasphemy. Her heart felt heavy upon contemplating that she'd involved the memory of her only son in these games.

But if Spiritualism was chicanery at its crassest, and Creation had been wrought with but a Word, then could not fervent hope make the Word tangible? This allowed the possibility that *her* Word could create tangible works.

And if the Transcendentalists of which Rose had spoken were correct, nature was sacred, so the land itself could hold spiritual vitality. Alice prayed it was so.

She truly wanted to speak with Noah.

"Were you listening, Alice? Are you opposed to another go?" Gregory's question held concern, his conciliatory tone offering her the opportunity to decline.

"I am not opposed," she said, her heart withering in defeat.

Lectures, meetings, and social gatherings accounted for, they all agreed to the date Gregory marked on the calendar for the next séance.

Alice had just three weeks to come up with a means to make her dead son appear.

All four sat at the new table Gregory had custom ordered, built to specific dimensions as instructed by Alice. It had a wide surface, but was lightweight as well, unencumbered with any wrought iron. As Rose had explained in a pedantic tone, that particular element would interfere with psychic magnetism, though spirits were, so it was said, known to be drawn to voltaic fields. But Alice had omitted the iron out of concern it would make the table too heavy to move on her own in the dark, not on any dishonest nonsense about fields and forces. A vase of roses sat on the table's center.

Alice had read *The Psychic Structures at the Goligher Circle* and visited the recently opened Honan-Allston library for various titles on Spiritualist practices. Over the weeks, she'd invented several methods to conjure false spirits by sleight of hand and trickery, as well as sussing out how Mina may have accomplished some of her fraud. Confident in her abilities, she was ready to astound her small audience.

The parlor was dimmed, the red lantern Howard provided emitted an eerie glow that saturated the room in an unctuous shade, though any physical manifestations would be visible in the gloom. The floorboards appeared slick and black as oil in the unusual lighting. Alice feared her feet might sink into an endless pool of tar if she were to stand.

The pale faces of her three companions were hazy, like photographs whose chemical development had been interrupted. Alice's heart ached with the immorality of what she was about to present. But this is what her husband wanted. This was what she'd give him.

The circle completed, Alice derived strength from her newfound authority. She experienced a kind of empathy with the room's crannies and nooks, the patterns of the streets outside, the city's layout in its entirety. A calm purpose suffused her soul. She was of some importance at that moment, as necessary as the streams and lakes, the sun and moon. She'd never before held such responsibility.

Only minutes passed when Alice released a gargling sound from deep down. She tensed her arms and shook in paroxysms of mediumistic fervor to make certain her limbs were restrained.

"I see a fluidic nimbus flowing through the vibrations of our love," Alice moaned loudly, so as to mask the sound of her foot sliding forward against the floor. She wedged the toe tip of her right Sally pump beneath a foot of the table leg.

Shoe firmly secured, she turned her ankle towards the floor, lifting her end of the table several inches. The vase slid across the smooth walnut surface onto Howard's lap. He released such a shout of astonishment Alice had to restrain herself from further raising her leg and flipping the table onto his head for emphasis.

"Do not release your hold on the person next to you!" Alice demanded. The thrill of fooling educated folk and their disproportionately excited response to such a simple feat motivated Alice to attempt another. It was all too easy. She threw her head back.

"Look there!" Howard exclaimed. "What's happened to her face?" Alice's forehead glowed a sickly yellow-green, the color of a rotten pear.

"This house, our thoughts, this circle allows spirits to travel towards me on vibrations of etheric light," she growled in a masculine voice.

Her body suddenly went limp, head lowered to the tabletop. She lay there, seemingly asleep.

The dark red room seemed to pulse with tension.

"I am here. I did not die. There is no death." Alice spoke in a strange husky voice.

A white face bobbed over the edge of the table.

What appeared to be moist clumps of primordial fluid streamed from the disembodied head, under Alice's skirt, trailing between her thighs. Despite the diluted light, Gregory recognized the face.

"You may touch him now, Gregory. But no one else is to release their grip." Alice whispered, her words sending shivering tremors through the tabletop.

Gregory did so, marveling at the ectoplasm's texture, like blancmange, but oily and slick.

"My son. My son," he murmured as he rubbed the substance between thumb and forefinger.

"Oh, my boy. Welcome home. Welcome."

Gregory moved to stroke the dead child's cheek, but Alice reached out and grabbed his wrist.

"This is done," she said. "Reform the circle, Gregory."

He reluctantly leaned away from Noah's spirit and returned his hand to his wife's wrist.

Noah's head lowered beneath the edge of the table.

"Now we must bow our heads in prayer." Alice said.

When the prayers ended, they all sat wide-eyed as if waking from a beautiful dream or perplexing nightmare. Gregory turned the light back on and extinguished the red lantern. He appeared calm, tranquil.

"Oh look! The flowers are no longer buds! They're plump as if kissed by cherubs!" Rose remarked on finding the unbroken vase on the floor, surrounded by long stemmed roses.

Rose didn't know that Alice herself had purchased the fully bloomed flowers and placed them in the vase that morning.

She despaired of the path she'd chosen. Every soul in this room was decaying, festering rags pretending to be alive, their foolishness reprehensible.

To think the dead could return.

Gregory knelt before her. Clasping Alice's hand with both of his, he looked into her eyes beseechingly.

"You brought our boy home, dearest. You truly reached our boy."

Alice thought of the last séance she'd attended at the Crandons. Mina's 12-year-old son had been locked away in his bedroom, while Walter spoke in tones of the mud-gutter through his sister Mina, in the very room adjacent. The poor child must have been terrified. The clash of cymbals, cacophony of moving furniture, and wailing of profane voices would have disturbed anyone, much more so a young boy.

The world ran thick with corruption, on whose currents Alice knew she'd soon be swept away.

In the parlor, Gregory paced while Alice sat on the couch. His soles snapped against the cold floors. The Boston skies were slate gray with drizzle. Every room in the house was stifling and dreary, as if choked with an asphyxiating fog.

"Why won't you summon Noah again?" Gregory paused in his relentless back and forth. His eyes were bloodshot, cheeks blotchy. His hands trembled, fingers nervously plucked at the buttons on his vest, the others gripped a bottle of whiskey.

"There's nothing there." It had only been three days since the séance, and Alice was no longer willing to cower and pretend anymore. The edifice of her faith was collapsing, and she didn't intend her life to remain untouched by the aftermath. Two séances had been more than enough, and she wasn't about to continue the charade.

"A séance. Just the two of us. I'm not asking much. You brought our boy back to this house. Do it again." He pleaded, a petulant whine.

She almost confessed, but the hurt in Gregory's voice was touched by a white-hot obstinance that would accept no disagreement. Alice couldn't abide this. It took a great effort to refrain from lashing out, striking back against her own lies and her husband's simpering need to accept anything she presented as proof of reaching their dead son.

"I don't know. It may have been Noah. I can't say."

"I saw him, *Alice*. We *all* saw him." Gregory rasped, his voice weakening.

"There is no hereafter."

"What of Mina? What of *our* two séances? Not just me, but Howard and Rose saw him as well."

She could no longer appease him with her deceptions. Confessing would cleanse her soul. "All lies. I'm sorry, Gregory. I deceived everyone. I am so very sorry."

"I cannot accept that! I *saw* Noah! You've given me hope, Alice. Why are you so eager to take that away?"

"You *needed* to see Noah. Christ forgive me, for I did what you asked!"

"This is insane, Alice. I can't understand why you're denying—"

"*Noah* was a muslin cloth draped over a child's toy ball. His face a photograph you took when we were picnicking at the Fens, May of '15 I believe. I attached a slipper to the gimmick, which I put on my foot unseen, then lifted it so the head seemed to be floating over the edge of the table."

"Alice..."

"The fake spirit was hidden beneath my skirt. All I required was to grasp it with my feet, slip it on and wave it about with that butter saturated coil of cloth clasped between my thighs. You thought it was an ectoplasmic umbilical. The red lantern made it that much more difficult to detect my trickery."

"This is—I can't accept, no, you've—" his words were laced with a growing despair. "None of it was real?" Gregory's grip on his bottle was precarious, as if his body threatened to cease functioning.

"A gimcrack ghost, now hidden away in the back of my closet. At the bottom of the old chest."

"But your face glowed with light and—"

"Zinc sulfide luminous paste applied to my forehead. My bangs covered it. A flip of my hair and it was revealed. Nobody saw me wipe it away when you put out the red lantern and turned the light back on."

"The table rose—"

"I used my foot to tilt the table. It was that simple."

Gregory opened his mouth to shout, to roar, but only managed a strangled cry. The bottle fell from his hands, bounced against the floor but didn't break. Amber drops of liquor spotted the wood. He stepped away from his wife, hand to mouth as if embarrassed he'd been capable of such a susceptible sound.

"It was what *you wanted*." Alice stood, her gaze meeting his. A fierceness churned within him, while a collected strength shone in her eyes. "What you *demanded*."

This was all false. The world had been reduced to celebrating floating trumpets in darkened rooms and being told what to think by spirits in place of relying on their wits and humbling themselves before the immensity of God's nature. She'd associated with coarse people, humbled herself before unpleasant acquaintances to mollify a need for superiority. This lovely Boston home, her expensive clothing, furniture and material items, every aspect of their lives subjected to others' scrutiny—her very faith had been dictated by whims, piety itself now incumbent on fashion.

No more.

"My days are swifter than a weaver's shuttle. And come to an end without hope," Alice said mournfully. The very room seemed ethereal, as if she were caught between two states of matter, the temporal and vaporous, neither of which comforted her.

Her husband turned without a word and strode out of the room.

Hours later, an odd sound from the parlor startled Gregory. He set his bottle of Scotch aside and rushed into the room.

Alice was sprawled across the couch. On seeing her, Gregory shouted something inarticulate, with such sorrow it moved Alice with the very same sadness she felt on first learning of the death of their son.

Her dress was bunched up around her waist. Viscous threads of a pallid substance coiled from between her thighs. A teleplasmic umbilical stretched across her bare stomach, concluding in a wet clump of fetal ectoplasm in her arms.

Raising her wan face from newly formed child to husband, Alice's eyes welled with tears. She panted like a beast dying of thirst, locks of auburn hair plastered to her forehead. She made a low guttural sound that altered slightly before concluding, as if she'd been in considerable pain, ameliorated by a state of such ecstasy physical discomfort was no longer a concern.

"I've made us a boy again, Gregory. Is this what you wanted?"

He reached out to the mass cradled in his wife's arms. His fingers brushed against its muslin cloth skin, damp with mucous and blood. He pressed down tenderly, the material yielding slightly, allowing the cartilaginous skeleton beneath to be detected. The cunningly crafted wire frame support felt biological, even to a trained surgeon.

"You've made our son again," Gregory said with awe.

Anticipating further requests for miraculous demonstrations, on the day after the previous séance, Alice had cunningly stitched together portions of cloth and various animal parts, including a trachea, and purple-gray liver. After slathering it in blood from the butcher's shop, she'd left the horrid creation outside, imbuing it with the acrid stench of the grave. Now she manipulated the fabric and organic matter with her hands, like a shoddy puppet, or a child pretending their stuffed toy was alive.

Gregory wept, convinced Noah had come back to do everything all over again. He didn't see a hideous doll, but the beauty of a perfectly formed life and his wife holding their newborn in a posture of maternal bliss. The moldy babe's limbs and skin stank, but Gregory thought them pristine and playful as Harriet Hosmer's sculpture of Puck.

Falling to his knees, he laid his head on Alice's stomach. He stared at his wife and child for quite some time before mumbling, "He's everything I prayed for."

"You've been drinking. Go to sleep, Gregory. You smell of death."

"How long will his ectoplasmic body remain?"

"An hour. Two at most before the aether calls his little soul back home."

"Should we pray for him?" Gregory asked.

"I see no need. We brought him into our world with prayer, so he may depart with those sweet prayers still singing in his ears."

Gregory nodded in drunken understanding, then rose, touched her forehead with genuine affection. Clumsy with alcohol, he snagged her hair as he moved his hand away. His inebriated gesture was a promise that the worst had passed. Everything was going to be wonderful once more.

Just as he reached a chair, he collapsed, slouching down, chin resting on his chest. His snores let Alice know he was deep asleep.

Pretense done, Alice left the couch, pulled her dress down, removed the umbilical she'd fashioned from linen and putty. Quietly walking across the parlor, she exited through a door into the back yard, leaving the cloth umbilical behind to be disposed of later. The butcher shop remnants remained in her arms.

The rain fell lightly. The square shrubs surrounding the private space no longer appeared symmetrical, as if someone had uprooted and replanted the vegetation in a subtly different pattern. A metal sundial stood in the middle, raindrops singing off it in metallic tones. The neighbor's houses glowed a muted blue behind Palladian windows, as if strange fires burned within. The city had never felt so peculiar to her before, yet an uncanny skein stitched into the very fabric of the town traced its path to her heart and made her feel as if she finally belonged. She retrieved a spade from the shed in the corner.

Kissing the clotted fabric child's cheek, she gently swayed it in her arms. She sang a song from her childhood, lyrics breathed where she could recall them, hummed when she did not. Here in the clean night air, the grotesque fabrication was less fragrant with rot and mold. She quoted Job 6:11, transforming the passage into a sing-song verse,

"What is my strength,

that I should wait?

And what is my end,

that I should endure?"

She wept at her crime, fingers digging into the inanimate thing in her arms as if this false child had actually meant something of importance. She hoped God would snatch her last breath away so everything could simply cease to be. She wanted to tear the fabricated baby into fragments, throw the bloody cloth and decomposing meat doll about the grass.

But she held it like a child. She would bear the brunt of all the misery and discomfort as all women had always done. She would continue to put forth the greatest efforts and receive the least in turn. There had to be rewards elsewhere; something waiting in the hereafter. There was little reason to perform as was expected if nothing was to come of it. There must be, or what use was anything?

Setting the fetid bundle on the wet grass, she began to dig a hole in the soft soil.

The sky pressed down, an atmosphere of apprehension grew inside her, a black syrup seeping through the air, what she assumed must be darker storm clouds. Wisps of pale fog slipped from the shadows at the far end of the yard, like a figure retreating from a window. Alice lifted the soiled rags of her fake child, now sopping with foul rainwater.

Her arms suddenly ran warm with black liquid. She immediately recognized it as the tarry substance meconium. A child's first stool outside the womb.

The overturned earth was as dark and furred as the mold growing on the cloth. The night was black and sticky as her child's excrement shining on her hands. She gave Noah one last kiss.

"Kindness, my sweet Noah. Kindness."

She buried the filthy thing before it began to cry.

PALLADIUM AT NIGHT
(FOR BOB LEMAN)

Irepani first heard about the Leman fire lookout tower from his fellow homeless. Rumor had it the structure was abandoned in the late 80s and no longer received any funds for upkeep. It used to be rented out to weekend campers, but budget cuts prevented regular maintenance and safety issues meant the place was now unavailable to the public.

His down-and-out companions whispered strange things about the tower and shared so many stories the structure had become something of an urban legend. They insisted the city, even with its traffic, crime, and pollution, was a safer place than out in the middle of nowhere with nothing to threaten you except wildlife and starvation. The city offered warmth where the determined could find it—sustenance, and relative safety in numbers huddled in makeshift camps off the freeways. The wild offered nothing but solitude and hunger.

But Irepani welcomed solitude. He'd wanted to spend a few nights in the tower ever since hearing about it. The idea of being far from civilization and its trappings appealed to him. The lookout was perfect; nothing to rent and no way anybody would know he'd squatted there for a few days. He'd be safe. Hopefully the wild would help quell those alcoholic naggings that refused to completely vacate his system. Just get away from it all. The city. The part-time job. The past. He was grateful for everything in his life, especially his cousin Lorena, his dog Cadejo the Third, and God, but he needed to get away.

God hadn't prevented him from stealing Lorena's battered Jeep Wrangler to head out to the unexplored forest for a weekend of camping and contemplation. Lorena was out of town with another in a long line of boyfriends whose name Irepani hadn't bothered to remember. She wouldn't be back until

Wednesday. *I'll fill up the tank and it'll be like I never took it out for a ride at all. And Cadejo needs to get out of that shitty cramped studio apartment anyway.*

This line of thought allowed him to still be good with Lorena, Cadejo, *and* God.

That Trinity had saved him. If not for those three he'd never have quit drinking eight months, two weeks, and four days ago. He'd kicked the addiction and wasn't about to relapse. Made it this far—no need to give in to those dark needs. He was past that. Step by step, hand in hand with God to help over the rockier parts. Life had thrown plenty of crags and peaks his way.

They rolled down the gravel road for what he thought must have been at least an hour before Cadejo began to whine and paw at the passenger window. Caressing her muzzle calmed her. The expanse of forested land gave Irepani pause, but his companion was due for a bathroom break.

He reluctantly pulled the jeep over. The dashboard clock's blue light was dim. It displayed dashes instead of numbers. Something wrong with the electrical probably. He made a silent prayer for the Jeep to avoid breaking down out here in the middle of nowhere. Lorena would be pissed if that happened.

"Alright, alright. We're making a pit stop."

He looked towards the woods. A branch wobbled, leaves fluttered to the ground. The birds he assumed were responsible made an odd sound.

Opening the door, Cadejo immediately leapt out and disappeared into the high yellow grass. Standing alongside the ditch, Irepani watched the stalks jerk erratically as his best friend ran off her pent-up energy.

He'd only had three pets in his 24 years, all of them dogs. Cadejo when he was eight, Cadejo the Second in High School, and now Cadejo the Third. Cadejo the Third had been his friend for nearly three-years. He'd found the puppy abandoned on the streets of Portland when he himself was homeless for several months, when drinking had brought him to his lowest point.

He'd rather be with her than anyone else—even his cousin if he had to choose. He liked the quiet; living on the streets was nothing but incessant chatter and noise. Sirens, horns, pedestrians on their phones, schizophrenics shrieking about God and others trying to strike up a conversation when all he wanted to do was seethe silently in his private bubble. Cadejo never engaged in pleasantries, never mentioned the weather or what was popular on TV that week. Irepani loved her with all his heart.

Despite it being early September, his breath trailed above in gossamer strands. If the weather didn't clear it'd be a cold night in the lookout tower. They'd survived worse. Anything was better than sleeping on concrete, huddled near a steaming grate for warmth. He could no longer count on the booze to warm his bones at night. Those days were done.

But he wanted a drink. This wasn't just a craving, but something far more primal, addiction stained into his very soul. It was a cliché to say alcohol numbed him from the realities of life, but there was that and something more—drinking helped retain those rare moments when he'd felt happy about being alive, slowed everything down, prolonged the good times, the joyful memories moving as if sinking in molasses. Blotted out the anger and loneliness. Everything else was pushed aside, speeding by so quickly his drunken brain couldn't acknowledge the struggles and pain.

Power over the clock. All that power within a bottle. Irepani quietly recited a prayer,

Obtain for us from your most holy Son the grace of keeping our faith of sweet hope in the midst of the bitterness of life...

Cadejo had been gone far too long. Irepani felt panic rise in his throat, released it as a sharp whistle.

She immediately bounded back. Silly dog-smile on her face, ears perked up, burrs in her fur. He pulled a few from her hide, then opened the door for her to jump back into Lorena's Jeep. He gave her a treat then started the vehicle.

His heart hammered in his chest. Why was he so riled up? Cadejo had never been in any danger. The hustle and bustle of the city was comforting; the vastness of the wild held too many unexplored regions, places dimly lit where only cloven hoof and paw had disturbed the carpets of moss. Too many places for Cadejo to get hurt or lost. That must be why he was so on edge.

"Good morning everyone. Sorry I'm late. Needed a few cups of coffee to jumpstart the ol' brain." Dr. Hyman smiled at the seated gathering of physicists, astronomers, geologists, neuro-psychics, and military before him.

"You the screwball-in-charge?" Major General Targ stood at the front of the group. He jabbed his lit cigar in Dr. Hyman's direction.

"Heh, well, yes, all things considered, I suppose I am. My associates call me Dr. Hyman, though I'm ok with plain ol' Andrew. I don't believe smoking is allow—"

"So, Dr. Screwball-in-charge, has any of this psychic witchcraft mumbo-jumbo research your team has invested a considerable sum courtesy the DIA led to any useful information?"

"Actually, and I hope I'm not speaking out of turn sir, we're mainly funded by the SRI. And we don't really think of any of this as 'witchcraft'. Further—"

"I'm not interested in discussing fiscal matters or hexes with you Dr. Screwball-in-charge. I've got my considerably large nuts twisted in a knot over national security matters. These fine folks sitting behind me are in the same boat. I'm very concerned about just how much the nature of your discovery threatens that security."

"Of course, sir. We've retrieved information from the PAN shrine."

The gravel became increasingly sparse the further Irepani drove. The soil eventually became looser, turning to silt the deeper they traveled into the mountains. Eventually the way became nothing but dirt so soft the Jeep's wheels had difficulty getting a grip. The absence of tire marks indicated no other soul had come this way in quite some time.

Further up the mountain, the road narrowed. A tall embankment on the right, a steep decline on the left guided them into a ravine filled with Pacific Silver fir trees. Irepani couldn't push the Jeep any faster than 25. He kept his full attention on driving.

Reaching a gate, he feared they were at the end of the line—the Forest Service website hadn't mentioned anything about a key or lock number in these parts. Reluctantly, he left the Jeep to check it out. He was relieved to find the gate unlocked. A rusted metal sign someone had used for target practice read LEMAN OBSERVATORY.

He'd read online that the abandoned Leman Observatory was 4- miles east of the Leman lookout tower. He planned on hiking out with Cadejo to investigate the old place. Rumor had it they'd once conducted highly classified astrophysics experiments there back in the early 90s, but funding had dried up and the scientific staff had dispersed to JPL, NASA, and various other lesser known industries. He left the gate open, returned to the Jeep, and drove onto an even narrower road that was little more than a path cleared of vegetation.

Cadejo gave a brief anxious bark out the back window, as if something was following them. Irepani glanced into the rear-view mirror but didn't see anything that would've upset her.

Half an hour later, the path branched. The right led to the old observatory, the left to the lookout tower. Irepani spun the wheel left. At the road's end, impeded by the woods, the area widened slightly into an open patch suitable for parking.

His watch had stopped at 2:37 p.m. This was about the time they'd first hit the gravel road. The phone was also dead, battery drained and the charger inactive for some reason. The Jeep's electrical must be on the fritz. Maybe it had shorted out his phone too. He couldn't explain why his watch had coincidentally died at the same time. The sun appeared to be lower than it should have been. He felt susceptible. There was no other way to describe his apprehension.

He checked his backpack once again even though he knew that the human and canine food supply and two-gallons of water had been packed— most fire lookout towers had no water supply and any wayward visitors had to supply their own. Fleetingly, he wished he'd packed a bottle of wine or gin.

Step by step. Another life.

Strapping down his sleeping bag and Cadejo's blanket to the top of the backpack, he hefted the heavy load over his broad shoulders. It was a little over a mile up the mountain to reach the fire lookout. His shoulders already ached at the prospect. Cadejo shook with nervous energy. She jumped up against his thighs, egged him on to get their adventure started.

They walked a narrow path barely defined by moist soil and scarce foliage. Old growth at his left and right had grown tall, gnarled by the winds. Douglas Fir formed a barrier on both sides, leading the hikers up the incline towards the mountain top. Bright purple larkspur flowers prospered. A brisk walk and Irepani could finally see the top of the lookout tower above the treetops.

They entered a slight clearing, though the ground still rose before them. A spread of copper wires was fastened to the lookout tower. They ran across the land to attract lightning strikes and disperse the electrical charge into the earth, away from the tower itself. The wires seemed to hum with something vibrant and deadly, like the apparatus in a mad scientist's laboratory in an old Frankenstein film. They continued to the tower.

A squat dark form lay in the middle of the path. Irepani thought it was just an animal sunning itself, though something of its size was best avoided. Maybe a black bear. He kept walking, but when the path turned slightly and they passed by a group of fir trees grown close together, he lost sight of it. When he could see straight up the path again, the dark shape was gone.

They arrived at a pair of Porta-Potties. Cadejo sniffed their perimeter. Irepani wasn't sure how any vehicles could make it up here to empty them, but he was grateful for the convenience. Approaching the lookout, Cadejo growled at a copse of spruce trees behind the tower. An animal ran through the brush, but Cadejo stayed by Irepani's side.

"Just a deer, girl."

Irepani thought about the shape on the path. If it'd been a black bear that meant there was a possibility of more of them. Cadejo continued to stare warily at the moving trees.

The tower's steps ascended, nearly vertical, more a tilted wide-runged ladder than stairs. Cadejo wagged her tail in anticipation. Irepani didn't look forward to what must be a good forty-foot trek to the top; the backpack's straps already chafed his shoulders. He was concerned about Cadejo falling over the side or tumbling down the stairs. He'd have to keep a close eye on her once they made it to the top.

They trudged up the stairs. Judging by the tower's dilapidated condition,

Irepani knew it couldn't possibly be up to code. He'd done some research before on lookout towers online and read that most came equipped with propane and electricity. But this one clearly had never boasted anything in the way of amenities, even before any upkeep had been decommissioned.

What year was this thing built?

No matter. It was a roof over their heads. Despite its appearance, he assumed it was structurally sound or the U.S. Forest Service would've torn it down by now. He walked the patio that ran all around the tower, then opened the unlocked glass door to view the inside.

The interior was about 12 x 12, windows on every side offered a spectacular view of Mount Hood to the north, Mt. McLaughlin and Crater Lake to the south, and the Cascade Range in all its splendor. A yellowed, torn map of the region was thumbtacked to the only wall space that wasn't window. A small card table and a short cabinet were the only other items left behind. An obsolete but functional Osborne Fire Finder alidade sat on a pedestal at the center of the room.

Standing before the window, Irepani looked down at the thin trail that led them here. The view sparked a memory:

Irepani was 8 years old, and he'd woken to a sound he wasn't sure he'd heard. His childhood home was at the top of a dirt path snaking its way a quarter of a mile to the main road. He remembered looking out the window, over the porch to the empty dirt field beyond.

The darkness was cut by flashing red and blue lights on the main road. He'd never forget feeling as if he were hovering before a great expanse made black by a starless night, the kaleidoscopic display of emergency vehicle lights, swirling colors hypnotic in the night, like a magic lantern with slides of red and blue stars. A silhouette was contrasted against the lights.

It appeared to be a man on all fours.

The man had been slowly crawling up the driveway. There must've been a car accident. An injured survivor had seen the house porch light and instinctively made his way towards it. Irepani must have been at the window for a minute, but in that moment the wounded man's progress up the driveway felt tortuous, as if he'd been frozen in a slow crawl for hours.

Something about his anguished movements, the way he held what must be a head up higher than a normal neck should allow, terrified Irepani. Now that the memory was more substantial, hadn't the survivor been far too bulky to be a person? Hadn't their limbs protruded longer than was possible, and bent at the wrong angle? Had his back jerked up and down, as if panting excessively like a wounded dog?

Irepani hadn't heard his mother walk up behind him. She'd startled him when she loudly insisted he go back to bed.

He tried to explain what was going on out there, but when he'd turned back to the window there'd only been blackness. No flashing lights. No man crawling up the driveway. Nothing out there.

The following morning, he walked to the end of the driveway. It must have been a dream; any remaining broken glass or puddles of oil or coolant was long gone. Nothing to indicate a car accident had happened anytime recently.

But an incongruous pile of gravel had caught his attention. He'd moved the rocks aside to uncover a Frisbee-sized puddle of coagulated blood someone had hidden. It was black and thick, though the cold morning prevented any insects from feasting on it.

Pushing the gravel back over the blood with the heel of his shoe, he'd seen an oddly shaped rock that made him hesitate. Reaching down to pick it up, he found it was a tooth. It was too long and sharp to be human. He tossed it into the field on the other side of the road then returned home.

But that was what, sixteen years ago? The wilderness excited his imagination, brought up old memories long dormant. In the distance, he saw the dome of the Leman Observatory poking above the trees like a rotten scalp. He'd take Cadejo along for a hike tomorrow morning to explore it. On a whim, he opened the cabinet to see if anybody had left something of interest behind.

Five mini-bottles of vodka were lined up neatly on a shelf. His hands shook. He should throw them into the woods. Dump the contents outside. Instead he pushed the bottles to the back of the cabinet. Their temptation would be a test. Proof he'd beat this.

His jaw clenched so tight his teeth ached.

Dr. Hyman wasn't used to speaking to anyone other than his associates. His audience, though only a dozen, represented some of the top minds in the military and scientific community. His hands danced in the air as he spoke. A nervous gesture he'd never been able to stifle.

"As you all probably heard in the briefing this morning, 2009-047A transmitted its invocation to Colonel Utts in her sleep last night. When she came to, the team translated her prayers into an algorithm we uploaded to INTEL's servers. The PAN satellite has received the data."

"It's operational?" Major General Targ spoke up.

"It is. But the Golgotha coordinates await further instruction, sir. Our ossiferous satellite's harmonics have—"

"See these two stars here, doctor? Didn't get these building huts for the Peace Corps. I'm of the mind that I've earned the respect that comes with these here stars, and I'd appreciate it if you began addressing me as 'Major General.' Not 'Sir.'"

"Oh. Understood. No offense intended, Major General Targ."

"This is a grand tradition you're continuing here. Frater 210 himself would be proud of what you've accomplished since his ascension."

Targ turned his prodigious bulk to look at those seated behind him. His folding chair groaned.

"You're all doing the Lord's work here, people. Praise Pan."

"Thank you, Major General. Pan be praised," Dr. Hyman said, though applause drowned out any possibility of anyone hearing him.

Irepani woke to Cadejo licking his face. He'd slept poorly. The forest had been particularly restless last night. Animals crashed through the foliage, snapped branches, critters leapt from tree to tree. They howled and moaned to a starry sky. But Cadejo hadn't seemed to notice. She'd kept quiet, not once growling at the activity outside.

"How'd you sleep, girl?"

She wagged her tail. Irepani's limbs ached from sleeping on the hard floor. Through the window he saw mist creeping high, obscuring the tops of the trees, filtering the rising sun's light into a weak trickle.

He warmed some water on the portable hot plate he'd brought along and made some instant coffee. Cadejo enjoyed a serving of dog food straight from the can. Breakfast finished, they left the tower for the Leman Observatory.

The sky was a dull chalkboard colored canopy. Irepani could see stratum in the cloud layers, each progressively darker from top to bottom. A sheet of rain smudged the distance. Judging by the breeze, a late summer storm was making its way toward the mountain.

He saw the shadowy form again. It had moved a bit further up the hill from where he'd seen it yesterday but was now motionless.

But once they reached the spot, he didn't see anything out of the ordinary. No hump, no dead animal, no pile of vegetation or shadows.

They descended the hill and entered a shallow valley. A brief hike led them to the foot of a mountain, the Leman Observatory perched at the top. Moving forward, Cadejo ran too far ahead only to be brought back by Irepani's exasperated cry for her to return.

A light drizzle arrived. The gentle mist compelled Irepani to close his eyes, face the sky, allow the moisture to coat his skin. He could smell the green and the dirt and the air, pristine, as if he was the first animal to experience it. He couldn't remember the last time he didn't have soot and concrete dust in his sinuses. He hadn't been this happy in quite some time.

It took about an hour to finally reach what was left of the Leman Observatory, though that was an estimate given his lack of a timepiece. The rusty barbed wire fence surrounding the property sagged low in several areas, so it was an easy matter to simply step over. The sole ELEVATION 3,310 FEET sign he saw was legible only after scraping away the moss.

The building's remains looked more like a dilapidated barn than a former observatory. There were no traces of the telescopic instruments once used for research here, much less any mechanical equipment. Empty beer cans testified to the previous presence of trespassers, though this must have been some time ago, for the faded labels were from brands available decades past. Walking by a skeletal office chair, its plush seat long destroyed by the elements, Cadejo whined nervously. Closer to the observatory, Irepani saw a filing cabinet on its side, the top rusted through. It was empty.

Nearer the structure, he saw all of the windows had been broken by vandals long ago. The frames were oddly octagonal shaped. FUCK THIS WORLD graffiti was emblazoned in bright yellow across the bricks. The gaping holes in the walls and openings where doors had been removed or rotted allowed the two to enter with no problem. Though Irepani wore hiking boots, he was careful to avoid stepping on any wood for fear it hid a rusty nail or two. Cracked ceiling panels littered the floor. The interior was overgrown with blackberry bushes.

Cadejo whimpered.

"What's up, killer? Stay by me. Don't want you getting cut."

Irepani rubbed his hands together for warmth. The air around his skin crackled with static electricity. Arm hair tickled. A metallic chill coated his tongue.

There was plenty of room to maneuver between the clumps of blackberry growth inside. He looked up through the roof where the stairway had collapsed to rubble in front of him. The drizzle pattered down, made soothing sounds against the warped wood floor. A stream ran over the lip of the open ceiling, flowing over the remaining staircase steps that led to the now useless observatory dome. Someone had spray painted BEWARE OF BITERS on the inside of the dome visible from the bottom floor.

Cadejo barked at the corner of the room where a massive bush formed a barrier. The dull gleam of a doorknob behind the green caught Irepani's eye. A door the vandals had apparently missed.

Cadejo slowly backed away, her yipping devolved into grunts of fear.

"Whoa, girl. Easy."

He grabbed her collar, gently guided her towards the door. She stopped just shy of it but didn't struggle. Irepani tore away clumps of vegetation to further expose the doorknob. He could sense every muscle in Cadejo's body strained to bolt. But she stayed put. Enough of the growth removed, he turned the knob and pushed it open.

The room was small, slightly larger than a broom closet. The walls and ceiling were coated in gray excrement, smeared and clumped on every surface, long dried and odorless.

A waist-high shrine stood in the center of the space. It had also been built up from shit. Irepani tapped it with his boot to find it was solid as plaster. The mound leveled off at the top to form a flat surface the circumference of a manhole cover.

A skull sat on top. Ram horns curled from its cranium, majestic and nightmarish like something from a book on Santeria his old high school friends had dabbled in as an ineffective act of rebellion. Teeth circled the skull in a pattern of grotesque decoration. Dried Hydrangea and Buttercups were strewn over it. Fallen petals lay on the floor like desiccated insects. Blobs of black and red candles surrounded the skull and base of the shrine. The wax looked wet, sweating a greasy tallow stain. Wax ran from the horns to the shrine in stiff mucousy strands.

Irepani had seen some beautiful *Nuestra Señora de la Santa Muerte* shrines back home, but the Skinny Lady gave healing and protection. This altar emanated something unclean. A malign wickedness he'd never encountered before.

He was certain the horned thing was a dog's skull, not a ram or goat. Leaving Cadejo just outside the door, he stepped closer. She whined but didn't follow. On inspection, he found that the horns had been sculpted from shit. If he had to guess, he'd peg the teeth as coming from a dog as well.

Several dogs in fact.

He'd never wanted a drink as badly as he did now. The need to stifle his fear with alcohol trembled inside like the prelude to a seizure.

Obtain for us from your most holy Son the grace of keeping our faith...

Elaborate occult symbols decorated every surface of the room. Irepani wasn't familiar with the meaning of any of them, except for the pentagrams of course, presumably drawn into the wet shit before it'd hardened. He was particularly baffled by the image of a rocket rising in a plume of smoke, a goat skull with enormous curved horns propped on the nose. Another dog skull? Irepani wasn't sure, but he was impressed that someone had managed that much artistic detail in such a disgusting medium.

Of course, it was a goat skull—why would a *dog* have horns? Then again, why would vandals make such an effort to dress up roadkill, and work so hard to create the rest of the symbols in the room? Kicking in windows and knocking holes in walls made sense to him. But a shrine?

The air was surprisingly arid in the closet. Little moisture intruded upon this ritualistic space. That must be why the shit had dried out and managed to keep everything intact. Irepani wondered why the ceiling hadn't leaked, when the rest of the observatory was barely standing.

Cadejo made a low growl. She barked once.

Irepani lifted the wax clotted skull. Excrement clung to it with a crackling, organic sound that turned his stomach.

Cadejo's barking became panicked.

"Hold on. Almost done, girl."

The skull felt warm and heavier than expected.

Cadejo's growl turned feral, aggressive.

The closet hummed. Air quivered. A vibration rippled through Irepani's head like a tainted transmission or an unclean energy. Pain, as that of a bee sting, a venom surge shuddered through his blood.

Retching, he backed away. Vomit gushed down his chest. His bowels ran wet, soaked his pants in foul liquid. The dog-goat skull fell to the floor. A horn snapped off.

He stumbled out of the closet, rolled onto his back. Cadejo was immediately on him, licking vomit off his face, whimpering in concern. He patted her on the scruff, spoke softly, let her know he wasn't hurt.

The room's confines had messed with his head. The shit was probably full of spores or something that made him violently ill. All that sickness sealed up in a tiny area. A lot of nasty pathogens floating around.

Still on his back, he kicked the door shut. Cadejo jumped up against it with her front paws, scratched its surface as if eager to prevent it from opening again.

Realizing nothing was going to come screaming out of the shrine room, Cadejo padded over and sat next to Irepani. Strands of drool dripped from her muzzle. Why hadn't the shrine been destroyed? And why leave the skull?

He stood, looked down at Cadejo with a weak smile. "I'm a fucking mess. Need to get out of these clothes."

Cadejo pranced in place, more than ready to leave the observatory. Irepani noticed her front right paw left a bloody print on the wood floor.

He knelt down to examine her. The pad was torn, a wide puncture wound punched deep. She must have stepped on a large nail or thick splinter. She bled profusely. Irepani was certain the risk of infection in this place was high. Ripping off his shirt sleeve, he wrapped her paw then tied a loose knot to hold it in place. It'd have to hold until they got back to the lookout tower.

The return hike seemed to take a fraction of the time it did to reach the Leman Observatory. Irepani chalked it up to knowing the lay of the land a bit better this time around and being so exhausted he'd fallen into a trance and lost track of time.

Cadejo playfully chased small animals into the forest but kept herself from leaving the path. She limped but seemed to be in good spirits despite the wound. Irepani got the impression she didn't want him out of her sight. He was sick twice on the way, vomiting clear liquid into the grass. His strength was slipping away.

Back at the lookout, halfway up the stairs, they passed through a heavy fog layer. For a few moments Irepani couldn't see the tower anymore, or the mountains beyond. He felt vulnerable, as if eyes watched from afar, a being whose gaze could pierce the fog.

Being out in the middle of nowhere made him feel exposed. Like something had followed them back from the remains of the Leman Observatory. He shook off the silly thought, but still moved as fast as he could manage up the stairs. He kept one hand on Cadejo's head to make sure she was still there.

The fog parted, briefly allowing Irepani to see all the way to the path. The black shape was there again, though a bit closer to the tower now. Irepani raced up the stairs with Cadejo into the relative safety of the tower.

"Contact was established at the Leman Observatory at approximately—?" Dr. Hyman tilted his head towards Colonel Utts.

She set her tablet aside and addressed the room, "2100 hours. The shrine's coordinates were established at 2100, inside the Observatory. There's some evidence that—"

Major General Targ interrupted, "Colonel, am I to understand that you're the psionics expert in charge?"

"I am." Utts replied with no small amount of annoyance. "If you'd rather read the report yourself...?" She handed the tablet to Major General Targ. "Though I'd like everyone to be aware of where we stand."

Targ ignored her, swiped a finger across the tablet, thumb and forefinger clenched around a cigar. The Palladium sigil, a rocket ship with a horned canine skull on its nose, filled the screen.

Realizing Targ was no longer listening, Colonel Utts spoke to the audience, "The shrine was adorned with the appropriate sigils to receive the satellite's crypto-occult transmissions. All written in horseshoe crab and canine blood as is necessary to establish my telepathic link. Prayer saturated shadows invoked a catalytic reaction, energizing the transmission. It looks like we've actually gone and cultivated a chain of Parson particles."

"What's that?" Major General Targ huffed a rancid cloud of cigar smoke.

"Parson particles. Similar to tachyons in that they travel faster than light."

"Meaning?" Targ glared at her.

"Meaning we've built a Parsons antitelephone capable of sending signals to the past. The perception of chronostasis events, as well as polychromic and monochromic time occurrences, has been initiated locally, and should proceed planet-wide."

"Still unclear on your accomplishment here."

"We've weaponized time."

The gathered crowd of military and scientists murmured excitedly.

Irepani spent the night puking into a trash bag. After returning from the Leman Observatory, he'd barely made it to the Porta-Potties outside. He'd been so weakened by the sickness, he'd done nothing but doze on and off well into late afternoon. The sun was on its way to setting.

He was glad he'd thought to bring a battery-operated heater. Huddling in front of it for warmth, he stared out the window at the gray skies while Cadejo rested her chin on her front paws, observing him with concern. Her paw was still neatly wrapped, though Irepani had neglected to bring a first aid kit so he hadn't been able to swap it for a proper bandage. He barely had the strength to prop himself up on one elbow to pet her.

He'd made so much progress in his life in so short a time. He'd even managed to save up a small amount of cash working at the diner. His manager said if he kept up the good work, he'd be on the grill full time. He was paid too little and had no health benefits but being undocumented meant he had to keep his head down and not draw any unnecessary attention.

It had taken several attempts, but he'd managed his way over the California border all the way up to Oregon where his American-born cousin lived. Lorena had put up with him for six years now.

Every other pad since leaving Mexico had been at a shelter, or in an alley covered in ratty blankets he'd picked up at a Mission. Here, in the wild, all of that seemed as if it'd been another man who'd crawled through the chaos and strife. He wouldn't let something as trivial as the flu bring him down.

Cadejo nuzzled his arm. The improvised bandage seeped a dark fluid. He unwrapped it to find her paw grotesquely swollen. The simple movement left him sweaty and breathless.

He gently spread her pads to see how infected the wound had become. The stench of rot hit his nostrils. Plump maggots squirmed in the hole. Irepani didn't understand how a wound could turn so quickly. He'd have to get her to a veterinarian as soon as possible, but he could barely stand, much less hike back to the Jeep. He couldn't allow himself to think of how he'd pay for a vet bill as well.

"I'm so sorry. One more night, girl."

He plucked the maggots from her paw with a safety pin that had held a pocket closed on his backpack. Once finished, he crawled over to the cabinet with great effort and grabbed a small vodka bottle. Returning to Cadejo, his face streaming an oily sick sweat, he twisted the bottle's cap with a satisfying sound. Hands trembling, he almost lost his grip.

Just one sip. Calm the edges. Chemical strength. Enough to help him help his best friend get through one more night.

... most holy Son the grace of keeping our faith, of sweet hope ...

He tilted the bottle over Cadejo's paw instead. She yipped once but didn't pull away. He poured half an inch of the liquid into the wound.

There was still plenty of vodka left. Mouth slick with saliva at the thought of draining the bottle, he replaced the cap and put it on the floor. He just wanted to go home now. Go back to work. Tell Lorena he loved her and thank her for everything she'd done for him. Apologize for borrowing the Jeep without her permission. The fever suffused his face and neck. His heart raced, his vision swam.

Tomorrow morning. Get to a vet. As soon as I can walk.

"We're not looking at another Montauk Project fiasco, are we?" Targ asked.

Colonel Utts shook her head, "The data indicates otherwise. Dr. Hyman can elaborate if need be."

"I'd be happy to. At first, I was skeptical of the previous attempts to psychokinetically manipulate tachyons. Harnessing time in geographically specific vectors as was attempted with the Philadelphia Project and telep—"

"I don't need a history lesson, doctor." Targ handed the tablet back to Utts. "Our ability to cultivate weapons out of time would allow a nation to send enemy soil back 1.5 billion years when their land was at the bottom of the ocean. That's

all the history I need to know."

Someone in the audience coughed. A young women Hyman recognized as a geologist from African University of Science and Technology shook her head in disapproval.

Targ focused on her, growled in an authoritarian voice, "Ecclesiastes chapter 3. 'He hath made every thing beautiful in his time: also he hath set the world in their heart, so that no man can find out the work that God maketh from the beginning to the end.'

"Once upon a time only God was omnitemporal. Now we're on the verge of wielding that same power. That's all I need to know."

A few offended sounds came from the audience, but nobody challenged Targ.

"Anything else you two have to give me?"

"Just one thing." Dr. Hyman said.

"Out with it then."

"A presence has been detected."

Cadejo was gone.

Scatter-brained from the fever, Irepani must have left the front door ajar. She'd run out last night, or earlier that morning. Irepani could move slowly now, but his best friend was missing, and this motivated him to get dressed as quickly as his weak limbs would allow. The sun was higher than he'd expected. He must've slept late.

Muscles protested every movement. He shouted *Cadejo* from the front door of the tower. After no response he moved down the stairs, hand over hand to support his feeble body. Feet dragging, pausing to catch his breath every few steps, he finally reached the bottom and headed towards the copse of spruce trees that had attracted Cadejo's attention when they'd first arrived.

The woods were quiet. Irepani picked up a crooked branch to use as a cane. Breath came sharp and ragged, steamed into the air. He shouted Cadejo's name again and again.

A deformed face peered out of the woods.

Irepani stood still, held his breath for several seconds. Once he was certain the face wasn't moving, he turned his head to the right to allow a clearer view between the branches.

It wasn't one face, but two.

Leaning a bit more to the side, he saw four heads, then a glimpse of a shoulder. A torso.

The plastic, expressionless faces of mannequins.

Relieved they were just damaged dummies, he still approached cautiously. It wasn't every day he came across battered dummies dumped in the deep dark woods.

Five mannequins stood before him, their feet buried in the ground for support. Torn clothing dangled like swamp moss from upraised arms. There was something of the supplicant in their pose, an attitude of veneration in their upturned faces. Their plastic bodies had been charred and melted, subjected to such intense energies features had slipped into amorphous anonymity. Peering closer, Irepani saw several impact sensors attached, the kind used to monitor shipped packages or damage from sports injuries. The stickers were clustered around their heads.

He'd lost track of time. The sun was already going down. Summer days were longer, but it couldn't have been much later than early afternoon, yet the light was already slipping away. He must have misjudged how long he'd been outside. If only he had a working watch or phone, he'd know exactly what was going on. He was happy to leave the mannequins behind.

Returning to the tower, he sat on the balcony, depleted of any vitality. He bellowed *Cadejo* until he lost his voice and the dark came on. There wasn't any light pollution from Cottage Hollow, though the town must've been less than 5-miles away. It didn't make any sense.

Cadejo *would* be back. He'd wait one more night and search again in the morning. She wouldn't leave him alone. *For fuck's sake, if I could only get my strength back.*

Irepani noticed the large lump on the path again. From this angle, it looked like a large man on all fours. But the sun had fully nestled behind the mountains and the shape was just a black mound. It was nothing. Nothing worth investigating until tomorrow morning, if at all.

He crawled back into the tower. Opening the cabinet, he noted the vodka bottles were where he'd left them. There was no reason they shouldn't be in the same position, but he was transfixed by their presence. Their arrangement. Their order.

The one bottle he'd opened to cleanse Cadejo's paw was still on the floor. He touched the cap. He wouldn't open it. He'd enough willpower to leave it be.

The waning light spilled across the treetops like molten honey. The glow stopped just shy of the path leading to the tower, a demarcation crisp and precise as if drawn with the aid of a ruler.

Irepani could see the thing down there a bit more clearly now. Though still a silhouette, it was clearly a person, or at least something built like one, though inadequately, far too massive to be mistaken for anyone without a disorder or deformity. It had moved several feet closer to the tower since last he'd glanced over at it.

But it wasn't moving now. At least it didn't appear to be. A lost hiker? Were they hurt? Something about its posture made Irepani think they were wounded, though he couldn't explain why he thought this.

He was a kid again. Red and blue lights swirling over the mangled form of a creature coming to get him.

Ridiculous. What if it was a person and they needed help?

He slowly hobbled down the tower stairs onto the path. The trees at the edge were massive, their thick branches cast a heavy shade cold as deep waters.

Drawing closer, Irepani could make out the shape wore a drab green military uniform.

The uniform was torn in several places, patches of dark moss spotted the cloth. The body wasn't formed right. Its bilateral symmetry was off. What must be their right arm and leg was puffy, the left angular and insect-like. Head tucked against chest, face buried in the decaying jacket, Irepani thought it might be a large trash bag filled with broken sticks piercing the plastic. He didn't want to imagine how tall it would be if it stood up.

This was absurd. Someone must have illegally dumped a load of trash. Nothing alive could look like this. Irepani glanced around the path nervously.

The wind parted a leafy branch, a spot of weak sunlight illuminated the dark heap. A service patch was briefly visible on its arm. It portrayed a rocket ascending above a plume of smoke. A horned skull was balanced on the nose.

The patch read **PALLADIUM AT NIGHT** in bright yellow letters.

Irepani reached out to touch it.

His mouth filled with sour vomit. The forest rippled like water before he lost consciousness.

"A new form of life? Co-existing alongside us? Never thought I'd live long enough to take something like this seriously," Major General Targ said.

"It's certainly a game changer. We find ourselves in something of a quandary: is this newly discovered intelligence so extraordinarily slow compared to life on our planet they lurk at our periphery, and we cannot possibly detect their intervention? Or do they traverse so quickly human senses cannot record what is occurring?"

"That's the million-dollar question, Dr. Hyman." Colonel Utts said.

Dr. Hyman spoke in a whisper, "Up to today, God was the only intelligence that possessed a Quasi-Temporal Eternality."

"Never took a philosophy course in college," Targ said impatiently.

"Sorry. A QTE is a being that experiences its entire life all at once, the past present and future simultaneously. With that in mind, an eternally existing God must experience everything that has ever been or will be."

"Is that how these creatures see the world?" Targ was genuinely intrigued now.

"Difficult to say. They are probably living time from a reference we are incapable of comprehending. Hell, even different Earth cultures see time differently. Off the top of my head, the Pirahã Tribe doesn't have any concept of time in their language."

"Humans we can handle. But this new discovery, we don't have any data on their biology, technology levels, language...?"

"All we know is that they're out there. And our poking around called them out."

"You're 100% certain?" Targ ran a large hand across his shaved head.

"Yes. Unfortunately," Colonel Utts said.

"Why is that unfortunate, Colonel?"

"Well Major General, it's because they now know we're watching them."

Irepani woke up inside the lookout tower. He guessed two hours had passed, though he didn't trust his interpretation of much anymore.

He knew rational explanations were few and far between when it came to whatever was going on. Something was wrong, above and beyond the presence of an impossible thing on the path.

It *had* moved. He'd touched it and something transported him back into the tower somehow.

What would happen when the thing eventually reached the tower? This was inevitable, though Irepani couldn't explain why. And where was Cadejo?

He had to find her.

He looked out the window. The creature on the path was now upright.

It walked, gradually, yet undeniably approaching the tower. It was so tall, what Irepani assumed was its head touched the higher tree branches.

Irepani screamed Cadejo's name because anything else seemed inconsequential. He cupped his hands to his mouth to trumpet his voice. Skin smelled of sweat. The forest. His dog's fur. Ethanol, burned into his skin, vodka molecules nestled in his pores. Integral sequences. Rhythms. He screamed his dog's name.

Time was an artificial construct, and constructs may be torn down.

Irepani stepped away from the window, the back of his knees bumped against the cabinet. He opened it. Picked up a vodka bottle. Swayed on wobbly legs. His right foot was asleep.

He shouted Cadejo's name again. The thing on the path looked up with a face hauntingly reminiscent of the ruined mannequins in the woods.

The forest burned.

Flames ran from mountain top to valley, as far as the eye could see. Blisters of sap within ancient oaks and conifers popped as fire consumed them. The sky filled with embers and a torrential blaze rose over the earth.

The entire planet was ablaze.

The conflagration spread quickly across the mountains, but the flames didn't cross the circumference around the tower and thing on the path. The land was reduced to ash in mere moments, like a time-lapse camera trick before Irepani's eyes.

The creature kept walking with a terribly measured pace.

The world was a vast landscape of cinders and dead earth, like the surface of another planet. But as Irepani watched, the gray suddenly gave way to green shoots pushing through the dead soil from fertile depths far below. New growth rose, the land covered in life and vitality. All in a matter of seconds from his frame of reference.

The thing was still coming up the path.

Irepani had stumbled into the radius of some bizarre experiment's aftershocks. Blundered onto a testing ground. In the middle of some clandestine experiment, a civilian who'd wandered onto something like the Nevada Test Site to witness a mushroom cloud in the distance. What else could this be? Existence tugged you down time streams whose current nobody could ever know they'd fallen into.

What else?

Irepani suddenly remembered what had yet to occur, while the past came to him as fresh as if he were experiencing it at that very moment.

They looked like dog bones.

He was 8 years old again and burying Cadejo the First in his mom's garden.

How could anyone possibly understand his despair? It was a special kind of sadness, a sorrow reserved for children who've lost their first pet. But this had happened years ago, and he was no longer that little boy who'd wept over a small grave, heart broken in so many ways it was never put back together quite right.

Irepani held his dead dog, but it wasn't Cadejo the First, but Cadejo the

Third. She was so small now, just a floppy little corpse and this simply couldn't be. All Irepani could say was *oh no, not yet.*

It's not time to go.

Not yet.

But once they were buried, they couldn't be unburied. Time was no longer reliable. Irepani desperately prayed it would loop around, backtrack to some moment on his path where he could once again feel Cadejo snoring on his lap.

Not yet.

It's not time to go.

He buried Cadejo beneath the lookout tower so many times he lost track of how often he'd already done so. There were so many dog bones to remove down there it took longer than he thought it would. He grew old in the years he spent burying her remains, but he continued on as the dying Earth's oceans turned into mist and planetary crust fragmented into desolate plates.

What worth this insatiable desire to drink? Addiction was just the consequence of bits of matter jumbled together to pretend it had some inherent value. None of him, the alcoholism, the love, the kindness, was of any relevance. Every star died. Every burst of radiation dimmed into senescence. Chemical tidbits accumulated into something greater than the sum of their parts. A steady congregation of atoms, their union increased in complexity, each piece ultimately inconsequential.

Time ceased to be.

What did any of this matter?

Irepani looked at the sky and saw the death of heat, the demise of matter. Galaxies decomposed, dead dwarf stars sputtered out, nuclear fuel depleted and drifted into the blackness like a child's shiny trinket fallen into a swollen river.

Not a river, but a void.

What could no longer be called time passed nonetheless, replaced by a cold, lightless void with no activity save for perpetual dilapidation, existence dwindled into inert useless particles. All Irepani could do was witness this reverse of Creation.

Photons degenerated. Mists of electrons froze, the universe was an icy useless waste. An olive-gray sky churned, hardened, then flowed like a thixotropic liquid. The color held an organic quality, as of lichen across a rocky landscape.

Lorena was gone. There was no restaurant job to return to. No shitty apartment waited for Irepani to fall asleep within. There were no words to describe the eras that had passed.

All of humanity was extinct. Life ceased to be.

Irepani knew that Cadejo was also long dead. Only he and the creature on the path remained.

A new sun broke through the gloom. Feeble, not anywhere as brilliant as his planet's original sun, but a welcome respite.

Irepani still held a vodka bottle, pinched between thumb and forefinger. Its weight balanced, as if made to nest between his fingers. He longed to swallow the liquor's perfect weight down his throat.

... most holy Son the grace of keeping our faith—

Such a small amount. Surely it wouldn't ruin him. He thought of that arduous trek across the border between Mexico and California, that leap into a mystery that presented something new every day. Holding the bottle against the new sun's light he thought about photons traveling from 150 million kilometers away to meet the bottle, flicker through to his eyes, well up inside him. Alcohol, heavy and sweet as time.

... our faith, of sweet hope—

"I'm so sorry, Cadejo."

But Irepani was good with God, his cousin, and Cadejo. That's all that ever mattered. His soul was suffused with such peace he had to close his eyes against the beauty of that newborn sun, such joy as to be had in relinquishing his grief.

The creature outside struck the lookout door with such force the tower shook. The vodka inside the bottle churned like a stormy ocean.

❋

Dr. Hyman dropped his phone into his lab coat pocket. "So, that was Dr. Mishluv with the results. This is where we stand.

"As you're all aware, United Launch Alliance Atlas V was delivered with classified satellite Palladium At Night. The launch occurred at 21:35 GMT on September 8, 2009. The specific agency responsible for operating the spacecraft has yet to be disclosed, even to those of us participating in the project. Real hush-hush stuff. Alright. Colonel Utts, would you mind expounding on the current situation?"

"My pleasure. Specialist (E4-KEVB), planted the Golgotha shrine at N 43° 21.618' W 122° 53.000'. It was confirmed as of the 12th of September, that Palladium At Night made contact with the shrine's sigils on the planet's surface. Per our Psionics team, the immense power of PAN was implemented to conjure a Parsons particle storm.

"The ensuing result was that time was altered within a five-mile radius of the test site."

Major General Targ looked relieved. "The experiment was successful?"

Colonel Utts nodded, "Definitely. The only problem—"

"Problem?"

Dr. Hyman stepped forward, a placating tone in his voice, "We lost contact with the paradimensional presence we encountered before. It simply disappeared. But it's nothing to worry about. We've existed alongside them for who knows how long, so there's no cause for alarm."

"Exactly. Dr. Hyman is correct. Even now, our psionics division is in the process of implementing remote viewing protocols. If this intelligence is still out there, we'll find it." Colonel Utts said.

"And if it's not found?" Major General Targ stood from his chair. His size was intimidating.

"That's... that's, well, that's the million-dollar question," Dr. Hyman stammered.

Targ stared at the seated group with something like fear in his eyes. "May Pan protect us all."

"Praise Pan," Dr. Hyman whispered.

"Praise Pan," the audience of military and scientists echoed.

DEVIL GONNA CATCH YOU IN THE CORNERS

HURSDAY, 8th March, 1849.—

It has been a trying journey over narrow deer-paths and rutted trails. Heavy branches of ancient oaks cast the way in shadow, yet I continue to write my thoughts in my diary—what Father mockingly refers to as "belles-lettres". When I was a child, I kept a daily record during the two- month emigration from New-England to the Willamette Valley where Father had been hired by the Hudson's Bay Company; as an adult, a mere two-days' travel will not dissuade me from continuing to write. These valleys, these streams that break the monotony of impenetrable alder and oak forests make the wagon's passage that much more difficult.

I have left home as my parents offered my services to Uncle Jon Sutton, who has taken ill and is convalescing in his isolated country estate. Being his only niece, it was decided to send me to assist with any daily tasks necessary to maintain his orderly domicile, while a nurse Marjorie attends to his health. I consider it fortunate I am bound for Uncle's distant place and not condemned to settle somewhere like Mudtown, for the tales of that city's squalor invite much hesitation.

I haven't visited Uncle in years. He is something of a legend our in family, for he has the faculty to command an auditory response from any inanimate object—that is, he was once a renowned ventriloquist and quite popular thirty years ago. He has since retired to the unexplored wilderness.

I am not particularly pleased to have been taken from my studies at the recently built school, as Miss Chloe Clark is an exemplary educator, and neither am I inclined to be a chambermaid. Though frowned upon by my parents, I am proud of my schooling and wish to attain a teaching position. I miss the sweet embrace of my fiancé Matthew, but he understands I have a family duty to uphold. I am not a rebellious daughter. I readily obey my parents' wishes.

The bracing air out here is invigorating; the black soil encourages the growth of tangled green that covers the land in such lavish amounts that I feel as if I'm within a faery tale. This is God's country indeed. I am weary, but the driver insists my destination is just over the hill.

As we draw near Uncle's home, I notice that the water pump I once frolicked around in my youth is gone. A hole is now in its stead. The pump must have grown soft with rot, for the remaining slimy rock foundation is split by lichen, and there is detritus where it once stood. Retrieving water from the gaping pit may prove an arduous task.

This is the first indication of my seclusion.

FRIDAY, 9th March, 1849.—
Uncle Sutton was most gracious on receiving me. He is still handsome, though a mysterious ailment has sunken his cheeks and furrowed his brow. His once resonant voice is now a despondent croak.

Nurse Marjorie has a kindness most beneficial to one of her profession.

I have been here less than one day, yet I already find the spacious house to be cold and impassive; the many unoccupied rooms give me alarm for reasons I am unable to articulate. Perhaps it is their advanced state of disrepair? The vines outside have pierced the walls, their growth evident as raised blisters beneath the wallpaper. An unpalatable gloom hangs over all.

Despite my reservations, I am quickly acclimated to my new station. Though not one to enjoy scullery work, I am an accomplished cook. This afternoon I prepare a supper of sorrel soup and skewered larks done to a turn, basted with sage butter. The birds have been provided by Daniel, the hunter Uncle hired to provide game and fowl and fish, as well as fruits and vegetables from the nearest town a day's tramp away. I assume he is also the one responsible for chopping and stacking the monstrous pile of cord wood out back. He reluctantly introduced himself this morning. Daniel is taciturn, a roughly hewn man with a tobacco-stained, bushy beard. His hands bear copious scars.

Uncle and Marjorie are appreciative of the meal—Uncle says he has subsisted on a diet of milk and hominy for far too long. Now he warms his aged blood before an oak and applewood roaring fire, imbibing a wine-and-honey concoction of his own invention, while Nurse Marjorie stands at his side. I would have preferred a cherry-bounce, as I find Uncle's cordial disagreeable, lingering on the tongue in a most unpleasant manner.

SATURDAY, 10th March, 1849.—
This morning, conversation with Uncle Sutton is difficult. He is withdrawn, occupied by thoughts known only to himself. His gaze constantly rests on the window framing the darkness of the forest before the sun has sufficiently risen to banish the hoar-frost and pall.

When Uncle does speak, he is pertinacious, only interested in reminiscing about his ventriloquist act. I was not yet born during his fame, but the posters and many reviews my mother preserved over the years attest to just how enthusiastically his unique gifts were received. He continues to talk of performing throughout Europe and America, astonishing thousands with his skill in manifesting words from gentlemen's pockets, gentlewomen's teacups, or from the mouth of his moppet Fox-Faced Rannie, which he carried in a pocket.

I remember one yellowed, crinkled theatre bill boasting of his holding spirited colloquies with that ill-shaped doll.

I recall touching the wax and cloth figure, during the last visit to Uncle's estate when I was but a girl of ten. Though not so long ago, my memories of that occasion are slight, and I retain an inexplicable air of anxiety on what transpired in this old home far from any village.

I ask Uncle if he still has Fox-Faced Rannie, perhaps exhibited with the other trophies and career memorabilia in one of the many rooms I've yet to investigate. But he becomes quite agitated and feigns his hearing is inadequate. Nurse Marjorie is silent and grim. I fear I have incurred offense.

Afternoon.—

A strange occurrence.

I enjoy the bird song from the woods as I prepare supper, but notice it is slightly queer sounding, as if mimicry is responsible for the tune.

I will speak to Uncle Sutton on this matter. I do not appreciate him practicing his auditory illusions in an attempt to frighten me. I am not comfortable attracting attention by malicious prank.

I find this odd however, as Uncle is in his study reading, while Nurse Marjorie prepares medicine. I cannot imagine how one could possibly project sounds through the thick walls and closed doors over such a distance.

But I am certain that birdsong is false.

A chill now resides within my breast. My demeanor is darkened. I will busy myself with peeling potatoes and gathering water from that foreboding well. The thought of chores illuminates my mood from black to gray. I have contracted a parching fever.

I never see any of the birds.

SUNDAY, 11th March, 1849.—

As there are no churches here to attend, I spend my morning exploring the house after my perfunctory duties are done. I have no hesitation in believing the Lord yet watches over me. The mellow waxing light further reveals the mansion's age and flaws. The heavy damask curtains have lightened in the direct sunlight, the jabot darkened by decay. There are many floorboards in desperate need of repair.

Roaming this place brings memories. I recall one rainy day when Uncle entertained by vociferating from a closet. He then escorted me outside where a queer voice came from the heart of the woodpile. Back in the kitchen, words enunciated echoingly from the belly of a cast iron stove.

But that was long ago.

It is a curious thing, this ventriloquist talent. To think that it was recently perceived a malefic art, a divine throat spoken, or, conversely, a gift from disreputable imps and devils! But now ventriloquism is all the rage with the public—jugglers and conjurers readily demonstrate its charms. The menacing Carwin of literature has become a thespian, his art a puzzle to be solved. Something to scoff at, as freethinkers are wont to do with the story of Balaam's ass.

Even so, despite my troubles with Uncle's cleverness, I still retain an emotional thrill on hearing voices from elsewhere. It is a splendid diversion.

Afternoon.—

In my explorations, I inadvertently come across the room where Uncle has stored his dollhouses.

A brief explanation: Uncle was celebrated for the biloquist skill of making his speeches echo from various dollhouses he'd place about the stage. Each and every doll's domicile delivered a variety of vocalizations—of children, of husbands and wives, of chickens and dogs, of dialects most unusual. He'd created a host of characters to interact with in his show, personalities that chattered from dollhouse to dollhouse.

Judging by the fresh paint and unblemished wood, Uncle has managed to carve several impressive structures during his convalescence. His carpentry skills remain unsurpassed; the woodwork is exquisite. Even now I look about the room and marvel at the hand-made craftsmanship, the meticulously designed appliques. Each house is attired in the architectural details appropriate to their era.

It is good that Uncle manages to busy himself with a pastime to cultivate his mind, as well as nurture his blood and muscles through physical exertion. His recovery has been a trying one, and I am pleased my visit has coincided with a lilt in his spirits—though I seem to have acquired an intestinal disorder. Such are the conditions one suffers when drinking well water in remote regions.

Several older dollhouses remain in a corner of the room. There are holes in their ceilings, paint peels from the exterior. I find sorrow in their neglected state, sobered by the inevitability of Time.

Late Evening.—

Those wondrous dollhouses have entered my sleep! I've taken to dreaming of living within those petite homes, supping from minuscule plates at tiny tables, sleeping on soft, delicate, inviting beds. I am small and happy and wander the halls freely.

I exit my blissful dream when I see something moving outside the dollhouse window. That moment of surprise jolts me awake. I immediately recorded these thoughts.

O, what wondrously crafted works!

MONDAY, 12th March, 1849.—

I have nothing of interest to document to-day.

TUESDAY, 13th March, 1849.—

To-night, while fetching water, I heard a child giggle my name within the well. I dropped the bason in surprise, but quickly became vexed and shouted into the hole, "I am not amused by your tricks Uncle!"

The child's tittering ceased, though I retained a distinct impression someone was down there, squatting in pitch darkness, waiting for me to leave before he continued whatever games he was playing below. I couldn't be sure of such, as it was too gloomy to see the bottom. It was a most disconcerting feeling, though I know it was only imagination made fervid by the falling sun thickening shadows between the trees, like a dark velvet sheet stretched across a proscenium arch as in one of the curtain-raising Black Art magic acts before Uncle's shows.

In fact, if I hadn't known they were sparrows returning to their nests for the night, I'd have said those pale shapes dancing in the air between the pine branches could have very well been bones held aloft by black clad assistants.

The thought persisted as I walked back to Uncle's house across the wide field, the gloaming dispersing curious shadows over the ground. On returning to my room, I quickly wrote this entry.

WEDNESDAY, 14th March, 1849.—

Despite what I fear may be a touch of bilious fever, I decide to enjoy the fresh air. I cross over the field in front of the house and walk deep into the woods.

After an hour's walk, I find an old round stone barn, reminiscent of a structure I'd once seen in Hancock.

I was unaware such architecture existed outside of New-England. Whatever its function, I am not convinced it is a barn; there are no ranches and no livestock in these parts which are uninhabited even by Indians or logging camps.

The entrance has collapsed, and grasses grow between the wreckage, reclaiming much of the ground. On further inspection, the building's strange walls and high roof seem church-like in design. A large fragment of stone shows PRAYERS FROM UNOCCUPIED SPACES engraved into its surface. The words before and after have been erased by time and weather.

But I cannot fathom why anyone would build a round church in such a faraway place, nor what congregation could possibly have been compelled to travel through such a dense forest to gather for worship. I expect a sexton to make his appearance any moment now!

Father once told me they built round barns so as to avoid corners, for evil spirits and demons hide in the shadows of such places. "Devil gonna catch you in the corners," he'd say to taunt me when I was a child. I am not aware if any churches have been raised with this superstition in mind. Perhaps I will ask Uncle Sutton.

I eagerly return through the woods, for that structure fills me with a rapturous fright, as if I am on a precipice yet unable to step away to safety. In my haste I pass the well. Nearby, a few feet distant, I discover a rock wrapped in twine. The cord dangles down into the well's depths.

I withdraw the string from the hole and find it attached to a decomposed opossum, the twine wrapped around its soft bloated neck. Who could have possibly committed such a dreadful sin? I hold the hunter Daniel accountable with nothing to substantiate my suspicions.

Fortunately, there remains a large supply of water in a cistern beneath the house's foundation.

THURSDAY, 15th March, 1849.—
My nightmare follows thus:

The ground is covered with many holes. I walk over the field towards the forest. In that certainty common to dreams, I sense that plumbing the hole's depths will prove futile, for they have no bottom. I hear whispers emanating from the openings.

I pass by these ominous depressions, stepping gingerly so as to avoid slipping into their breadth. The nearer I draw, the more frantic the whispers grow. They repeat my name, "Charlotte! Charlotte!"

I see movement between the trees.

I move closer, so quietly I float above the grass and dirt and alder cones. I peer between a fan of branches.

Fox-Faced Rannie stands in a clearing.

I remain as still as a sparrow on a twig with a skulk of predators below.

Fox-Faced Rannie tilts his disconcertingly vulpine head, as if detecting the arrival of an unexpected visitor. "Big boys will grease our heads and swallow us whole!" he says in Uncle's cadence.

I awake.

I became very ill this night, vomiting with such severity that I fainted back into a sleep so profound no further nightmares could reach me. In the morning, when I went to clean away my sick, I found it wriggling with worms. Perhaps Nurse Marjorie has something to ease my discomfort.

Early Morning—
Though still recovering from the nightmare, as well as a bout of quick step, I put on my cloak and go for a walk in the woods. I had hoped to acquire medicine from Nurse Marjorie, but she must be assisting Uncle, for I cannot find her anywhere in the house and Uncle's bedroom door is tightly closed. Nobody answered when I knocked.

I normally cherish the landscape during these moments, when it reveals its refinery at dawn, those seconds the sky luridly divulges its magnificence, sun touching the tips of distant wooded peaks, forest magically transforming into a world much more splendid than it normally expresses on its dull face. But I am of a bilious nature; the odor of the mountain air aggravates my dyspepsia.

I find Fox-Faced Rannie swaying in a gentle breeze.

His tiny fabric jacket and trousers are smothered in a coat of moss. The cord around his throat is frayed and rotten. I looked to the branch from which he was hanged. The bark had grown over the twine in such a thick layer it must have been here many years.

I am perplexed as to why Uncle came this far to clamber up a tree to hang his moppet. I am disturbed as to why he committed such a deed.

I may inquire as to why he has done this, but do not wish to upset Uncle's delicate constitution with frivolous investigations. I want to avoid angering him as I did before on mentioning the doll.

I return to the house. I take a path that keeps me from passing near the well.

FRIDAY, 16th March, 1849.—
I have nothing of interest to document to-day.

SATURDAY, 17th March, 1849.—
While preparing Uncle Sutton's bed after a restless night's sleep, I find a diary beneath a pillow. He is currently outside, taking his constitutional with the assistance of Nurse Marjorie.

I am ashamed to admit I peeked inside the book. It is a shocking and gratuitously carnal account of Uncle's dreams and hallucinations. I feel rather ill on exposing myself to these lascivious musings. I will only record a brief excerpt of what I can recall; I am loathe to elaborate with such language:

> *Fox-Faced Rannie stands over my bed. He possesses the*
> *soft features of youth, plump faced and wide-eyed, but*
> *his tiny body is withered with age, spoiled and wrinkled*
> *as the overripe skin of an apple.*
>
> *His prick is erect.*
>
> *He hovers in the air at the side of my bed, moaning*

most disagreeably. A plaintive cry, as if my knee-figure has yet to master his vocal cords, heartily practicing for my benefit. I am paralyzed during this vision and pray the waking nightmare will cease.

Rannie grunts and squeaks. I recognize my own voice channeled from the depths of his belly.

I awake, but my words curiously distorted still resonate within the walls. I must be mistaken, for I hear "As the acorn is to stately trees, dollhouses are to sprawling mansions".

I know not what this is meant to convey.

I close the diary and return it beneath the pillow. This is the gibberish of a man gravely ill, but I am not one to judge my Uncle's physical and mental fortitude. I pray no unclean thoughts intrude my sleep to-night.

I haven't heard any birds this morning. The forest has fallen silent. Marjorie is laughing outside, far too long and loud for my comfort.

Early Evening.—
I have confronted Uncle Sutton.

I broached the subject of his emulating birdsong, of frightening me by casting his voice into the well, of Daniel and the opossum; of the stone building in the woods; of Fox-Faced Rannie. I dare not mention the journal.

On hearing this, Uncle's physiognomy altered most remarkably.

His countenance was tainted with malignancy, like that of the old man tormenting the Savior in Bosch's Christ Crowned with Thorns. His incoherent response was the apoplectic rant of a deacon overwhelmed with the Holy Ghost.

I've noticed that Uncle lapses into these dreadful moods when the sun sets in the beyond, and the chill of night breezes brings the chorus of wildlife through the open windows. But my questions have made him far more agitated than usual at this hour.

His outburst is unprecedented in its passion. Sallow skin and sunken eyes attest to the progression of his disease. I must speak with Nurse Marjorie to determine if she too has witnessed Uncle's strange fits. I pray she may provide succor.

SUNDAY, 18th March, 1849.—

It is late morning when I find Uncle in his study. He notifies me that Nurse Marjorie's services were no longer needed. He has dismissed her.

He will not hear my protests, that I am untrained in any form of nursing. He ignores my pleas and resumes reading.

On returning to my room I hear a tumultuous din. It comes from the storage room filled with dollhouses. I run to throw open the door and find his creations have been shattered into fragments.

I don't know who could have committed this act of vandalism and evaded notice. There are no other doors, and as far as I'm aware, only Uncle and I now reside between these walls. I am confounded as to how he could have left his study, destroyed his dollhouses, then escaped the room without my detection.

Curiously, only the old, dilapidated dollhouses remain intact. I now realize they look like small, round churches.

I desire nothing more than to return to my very own home.

Late Evening.—

I fear my prying into Uncle's journal has forever poisoned my sleep. I dreamt this night of such repugnant images that I am hesitant to write them down. I am compelled to do so nonetheless:

Fox-Faced Rannie stands at the foot of my bed. His erection is coiled like a fiddle fern found in great abundance during spring in these parts.

His prick unfurls against his jaundiced, splotchy paunch, slaps against the navel as if it is a newly grown cunny.

Rannie is tall as a full-grown man, hovering just above the floor. Toenails sharp as the devil's talons scratch at the wood.

His navel opens like a sopping cunt. A stench escapes from its depths.

Something moves inside.

Uncle's voice projects from the maw, "Charlotte dear, big boys will grease our heads and swallow us whole!"

A malevolent face peers out at me.

I've hurriedly written this obscenity down. I hope I may return to sleep. These are not my words. Someone else has scripted this vile passage. I feel a corruption seething in my blood, in my soul.

MONDAY, 19th March, 1849.—

My heart is broken. Daniel returned from town early this morning, bearing a missive from my parents. My sweet sweet Matthew has hanged himself. Daniel does his best to console me in his rough and uncultured way, but I am inconsolable.

I cannot understand why the Lord has taken my love from me.

MIDNIGHT.—

I awaken to hear myself concluding a sentence whose precise words escape me. Perhaps I've been repeating a litany in my sleep, for I sense I've spoken a prayer of sorts, unbidden, as if quoting a beloved poem.

I search the house. Uncle Sutton is nowhere to be found. I know not where he has taken leave.

I found a note in the study. It is written in Uncle's trembling hand:

Daniel has gone far away. I know not where. I fear for Marjorie's safe transition. I am no longer who I once was, and the new me speaks such atrocities. May the Lord preserve us from that which sullies the blank spaces that were once blissfully unoccupied.

Goodbye, dear Charlotte. Pray for me.

Despite my concern, I am exhausted and struggle with an aggressive fever. I relax in Uncle's study and read until sunrise amongst the volumes of blotted sheepskin, moldering manuscripts, and bound editions. I'm distracted by odd sounds deep within the house. Unable to finish any sentences, I find myself plucking at the spines losing their stitch. Curiously, I no longer lament my dear Matthew's tragic fate.

I will worry about Uncle Sutton to-morrow, for I can do little in my state. I dare not leave the house; the nearest haven of civilization would take me far too long to reach, and I must stay here in case Daniel returns with game, or perhaps even Marjorie, forgetting some item necessary for her work. I pray they will bring news of Uncle's whereabouts.

I am filled with a strange apathy. I regret not becoming a rebellious daughter long ago. I'm no longer a meek girl; I am anxious to accept my independence. My waning health and the dimming sun send me back to bed.

SUNDAY, 25th March, 1849.——
Daniel the hunter has yet to visit again.

Marjorie has yet to return.

I've seen no other soul for many days. The larder is more than sufficiently stocked with jarred foods and canned meats. If necessary, I may stay for months. The house is covered with layers of grime and soot. I do not know why there has been such a hasty accumulation. My hair is tangled, my clothing clotted with filth. The wind whispers my name.

I am no longer filled with an acute longing to leave this house, to return to my studies, to go home again. I have little but sorrow awaiting me there. I look out the window as I prepare tea.

The oaks and cedars have formed a strangely circular pattern, as if aspiring to become curved walls.

A clump of bushes at the forest's entrance suggests a wide entryway, the trunks beyond a sturdy door. There is a delicacy to the manner the branches and leaves and saplings spread, their varied colors interwoven to create side gables and many windows arranged in strict symmetry. The forest canopy is now a roof. A thought comes to me:

As the acorn is to stately trees, dollhouses are to sprawling mansions.

There is movement in the forest. I no longer believe those pale shapes I viewed several days ago to be birds.

I pray aloud. I am suffused with a sacred thrill on wondering how sweetly the Lord's numinous pronouncements will saturate my soul with such great love. As my pitch rises, I hear my prayers emerge from deep within the forest, reflected back to me in a multitude of utterances.

I do not recognize any of the voices. Not even my own.

PROFESSOR COGNOSCENTE'S CALIGINOUS CHARMS CARNIVAL

John reached into the dog-faced gargoyle's mouth and gently rapped the animal's tongue against its brass palate. He was about to retreat to the relative warmth of his car when Professor Cognoscente opened the rain warped door.

The elderly magician had donned his crisp tailored tuxedo and antique conical hat, as if he'd expected company. The years had added stains and thin patches to the uniform, but John thought the Professor still fit the role perfectly.

He hesitated, the desire to return to the warmth of his car needled him like post-stroke pain. It had been irrational to embark on a twenty-hour drive just to knock on the door of a stranger unannounced, but seeing the Professor again revived intense memories of that night:

Shouts of barkers summoning the unwary to try their luck at rigged carny games. Museum Shows displaying deformed livestock and rows of pickled oddities. Hoofed things with beaks floating in amber liquid reeking of formaldehyde.

"I'm sorry to intrude," John was painfully aware of his stilted speech, a consequence of the blood clot that had damaged a small portion of his brain, "but are you *the* Professor Cognoscente?"

The old man stroked his white goatee. Gloved hands touched the brim of his odd hat. "I suppose my denying said accusation would be futile as I am hardly attired in a manner contrary to my identity."

John gave a small hesitant laugh. "I saw Professor Cognoscente's Caliginous Charms at the Cottage Hollow carnival 50 years ago. Tonight. I'm a magician because of your act. I mean amateur magician but, well, I've been waiting to tell you since I was a kid. It was a helluva show." The cold was invasive. He pulled his moth-eaten fleece jacket tighter against his chest.

There was a terrible moment when the Professor's body language suggested he was going to close the door and be done with this interruption. But he surprised John with a delighted grin. "It would be a mistake and breach of etiquette to turn a fellow sorcerer away on such a meaningful anniversary."

The Professor gestured for him to step into the foyer, a display punctuated by the glint of a silver ring adorned with an owl's face. John found it odd that it was slipped over a gloved finger.

"Please, come this way. Your timing is impeccable. I have a brief reprieve from my studies. There is wine and coffee in my study."

The Professor moved with a confidence and dexterity that belied his age. They entered the vestibule and the next indication this evening would be unique were the misleading dimensions of the hall lined with portraits of history's greatest conjurors. Here John was perplexed, for the unusually lengthy period it took them to travel what must have been less than 15 feet hinted at greater illusions to come.

They neared a cherry wood stairwell with tiny toad-like creatures carved into the banister—their faces were most certainly not scowling as John passed, nor were their moist jittery eyeballs anything other than an optical deceit produced by the subtle collusion of light and shadow.

John's curiosity faded slightly. He wished the wild-eyed things looked more like real frogs than something that only mimicked a batrachian origin. The trickery involved in creating the impression of their frowns turning into grins was exceptional.

Once in the vast study, Professor Cognoscente removed his hat. With a flick of his wrist he sailed it onto a table. His shock of dyed black hair reflected the dim light like an obsidian mirror. The room held the musk of old books, old wine, old secrets.

John was confronted by ceiling high bookshelves, towers of manuscripts, a chaotic accumulation of magic gimmicks weighed down the shelves. The book's spines boasted titles like *Occult Mentalism* and *Cold Reading for Fun and Prophet*. First editions and museum quality rarities on display under glass, volumes like *Wirkungen der Leiche,* masterpieces of legerdemain by Francois-Honore Balfour and Ah Uincir Dz'acab. Modern classics by Annemann, Punx and Kellar.

Meager scraps of light from the dust furred lamps fell onto the conjuring literature. The angles of the rows of bookshelves created the illusion they extended deeper than the room could accommodate. John couldn't get the stairwell out of his mind. He was puzzled as to why he'd only seen one floor on first arriving at the house.

"This is incredible." he whispered with admiration. "Is that a real Buatier de Kolta? I didn't know he'd published anything."

"That is a unique item, a manuscript Kolta penned that I managed to acquire. It's one of a kind."

John shook his head in bewilderment.

"So, shall we begin your lessons?" Professor Cognoscente tilted his head towards an oxblood leather couch, scuffed and faded from countless guests.

John was confused, but his giddy smile refused to relax. "Lessons?"

"Why yes. Lessons in the magical arts. That is why you've traveled so far and made such an effort over such a span of time to find me. Correct?"

"I just wanted to thank you for your Caliginous Charms Carnival."

The Professor gave a slight nod. "You're welcome. Now, there is coffee here. Wine there. If there's no lesson, shall we discuss our occult proclivities?" He clapped his hands in delight.

They discussed arcane matters deep into the evening. The old trickster related anecdotes about his career, but only glossed over the circumstances that led to his retirement. John bared his soul, confessed that the Caliginous Charms Carnival had altered his worldview by elevating magic from frivolous amusement to an art. Inspired by Victorian séances, traveling freak shows and psychic chicanery, the Professor's act transcended its roots and transformed trickery into avant-garde spectacle. But the magician dismissed the persistent inquiries and refused to discuss any of the illusions he'd performed that night when John was just a boy.

John was frustrated, but his host had been more than accommodating.

He'd offered hints and tips, such as the proper angle to hold one's thumb when performing sleights with florin coins, and the varied approaches to cutting and restoring objects like ropes, snakes and tongues. They spoke of psychological deceptions, of hypnosis and trance states. The Professor even described a performance where he charmed an audience member into believing a shadow was sitting on their lap, suckling them like a baby.

Tiny footsteps tapped across the floor upstairs.

"I'm sorry. I wouldn't have taken all your time if I'd known you had a guest." John said.

The Professor set his wineglass on top of an old book, the cover separating like flaky pastry. "No. Just you and me. Old houses make strange noises, as old magicians tell strange stories."

John heard something creak near the bannister in the hallway.

"I must apologize, I feel I've monopolized the conversation." The Professor touched his silver owl ring contemplatively.

"Oh no, no. Really, the honor is all mine. I can't thank you enough for tonight." John paused, listened for any further movement in the house before continuing,

"I hate to dwell on it, and I respect your reluctance to talk about the Caliginous Charms, but I've only been able to replicate *some* of your illusions from that night. It's like it was all a dream, as if the audience, as if we all were hypnotized or—" John shook his head, laughed at the idea.

The Professor leaned in so close John could smell the wine on his breath. Outside, near the front door, branches rattled against each other, though he hadn't noticed any trees planted that close to the house. The Professor's teeth were very white and quite small. This summoned the once submerged memory all those decades ago of a dwarf crawling from the small opening of the Professor's hat.

"Illusions? Well yes, but also much more. So, John, in answer to your persistent inquiries, I ask you this as it is a concern of mine: why did you feel the need to find me?" His question held an accusatory tone.

John couldn't accept that he'd made a mistake in coming here even though the conversation was quickly becoming uncomfortable. He was just a pathetic stroke victim who'd puttered his life away in pursuing magic, in practicing a child's hobby. He couldn't believe this was how his perfect evening was going to end. His voice was as tremulous as his nerve damaged left hand, "I just wanted to thank you. That's all."

The Professor's voice lowered threateningly. "No. You want *more*. You want to know what transpired the night I presented my Caliginous Charms ritual. You want me to expose all of the things you saw. You want me to describe in intimate detail how I accomplished them. Am I correct? Remember John, I'm a magician, I know all." He smiled at his joke.

John responded with more passion than intended, "That night—your performance, your tricks—it was the single most important event in my life. You're the reason why I wanted to become a magician."

"If that is so then answer me this, John." The Professor's face seemed to contort and shift as if it were a mask slightly askew. "Are we mere prestidigitators?"

"I don't—"

The Professor interrupted, "Do magicians lie to the audience? Pull the wool over their eyes with sham cards and crude props and crass chicanery? Or do we fill them with awe?"

"Oh, I see. I do think magicians should use a disclaimer admitting their hocus pocus is just tricks and not really supernatural."

Professor Cognoscente turned away, stared out the dark rectangle of the window. The stars seemed unusually bright tonight, clumped in a spiral within one portion of the sky, like foam around a drain.

John wished he'd opted for the coffee instead of wine. He wasn't much of a drinker, and the half glass he'd nursed was having a pronounced influence. It was difficult to focus on the back of Professor Cognoscente's head. It appeared to be a smear hopping at the end of a stump.

The sight awakened something new in John, something from the Professor's show smothered under the passage of years.

The Professor entices a reluctant volunteer to step into an oddly segmented box. He bisects her body, does unusual things to the torso. A parade of deformed performers peek out from the narrow dimensions of ornate props. Strange animals vanish and manifest in the nooks and crannies of the carnival booth.

"You disappoint." The Professor's admonition pulled John from his reverie. "We invite the spectators to briefly forget their mediocrity, their stinking skin and teeth and hair, their anchors to these rotting garments of reality. Why shouldn't we tear that away and allow the cosmos to gaze back at the audience?"

John didn't know how to respond. He shouldn't have wasted the gas money to drive all this way, and he certainly shouldn't have wasted all this time pursuing Professor Cognoscente like some celebrity besotted teenager. A sickly dread filled his throat, like rising stomach acid.

"We are archetypes of the shaman, John." He tapped his owl ring against a glass for emphasis.

John wanted to get back into his car and drive far away from this crazy magician, back to his one-bedroom apartment and collection of magic books. He'd just spent the best hours of his life talking with his childhood hero, but his joy was swiftly bleeding away as the old man continued ranting. This wasn't what he'd wanted. This dream had become sour and corrupt.

"We are enchanters, my friend."

John stood up. "Look Professor, I'm not here to—"

"This," the Professor persisted, pointed to the window now streaked with star shine, "is a balsa wood world built up and torn down at the magician's whim. A cheap theatrical backdrop. And this," he ran his hand over his face as if wiping away sweat, "is nothing more than wax and stage makeup. Existence is malleable, John."

Something moved along the stairs, flopped about with a muscular, sinuous disturbance.

John glanced towards the doorway that led to the hall which connected to the front door. "I'm sorry. I don't mean to be rude, but I have a long drive—"

The Professor placed his forefinger against John's mouth. "I have one more secret to reveal to you."

"Professor, I appreciate your hosp—"

He slipped his fingers between John's lips.

An intimate violation, a penetration of his privacy. John could taste wine on the flesh, feel the skin folds of knuckles and tickle of hairs on the back of a thumb.

Professor Cognoscente punched his fist down John's throat. He spoke in his resplendent stage voice, "Are we entertainers or are we shamans?"

John stood in rapt attention, his breath shallow, his body a boneless mannequin. A small voice in the back of his head castigated him for knocking on the Professor's front door in the first place. But a louder voice imbued with the thrill of childhood curiosity was unable to contain its excitement over just how this revival of Professor Cognoscente's Caliginous Charms Carnival would play out.

John is 8 years old again. The creaking and groaning from the tent's canvas roof are most certainly due to the encroaching storm lowering the carnival booth's temperature and not something pacing up there. When he hears voices in the ceiling, he knows it isn't the weather but Professor Cognoscente's magic that's responsible for the miracle.

John's gorge rose as the Professor wiggled his fingers deep within his neck. He withdrew a fragile length of chain attached to a silver locket and dangled the artifact before John's eyes. The chain became eerily motionless, like a projector that had frozen on a single frame. He couldn't look away from the intricate whorls of brambles and ivy etched into the locket's metal. Foliage writhed across the surface.

The Professor twitched his fingers in such a subtle motion John was scarcely aware he'd done so. Hinges as thin as eyelashes slid open to reveal the locket's interior.

Inside was a silver skeleton key far too large to fit within that space. The trick was flawless. John had no clue as to how this displacement of mass and volume was achieved.

"My friend, are you ready to once again experience my *Carnival?*" John could only moan a guttural response. He was both horrified and relieved to hear his voice reply emphatically.

Yes...

The Professor swung the locket in a methodical arc, like some 18th century mesmerist. John saw silvery tangles of furcated snakes, shadows with milky lips, brambles that flowered with silver keys. The key touched John's forehead, penetrated the skull, spilled coils of dream wetly onto his lap. The locket and key gleamed while the house plunged into darkness. The study's interior seemed to grow larger than the outside world blazing with starlight that failed to brighten the room.

The Professor unlocked John's memory of feeling small and vulnerable as he sat on a cold metal chair before a small stage where a dwarf demonstrated his acrobatic skills. A gaunt woman floated in the air before Professor Cognoscente. He made ostentatious gestures around her malnourished body. He bellowed at the small audience, challenged them to witness the delights he was about to offer.

John follows the audience's gaze to the chattering above. There is nothing there, the roof is gone, like a prop vanished with a theatrical flourish. The crowd stares into the carnival of the night sky, a vast region populated by bulbous objects tented by a smattering of stars. The spiral arms of galaxies pinwheel around dense bloated masses, shadows cavort in space, pursuing voracious grinning things. Existence is nothing but a hollow facade, a prop with hidden compartments bustling with secrets. John's life's purpose is fulfilled.

He was back in the study, entombed within his inert body again. The Professor's shadow merged with the dark room like ink spilled on a mahogany table. The key and locket were all that could be seen until the area was spontaneously illuminated by a single lamp. Even then the shadows behaved curiously, excitedly hopping about like something pulled out of a magician's hat.

John collapsed onto the couch. The Professor sagged into a leather chair with a discarded rag doll's clumsiness. Something curly and night black slid from his scalp, splashed onto the floor, bald pate glistening like smooth plastic reflecting the lamp's glow. His head flopped down at an angle contrary to the anatomy of his neck. A wobbling plump bulb at the end of a stem.

John still couldn't move, couldn't even scream. His eyes detected movement from the far side of the room. The old conical hat hopped jerkily across the floor, as if it were being tugged by an invisible thread. It concluded its passage by leaping onto the Professor's quivering bald head while his face remained hidden by the flitting shadows.

There was one moment when Professor Cognoscente's head was no longer obscured. A brief instant when his whole body slumped forward into a less murky patch of space and his featureless face flipped open on delicate hinges to reveal a chasm that extended eternally.

In that moment, something resembling a grin rippled across the flap of his smooth-as-an-egg face. An insinuation of deep-set eyes marred the surface like the blur of an insect's wings fluttering against frosted glass.

This brief flicker of expression conveyed all the awe that John had long suspected lurked behind the universe's curtain. A suggestion of the limitless wonder he was about to witness as the grinning bulb jerked hypnotically on its thick stalk and lowered itself to stare at his face forever.

THE ANTHROPARIAN
INTEGRATION TECHNIQUE

Bian's first suicide attempt was a fistful of sleeping pills shoplifted from a nearby convenience store. There were three more attempts in as many years, each successively more innovative, but none resulting in death. This had set her on a routine of obsessive-compulsive mutilations, primarily inflicted against the regions of her body she found most flabby and disgusting.

She'd been exposed to more therapies than she could remember. Light therapy, Hakomi, re-experiencing birth by being wrapped in warm, damp blankets and struggling to free herself before suffocating. Pre-birth emotional poisons rooted out, psychological trauma in the womb, an accumulation in her psyche until the pain and sorrow manifested as depression and hopelessness. Hope for a normal life was as ephemeral as ash.

At their wit's end, Bian's parents took her to visit Dr. Silvert.

Bian had heard her parents discussing Dr. Silvert several months before the visit. From what she'd picked up, they considered him a last resort, and an unappealing one at that. He was an "occult quack," and rumors of illegal therapies plagued his practice. But drastic circumstances necessitated drastic treatments—and considering every other therapy had been a dead end, they'd arranged a session.

The doctor's office was located at the end of a lonely strip mall, the last retail building on the outskirts of town before hitting the few remaining establishments—an auto parts salvage business and a water reclamation plant that appeared to have been condemned and closed. Bian knew that nobody from town ever came out to the outskirts except for the bad kids who fought over drugs and sold their stolen goods.

She was hesitant to accept that this empty mall, blurred by a haze she assumed was from the water reclamation place, was where any reputable professional plied their trade. But she'd no say in the matter. Once arrived, she saw there was no name on the door, though her parents were confident they'd located the correct place.

The office was a small, windowless space. A single desk and chair sat in the center. An old-fashioned intercom on the desktop, a tangle of frayed cords running from it to an electrical box haloed by black scorch marks, gave an electronic purr. There was nobody present. A dark wood panel door at the back of the room led to what must be where Dr. Silvert waited in his main office.

Bian had seen a corner window looking out onto the parking lot, but she couldn't locate the window now. Was that raised area a plastered over rectangle where the window should be?

The office was claustrophobic, not conducive to a calm therapeutic environment. In Bian's mind, it seemed as if it was designed to seal itself from anything intrusive, including new patients.

Her mother pushed the intercom button.

"Hello? We're here for Bian's appointment."

A wordless static responded.

She pushed the button again and repeated herself. This time, the static was subdued, and they could hear a sonorous voice on the other end.

I'm ready now. Send Bian in please.

The three moved to the door, but the intercom voice spoke abruptly,

Just Bian. No one else.

They were hesitant, not sure how he could see them, but remained silent. Bian took the initiative, nodded to her parents, and entered alone.

It was gloomy inside. The wallpaper was dated, striped and colorful, shiny like ribbon candy. A single table lamp on an oval desk left a faint green spill in a small circumference. The lampshade was tattered and stringy, as if threaded together by glowworms. A folding chair was the only other piece of furniture.

Dr. Silvert sat behind the desk, his thin fingers resting on an intercom.

His suit was faded and patchy. Bald, his pate looked soft as pudding in the light. Bian looked back at her parents.

"Please close the door and sit down." Dr. Silvert insisted. Bian did as she was told. Her eyes adjusted to the dim interior. The folding chair was cold and hard.

"I've heard quite a bit about you, Bian." Dr. Silvert leaned across the desk, large eyes fogged like antique glass, comical in such a stern countenance.

"I've been to a lot of therapists."

"I've read your records. Your parents made the right decision in reaching out to me."

"I hope so." she said quietly.

"How does your mind work, Bian?"

"I don't know."

"Is it physical or spiritual?"

"I don't know."

"Most people don't know."

Bian wanted to answer the doctor's questions correctly, to impress him with how much she wanted to get better. But she already felt as if she were a failure.

"Depression is like cancerous cells." Dr. Silvert continued, his long hands together, palms up. The gesture made Bian think of a child holding a dead animal he'd discovered on a nature romp.

"Both take over everything. Grow in malignant proliferation." Hands parted, fingers spread as if signing a diaspora. "Remake what you are in their own corrupt image." This was new. Counseling and a copious supply of pharmaceuticals had done little to stave off Bian's persistent morbid thoughts. But she'd never heard of the approach Dr. Silvert was taking. She felt ugly, a bloated monster unworthy of living. Maybe she'd finally found a way out.

"I want to be someone else." Bian said in monotone, as if reciting a phone number.

"You're not comfortable in your skin, Bian! Because you think that *you're nothing but your skin.*"

Bian began to cry. His words made sense. A bizarre, elusive sense, yet redemptive in what she could understand so far.

"We are not simply physical beings filled with chemicals and sinew." Dr. Silvert whispered.

"What are we then?" Bian wiped a sleeve across her wet cheeks.

"We have a Seraph inside." He tapped his head, then pointed at Bian's forehead. "We're all burdened with a blessed warmth. Hosts to a luminous immaterial resident."

"A soul?" Bian asked.

"Not a soul. Something *more*."

"More?"

"*More*. An angelic being nestled inside you, the very *you* that makes what constitutes you, *you*." Dr. Silvert's voice was triumphant.

"Inside me?"

"Yes. We call it *Anthroparian Integration*. A new psychotherapeutic tool. You're experiencing Stage One now, the *Revelation Phase*. You're doing remarkably well, Bian."

"I don't know anything about that."

"It's a new method to somatic therapies. I'm one of a select few trained in it."

"Angel? Like actual angels? From the Bible?"

"*Seraphim*. And I wouldn't want to impose any specific cultural interpretations." His eyelids rapidly opened and closed, not a complete blink, but a nervous tic.

"Seraphim are universal. Every culture has some variation. Suffice it to say they're terrifying in their magnificence."

Bian allowed herself a fleeting moment of hope. She'd never heard of such an odd therapy before, but it was appealing. She liked the idea of secular Seraphim. Maybe this strange doctor and his weird *Anthroparian Integration* treatment was for her.

"Bian, the important thing is to realize that we're tubes of cancerous cells hastily slopped together. Shit in one end, shit out the other. *But* we're clever cancerous cells. And within, you hold a living Seraph."

Bian giggled at the profanity. "Seraph?"

"Seraph." Dr. Silvert reiterated with an ecstatic smile. He spread his arms wide to demonstrate the joyous enormity of his revelation.

A heavy flow of blood darkened the porcelain. The broken plastic hairbrush handle had slid near the drain, the end serrated and knife sharp. An angry gouge in Bian's wrist seeped with each pulse. A tube emptying itself.

Out. Out of me. Go away. Make me go away.

The bathroom stank, sour and raw. She turned the cold water on to rinse her arm clean. The wound was ugly, but not deep enough to be fatal. The waste from her veins ran thin in the water, slipped down the drain.

I'm a foul thing. I'm ugly. Unworthy of happiness.

Sick.

Dr. Silvert had given her stacks of psychotherapeutic literature. Pamphlets, books, photocopied papers from psychology journals with names like *Neuromyth: Journal of Spiritual Gnosis,* and *Esoteric Experimental Psychology.* Much of it was baffling, but Bian was intelligent and read everything.

She was familiar with religions that shared a superficial ideology with the Anthroparian Integration Technique—faiths like Christian Science, which insisted illness was an illusion and sickness a mental aberration. The Technique, too, saw material existence as a disgusting falsehood.

From what she could gather, Anthroparian Integration presupposed the birth of the cosmos as the metastasis of existence. Atoms were composed of cancerous particles, and consequently, matter was inherently corrupt. The material universe was a pathology, a decomposing skin festering around the ethereal nature of Seraphim.

There were only three stages to the therapy: the *Revelation Phase,* which she'd finished, *Extrapolation Technique,* and the *Numinous Exuviation Method.* Each one further opened up the patient to their potential within, allowing a profound communication with the Seraphim.

The final step, the *Numinous Exuviation Method,* filled her with a strange sense of elation and fear despite not knowing what it entailed. None of Dr.

Silvert's literature gave any descriptions.

But she was still hurting herself. She felt she was on the road to recovery, but the journey had only just begun. A glimmer rippled in the mirror. A gleam like star shine on moist eyes. Bian quickly looked up and around the small bathroom.

But nothing moved. A sound deep within the maze of the plumbing startled her. She looked into the sink at her blood.

I am more than an abnormal thing. I have something intangible within. I have a Seraph inside.

Her blood had coagulated around the drain in a strange shape. She was made of phlegm and blood and shit—no right to dream of becoming anything else. The world was teetering building blocks and no amount of poetry or faith could make it otherwise. Filth frantically reproducing filth.

I am nothing more than that which can be disposed of into sewage systems and clotted around drains.

She turned the faucet up full blast. Water washed away the vestiges of blood. *No.*

I am a host to primordial glory, incubator to the ceaseless activities of an immortal being eternally blazing with fervid grace. I am made of bodiless star shine.

That is not me. I am not the sum of my body.

I am companion to a Seraph.

Bian's parents dropped her off at the strip mall with the promise to return an hour later after running errands. Once again, the office was empty save for the desk and intercom. Nobody responded when she pushed the button. Dr. Silvert's main office door was ajar, so she stepped inside, uninvited.

Dr. Silvert was gone. In his place, four Styrofoam mannequin heads sat in a row on the desk. Each was topped, from left to right, with a mauve, pink, red, and white wig. The faces were gray and vacant. Their only characteristic was a slight depression where eyes should be.

Dr. Silvert's voice suddenly encompassed the room, like a spongy growth on the walls and ceiling.

Please shut the door, Bian.

The intercom was missing. There weren't any speakers visible on the walls. Bian closed the door.

The Styrofoam heads lit up, illuminated by a beam of light from hidden projectors. Faces of strangers were projected against the Styrofoam. Light dripped down distorted noses and eyes, warped mouths into condescending sneers and dejected frowns. Their distressing features suggested something evil to Bian, a viciousness made all the more poignant in contrast to the brightly colored wigs.

Today we are going to try something called the 'Extrapolation Technique.' Is that to your satisfaction Bian?

"Ok."

Do you know these people, Bian? Do you recognize their faces?

"Nuh uh."

They are the faces of Seraphim, imposed on silly human heads.

She looked around the room but couldn't locate any projectors. The shafts of light simply trailed off into the dark, their origin clandestine.

Seraphim are light cast against foul superficial bodies. An impalpable terrible beauty denigrating itself by inhabiting human shells. But sometimes Seraphim too take on aspects of our world. When this occurs, they may become tainted.

"What do I need to do?" Bian pleaded, fear of disappointing Dr. Silvert making her frantic. She was so close to achieving a breakthrough, so near to discovering a path to happiness.

Your Seraph is spoiled, Bian. Its star shine has been invaded by matter. By rot.

"What do I do?"

What do you think you need to do, Bian?

Was this why she'd hurt herself? Had her body known its symbiotic relationship with the Seraph was sick as well?

The radiant Styrofoam heads flickered. Bian thought the pink-haired one bared its teeth. It was so quick she wasn't sure she hadn't imagined it, but the possibility filled her with horror.

"I need to cure it," she mumbled.

Yes. How might you accomplish this, Bian?

The glowing faces grew brighter. The Styrofoam heads wobbled slightly from what Bian assumed must be a semi-truck driving by outside.

"Please tell me, doctor."

The projected light-faces dimmed, then disappeared. The room was impossibly dark. Bian reached for where she thought the doorknob might be, but her hand passed through emptiness.

Before we conclude our session, Bian, please tell me how you might go about curing yourself and the Seraph.

"I don't know! I already said I don't know!"

You must imagine your Seraph's visage over your own face, Bian.

"My face?"

You must conjure it.

"How?"

You must confront your Seraph. You must face it with your dull, dead gaze.

The room hummed with the din of machinery, metal against glass against muscle against bone. A skull full of industrial noise, the cacophony of the universe. Bian shook at the awesome hymn. She wanted to scream, but pressed fists against her ears to deafen herself. The noise died to a piercing note, then that too faded away.

Come back next week, and we'll conclude with Stage Three. When Bian fully regained her composure, she drew a deep breath and found the door. Opening it, she saw that the pink wig had fallen off. She grabbed the Styrofoam head and hurried outside to wait in the dismal haze for her parents to pick her up.

Back home, in the privacy of her bedroom late at night, Bian removed the stolen mannequin head from its hiding place wrapped in her jacket. She regretted not grabbing the wig.

Dr. Silvert would never know she'd dabbled in therapy without him. If he accused her of stealing the head, she'd deny it. What could he possibly do to her? And what harm was there in trying the final stage of the *Numinous Exuviation Method* on her own?

She'd no idea how to go about performing the method, but assumed the head was involved somehow. Maybe if she visualized her Seraph's face onto the Styrofoam, she'd attain some sort of revelation. A vision.

Bian stared into the shallows of the head's eyes, scrutinized its dull gray color, wondered at the tactile sensation of Styrofoam, gritty yet soft like fine sandpaper. Willing her Seraph's presence onto the Styrofoam bust, she imagined it a lifeless template of her own skin. She smiled at the thought this was a spooky game of gazing into candle lit mirrors to summon spirits—a frivolity she imagined other children played at slumber parties.

An electrical thrill shot through her. She was doing something wrong, violating a mysterious sacred rite. Like standing on a length of old train tracks, rails stippled with lichen, wooden ties crumbling from time. But a train was coming, the tracks vibrating as something massive hurtled its way down a path long abandoned. The anxiety was crushing. She prayed the Seraph would suddenly appear at her side, bronze hands on her shoulders, six wings spread so wide the planet would tilt under their magnificence.

Bian concentrated, unblinking until her eyes burned, and tears ran down her cheeks.

The mannequin head glowed from within.

Something stirred inside the Styrofoam like an animal beneath a thin eggshell cage.

Bian gripped the head with such strength her fingers sank into the Styrofoam. She closed her eyes. The head's glow was so bright she could see it behind her eyelids. It burned with such sublime beauty, she'd no means to describe it.

Behind her closed eyes, the Seraph's eyes opened.

Bian studied it in her mind's eye. She was such a useless thing. So useless.

This being deserved more than her. More than this ugly, sweaty, stupid girl. A Seraph, born inside luminous spheres forged before the cosmos existed was impossible to touch, to see, to hear, to comprehend. She would never deserve this.

The Styrofoam head bucked and thrashed in Bian's grip, but she didn't let go or even open her eyes. She was no longer weak. What was her debilitating depression in contrast to such wonders to come?

The World was not made up of ghosts and breath. The World was brute force, elegant in its efficiency. Chaos blundered its way through space with wanton cruelty, tossing aside the toys of Creation. Her Seraph would never fade in potency, its light so wondrous it would forever remain like the memory of a color she couldn't name. On finishing the *Numinous Exuviation Method,* she'd behold her glorious Seraph.

She opened her eyes.

The Styrofoam head was gone. In its place she held a fetus. Its body was desiccated like dead leaves, shriveled and decayed as stillborn dreams.

FROM A PEOPLE OF STRANGE LANGUAGE

A Play in One Act

But so long as we think in human language, we shall never arrive at a truer expression than breath or spirit, unless we rise to a higher octave of thought altogether, and agree to call it the Infinite in Man, as we recognized in the gods of nature the ancient names for the Infinite in Nature.
—Max Müller, *Anthropological Religion*, p. 229

CAST OF CHARACTERS

HELEN POWELL: *The medium; Catherine's aunt.*
PROF. WILLIAM COSTOCK: *The philologist; a scholar.*
MILDRED GAVESTON: *The naturalist; Nellie's lover.*
NELLIE DENSMORE: *The addict; Mildred's lover.*
CATHERINE: *The lost; Helen's niece.*

SCENES

Scene I	The forest, lost
Scene II	The study, evening
Scene III	The forest, a stranger
Scene IV	The study, séance
Scene V	The forest, language
Scene VI	The study, extinction
Scene VII	The forest, void

SCENE I

SETTING: The forest, dark and mysterious. A white expanse of snow covers everything. The wind shakes trees. Branches lash the black, whistling air.

AT RISE: A young girl, about 10 years old, wanders in the woods, clearly lost. She is wearing a black wool long coat, trimmed with silk velveteen, wool gloves and a hat, though this is insufficient protection against the cold. Her blond hair whips against her face in the gusty night. Ankle deep in snow, she trudges from stage right to left. She is barefoot. Once she reaches stage left, she pauses, looks behind as if hearing a voice, then proceeds off stage.

(BLACKOUT)
(END OF SCENE)

SCENE II

SETTING: A vast room too grand to adequately light. The sole window looks out onto the white nothingness of snow. Bookcases stand from floor to raftered ceiling. Mahogany carvings of saints and strange creatures, their abdomens split open on hinged flaps to display innards like pages from a naturalist's book, stand vigil along the walls.

Situated at stage right, tables arrayed with microscopes and telescopes, geological specimens, various minerals and unusual fossils preserve the impression of unknown life- forms. A galvanic battery's coils heat crucibles hissing with molten substances. An antique faded rug covers the floor.

Opium paraphernalia rests on every surface. Bamboo pipes adorned with ivory saddles, glass cones of opium lamps, and mother-of-pearl opium trays. The scene suggests a former opulence, now neglected and covered in dust. The residence of a wealthy hobbyist displaying an interest in naturalism, long succumbed to vice, and their home has become a decadent opium den.

AT RISE:

A carbon arc lamp illuminates a spirit cabinet at stage center. The cabinet is constructed from a dark tarp suspended by a skeleton of wooden frames held together with bands of hammered metal. The cabinet 's curtain is closed. Four plush but rickety chairs circle the tall box. Seated, PROFESSOR WILLIAM COSTOCK, NELLIE DENSMORE, and MILDRED GAVESTON. HELEN POWELL stands at the cabinet's left.

HELEN POWELL : 25 years old, a blond white woman, smartly attired in a black gored skirt, her neck thinned by a high lace collar, pale hair done up in Gibson Girl fashion. Her accent suggests Oregon, circa 1900.

HELEN

Tonight is unfit for any soul to be out-of-doors; the snow is relentless, the sky black as pitch. My motor carriage passed through a web so vast I shudder to contemplate the size of the spider responsible!

MILDRED GAVESTON: a pale redhead, well dressed in fashionable clothes, but wrinkled and stained as if she has worn them for several days. She is in her late 40s and quite striking. The impression is that her fortune is slowly declining, though she retains as much of the finer things in life as long as she's able. Her fingers are scarred from opium lamp oil burns. She gestures for HELEN to approach.

MILDRED

Please come over here so Nellie and I can see you dearest. Ugh, are these dark strands webs? I've never seen such a thing...

(*plucks sticky threads from HELEN's clothes*)

NELLIE DENSMORE: MILDRED's companion, early 50s, a portly white woman with rosy cheeks, attired in an ill-fitting threadbare suit, hair gray and unruly. She is lugubrious, with a perpetual scowl. Her speech is relaxed, excessively calm from an opium high. She takes HELEN 's hand and kisses it.

NELLIE

A pleasure to have such an esteemed medium demonstrate her talents in our very home.

WILLIAM COSTOCK: a 30-year-old black man in a charcoal Newbury suit and bowtie. Wire rimmed glasses rest bent and lopsided on his nose. There is an air of coldness about him, an aloof intelligence not just academic, but that gained from traveling the world. He is bookish, yet has clearly faced violence and adversity in life.

WILLIAM

I've yet to make your acquaintance Miss Powell. I'm Prof. William Costock.

HELEN

(Visibly nervous, she glances at the window as if anticipating something.)
Miss Gaveston mentioned that a brilliant Negro professor from Dartmouth College would be attending.

WILLIAM

Am I a testament to Virchow's study debunking demarcations of race?

HELEN

I'm sorry if I've offended, but I know not what you mean.

WILLIAM

(distantly)
No need to apologize. And did Miss Gaveston explain as to why I'm here?

HELEN

Only that you're an academic. And a believer. Is this why you were invited tonight?

WILLIAM

It is. I'm a reluctant skeptic, and an obstinate believer. I've seen many things of which I cannot explain.

NELLIE

Do tell.

WILLIAM

I once attended a Tchokwe ceremony in Angola where their sacred wooden masks frowned, grinned, sang in a strange language all on their own. It was a terrible sight of which I've no explanation.

NELLIE

Inexplicable.

WILLIAM

And I swear that mask...

MILDRED

Yes?

WILLIAM

I swear it took on the aspects of my features, like a mirror, reflecting my terror from an inanimate wooden face.

MILDRED

Mirrors! So like that Rachilde play—
(to NELLIE)

...the one with the spiders?

NELLIE
(disinterested)

L'Araignée de Cristal.

MILDRED

Thank you dear. Yes, a decadent masterpiece.

HELEN

Decadence? This world forever frustrates my immolations.

NELLIE
(amused)

Immolations?

HELEN

Oh! I misspoke. I meant to say *assumptions*.

NELLIE

You are an odd creature, dear.

HELEN

Why, I'm—

MILDRED

(interrupting)

The professor here is also a polylinguist.

NELLIE

(attention diverted from HELEN)

You're a... what's the word?

WILLIAM

A philologist.

NELLIE

(snaps fingers in excitement)

Yes!

HELEN

Why would a philologist be interested in a séance?

WILLIAM

My hypothesis is that in the spirit world all speak the same idyllic tongue, as of that spoken before a scattered Babel. Perhaps every language on this planet is rooted in that realm. I hope to speak to the dead tonight so as to gather more evidence.

HELEN

A dead language?

WILLIAM

A language of the dead. Tell me Miss Powell, how do the spirits normally communicate to you?

HELEN

Why, in actions, in cold grave breath, in levitations, in song.

WILLIAM

(impatiently)

Yes. Yes. But what *language?*

HELEN

English of course.

WILLIAM

I've attended several séances where the dead spoke English, Japanese, Haryanvi, Spanish, Yoruba—I could name dozens. But do you know the common web connecting all?

HELEN

I can't imagine why I'd know.

WILLIAM

They're all the native tongue spoken by the medium who'd arranged each séance.

HELEN

So, you *are* a skeptic.

WILLIAM

On the contrary; I emphatically know there *is* an afterlife, but I don't believe heaven is as monosyllabic as most psychics would have us believe.

MILDRED

(laughing)

Oh professor, I've come to the conclusion you've taken too much of a liking to Müller's anthropological religion.

WILLIAM

Müller *was* correct. Language is integral to how we interpret our existence, and how that reality is projected to us. "Man lives in the world about him principally, indeed exclusively, as language presents it to him."

(abruptly turns to HELEN)

But I ramble on. What of you Miss Powell? You built this spirit cabinet?

HELEN

I did indeed. The chair and table as well.

NELLIE

(sarcastically)

Extraordinary carpentry skills, kiddo.

HELEN

(nonplussed)

Thank you. My father was a skilled woodworker. He taught me well.

WILLIAM

(gesturing towards the spirit cabinet)

I very much look forward to seeing what you produce from the veiled Beyond, whether ghostly skulls or rattling chains.

HELEN

Chains! Skulls! My summonings are of a more, *cherubic* nature. Tonight, you're more likely to be presented a fragrant bouquet than a shrieking skull, Professor.

WILLIAM

(jovially)

A pity. Cephalometry is an amusing pastime.

MILDRED

Speaking of which, when last we spoke Professor, it was in disagreement over the Calaveras skull.

WILLIAM

(amused)

Oh, you and that damned skull!

MILDRED

I maintain it genuine, and not an autochthonous relic. I think we've an honest to God Pliocene man in North America.

WILLIAM

If I may borrow John Powell's term, the skull is that of an *Amerindian*. Not a *new man* of any sort.

NELLIE

(pulling on opium pipe, addressing MILDRED)

Forgive the question, love—my drug addled state has me confused. Is this related to that strange fossil your friend Dr. Zaldívar dug up in South America last summer?

MILDRED

Related in that both testify to the antiquity of Man, though at different sites. That

Jalisco find had the most remarkably shaped skull, not even remotely sapien in appearance. Zaldívar dubbed it *Pithecanoús*. A real blow to the pithecometra thesis, right Professor?

WILLIAM

(coldly)

Zaldívar's ideas are as unscientific as Buchanan's sarcognomy ravings. Pithecanoús? The "thinking ape"? Nonsense!

MILDRED

I cannot disagree enough. We are reluctant to consider the possibility that there are, or were, antediluvian beings superior to us in mind, skill, technologies. The world was preceded by such minds as we can only wonder at. Our races' extinction will be followed by intelligences that will make our trash midden's contents quaint in comparison.

WILLIAM

Pithecanoús is nothing more than the Calaveras skull nonsense wrapped in the mantle of mysticism and Zaldívar's eccentric faith.

MILDRED

(tilting her head in acquiescence)

I am at an impasse. I cannot disagree with your assessment. Or with Dr. Zaldívar's for that matter.

WILLIAM

And what of Zaldívar's proposal that there's something further up the Great Chain of Being? A being he has dubbed *"Phainothropus"*?

MILDRED

I've no stance. Is this related to your interest in the Enochian language?

WILLIAM

I believe there may be some connection. I'm not convinced any such language is attributable to angels, though I am *most* curious as to what tongue the dead choose to correspond. My interest in languages, and of my recent inquiry into the speech of ghosts, well, the possibility I may communicate and gather some indication of how cultures manifest in the afterlife is of paramount interest.

MILDRED

Was it Charlemagne who proposed that to have a second language is to have a second soul? If so, the afterlife must be as confused as the land of Shinar after God kicked out its inhabitants.

WILLIAM

(laughing)

And all the more confused for language's peculiarities. My friend Frank Cushing and I lived with the Zuni for a length of time. They taught me their language, though I only possess modest fluency. The curious thing is that Zuni speakers do not differentiate "yellow" from "orange," but instead discriminate based on the object being spoken of, not its precise hue. An orange leaf and a yellow sky are differentiated by the subjects, not the shade or hue itself.

NELLIE

(dismissively)

I cannot understand such intricacies.

WILLIAM

(condescending)

Language is a veil. Only by lifting it may we see what it insists on hiding.

MILDRED

Language may *alter* us.

WILLIAM

Well said. And what better place to explore this notion than in a town that not only welcomes mediums and spiritualists, but celebrates them.

MILDRED

Have any of you had time to appreciate our town? Talent is a unique place with a curious history.

WILLIAM

I'm afraid I've only just arrived, having travelled from Linkville, though Talent's reputation is known to me.

HELEN

(distracted, looking out a window, wringing her hands in consternation)
I am newly arrived as well, but have heard of psychics performing good deeds here.

NELLIE

Talent is a colorful collective of intellectuals, woman's suffragists, psychics, spiritualists of all sorts. We are proud of our unconventional ways.

WILLIAM

You've had other psychics here? In your home?

NELLIE

Of course. Though none as celebrated as our Miss Powell here.
(conspiratorially, smiling at HELEN)
I hear this one can convince spirits to make flowers float in the air and guitars to strum themselves.

MILDRED

And the tapping of dainty spirit hands about the room!

NELLIE

Tappings! Charming.

HELEN

That and more.

WILLIAM

If so, let us say I accept Miss Powell's expertise and she produces, or summons as it were, tapping sounds from various corners of the room uninhabited, save for the participants seated round a table. The scientist is perfectly justified in inquiring as to whether these rappings may be reproduced on, say, for argument's sake, the taut membrane of a phonoautograph.

MILDRED

(intrigued)

Reasonable I would say. What are you getting at?

WILLIAM

What of heavy tables elevated and propelled across a floor without human agency? The scientist merely requires an instrument to measure this alleged movement, a means to ascertain whether the furniture actually became animated, or whether the suggestion was brought on by a dimly lit room and the inebriation of its participants.

NELLIE

Heh. Clever.

WILLIAM

Spirits reach through walls and tables yet retain the ability to pluck at a sleeve or tousle hair from their spectral realm. How do they commit such acts if insubstantial? How to snatch a beloved locket left by a long-deceased relation? If capable of such, I ask, would said spirit be capable of reaching through a bell jar to retrieve the 1000th of a grain of arsenic, drawing this minuscule speck through glass as well as the solid surface of a mahogany table? If incapable, why is the cumbersome locket accessible but not the barely detectable grain?

MILDRED

What you're saying is that if spirits are capable of intervening in the material world, their meddling in our physical realm means they must be amendable to scientific verification?

WILLIAM

Yes! How would such an entity speak without vocal cords—what can be said if the physical trappings to vibrate is absent? Do the dead have a culture? Religion? Language?

MILDRED

(looks towards opium paraphernalia)

I imagine they retain the faith they practiced in life. Lord knows I look forward to my vices after death.

WILLIAM

If Miss Powell is able to entice the dead to speak, the evidence of such should be attainable. This raises another question...

(pauses)

MILDRED

What's that?

WILLIAM

Are spirits subject to organic evolution?

NELLIE

Such a nimble minded Professor!

HELEN

What an unusual thought.

WILLIAM

Think of it! Are the dead subject to natural selection? What of the millennia that Man has occupied this Earth, each and every soul continuing on? If Darwin is correct, and this world's diversity of life is attributable to his theory, then what of the afterlife? There must be something similar that occurs with the deceased.

MILDRED

From so simple a beginning...

WILLIAM

Precisely! Languages must have something analogous with nature's animalcules, a paramecium speck of communication that started it all. Not to mention the myriads of languages that sprang into existence only to become extinct over the millennia.

HELEN

(distraught, looking out window)

May we dispense with such talk and continue the séance?

MILDRED

(concerned)

Of course. Are you well, Miss Powell? You seem...distracted.

HELEN

(attention elsewhere)

I... I'm quite well. And eager to begin the summoning.

MILDRED

(satisfied at HELEN's response)

Then let us proceed!

(BLACKOUT)
(END OF SCENE)

SCENE III

SETTING: Back in the dark snow-covered forest.

AT RISE: The girl stands hesitantly, afraid of something she thought she saw. The audience now sees it too—a glimmer of light in the distance, as that of a lamp. She leans forward, squinting, rubs her arms for warmth.

GIRL
(cautiously)

Hello?

(The radius of light grows more expansive, like the headlamp of an approaching automobile.)

GIRL

Did you call my name? I know you're out there. Please don't frighten me! I'm lost!

(Waits a few moments. On hearing no response, she continues to slowly walk towards the distant glow.)

(BLACKOUT)
(END OF SCENE)

SCENE IV

SETTING: Back in the study.

AT RISE: HELEN, MILDRED, NELLIE, and WILLIAM stand in front of the spirit cabinet. One side of the cabinet has been cut-away, revealing the interior to the audience, though the box is at such an angle those on stage cannot see inside. The cabinet's interior is simply decorated with a wooden chair and a small ornate table, of suitable size to display a vase of flowers and a guitar. HELEN moves to open the curtain.

WILLIAM
(interrupting, stepping in front of HELEN)

One moment. Having consulted a magician acquaintance the other week, I am aware of the various ways trickery could be utilized to produce spirit manifestations.

HELEN
(insulted)

I assure you no trickery is involved.

WILLIAM
(placating)

It is not my intent to disparage your mediumship Miss Powell, I am merely searching for any deficiencies which may allow the practice of deceit. A shallow chamber, or—

(running his palm across the wood of the table)

—any defect, subtle bulge, or seam which could potentially betray a secret compartment.

(gripping the curtains)

No flaps or slits to allow a slight girl to slip in or out undetected. I am convinced the spirit cabinet is genuine and hoax-proof. You may resume.

HELEN

(nervous, speaking warily) A slight girl you say?

WILLIAM

Yes, I mean perhaps a girl, if trickery is utilized—oh! I do not point any fingers! I did not mean to imply there's an intruder in this home. Lurking in the shadows—

MILDRED

I assure you both that you're my only guests tonight.

NELLIE

(holding a length of rope)
May I take the liberty Miss Powell?

HELEN

(pushes the curtain aside and sits on the chair within. Posture straight, dignified, unruffled by WILLIAM's insinuations.)
You may. Let us speak. And be spoken to. By the dead. Please make sure the knots are quite tight.

(NELLIE ties HELEN's hands and ankles to the chair. MILDRED steps forward to verify the veracity of the knots.)

MILDRED

(mollified)

There is no method available to man or woman that would allow them to escape from such bonds. I'd bet my life on it.

NELLIE

I'd bet *Miss Powell's* life.

MILDRED

Professor?

WILLIAM

(tugs at the rope)

I cannot imagine anyone escaping such secure bonds.

HELEN

I am ready.

(MILDRED closes the curtain and takes a chair. WILLIAM and NELLIE accompany her.)

HELEN

(The others can only hear her voice from behind the curtain, though the audience still has a clear view through the cut-away cabinet.)

Join us ancient spirits!

(The audience sees HELEN remove a chair spindle that has clearly been gimmicked to easily slip loose. She frees herself of the rope, but keeps it knotted. She picks up the guitar and strums several discordant chords.)

NELLIE
(*applauding*)

Wonderful!

WILLIAM

Spirits! A colloquy! A poem! A sonnet!

(*HELEN sets the guitar back on the table and throws a rose over the cabinet onto the floor. She follows with another rose, then another, until the entire bouquet is gone.*)

WILLIAM

Impressive! But are the spirits mute?

(*Helen grabs and shakes the curtains, so they quiver in an odd manner.*)

MILDRED

(*tilts her head towards WILLIAM, but holds her gaze on the cabinet*)
You cannot deny the miraculous intervention of the spirits here, William, speeches or not.

WILLIAM

I cannot deny or confirm anything as of yet. I am disappointed they are reluctant to join us in conversation.

HELEN

(*Sits back down, slips into the ropes and wedges the chair spindle back in place to make it appear as if she'd been captive the whole time*).
The spirits are retreating.

NELLIE

So soon, kiddo?

MILDRED

There is always tomorrow, dear.

WILLIAM

Was my request for a word or two presumptuous?

(A roar rumbles through the room, a blaring trumpet, though far louder, with an insinuation of words. The bellowing increases in volume until the very stage shakes as if an earthquake grips the theater. HELEN is visibly stunned, though she sits unmoving, not daring to reveal that she can easily free herself from the bonds.)

NELLIE

What in God's name?

MILDRED

That voice! In the air itself!

WILLIAM

Miss Powell? Is this your doing?

HELEN

It is not! Release me! I cannot remain in this cabinet!

WILLIAM

(pushes curtain aside and hurriedly unties HELEN)

How can this be?

HELEN

(Rubbing wrists to falsely demonstrate that the loose bonds were secure.)
I can't explain... Nothing in my previous experience...
(Now outside, she quickly draws the cabinet curtain shut, afraid of its contents.)
No more! No more for today.

NELLIE

If not spirits, what else?

WILLIAM

It was a sentence. A colloquy. I cannot place its origin, but those *were* words in that blast of sound. I am certain of it.

MILDRED

A speech, a song, a poem. What does it matter? It was a voice unlike anything I've ever heard.

HELEN

This is not my doing!

WILLIAM

Not your doing? But the spirits—

(Suddenly, an ethereal light sprays out of the opening at the top of the spirit cabinet, flows from beneath the closed curtains like molten starlight. The audience can no longer see into the cutaway portion of the cabinet, for the illumination is too intense. A warbling yet magnificent voice shakes the room.)

VOICE

AITITSIRT XE ERECSID ÓTIC...

(They all stand frozen in place, stunned by this turn of events.)

MILDRED
(reluctantly breaking the silence)

Latin?

WILLIAM

(*shaking his head in confusion*)

No. Not Latin.

NELLIE

(*trying to open the door to leave the study*)

The doors are locked!

MILDRED

How can that be? It locks on our side, and I have the sole key.

NELLIE

Open the damned thing!

MILDRED

(*Hurriedly retrieves a key and fits it into the keyhole. After desperately twisting it, she turns in exasperation to the others.*)

I cannot unlock it. There must be something on the other side.

HELEN

The windows. Look to the windows...

(*A black fog presses against the windows, contrasting against the snowfall like ink in milk.*)

WILLIAM

(*Tries to open the pane, but it won't budge.*)

It is not fog...

HELEN

What is it?

WILLIAM

Black threads. A downpour of... shadowy strands. Like those removed from your clothing by Mrs. Gaveston earlier. It's sealing the windows shut. This must be what has intruded the mansion's main hallway, pressing its bulk against the study door, preventing our escape.

HELEN

I don't understand...

NELLIE

Miss Powell, please stop this! Make that cabinet cease its infernal activity!

HELEN

I am *not* responsible for this!

(They all halt, as if hearing something skulking near, or detecting a presence that should not be.)

NELLIE

Can you sense it as well? A palpable evil has been let loose.

MILDRED

I do. That voice's tone, its timbre... It leaves me soul-stained. Violates my very-

NELLIE

We must leave.

MILDRED

You've strength yet my dear.

NELLIE

Strength? You prattle me, my love.

WILLIAM

What's that?

NELLIE

Oh, I mean my love flatters me. I mean... I don't understand... My mind is... My words...

WILLIAM

(interrupting, pointing at the cabinet)

Its words have already infected us. If speech begins as a child's cry, a cry that becomes more sophisticated over time, might this voice be the wailing of an infant soul? A mind crying out to communicate with us?

NELLIE

This is no time for your cleverness Professor!

WILLIAM

(ignoring NELLIE)

Descriptive grammars. Linguistic families. What could this be? If the structure of language mirrors thought, different languages produce different minds, separate dimensions of thought. What sort of mind is responsible for this voice? And what *has been* spoken?

NELLIE

(frantically)

What could it possibly have meant to convey? Why would its words change my words? I do not understand!

MILDRED

It said something like "aititsirt xe erecsid ótic". But how could one decipher what that means devoid of any Rosetta Stone?

NELLIE
(retrieves an opium pipe and candle)
My nerves are assaulted. I cannot bear this any longer.

(MILDRED joins her. Both sit down to prepare the opium pipes.)

WILLIAM
This entity unsettles me like no other encounter. I cannot express the depths of abject trepidation I feel on hearing that voice.

HELEN
Let us leave this room! We can break down the door and wait elsewhere until daybreak. Anywhere out of sight of that cabinet.

WILLIAM
(Continuing manically)
If I may once more borrow Humboldt's idea that language itself is a "formative organ of thought", we can see how unique languages provoke unique thoughts. How strange must be an evolved mind that speaks from the grave!

(The cabinet wobbles left and right. A banging sound from within, so loud windows crack, and bottles fall from the shelves.)

VOICE
OGE SUNUM MUUTEPREP...

WILLIAM
I will open that curtain...

HELEN
(in desperation)
No! This is not my doing! We must leave!

MILDRED

Then command the spirit to relent! To leave us be!

HELEN

I cannot...

NELLIE

Why? For God's sake Miss Powell, end this nightmare!

HELEN

Because I am a fraud! I am a cheat. I do not establish a pious rapport with angelic souls, but perform legerdemain.

MILDRED

(confused)

I'm at my wit's end. Explain!

HELEN

My dear Catherine is missing.

MILDRED

Who?

HELEN

(sheepishly)

I drove to your mansion with my niece Catherine. I stopped once we glimpsed your house's lights, for Catherine slipped away into the woods and I was to allow her surreptitious entrance through a window at the hour. She was to sneak into this very cabinet and assist in my deceptions.

MILDRED

Deceptions?

HELEN

Yes. We practiced extensively. Catherine was to step out of her concealment within the cabinet, draped in a gown I'd soaked in oil of phosphorous so as to acquire the viridescent radiance of a soul from Beyond.

NELLIE

(Bleary eyed, the opium taking effect.

Apparently, we were to be host to a fake ghost, my love.

(shakes head in astonishment)

What happened to Catherine?

HELEN

She never gave the signal to open the window. She is gone. I know not where.

WILLIAM

(ceases agitated pacing)

So, this phenomenon exists independent of you?

HELEN

I've nothing to do with this. Please do not open that cabinet curtain.

VOICE

VOS SITSE NON...

MILDRED

(shaking, reaches for opium pipe)

I refuse to listen to that any longer. Its tone fills my mouth with coppery flavor. My nose with ozone stench.

NELLIE

I want to slip away into dream and leave this evening a forgotten memory.

MILDRED
(exhaling opium fumes, speech slurred)
...a forgotten memory.

HELEN
(watching MILDRED and NELLIE prepare their pipes)
I did not conjure this voice.

WILLIAM
I'm uncertain as to which is the conjurer and which the conjured.

> Black gossamer strands fall from the darkness above, past the catwalks, onto the auditorium. Gummy threads gather on the audience's clothes, in their hair, and upturned faces.
>
> Within moments the air is fuzzy with threads connected to chairs, the floor, bodies, their origin anchored to some unfathomable point in the shadows above. Strings cluster in the audience's open mouths, like loosely wound balls of blackened yarn.
>
> Darkness settles. The stage turns black.
>
> Crashing sounds in the dark. Screams. That trumpeting **VOICE**, now speaking in a manner that suggests it's attaining a grasp of a new language.

VOICE
CHYLDE UF SAPIENS, THY TUNG IS STRAYNJ TO SPEEK. LYFT THY GAYZE CHYLDE UF SAPIENS, SO THAT YURE SOULLS SHALLT BE ILLUMYNAT'D WYTH ALL THAT I HAVV TO GIVV...
(BLACKOUT)
(END OF SCENE)

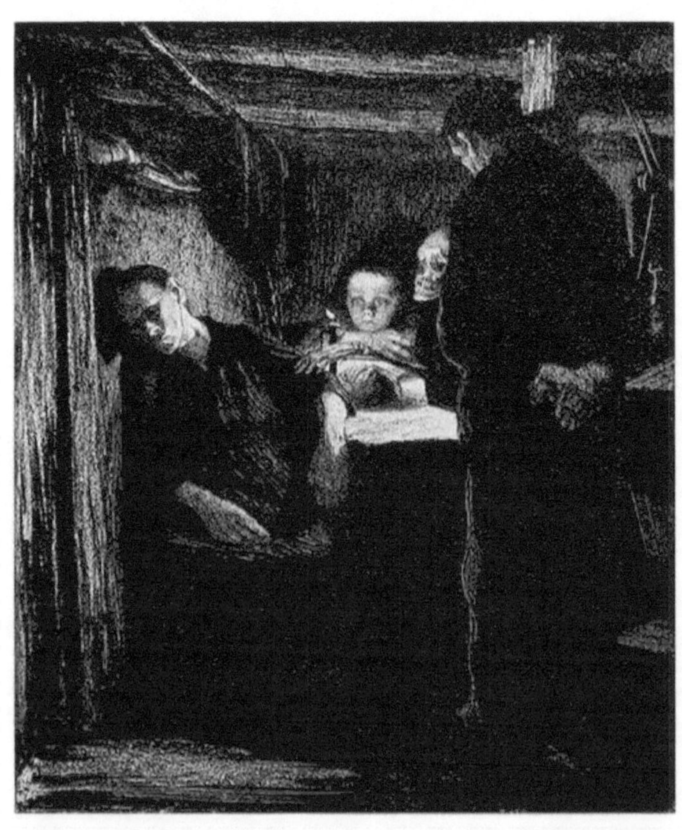

SCENE V

SETTING: The snowy woods.

AT RISE: The lost girl the audience now knows
                   to be CATHERINE stands in the snow.
                   An oval light the size of a full-length
                   mirror hovers before her. She is deep in
                   conversation with the light.

CATHERINE

Aititsirt xe erescif ótic...

(BLACKOUT)
(END OF SCENE)

SCENE VI

SETTING: The study.

AT RISE: When the curtain rises it's clear a period of time has passed. Only HELEN and WILLIAM remain standing, exhausted, breathless. Those weird black threads make it appear as if the actors are smoky ghosts performing behind a thin curtain. A carbon amp light focuses on WILLIAM.

WILLIAM
(to audience)

I am still Prof. William Costock. My mind is my mind. My speech is my own. We have been trapped in this room for two days now. The remaining water runs low, I am deprived of sustenance. Wretched. I am wretched. The cabinet will not cease its infernal activities.

(warily glances stage left)

The cabinet's entity has acquired several human languages in the time we've been imprisoned. It's words... befuddle. I fear its native tongue has twisted some intimate component of what constitutes myself, that indescribable seed that brands every soul with a unique character. Merely hearing its speech has irrevocably changed me.

(the light dims, switches to HELEN)

HELEN
(nervously)

My name is Helen Powell. Of this I am still certain.

(glances back at cabinet)

I pray I do not see its face. I do not wish to gaze upon that creature, but that damned cabinet's curtain will not remain still. It sways and ripples in hideous suggestion. I heard it speak. That thing which is within. I heard it speak again and again!

(imploringly to audience)

I fear I've seen an eyelash. The tip of a fingernail. Whatever I've spied, it is slight, a suggestion of the immensity that lurks within! Oh God! My God! It is only Prof. Costock and I now. Oh, my poor niece Catherine! I wish her safely in my company once more. I cannot imagine where she has disappeared to.

(The stage is lit in its entirety, revealing MILDRED and NELLIE in their chairs unconscious, succumbed to opiate overdoses.)

WILLIAM
(to cabinet)
What are you?

VOICE

I AM BROKEN. I AM A SHUDDERING THING. I AM WITHOUT THOUGHT. I AM WITHOUT.

HELEN

Are you responsible for Catherine's fate?

VOICE

OF WHAT FEARFUL REALM WOULD ONE MOST LIKE ILL FOR ANY CHILD TO GO? WITHIN THE SICKLY BOWELS OF THIS EARTH? AMONGST THE GAPS BETWEEN THE STARS, SPLIT LIKE PETRIFIED SPACE, TUMBLING

THROUGH THE AETHER? FOREVER OUT OF REACH?

HELEN

Oh, my Catherine...

VOICE

TO THIS I SOLEMNLY SAY THERE ARE FAR MORE SHADOW-HAUNTED REALMS TO SLIP LOOSE FROM UNDER THE SHELTER OF SUBLUNARY BONDS, TO WANDER IN SPIRITUAL SQUALOR, IN PERPETUAL HOPELESSNESS.

(The cabinet curtains sway. A harsh luminescence pours out.)

WILLIAM

(in a rattling, croaking voice, addressing the audience)

Words make things so. If these words reach you, then language has already taken root. If alien thoughts and strange comprehensions afflict, then corrupt glossolalia has infected our world. As the prattling cries of a newborn eventually become eloquent speech on evolutionary paths, so to do the meager, torpid stirrings of your dull mind become something far more magnificent than you'd ever dreamt possible.

HELEN

Professor?

(WILLIAM is still standing, though it's clear he's dead. His corpse has delivered a final colloquy. His mouth remains open, eyes rolled into the back of his head, arms limp though his legs still support his body standing upright.

HELEN looks out to the seats.

Each and every row is occupied by a festering cadaver. Their mouths remain agape in rapture. Black threads ascend from their mouths to the darkened ceiling, as if nests spun by a nightmare species of spider.)

VOICE

I AM WHERE DECAPITATED GODS RUMINATE UPON DECAYED THRONES, WHERE ANGELS TREMBLE BEFORE ENDLESS ASCENDING SUNS. I AM PRESENT WHEN THEIR SIMPLE DREAMS MAY NO MORE STAVE OFF THE PURIFYING LIGHT, THAN A SURFEIT OF BLISS MAY KEEP THE VOID AT REST.

(The spirit cabinet's curtain parts. The cabinet tilts back and forth precariously, emitting a light so profound it darkens the sun. Eyeballs melt. Skin crisps and smokes.

The stage collapses into seared ruins. Seats crumble, floors sink into the earth. Roasted corpses tumble like raggedy dollies, dormant limbs flail comically. An ominous absence suffuses the house.

This nothingness is broken by a pinprick of light so potent its terrible luminosity reveals a paramecium shaped creature squirming within its radiant heart.

The cabinet and HELEN's burnt corpse are the only things remaining in the space that was once a stage. HELEN is an ashen pillar, in the same pose as Edith glancing back at Sodom. A corpse bearing witness to the birth of extinction.)

(BLACKOUT)
(END OF SCENE)

SCENE VII

SETTING: The spirit cabinet is all that remains
on a soot black stage.

AT RISE: The stage curtain rises to reveal a void
black as a spider's body.

(The cabinet's curtain moves. A pale hand reaches out from within to part it. CATHERINE peeks out tentatively, making sure there's nobody around. She steps out, glances left, then right. She's wearing a diaphanous glowing gown. It casts an eerie spectral light around her. She bows to the void that was once an audience, then casually walks across the soot black stage to exit on the left.

The tattered, scorched remains of the curtain closes.)

(BLACKOUT)

THE FIGURINE

Nathan finds the first figurine under Sylvia's bed. He tells himself that he's looking for old drawings, abandoned costume jewelry, any memento to retain the presence of his little sister. But deep down he's fully aware he does this to assuage his guilt, though no trinket can ever erase the past.

He traces a finger across the stone surface of the object. It nestles comfortably on his palm, from wrist to fingertips. A shudder runs through his bones—concern, anger, bewilderment; a cocktail of conflicting emotions, as if he'd discovered contraband in Sylvia's room. He wishes he'd found something illicit hidden away. This might prove she is still part of his life. But she's gone, taking all her secrets into the emptiness.

The figurine is of indeterminate cultural origin. There is something reminiscent of old American rural crafts about it. A thin layer of grime coats the stone as if it'd been preserved in used oil. It's smooth, like pale marble.

It has twig arms and legs lashed to the torso with thin twine, and an oval head sculpted so out of proportion to the body it feels as if it will fall off. Subtle depressions mark where eyes should be. It's wearing a rough burlap sack tunic, soft and fragrant with age. The form insinuates something feminine, though Nathan can't say why. He has no idea how his little sister had gotten ahold of such a thing, much less why she'd kept it. Maybe Pastor Rios gave it to her. It's an odd carved objet d'art that doesn't belong here. The sculpture doesn't feel real. Diaphanous, sunlight on his hand, a fragment of dream made tangible.

The house he'd grown up in is unfamiliar after being away at college for the last year. Sylvia's room is hollow after her death. He's ashamed it has taken him so long to gather enough courage to go into his little sister's bedroom.

Home trembles with abject misery, as if the walls are so contaminated with despair they'll split under their own grieving mass. Nathan feels unclean. Fingernails crusted with filth, breath sour, scraggly hair greasy and odorous. He hasn't showered in a week. His mind is clogged, the world distorted with a sepia taint, as if he's trapped inside one of the many amber beer bottles strewn about his dorm room at the University upstate.

He opens an e-mail app on his phone while idly rubbing the figurine with his thumb, both repulsed and soothed by the greasy texture. There are 28 new messages just this morning from the website he'd initially set up as a Crowdfundtastic account to help families pay for their children's funerals. It has gradually become a memorial site over the last few weeks.

Nathan knows most of the messages will be hateful, conspiratorial rants. Accusations of fraud. Lengthy dissertations insisting the slaughter of a classroom full of ten-year-olds was faked by the government. He has seen it all already.

He prays something will cease working inside his head. Anything to take him away from this increasing misery with a swift and sympathetic finality. Thinking back to that Thursday earlier in the month, Nathan can't help but picture eighteen elementary school students sprawled in awkward, undignified poses. He'd seen some survivors on the news describe the shooting in explicit detail—the panicked horror, the stench of astringent vomit smeared across a breezeway where the wounded dragged themselves away in an attempt to hide. Pools of blood beneath faces like wet pillows. Screams. Crying. Slivers of his sister's shattered head strewn across the classroom floor.

Their mom had initially been reluctant to give her 10-year-old daughter her own smartphone, but Nathan convinced her that Sylvia was mature enough to handle the responsibility. Besides, it'd make everyone feel better about her ability to contact her mother or big brother in case of an emergency. He argued it'd be nice to keep tabs on his little sister all those miles away while he was at college, to make sure she was safe and sound. Send him selfies. Videos of what she was up to.

Less than a month ago now. That Thursday, Nathan had ignored his phone after seeing Sylvia's number, surprised she hadn't just texted. Assuming she'd be asking if he was going to make the four-hour commute to visit that weekend, he'd hit the decline button and went back to his studying. Once the phone convulsed to notify him he had voice mail, an ominous sensation warned him that it might be important. He listened to the recording.

All that screaming in the background. All those gunshots. Pained shrieks, desperate and so hopelessly sad. His little sister shouted one sentence. Her final words, the last thing Sylvia said in a breathless rush before she was decapitated at close range by a rifle,

Nathan mom isn't answering her phone please I'm still hiding under my desk.

He isn't ready yet to delete the message. Listening to it has become a daily ritual. The phone is returned to his pocket. He continues to run fingers over the figurine's cold, slick body. He wonders why Sylvia hid it underneath her bed. He wonders if anyone suspects anything. An unctuous film coats his clammy hands.

Nathan finds it difficult to sleep in his old room. He hears what sounds like whispering somewhere inside the ceiling. And when he finally does fall asleep, the nightmare ruins his slumber. He has had the same nightmare several nights now. He's swimming in an ocean of raw sewage, fighting heavy currents of waste that slop into his mouth, nose, and eyes. He sees a shore ahead, and struggles against the porridge thick liquid to reach solid ground dotted with tufts of foliage waving in the wind. Some aspect of his mind knows there are guns on the land, and he needs to reach them so he can kill the man who murdered the children.

But as he swims closer, he realizes the shore is a wasteland of shattered bone bits and partially intact skulls. The foliage are hanks of hair protruding from the carnage. Nathan wakes up stifling his gag reflex, the stench and foul flavors a lingering memory on his tongue. He wakes up knowing he deserves to choke to death on feces and piss.

The anger remains as virulent as ever. It's a fiery angel in his breast, a potent fist of caustic rage that fills his veins with hope. He wishes the gunman hadn't shot himself in the head. The murderer's suicide was a cowardly act that robbed Nathan of any chance for revenge, no matter how unlikely that would have been. He not only took Sylvia, but also any chance of Nathan finding peace in his soul for his own sins.

He sits up in his old bed, underwear uncomfortably damp with sweat. His mom hadn't changed the bedroom much since he left for college. A few boxes in the corner. Dry cleaning in plastic cocoons waiting to be put back in the closet. An ironing board. That's all.

But the room's new occupants are menacing in the night. Boxes crouch and blouses rustle from the heater vent's gusts and the ironing board leans forward as if interrogating him. He doesn't want to stay here. He wants to go back to his dorm, but fears for his mother's health. She needs her only surviving child to get through the coming days. Nathan isn't sure this is the case, but he wants it to be so.

Sylvia should still be sleeping in her own room not 15 feet away. He misses hearing her talk in her sleep at night. A disgruntled parent and his obsession with guns put an end to that ever happening again. Nathan can no longer even consider the murderer's motivation for the attack—the why never mattered. The heft of this tragedy presses down against his skull with such maliciousness he wants to punch himself in the head until something cracks and releases the pressure. The ubiquitous nature of school shootings dulls his brain, turns his sister's death into something unreal yet inevitable. This type of thing only happens in the big city. Not in tiny towns in the middle of nowhere. This type of thing happens all the time now. His anger is a beacon.

He hears the noise again. A hushed voice, as if tiny people are having tiny, secretive conversations. He quietly slides the bed covers aside and steps out into the hallway to investigate. He doesn't want to wake his mom or her boyfriend, Jeremiah.

Nothing moves. The hallway is devoid of anything alive. Something speaks above his head, a hushed breath, not truly words but noise that draws his attention there. He looks up, detects the faint, dark lines of a trapdoor etched in the ceiling. Has it always been there? At nineteen, he has never known any other home than this one. He has no memory of an attic.

Sleep and grief are rewiring his brain in dangerous ways. He's hearing things. He has to take better care of himself if he's going to be a pillar of strength for his mother.

He'll explore the trap door in the morning, after his mom and Jeremiah attend another memorial at the nondenominational church whose name he can never remember. He can't sit through another sermon, having suffered through too many of Pastor Rios' speeches as of late.

The Pastor's pious platitudes and sympathies felt oddly detached, leaving Nathan colder and angrier than ever. They'd started going to the church a couple of years ago, but Nathan has never been very religious, and the church's folk aesthetic and porcelain-smooth Virgin Mary statues, their emaciated bodies draped in sackcloth clothing, was off-putting. The elegantly arranged branches lashed together as limbs didn't seem particularly traditional to him either. It wasn't a comfortable place of worship in his mind.

Tomorrow he'll have the house all to himself.

Nathan doubts he'll go back to school this semester, if ever, but he studies for his sociology test next week anyway. He reads about a primate study conducted in Japan in the '50s. The researchers observed monkeys from one troop washing their wheat and sweet potato supplies—a behavior no other primates had demonstrated before. This washing method was picked up by another troop, and several others were subsequently recorded doing the same, even though they were geographically isolated from each other. When the practice reached roughly a hundred monkey participants, the phenomenon seemed to spread by some unknown means.

But the research was poorly done, and the Hundredth Monkey effect has never been substantiated, though it did find footing in the annals of new age philosophies. Recent sociological studies proposed something similar, though devoid of any supernatural pretense—a minority view may pass some defined demarcation then leap into the majority, that demarcation being the *tipping point*. If 10% of a population adopts a dogmatic belief, the majority of that society will follow suit. Social and political ideologies, pop culture, violent crime, religious trends—all are susceptible to this tipping point.

Nathan rubs his tired eyes and reads the paragraph again. His vision streams the words into liquid sentences, everything bleeding together into, *the majority of that society will follow suit with violent religious trends.*

He needs a break, and since he's the only one home now, decides there's no better time to explore the trapdoor. Returning to the hallway, he unfolds a step stool he retrieved from the pantry and carefully places a bare foot against each step. The hatch has been painted over many times, the thick latex fusing it shut. He picks at the edges of the door and manages to peel several scabby layers away. A strong push and the panel swings upwards on creaky hinges. He raises himself into the dark opening.

It's a nondescript bare area, though Nathan is surprised that even though the ceiling is low, he can stand without bumping his head. A pristine layer of dust carpets the floor, unmarred by tiny rodent feet. A floor to roof window looks out onto the front yard. Nathan has looked up at it countless times over the years, but always assumed it was decorative, not that there was an actual room behind it.

He takes a step forward, excited yet slightly saddened on disturbing the perfect strata of dust, like a child disappointed to see their boot holes punched into the wild expanse of untouched ice on a snow day. He notices a floorboard warped slightly where it meets the skirting board below the window. The floor is so cold it hurts the soles of his feet.

Dropping to one knee, the cold soaks through his jeans. Prickles run down his shin. He tugs at the upturned edge of the board. It shifts slightly with an ominous creak. He pulls it further, exposes a black gap beneath. Something small and pale within glows from the gentle radiance of sunlight through the window. Nathan reaches in and removes a figurine.

It's similar to the one he found in Sylvia's room yesterday. This find is slightly thinner, a bit more intricate in design than the other. The sculptor has given great attention to its large eyes and gently smiling mouth. Its burlap sack garb is delicately stitched, fitting the object snugly like real clothing. The twig legs have been snapped off, though both arms are intact.

Nathan sits down before the window and pulls out his phone. There are more messages on the memorial site, but he doesn't read them. A car glides by on the street in front. He listens to his sister's voice on the saved message.

...I'm still hiding under my desk.

Sorrow is a given, but his hatred is more powerful now. He seethes at all hours, and constantly fantasizes about killing the murderer before he has a chance to off himself. Nathan cries quietly for a good hour before deciding to go back downstairs. He stands, and on a whim, glances above.

There's a trap door in the ceiling.

He can't imagine where it leads to. It would have to open onto the roof. What use could it be? Hands flat, he leans against it, but the panel refuses to budge. The grooves around the square are proof it's not just painted on, but it's so tightly closed it doesn't even shift when he pushes against it with all his strength. He gives up.

Now thirsty and hungry, Nathan lowers himself down through the attic door's opening. He pulls the hatch down, then steps onto the floor. Back in his bedroom, he places the figurine with the previous one in the suitcase he is still not sure he will ever unpack.

At dinner, Nathan sits and surreptitiously watches his mother and Jeremiah eat. Their faces are sallow, eyes irritated with tears, mouths grinding tasteless food between teeth, across gums, down throats. The basic requirements of day-to-day life have become a chore. So much misfortune in such a short period of time. Living has become an ordeal.

His mom had met Jeremiah shortly after Nathan's father died of a brain tumor. The relationship was difficult for Nathan and Sylvia to accept—the fact their mother had moved on so quickly upset the siblings. Jeremiah had initially been kind and supportive, but transformed into a violent, unpredictable drunk as his addictions intensified. And now, with Sylvia's murder, Nathan feels marked, chosen to suffer as everything around him is in free-fall. No longer able to tolerate the quiet, Nathan speaks up.

"I didn't know we had an attic."

"We do?" His mother responds dreamily, as if not fully comprehending what her son has said.

"There's a trap door in the hallway ceiling."

"Hm," Jeremiah grunts.

"Nobody's been up there?"

"Not me," his mom says. Jeremiah shakes his head.

"Really? Mom, you've lived here, what, twenty-five years and never noticed it?"

"Never noticed," she says as if her thought processes are just catching up with the conversation.

"Maybe I'll check it out later." Nathan says to see if they'll react.

Nervously, as if attempting to deflect Nathan's interest, Jeremiah interjects, "Oh, *that*. I think it's the entrance to a crawlspace. To get access to all the wiring and insulation and all that kind of thing. Just a small area. Don't go up there. You might get hurt."

Nathan doesn't contradict him. Doesn't confess to opening the door already and entering the attic. The other mysterious trapdoor is his secret. He doubts he'll ever mention it to anyone else.

"I heard something up there." Nathan persists.

"Oh no!" His mother says, mortified. "We've never had a rat problem."

Jeremiah covers his food-filled mouth with a paper towel and says, "Remember last Spring when that family of raccoons moved into the garden shed? Maybe we have raccoons in the ceiling now."

Jeremiah laughs, but it's an odd sound, touched with sorrow and hysteria.

Nathan has never heard him make such a noise before. It's deeply unsettling coming from such a large man. He can't say Jeremiah and his mom are lying, but he's certain they're pretending. The grief and devastation of Sylvia's death changed everything, but he finds these performances unsettling.

"Found this." Nathan triumphantly sets the figurine he discovered in the attic onto the tabletop as if he's checkmating them both.

"Where did you get that dirty old thing?" Jeremiah asks, disgust on his face. Did he just lower his voice to be more threatening, or perhaps even impersonate someone else?

"Ever see it before?" Nathan pushes it forward an inch across the table.

"I'm still finding old doll heads and LEGOs in the yard where you and Sylvia buried them when you were just babies." His mom replies, her sentence trailing off like a lost child.

"I remember those. Sylvia and I used to pretend we were archaeologists finding ancient artifacts."

"Such an active imagination. Sylvia was acting so differently the last year or two. She just changed overnight."

Jeremiah nods reflectively. "Poor thing with her night terrors."

Nathan closes a hand over the figurine. A profound sense of shame heats his forehead. He was a child then too. He hurriedly finishes his dinner then excuses himself to the bedroom.

Later that evening, when Nathan's mom and Jeremiah are asleep in their bedroom, he quietly climbs into the attic and tries to open the peculiar second trapdoor. Rapping his knuckles against it produces a hollow sound as if there's a space above. But this can't be. There can only be the roof beyond it. After half an hour of unsuccessfully pushing and stabbing a screwdriver into the grooves to see if he can loosen anything, he resigns in frustration. He decides to go outside and see if he can determine exactly where the door might be located on the roof.

From Nathan's vantage point on the front lawn and his flashlight beam aimed at the roof, he can't see how there could possibly be another room. The roof slopes at an abrupt angle where the door should be, and there's simply no way any additional area could have been built on top of the house. Maybe it's a trick of the eye in the way it's constructed, like the Ames optical illusion where it seems as if objects on one side of the room are a vastly different size than the other side. He considers borrowing a tall ladder from the neighbors in the morning so he can actually climb up there for a closer look.

Circling his home several times, scrutinizing every curve and slant in a vain attempt to detect anything unusual, Nathan finally accepts that he's wasting his time and goes to bed.

In the morning, Nathan is surprised to find his mother, Jeremiah, and Pastor Rios seated at the table in the kitchen. They're drinking coffee over boxes of pastries.

"Good morning, kiddo. Breakfast is on me." Pastor Rios says with a grin as he swivels a box of apple fritters towards him.

"What's going on?" Nathan's voice is raspy with fatigue. His eyes are gummy.

"Just having a chat." Jeremiah sips his coffee, peers over the rim of his mug.

"I haven't seen you at any services lately." Pastor Rios says with a stern concern Nathan finds forced.

"No reason to go."

"You don't need a reason." Pastor Rios says, helping himself to another donut.

"Sure I do." Nathan mumbles.

Pastor Rios holds a hand up as if requesting permission to speak. Nobody responds, so he continues. "You don't need a reason, Nathan, because rituals have always been important to folks. And in times of need, rituals are needed more than ever. I'd say this qualifies as a time in need."

Nathan pours himself a cup of black coffee. The smell is earthy and repugnant. "If God cared, Sylvia would still be alive. That's why I have no reason to go."

His mom stares into her coffee cup, eyes wide and wet. Jeremiah taps a cracked thumbnail against his ceramic mug. Nathan notices his nail bed is deeply bruised, wet and dark.

"That is a concern. It really is, Nathan. But trying to decipher the problem of why God allows evil is, well, too much for our little brains to solve." The pastor protrudes the tip of his tongue from between his lips. Nathan thinks it looks like a pink fish poking out of its habitat.

Pastor Rios rolls his eyes up into his head. Makes a mewling sound.

Nathan finds the whole thing disconcerting. The pastor has always tried to be the young, hip religious figure in the small town, but this outburst worries Nathan. His mother and Jeremiah don't appear to be as concerned about the pastor's strange demonstration as he is.

"So, you don't have a real answer then." Nathan says bluntly. He points his middle and index fingers at the Pastor, though he's not sure why he makes the gesture. "You're a fucking joke."

"Goddamnit!" Jeremiah exclaims. Nathan's mother focuses on her coffee mug and refuses to make eye contact with anyone in the room.

"No, no. That's alright. I get it." Pastor Rios laughs good-naturedly.

"Let me put it this way, Nathan. Think of it like this: a parasite invades a host. The host can't consider itself a victim here; there's a mutual benefit even if the host cannot understand why."

Nathan nods to acknowledge he's listening, if only just.

"We are all subject to the majesty of cruelty, the unknowable aspect of the origins of our suffering."

"I can't believe that."

Pastor Rios folds his hands together, rests his elbows on the table. "School shootings are rare, statistically speaking."

Nathan leans forward, inches from the Pastor's face. "So, you're saying Sylvia won a fucking lottery?"

"Nathan. Last warning." Jeremiah drums his thick fingers against the tabletop to emphasize his seriousness.

"Goodness no, Nathan. Of course not. I just wanted to make it clear that these sorts of tragedies shouldn't determine how you continue with your life. Rituals can change things. For the worse. For the better. But no matter what, they're important."

Nathan quickly turns towards his mother, a glob of coffee jumping from his cup to the linoleum floor. He is so angry he can't think of anything to say.

His mother speaks meekly, "I just don't want you to be afraid to return back to college. That's all."

Nathan's temper makes his voice sound childish and high pitched in his own head. "You want me to leave? I can. Now. No problem."

"You know we don't want that, Nathan." His mom says, though her expression contradicts her words.

Pastor Rios stares at Nathan accusingly. He speaks softly, carefully. "There are some things we don't want to know, but can't ignore."

Nathan slams his coffee cup down against the counter and leaves the kitchen.

That night, Nathan doesn't dream about swimming through sewage to reach a dead coastline. Instead, he dreams about Sylvia.

He embraces his sister, now perfect in every way. Tangible meat and bone, soft skin scuffed by playing outside, rough and tumble at the park with her friends. Shaggy hair in need of a trim. She smells of green grass and sweat that still has the scent of a child before the onset of puberty.

Sylvia rests her head on Nathan's shoulder, at that perfectly balanced location, warm and strong and kind. Her breath tickles the hairs on the back of his neck. She stays in that position for several minutes, in the company of her big brother.

Nathan luxuriates in the contact, real or imagined. The solidity of his sister he'd thought long gone is a reprieve from the nightmare of being awake. She is here, brimming with warm blood just below her skin and a kind smile with perfect teeth. He'd almost forgotten how tall she was at ten years old.

This was never real. You ruined it all.

He ignores the thought. Sylvia's body trembles violently as she struggles to speak. Her embrace is painfully urgent. She shudders with such severity her teeth chatter. Nathan is afraid she might crack a tooth.

She turns her mouth to Nathan's ear and whispers with great effort, but he wakes up before he hears what his little sister has to say.

Nathan stays still in bed. Holds his breath. Someone speaking up in the attic woke him. He is sure of this.

Suddenly, he hears several things chattering in the attic.

Filled with adrenalin, he runs out of his room, down the hall, and clambers up the stepstool he'd left there. Inside the attic, the air is chillier than it should be. The room is empty.

He realizes he's holding the figurine he'd found up here the day before, though he has no memory of grabbing it. He turns his attention to the mysterious second trapdoor.

But it has already been opened. An exhalation of cold flows through the gap.

Who's there? Nathan whispers with enough force to shove his words into the darkness above. The trapdoor doesn't access the roof; he can't see any stars beyond the black square. But that cannot be.

He breathes deeply. Gathers his courage. Is whoever opened it still up there? Since the ceiling is so low here, he has no trouble reaching the aperture and pulling himself inside. He expects to be snatched away by something dark and loathsome, float heavenward, to a place both terrible and miraculous. Somewhere wonderful and tragic. He hefts his body through the space.

But nothing swoops down to destroy him. The second attic's layout is not much different than the one beneath him. The ceiling is lower, but he can still stand if slightly hunched over. A floor to ceiling window that shouldn't be there allows moonlight to illuminate dozens of figurines arranged around the room.

Pale, enigmatic stone effigies of various heights stand as if awaiting a command to wake them. Some are knee high, others as long as his thumb, most are in-between. They all have simple faces with simple eyes and simple mouths. A few have had their missing arms replaced with twigs. Their burlap cloth gowns are slightly faded and dusted in layers of time.

The impossible attic is silent as death. Nathan looks out the window that violates any rational notion of geometry he retained from his classes. A trickle of stars glimmer like droplets of dew the more distant they are. Nathan looks out onto the lawn below him.

The townsfolk are all gathered outside.

Nathan sees the neighbors whose names he'd never bothered to learn. The manager of the only convenience store in town. The librarian, elementary school teachers, and surviving students. Pastor Rios is down there too, serene and contemplative. Nathan's mother stands eerily still next to Jeremiah. They both stare up at the attic window with blank expressions. Nathan knows everyone is aware of what he did. The moon swells as big and bright as a wide-eyed child before their death.

A small figure, probably a girl, steps in front of the crowd. The child is dressed in an oversized burlap feed sack. Her thin arms jut out like wooden stems. Maybe it's not a child. They don't have legs.

Nathan tastes shit in his mouth. He doubles over, retches dryly. Specks of gummy saliva spatter curious patterns in the dust.

The amputee somersaults across the grass. Hands and stumps touch the ground with a seasoned acrobat's skill. The girl waves her arms in the air in celebration of something Nathan feels must be ancient and pious. Before the silent, grim crowd, the child prances across the lawn maniacally, spinning and tumbling in a distraction of activity. The child's burlap sack is hooded so it obscures her head. Nathan isn't sure why, but he's certain her face is as smooth and pale as the figurines in the attic.

The rest of the town remain motionless and mute on the lawn. Nathan wipes a wrist across his mouth, then pulls out his phone to perform his daily ritual of playing Sylvia's message. He listens to it one last time.

Then deletes it.

They were both so young. He can no longer lie to himself and pretend he didn't know it was immoral then. He helped Sylvia take off all of her clothes and kissed her on the mouth and everything that followed was wrong. He knows he is a monster.

He reaches out and touches the window that should not be. Sylvia used to root for him at his soccer games, voice raised in encouragement. She used to make jokes with him at dinner and they watched the same TV shows and laughed at the same parts despite their age difference.

"I can change." Nathan says to no one. The glass is ice cold. Other than the legless acrobat, the crowd outside are still as statues.

The figurine in his hand is weighty. A burden. An anchor holding him back. Impossibly heavy. He slams it against his temple several times, each impact reverberating inside his skull. But neither the figurine nor his skull breaks. He feels blood pool in his sinuses, drip down, tastes it in the back of his throat.

He carefully sets the object on the floor with the others. He is no longer furious. There is an immortal sorrow within that will carry him on for the scant moments he has left in this life.

Eighteen victims. Girls and boys with their bikes and pets and favorite foods. Eighteen innocent souls with backpacks and game nights and cherished books.

And Sylvia victimized twice.

Nathan thought the gunman erased any chance of his terrible secret being revealed. He knows he's sick and a coward and deserves what's coming to him, and far worse.

The townsfolk raise their faces to the attic window. Only Nathan's mother drops to her knees. She topples forward, her face buried in the grass. Her shoulders shake with grief. Nathan doesn't need to count the crowd to know there are now exactly a hundred people staring up at him.

He feels a tiny, cold hand slip into his. Startled, he immediately looks down. A figurine stares up at him with a joyous expression. It speaks in his little sister's voice,

...I'm still hiding under my desk.

AFFIRMATION OF THE SPIRIT: CONSCIOUSNESS, TRANSFORMATION, AND THE FOURTH WORLD IN FILM

(originally published in *Cinemassacre*, v. 1, issue 3)

A projector spits dirty light against a torn screen in a run-down Los Angeles theater that screens art films by day, pornos at night. A jumbled Vorkapich sequence depicts various species being slaughtered by a dozen figures clad in rain gear. The scene is followed by a medium long shot of a man crucified on the slaughterhouse's grime bespattered door. A forward zoom reveals that the body is nailed to the sheet metal with long iron spikes impaling his wrists, ankles and throat. Hundreds of smaller, thinner silver nails protrude from his naked body in such abundance he could be mistaken for a shining metal sculpture if not for the subtle swaying of his head. The soundtrack consists solely of animals shrieking.

Given the amateurish performances, poorly recorded dialogue, and inexpertly framed shots (likely using a Bolex H16), the audience may be excused for assuming they were watching a snuff film, or more charitably, a clumsily produced amateur movie. But this is the opening scene to *The Powdery Man* (less commonly titled *Film Maudit*), a little-known experimental art film from 1974, give or take, as the production history is notoriously muddled and mysteriously unverified.

The Powdery Man had a brief limited release before passing into obscurity. There were rumors that any existing complete prints were destroyed after the initial showing, but a dozen or so heavily edited bootlegs continued to circulate in collector's circles throughout the 80s and 90s, so rare the extant copies went for a hefty price if they could be found at all. I myself was only able to view a battered VHS tape, the images obscured by tracking lines and faded from countless recopying.

In short, a veritable cult has conglomerated around an obscure, nasty little flick. But a rare few who experienced a screening in that original Los Angeles theater during the summer of '74 insist there was nothing quite like it. And the one person I managed to speak with who retained any memory of their viewing emphatically insists there will never again be anything even remotely like it.

But my interest goes beyond a single film; considering such cinematic trash raises the question of how and why the Big Screen manages to allow the emotional, intellectual, and spiritual vitality of cinema to be that much more palpable, even with a less than Oscar-worthy product. What is the allure of filmed depravity, of viewing violence and dread and discomfort? Is there some innate need to be *challenged?* Are we actively seeking to threaten and subvert our very moral and spiritual foundations through art? Excluding politics, of every human creation, religion and art rise to the surface as the most contentious. Consequently, why does film seem to be the most *magical* of the arts? Are film and religion more alike than we realize?

Film and religion celebrate as well as condemn the basest of human desires. Both exalt the darkest impulses and grandest accomplishments. There's little controversy in my asserting that religion has brought the world great things as well as atrocities (see Bataille's assertion that the sacred has intimate connections to eroticism, violence, and religion[1]). Film tends to focus on these extremes of the human condition as well. I'm certainly not walking on untrodden ground when I assert similarities between the Church and Cinema.

With faith and art, atavistic acts may become transcendent in their savagery, looping back to approach the illimitable, the dichotomy of the infinite and infinitesimal. The faithful and cineastes have mutual interests, overlapping philosophical and theological inquiries. Both boldly examine the sewers of the human soul in an attempt to find pious or artistic enlightenment. In this I think

---

[1] Georges Bataille, *Theory of Religion*, (New York: Zone Books, 1989).

there's something new to present.

II

As early as 1910, Minister Herbert Atchinson Jump extolled the link between film and religion within his self-published pamphlet, *The Religious Possibilities of the Motion Picture:*

> The pulpit orators and evangelists use 'moving pictures' in one sense of the term, pictures that move the heart by their thrilling quality; but the picture that literally is moving, that portrays dramatic sequence and life-like action, possesses tenfold more vividness and becomes therefore a more convincing medium of education.[2]

Religion and film have been inexorably linked since the first Kinetoscope. There's a dark glamor at the heart of both, a quality that makes them eminently transformative. To watch a movie is to stare into the eye of the cosmos and contemplate infinity; to participate in rituals and listen to a priest ruminate on faith is to go through something similar and to be a different person than you were before entering the scared space, whether mosque, church, synagogue—all theaters of human creativity. Film and faith are means of inspiring wonder on viewing the illimitable as an impetus for *astonishment*. We are irrevocably different beings after these liminal journeys.

III

Filmmaker Stan Barkhage famously wrote, "The stars are the optical nerve-endings of the eye which the universe is."[3]

---

[2] Herbert A. Jump, *The Religious Possibilities of the Motion Picture* (n.p.: 1910), 7-8.

[3] Stan Brakhage, "The Stars are Beautiful," in *Essential Brakhage*, ed. Bruce McPherson (New York: McPherson, 2001), 134.

I cannot disagree. Filmgoers participate in an activity that began when the first cognitive primate stared into the night sky and marveled at what it could never fully comprehend—that is, to wonder about its position in the world and thus be consumed within the whirlpool of existentialist angst or else be motivated to ascend to celebratory optimism. Film is philosophy cloaked in the mantle of literature, shorn of the shackles of live theater.

There is an intimate connection between humanity's gaze and the night sky. How many billions of eyes have stared into the heavens? Natural selection has sculpted your vision to adapt to star gazing, and since the movie screen is far too recent an invention to have been shaped by evolutionary pressures, your biology hasn't fully grasped the images splashed in light on the screen. As filmgoers, you are still an ape captivated by stars. Your ancient nature hasn't evolved adequately to comprehend the spectacle of the heavens, so you react with *awe* at films.

This all suggests the medieval pilgrim in a gloomy church interior, dumbstruck at the beauty and ephemeral wonder of stained-glass windows, their holy narrative encompassing a vast church wall, vividly illuminated by streaming sunlight. The blazing colors of divinity are a clear analogy to the dark theater's luminous Big Screen and its spectacle. All it lacks is motion. Upturned faces in rapt attention receiving a narrative, soul-stirring music moving the audience to emotional extremes, both settings ebbing with spiritual grandeur, the actors beautiful beings composed of light projected through celluloid, the deification of thespians, "those modern vestiges of the Greek divinities."[4]

All-consuming experiences, religious observances and the cinema envelop you in promises of other worlds beyond the mechanistic, the visceral, this rubbish heap of a world. Both take "mortal aging flesh and convert it into ageless columns of dancing light."[5] They offer unreal creatures of fantasy, seraphim on the Silver Screen that lure you into becoming something different

---

[4] Tyler Parker, *Magic and Myth of the Movies* (London: Secker & Warburg, 1971, 31.

[5] Colin McGinn, *The Power of Movies: How Screen and Mind Interact* (New York: Pantheon 2005), 82.

than what you were before entering that sacred space.

So, we've arrived at the point where you *transform* into spectators within cathedrals of light and imagination, observers of terror and bliss in the theater. But analogies between churchgoers and filmgoers can only go so far before one may be accused of stretching a metaphor too far or straining to make connections where they are tenuous at best. I will make one more leap that will likely offend, but which I hope to substantiate.

IV

At their root level, religions exist to justify the existence of a soul, or as the secularist contends, a mind. The innate need to distance oneself from the natural world by concocting beliefs that inculcate you with an intangible, immortal aspect is the strongest link religion shares with film. You strenuously resist your bodies, rebel against the prospect that your decomposing forms are all there is, blanch at the prospect that there's nothing cocooned inside your filthy shell to transcend disgusting flesh. Religions and art and dreams are all plaintive cries to *transform* once your body sickens and dilapidates into compost.

Psychologist Bertram D. Lewin postulated in *The Yearbook of Psychoanalysis* journal that:

> In a previous communication, a special structure, the dream screen was distinguished from the rest of the dream and defined as the blank background upon which the dream picture appears to be projected. The term was suggested by the action pictures because, like the analogue in the cinema, the dream screen is either not noted by the dreaming spectator, or it is ignored due to the interest in the pictures and actions that appear on it.[6]

---

[6] Bertram D. Lewin, "Interferences from the Dream Screen," *The Yearbook of Psychoanalysis* 6 (New York: International University Press, 1950), 104.

Brains have evolved to accommodate this inner screen. The very systems in your heads come equipped with a "viewing theater," if you will.

Film theorist Bruce F. Kawin built upon Lewin's ideas with a concept he termed "Mindscreen"—that is, excluding the occasional gimmick, films are overwhelmingly thought of as third-person omniscient narratives. But film is more like the dreaming mind in that it becomes a first-person thinking being, a self-conscious independent thing, estranged from the contributions of any audience's interpretation. As Kawin succinctly puts it, "Film is a dream—but whose?"[7]

This obviously raises questions about the nature of the human mind itself. The mind-body problem (or mind-film problem? has generated a vast literature beyond the scope of this essay. Suffice it to say for our purposes that neurophilosophers remain skeptical that a physical brain, and the audience by extension, *even possess the potential for consciousness.*

Again, Kawin:

> [A]lthough a camera does not have consciousness, and cannot therefore literally be an I, it is possible to encode the image in such a way that it gives the impression of being perceived or generated by a consciousness. Although this mind remains off- screen, its existence is implicit and can be integrated into the fiction, with the result that the field is properly termed first person.[8]

Human consciousness and the cinematic consciousness work as poetic descriptions *and* philosophical avenues in which to explore this religious and artistic need to inject a ghost or mind between the molecules of your blood and bone. Like the physical medium of film, human activities, creative expressions, and musings generated from meat-dependent brains also give the "impression

---

[7] Bruce F. Kawin, *Mindscreen: Bergman and First-Person Film* (Dalkey Archive Press, 1978), 3.

[8] Ibid., 11.

of being perceived or generated by a consciousness." But minds only work as metaphors for mechanistic processes, and this begs an explanation as to the idea of just what is meant by a film's "consciousness."

The screenwriter, actors, and director may be the focal point for filmmakers, but a film in its entirety exists as a comprehensive whole, a self-sufficient "mind" that unveils its imagery and story onto a screen. Consciousness, or a convincing facsimile of such, suffuses the very screen.

Granted, a film exists as the holistic work of many, but can safely be boiled down to the screenplay, director and performers. But the resulting product is an entity *unto itself*, a distinguished, thinking thing unconfined by the strictures of its creator(s). Film is a "mind" of photons projected against a screen accompanied by noise, all caught in an endless loop with a beginning, middle, and an end.

Descartes famously posited the existence of a world composed of physical bodies and a world of incorporeal mental states. But Karl Popper argued for the existence of a third world, one which is the *sum of human minds*.[9] I propose that film is the fourth world.

Popper also described determinism as a logical progression from this, as a motion-picture where the images currently being projected are the present, scenes already viewed were in the past, and those yet to be seen remain in the future.

> In the film, the future co-exists with the past; and the future is fixed, in exactly the same sense as the past. Though the spectator may not know the future, every future event, without exception, might in principle be known with certainty, exactly like the past, since it exists in the same sense in which the past exists. In fact, the future will be known to the producer of the film— to the Creator of the World.[10]

[9] Karl Popper, *Objective Knowledge: An Evolutionary Approach* (Oxford: Clarendon Press, 1979), 106.

[10] Karl Popper, *The Open Universe: An Argument for Indeterminism* (London: Rowman & Littlefield, 1982), 5.

If the "producer of the film" and the very "Creator of the World" know what has been, what is, and what will be, why pretend you've *chosen* anything in your life? You've no choice, and nothing is under your control. Why bother pursuing your dreams? Have children? Fall in love? Out of love? You're incapable of making decisions, you've crossed this trail previously, and you're condemned to pass over the same ground again and again. You're at the mercy of the fourth world, and everything you have been or will be has already been filmed.

V

Since we've established a fourth world "film-mind," I ask whether or not the theatergoer is even *real?* Is there an actual, substantive *mind* (whether metaphorical or literal) processing the narrative in a film? Or is the viewer an unthinking mannequin reacting to the brightly lit spectacle on the screen in the same manner a plant reacts to photons?

What of this?

As I type, I am pestered by the notion I may not be a *me* typing these words. Am I a person with a brain and nervous system in charge of my diction? If so, what in turn is nestled within that brain, dictating its secret diction to my brain, and another mind inside that mind, in infinite regress ultimately concluding in a celestial mind? There must either be a beginning, an uncaused first mind, or no mind at all. Dregs and trash dressed up as angelic beings are still garbage, and we all know what Rilke thought of Angels.

If humanity truly are automatons, you are relieved of anything other than a reaction based on ages of evolutionary coding stamped into your DNA. Your species is subject to physical laws dictating your behavior as precisely as plants are to phototropic influences. *Choice* is an illusion, as "inescapable" and "repulsive" as semiotician Kristeva postulates:

> What is the demoniacal—an inescapable, repulsive, and
> yet nurtured abomination? The fantasy of an archaic force, on
> the near side of separation, unconscious, tempting us to the
> point of losing our differences, our speech, our life; to the point

of aphasia, decay, opprobrium, and death?[11]

There is no evidence of reality outside the domino effect of chunks bashing into bits and the resulting physical processes being revered as something other than the mechanistic drudgery they are. Even film, despite its potentially being a thinking thing, may also be caught in the web of the mind-body problem. Free-will is nonsense, you

> are pure material machines, [a]collateral product of [your] nervous processes, unable to react upon them any more than a shadow reacts on the steps of the traveler whom it accompanies. Inert, uninfluential, a simple passenger in the voyage of life, it is allowed to remain on board, but not to touch the helm or handle the rigging.[12]

Did you notice that your hand is the texture and color of putty?

Your every decision has been plotted by Popper's film producer. or, less poetically, unthinking materialistic properties. Regardless, you've no say in any matter, as physical matter says it all for you(!). Everything inevitably collapses into the scripture of entropy, your every move a bio-molecular clockwork spasm, a stopwatch set millennia ago by mindless selective forces. A windup doll with bad breath, aching back, and a hankering for watching bad movies in dimly lit rooms. There simply is no *you* to process the sights and sounds from the screen, sluiced through your retinas and dumped into an empty (plastic) brain.

Now it's perfectly natural for you to question whether you're transforming into a special effects stunt dummy. Evolving into a corpse prop to be dropped from great heights just might be the best application for a useless mannequin like you. This is the logical conclusion of an inert thing acting as if it's conscious.

[11] Julia Kristeva, *Powers of Horror: An Essay on Abjection* (New York: Columbia University Press, 1982), 107.

[12] William James, "Are We Automata?" *Mind*, vol.4 (13: January, 1879), 1.

Speaking of mannequins and special effects stunt dummies, and given your lack of a mind and the potential for a consciousness to *exist on film* only (our fourth world), even those "two-dimensional puppets on the screen" may be deprived of sentience:

> Puppets provide an interesting case: no one would mistake them for a real person, yet they aim for a certain kind of naturalism. They resemble movie images in respect to ventriloquism: a voice is thrown into the puppet's mouth in much the same way speech appears to emanate from the mouths of those two-dimensional puppets on the screen. The voice is pretty much a normal human voice in both cases, but the apparent source of the voice is a transformed human—large and flat in the one case, small and knobby in the other. The Punch and Judy show is not a million miles away from the film: patently unreal figures, of altered dimensions, spouting their lines—or seeming to. Both convey a startling animation, in the sense that we quickly forget that they are only effigies of real people; they "take on a life of their own." And I think that both demonstrate a kinship with the uncanny—they seem to move of their own volition, despite their lack of inner agency. It is uncanny if inanimate objects began to move as if they had a will of their own, and both puppets and movie images do this—it is as if they were alive, while clearly not being so.[13]

The similarities to you are striking, are they not? Pay attention to this scene. This is where the Powdery Man hovers in the background while a poorly constructed dummy is torn limb from limb by unseen assailants. The effect is cheap, a shoddy effort to produce gouts of gore that are far too red and thin to be real blood. But there is still a sense

---

[13] McGinn, *The Power of Movies*, 92-93.

of the *uncanny* in viewing such violence against emotionless, insensate plastic. The viewers cannot help but place themselves in the dummy's position, stuffed with rubber viscera and fake fluids and unblinking eyes. Does it really matter what's inside since it's all tactile, free of any wispy souls? You are just an effigy of a real person.

Let us return to the film.

Jaws warble and mouths clack in laughter at the antics of the Powdery Man on the big screen. You thrill at the sight of mannequins falling from a gray sky, piling up like cordwood, their dead limbs and artificial smiles still intact. The dialogue is gibberish, but why assume empty-headed things are capable of making sense?

When all is said and done, when **THE END** eventually rolls across the universe's screen your mannequin hands will clap, your glass eyes well up with emotion, and unseen strings will tug you upright. You'll move down the aisle to the lobby where you'll chat with your fellow cineastes about the screening of *The Powdery Man* you just sat through, maybe even discuss other trivial ideas. Incessant dummy talk. This is a certainty.

It *will* happen.

But for now, good ol' corpse prop takes in a show. Does it enjoy the movie? Is the narrative entertaining? Do photons bounce against your plastic retinas and send signals to your plastic brain? Is it even possible for you to enjoy a film?

To enjoy anything? To *be* anything?

Your script was written ages ago. The storyboards place you precisely where you're destined to be. You cannot deviate from the screenplay. The cameras roll. Mouth the banal dialogue. It doesn't matter if you understand what you're saying or not; you're a vessel for a story you had no hand in writing.

Existence is in the can. The world is a theater of empty-headed viewers, wanting nothing more than to be like that mind up there on the screen. You yearn to break free of the putrid matter that constitutes your parody of a body. But that's as ridiculous as a shadow dreaming it can exist independent of what casts it.

Stand on the X, dummy.

You are composed of still shots spooling through a void at 24 frames per second. Flickering matter frozen in place and artificially manipulated to appear to be cognizant things capable of making decisions. But you are not capable. You don't have the equipment.

There is no Auteur.

But oh, the screen! There is something like a soul revealed when the curtain parts and the blank surface is illuminated. There's nothing as transcendental as film! As *transformative* as a good movie!

The fourth world is glorious indeed!

The movie is starting. Of course, it began and ended long ago. Here begins another showing.

It's time to watch and be *transformed*.

VI

The spirit is so closely linked to the body as a thing that the body never ceases to be haunted, is never a thing except virtually, so much so that if death reduces it to the condition of a thing, the spirit is more present than ever: the body that has betrayed it reveals it more clearly than when it served it. In a sense, the corpse is the most perfect affirmation of the spirit.[14]

[14] Bataille, *Theory of Religion*, 305.

BIBLIOGRAPHY

Bataille, Georges. *Theory of Religion*. Translated by Robert Hurley. New York: Zone Books, 1989.

Brakhage, Stan. "The Stars are Beautiful." In *Essential Brakhage*, edited by Bruce McPherson, New York: McPherson, 2001:37.

James, William. "Are We Automata?" *Mind*, 4, no. 13 (January 1879): 1-22.

Jump, Herbert A. *The Religious Possibilities of the Motion Picture*. N.p.: 1910.

Kawin, Bruce F. *Mindscreen: Bergman and First-Person Film*. N.p.: Dalkey Archive Press, 2006.

Kristeva, Julia. *Powers of Horror: An Essay on Abjection*. New York: Columbia University Press, 1982.

Lewin, Bertram D. "Interferences from the Dream Screen." *The Yearbook of Psychoanalysis 6*. New York: International University Press, 1950.

McGinn, Colin. *The Power of Movies: How Screen and Mind Interact*. New York: Pantheon, 2005.

Parker, Tyler. *Magic and Myth of the Movies*. London: Secker & Warburg, 1971.

Popper, Karl. *Objective Knowledge: An Evolutionary Approach*. Oxford: Clarendon Press, 1979.

—. *The Open Universe: An Argument for Indeterminism*. London: Rowman & Littlefield, 1982.

Three years, two months, four days ago:

G-L-E-N S-T...

Glen Steinman paused, hand shaking above the page, unsure how to proceed.

"Go ahead, dad. Just sign it, and we're done with this." Alex said.

Glen gripped the pen tighter, the skin beneath his fingernails paling with the effort.

"Dad? Sign it." Candace insisted.

Glen placed his right hand over the failed signature, hiding the letter to his primary care physician concerning his end-of-life decisions. He spread his fingers, glimpsed a portion of the page,

Please accept this statement as a fully considered decision, as a testament to my personal choices regarding the circumstances of my death. If you feel you would not be able to honor such requests, please let me know now, while I am able to make choices about my care before my mental facilities are no longer sufficient.

Glen smiled at his daughter, Candace. Setting the pen aside, he lowered his gaze to rest on his son Alex's tie. The knot was as perfect as a fancy confectionary.

...while I am able to make choices about my care before my mental facilities are no longer sufficient.

Embarrassed, Glen lowered his voice to a whisper.

"I don't remember how to spell my name."

❋

Two months, six days ago:

Glen Steinman consulted his journal. The radio talk show sputtered nonsense.

...outside town, 6-year-old Jerry Grace holds the decapitated head of his friend while his father looks on proudly.

But that couldn't be correct. Glen tried to record everything in his journal, wrote down questions which he answered first thing every morning. He filled in crossword puzzles, practiced spelling tests to hone his mental acuity. Dementia couldn't win as long as he kept writing everything down. He'd beat this.

But the nonsense world kept intruding, filling his head with silly notions, warping his favorite shows and magazines into grotesque parodies of what was happening in the real world. He used to be an avid reader, but the disease meant he could no longer remember what he'd been reading. Yellowed mass markets littered the living room.

Standing in his kitchen, cigarette in hand, he scrutinized the piles of dishes crowding the sink. They'd spilled over onto the grimy countertops. Why hadn't his children visited? He knew they hadn't been by in a long time as there was no mention of them in the journal for several pages.

He wasn't sure he ever had children.

A diseased memory, a mental snapshot of his children's faces was smeared like a drop of water on ink in his notebook. But he couldn't forget about them. Not yet. He had to find his way to the center of the maze first.

A reporter on the radio said,

...baby carriage filled with frog eggs.

But he'd heard them incorrectly. Words were no longer processed in his brain correctly. Language had become a creaking, tilting Tower of Babel, threatening to scatter all coherence to the wind. Dementia had perverted his ability to understand. He turned the radio's volume down.

A stream of smoke spilled out of the corner of his mouth. Shapes within the smoke coalesced, something that may have been a memory, whether real or not. Cigarette burnt low. Thick, calloused knuckle skin prevented Glen from registering the pain immediately. He stubbed the butt out on a dish crusted with dried egg yolk.

Opening his journal to the latest entry, he read:

Mild weather. Someone is speaking to me through the radio, but I don't speak back. SPARAGMOS drives by my house. They want to take everything away.

He lifted a window curtain soft with mold. The fabric draped over his hand like moist dough. A portion of glass that had yet to be obscured by a film of nicotine grease allowed him to see something moving around in the night.

SPARAGMOS was driving their truck down the street.

He was certain they were going to tear down his home. Hoarder or not, this was *his* house. These were *his* possessions. Nobody had the right to impose *their* will on him. How long had it been since he and his neighbors began accumulating items to construct the maze's walls? All that hard work. He'd be damned if anyone was going to take that away.

A magnetic sign attached to the driver's door spelled SPARAGMOS in neon-orange letters. The two employees inside the cab wore orange jumpsuits. Maybe they worked for the city in some capacity. If so, they'd yet to remove the maze's stacks of old vehicle parts, inactive appliances, and broken furniture discarded on the roads. The workers seemed concerned about the alignment of the trash.

They stepped out of their vehicle, clipboards in hand, took photographs of the area and jotted down notes or directions or instructions. Glen imagined intricate maps and complicated schematics like a blueprint for a circuit board. He had no idea what they were recording, but he assumed it was a detailed layout of the maze.

SPARAGMOS's respirators, goggles and hardhats with built in lamps made them look like a species of insect found deep underground. Or cavers who'd lost their way.

Glen no longer thought they worked for the city.

The shorter of the two climbed onto the truck's bed, then ran a spotlight across nearby houses. The taller one returned to the driver's seat and carefully maneuvered the vehicle between piles of junk. The lamp convulsed when the beam caught on a particularly scabrous surface. Glen couldn't explain why the light behaved in this manner.

They stopped in front of a house. Glen didn't remember who lived there. When no one answered their knocking, the driver did something to the knob and the door swung open.

Sipping room temperature black coffee from a chipped mug, Glen watched the house. He wished he had milk, but the fridge stopped working long ago. It now held a dozen bottles and containers rimmed with black mold.

He waited.

Eventually, SPARAGMOS left the house. They had nothing with them. The driver spoke into his radio. His words were difficult to make out, like a voice mumbling through an intercom, *...SPARAGMOS is proceeding—*

The rest was a fuzz of static.

Glen tried to write down the license plate as they drove away, but there were far too many numbers and letters. Foreign squiggles. An upside-down *A* followed by numbers he had never seen before. He looked through his journal to find he'd attempted to record their plates many times before. All to no avail.

He turned the radio volume up,

...an old lover's voice speaking through a keyhole? Recent reports of the townsfolk stockpiling...

The nonsense broadcast was interrupted by an unusual sound. Scraping. Rasping. Like a splintery rocking chair nudged by wind. This had happened before; Glen's radio often picked up other conversations, hijacked frequencies, phone calls, transmissions from who knows where. But this noise, this strange creaking in the middle of the newscast, was new.

He recognized it as the monotonous groan of an old door slowly opening.

One month, nine days ago:

Glen was still in his dingy bathrobe when he opened the front door. Cigarette burn on his lapel. Coffee stained sleeves. A young woman and man greeted him from the porch. They appeared alike. They claimed to be his daughter and son. He didn't recognize them.

"What do you want?" Glen tried to make himself presentable. Smoothed his hair back, scratched his beard to dislodge any crumbs. Clutched at his bathrobe to keep it from falling open, exposing his ill- fitting underwear.

"You decent, dad?" The man smiled. Teeth thin as needles. Pushing past Glen uninvited, he moved a box packed with plastic odds and ends from the couch to the floor. He sat down, rested his hands primly on his lap. The woman hesitantly followed suit. She didn't speak but nodded at Glen. Her teeth were normal. Glen thought her eyebrows must be so blond he couldn't see them against her pale flesh.

"Why wouldn't I be decent? I'm no pervert." Glen was angry that he could be so easily shoved aside, like a hollow thing still held together because it doesn't know any better.

"Easy there, *pops*. No need to get upset. Just wondering how you're doing." The man's left eye appeared to be larger than the other.

"Have you emptied those buckets from the bathroom? It's not hygienic. You can't hoard that kind of thing." The woman was clearly appalled by Glen's living conditions.

"My fucking property." Glen didn't mean to sound so angry. He said shocking things these days, his filters no longer strong enough to prevent offensive outbursts. He was embarrassed, appalled that anyone could think him an ugly, bitter old man. *It's the disease!* he wanted to shout. His mind was traveling to an unseen destination, slated to arrive long before the rest of his body caught up. Rage and frustration were constants.

"We're here to see how you're doing, dad. That's all." Glen noticed the woman had a receding hairline. Her forehead was smooth. Like glass shiny with sweat.

"It's not junk," Glen said.

"These old newspapers?" The man patted a yellowed, musty newsprint tower. It swayed precariously. Something scurried beneath the thick refuse on the floor.

The newspapers and magazines were an incentive; Glen would read the entire backlog once he'd beaten his dementia. He'd catch up on world events, read about the political strife in other countries, and the economy here at home. Everything was kept for a reason.

"I don't expect you to understand what it's like to lose someone."

"*Pops*. I get it. But mom has been gone for years."

This couldn't be right. Glen had recently made a new piece of furniture for his wife's birthday. A beautiful dark wood cabinet to display her glass collectibles. They'd gone out to see *Dance With Me*. It had been a wonderful evening.

He fumbled through his notebook, but couldn't find anything about his wife. He went back through a year of entries. Three years. Rifled through more.

Nothing.

Nearing panic, he shuffled through a box of old notebooks, going back even further.

Why were there so many empty pages?

His short-term memories had been the first to diminish when his brain betrayed him, but childhood exploits, decades of teaching, the death of his parents—they were all there in substance if not form. Deeply buried, yet vibrant, alive.

"Something wrong, pops?"

Glen couldn't imagine forgetting his daughter and son's faces, or how proud he was of them both.

But these two claiming to be his children had made a lie of this. Their presence was a testament to what little history Glen had retained. His personal deterioration was both withering and hateful. A mortifying descent into irrelevance.

"Why are you bothering me?"

"C'mon. Work. Research. That's why we're on this side of the tracks."

The man laughed, slid unnaturally long fingers against his trousers. He continued chuckling, as if used to Glen's mood swings and vicious demeanor. The woman stared at the front door, impatient for all of this to be done. Her eyes were all pupil now.

"Research?"

The woman cleared her throat. "You remember we talked about it, dad? Our project on exaptations?" Turning towards the front door again, she focused her attention where the frame neared the ceiling.

A tantalizing part of Glen was certain he'd once known. Bits and pieces from his years of academic work in biology remained, but the details had faded. He couldn't bear to admit his failing to this young woman that may or may not be blood.

"Of course I do," Glen lied.

"We talked about the goby fish? Their feeding behavior? Their ability to travel up waterfalls? Shared *exaptation*. One function originated with the other. Ended up being used in a different way than the original function."

"Like feathers," Glen said triumphantly.

"Just like feathers. Insulation and flight." There was a touch of sadness in her voice.

The man who may or may not have been Glen's son looked distractedly at the unwashed clothes filling the hallway.

Glen didn't know why they were studying a subject like exaptations in his neck of the woods. As far as he knew there weren't any animals around anymore. Birds, squirrels, even insects seemed to have vanished from the region. He hadn't heard any dogs in several weeks. The last time he'd seen a stray cat it seemed to have lost use of its vocal cords.

"But there aren't any lakes around," Glen insisted.

The man looked surprised. "Not studying goby fish."

"Then why are you here?"

"We don't care about little fish. Just big fish," he playfully stabbed a thin digit against Glen's ribs, grinning with that awful mouth.

The woman quickly redirected the conversation. "Too beautiful a day to stay cooped up inside, dad."

"That it is, that it is," Glen agreed. He looked outside, at a lawn that had once been a deep lush green.

A memory of his daughter falling down on the grass.

Her bloody nose.

The color of her blood and grass stained new dress.

His son crying in terror at his sister being hurt.

The smell of blood and the sun.

A dog barking in the distance.

Everything viewed through the cataracts of time.

All Glen saw at that moment were disassembled bicycle parts stored in a rusted wheelbarrow. Bent lawn furniture he'd kept in hopes the parts could be reconfigured into tables or chairs. He was protective of this mess. Each and every bit represented a piece in the jigsaw puzzle of who he'd once been.

The man followed Glen's gaze, whistled softly. "You and your neighbors have been busy bees."

Flustered, Glen's words trickled past his teeth like sand through a sieve. "That, that fucking, *maze*." His upper lip quivered, right eyelid slipped down over an eyeball independently. A conscious effort raised it halfway, vision only slightly blurred. Glen couldn't control his emotional outbursts. Rage often exhibited as sorrow, sadness as a petulant tantrum.

"Calm down, old timer. We'll get to the heart of this." The man touched Glen's arm. The woman continued to stand silently. Sliding his hand to Glen's shoulder, the man's oddly jointed fingers slopped over as if boneless.

"All I ask is that you remember we did everything here because it was necessary."

"I'm afraid of losing everything," Glen's voice cracked. He wasn't even sure what he had left to lose. He wrote everything down in his journal. Dementia couldn't win as long as he kept writing everything down.

"We'll check back tomorrow," the woman promised.

Twelve days ago:

It was difficult for Glen to move about in his home what with all the clutter. The dishes in the sink confused him; breakfasts were never more involved than several cups of coffee and a cigarette. Was this all here yesterday?

He handwashed a few dishes but gave up after realizing there were months' worth of food spackled plates. He smoked a cigarette as a reward for what he'd managed to clean.

After finishing three cigarettes, he spent time working in the flower bed. These were the only moments free from the weight of his compulsive hoarding. Here, knees and hands in soil, the vastness of the sky made him feel so unimportant he could barely muster the memory to exist.

He plucked a yellow pebble out of the dirt. It took a few moments to realize it was a tooth.

Inside the house, he checked on his mouth. He wiped a dirty hand across the cracked bathroom mirror. All of his teeth were intact. This was excuse enough to relax in the kitchen with another cigarette. He left the tooth in a scum frosted soap dish where it was quickly forgotten.

The radio was intercepting signals again. Adjusting the dial, the strange voices persisted, ...*houses torn down, uprooted everything to make room for the maze's core-*

Glen had the discomfiting image of a house tearing itself away from the foundation, plumbing dragged behind like a disemboweled animal.

Dementia was linked to the hoarding behavior. Glen accepted this deep down, suppressed it beneath the fear and the loneliness. But it was always there. Lapping at his mind like stagnant water at the bottom of a well.

It was all so dull and perfunctory. Life just a series of curt sentences scribbled into dog-eared notebooks, most of the messages having little meaning absent context. Glen had chronicled his transformation from Alzheimer's and the results were depressingly banal.

Wandering into the living room, he found polystyrene food containers covering the floor. Most were missing lids. He'd attempted to arrange the nails and screws in the receptacles, but like all else, the task had fallen by the wayside.

The people suspended in frames on the walls were only vaguely familiar. A box of photo albums in the attic could offer more information on their identities, but Glen was reluctant to climb up there by himself; the small space was lit by a single bulb, and he never felt as if he was alone inside.

The radio's volume increased though he was certain he hadn't touched it. The broadcaster said,

...just West of the burnt down slaughterhouse, a crinoline sack sat up, hopped three steps, then collapsed into a heap.

In the kitchen, Glen switched the radio off. He returned to his bed for a nap and dreamt about piles of hoarded refuse growing until the towns' maze wound its way across the planet. Meandering its corridors, anticipation set in as he drew closer to the middle. When the hoarders came out to visit the thing that sat meditating at the center of the labyrinth, Glen woke up.

Five days ago:

The radio voice was cheerful,

...has turned to milk, and authorities are discussing the available methods to drain the reservoir. In other news, we've spoken to researchers studying the hoarders in the quarantined region...

The shriek of rusty hinges emanated from the speaker.

Glen unplugged it.

Consulting his notebook, he caught up on what he'd done recently:

Failed again. The maze won't let me through.

He had written this dozens of times over the last month's entries.

He'd try again today. Make another attempt to reach the center. It was right there in his book. If he kept trying, that must mean there was a reason for his stubbornness. Bending the notebook in half, he slipped it into a jacket pocket. Picking up a box full of empty juice bottles, grocery store plastic bags, and bare thread spools, he headed outside.

The morning sky was laced with plum colored clouds that floated in such an odd manner Glen was compelled to keep glancing up to see if he could catch them doing something they shouldn't. There would be rain soon.

He continued along a sidewalk lined with bundles of newspapers and periodicals tightly bound by frayed string, stacks rising far above Glen's head. The fruits of his and his neighbor's diligence. A pile of air conditioning units and chairs blocked the path, rerouted him along a lane segregated by battered plastic bins.

He slid the box into an empty space on the wall. This was an enormously satisfying accomplishment. He continued along the maze.

The route was perplexing. Abrupt angles and branching intersections were bewildering. According to his journal, in the past he'd tried to track his progress with chalk, but the marks were always gone when he'd passed the area again. The sky ran darker, released a trickle of rain. Glen sensed he'd make real progress this morning.

He arrived at the main wall. Rising thirty feet into the air, a plastic lip drooped down over his side of the partition to prevent anyone from climbing out. The structure was constructed of several sheets of a mesh material, layered to create a thick boundary.

Machines purred on the other side. People chatted over the electronic hustle and bustle that reminded him of the mission control center of a space flight project.

Glen called out, but nobody responded. When the vibration of his voice touched the surface, the wall's material oozed like motor oil in water. His shouts spread so thin against the barrier words became inconsequential.

Moving on, he suddenly remembered addresses, street names. Progress through the streets had sparked something. The very act of navigating the maze ignited synapses long dormant.

In all the time living here he'd failed to notice the homes were so damaged the foundations had buckled. These were the skeletal remains where he'd grown up, married, had children. It must have taken some time to reach this level of disarray, but he couldn't recall stages of deterioration. It had always been this way. The present was as intangible as the distant past.

He walked until the air grew heavier, tinged with something electrical. The daylight washed out, like watercolors bleeding into canvas. This change didn't come from the cloudy sky, but a distortion of the landscape itself.

Glen arrived at the heart of the maze.

Something in the sky moved. The ground was unreliable, thin sheets all the way down, the center a tumultuous ocean of chaos. He imagined breaking through the crust, plummeting 4,000 miles to his death. An insignificant speck tossed into vast depths he could scarcely comprehend.

But the ground was solid. The sky wasn't alive. He walked onto the street. It was disappointingly suburban. His quest was over, but he'd expected to be overcome with joy at his success. He only felt content, no trace of elation.

Just an open area, not quite as littered with trash as it was in his old neighborhood. An unfamiliar house cast a large shadow across the street. It didn't look much different from any of the other homes, save for its size. A hazy aura floated from it, like gas fumes from an unlit stove. Glen wondered if something was waiting for him inside.

He noticed a SPARAGMOS truck parked up the street.

Ducking behind a low wall of broken gardening equipment and old ovens, he could smell years of stains and odors. The truck's dispatch radio emitted a high-pitched squeal.

The SPARAGMOS workers suddenly came into view.

They moved further down the road, splotches of motion keeping to the sidewalk. Glen wasn't sure if they'd seen him but took no chances and quickly crouched behind a rusted fence separating the house from a weed filled plot of land. He ran up the path to the front door. It wasn't locked.

Inside, the home was gloomy, the skylight blanketed in a thick pelt of dead leaves. The floor was marked with child-sized dried mud footprints leading up the stairs where the hall concluded at a bare wall.

Following the footprint trail, Glen was acutely aware of the sound his shoes made against the hardwood floors. Something crinkled under his foot.

An old-fashioned glass syringe. There wasn't any liquid inside.

He opened the first door he found.

Dull light poured through the bedroom window. The closet was open. Petite girls' clothes pushed aside as if someone had been in a hurry. The room held the faint aroma of apple juice and a sour undercurrent, like spoilt milk.

Compelled to move the oddly shaped pile of blankets on the bed, he half expected to find himself curled up there, wet with his own filth, mumbling nonsense. Grabbing the corner of a sheet, he pulled it onto the floor.

There was nothing on the mattress.

Something shifted in the closet. He turned just as a gray shape squatted into view. The mass slid towards him, weight altering its shape along the floor.

Glen nudged it with a shoe tip. It seemed to be dirty laundry that had fallen over.

But the clothes had fingernails.

He used a hanger to drag the material towards him. The substance was papery, crackling slightly. It looked to have once been whole, but was now dismembered, torn into the flabby outline of a face with vacant eyeholes, a hollow arm, an impression where thick veins once funneled blood. A leg, frayed bits where it once connected to a hip. An abandoned Halloween costume? Prop for a school play? Glen couldn't imagine what else it could be.

He remembered the outfits he and his wife used to put together for their children's school plays. They'd dress the kids up in such outrageously ornate get-ups the other children were envious, their parents abashed at their own lack of enthusiasm.

Glen couldn't bear to look at the skins anymore.

He explored the rest of the house. Hours passed. He found several other rooms with the desiccated skins as well. Loathe to touch them, he left the husks in their respective resting places.

In the cellar, he discovered a bare concrete room with a wooden trap door at the center of the floor. He tugged at the handle, but it was locked.

He paced back upstairs to the child's room. The sun had set long ago, the night as dark as Glen was capable of remembering. Was he supposed to meet his son and daughter? Was he expected to wait for them at home? Memory was liquid, dissolving into an amorphous string of events.

A searchlight lit up the house. A vehicle's radio blared its broadcast outside,

...in a copse of trees developers have yet to raze, a woman with burlap skin cries as she frantically digs into the soil looking for something she holds dear. If you are just joining us, a wall of unknown-

The radio switched off. A door slammed shut. Then another.

Boots hit the stairs inside the house.

Glen dropped to the floor, crawled under the bed. The space was low, but he sucked in his belly and managed to slide under the box- spring. A rectangular gap offered a clear view from the floor up to the room's light switch.

SPARAGMOS walked into the bedroom. Their heavy orange boots and jumpsuits glowed in the dark, like a heater's coils in the middle of the night. Their presence felt sacrilegious, a violation of a child's sanctuary. Glen silently prayed that they wouldn't check under the bed.

Gather the transitional materials, the shorter one commanded, her electric voice sputtering. The other turned to the closet, retrieving the skins. The night air flowed into the room, cool and sweet.

The tall one spoke into a clunky walkie-talkie, *proceeding on schedule.* He clipped the device onto his belt, then leaned down as if considering there might be something worth investigating under the bed.

His walkie-talkie suddenly erupted with static. A new voice said, *assistance required beyond the door.*

He straightened, motioned to his companion to move on. They left back down the stairs. Glen heard them rummaging around throughout the house, exploring each and every room.

He knew they were gathering the skins.

Their walking became fainter, though Glen could tell they were now on concrete, in the cellar, deep below the house's ground level.

A subterranean door creaked open, then slammed shut. He recognized that sound from the radio. Footsteps descended until the entire house settled into silence.

Glen crawled out from under the bed and sat down on the mattress. He curled up against the blankets that smelled clean and fresh as if just laundered.

If not for the chorus of bird song and the heat of the sun flushing his skin, Glen would have kept sleeping. He sat up in the unfamiliar child's room. Confused, he hurriedly left the house, locking the door behind. The morning air was such a deep shade of turquoise his eyes watered.

It was not an easy matter backtracking through the maze. A memory of the path had faded, and he was quickly lost.

Panic set in. He called out for assistance, but there was no answer. He ran. The direction didn't matter, the need to be elsewhere motivated him.

The neighborhoods he passed through were strange, unfamiliar architectures and unusual lawns laid out in patterns he'd never seen before. But there was something distinctly familiar, a sense that he was nearing recognizable territory.

He hesitated in front of his home.

But the foliage was different, the grass bristly and a lighter shade. The front door was thin and weak, the windows flimsy like plastic wrap. A poorly constructed quality to the whole thing, as if hastily built in his absence. The flowerbed appeared to be synthetic, bright with vinyl roses of various hues he was certain hadn't been there before. But this had to be home. Where else could he be?

Inside, he found the dishes clean and neatly arranged on the countertops. The radio was plugged in and blaring at full volume. Errant bits of conversation passed through the speaker,

...traveling, pearly babies moving quickly through—

He unplugged it again.

After his wife had been diagnosed, a shared suicide seemed the obvious solution. But the years rolled by and his terrible sorrow was dulled beneath the comfort of routine. When her senility progressed to the point her existence was meaningless, Glen thought of the pills he'd saved. But he no longer knew where he'd stored the medications. Now there was little chance of finding them amongst the accumulation of prescription bottles.

In the bedroom, he was certain that the bed was in a different position. The door's hinges were on the wrong side. The walls a different color. Feeling far too tired to work in the flowerbed, Glen slept off and on the rest of the day.

One day ago:

Glen woke to darkness. Mouth dry. Craving a cigarette. The radio chattered an unpleasant sound. Hadn't he unplugged it?

He walked downstairs intending to turn it off. Passing through the kitchen, he found the cord wasn't in the socket.

A walkie-talkie on the counter shrieked. A glass syringe was next to it. A blinking light on the walkie-talkie turned the plunger's medicine a sickly ochre.

Glen hurriedly checked the rooms, but there was nobody in his home. No SPARAGMOS employees snooping around. No one inside but him.

He picked up the walkie-talkie, pushed a button. The only response was an electronic squeal. He gingerly placed it back down next to the syringe, as if it were something disgusting he'd dug up in the flowerbed.

He stepped outside. One of the house's shutters was lopsided, like a tooth dangling from a thread of gingiva. The street was empty. He lit a cigarette. The distortion of the sky made it seem as if the garbage had risen as high as the hills, a maze of discarded items growing exponentially.

None of this was trash. These were the remains of people's aspirations. Gifts and reflections of cashed paychecks. Small yet substantial attempts to better lives, to ease the perpetual hopelessness and allow brief moments of happiness through the acquisition of useless junk. The thought of losing all of this filled him with sorrow.

The walkie-talkie's chatter wafted out of the open window. Glen was reminded of his overwhelming loneliness. Voices were just another indication the world was inhabited by strangers, memories less than ghosts. Hints of histories eroded by the past. He was fairly sure his home was a facsimile of the house he'd lived in for so long.

He desperately wanted to shed his body, slip out of this wrinkled flesh, leave nothing behind except sloughed off sheets of memories thin as time. Everything he'd ever wanted passed by long ago.

The night became so thick Glen feared the rising sun would be too weak to illuminate anything in the morning. There was nothing more to do anymore except continue into a hell of fading memories.

Dropping the cigarette to the asphalt, Glen returned to the house. He ignored the strange colloquy babbling from the walkie-talkie. Moving up the stairs, he briefly lost his way in the small two-story house. He eventually found the bedroom.

Someone was tightly wrapped up in the bed's sheets.

Was his wife still alive? Were his children finally visiting?

There was a time when his wife was healthy, before the Alzheimer's progressed to the point her body no longer remembered how to keep itself alive. Glen had grown accustomed to her clumsy attempts at affection then, like a child who'd learned how to kiss from a scene in a movie she'd long forgotten. There were times when he thought his wife relinquishing any vestige of her past was a gift, the dissolution of memory a kindness. He hoped that when he eventually forgot everything his death would come as quickly and mercifully as it did for her.

What if even God was capable of forgetting? Everything was dependent on memory. Without memory, the world had no meaning.

Glen pulled the sheets off the mattress.

The bed's occupant gaped at him with empty eye sockets. Papery skin rustled in a breeze from the open window. The mouth fluttered as if about to speak.

The walkie-talkie in the kitchen roared with the din of screeching hinges.

Today:

Glen no longer had the strength to get out of bed. He wanted to go downstairs and turn the walkie-talkie off. The sound of that old creaky door opening and closing had given him a headache. But he was so tired.

Someone shouted his name. Glen didn't dare answer back.

People were coming up the stairs. Glen nervously patted his head to make sure his hair wasn't too disorderly.

The two who claimed to be his children entered the bedroom. They both wore SPARAGMOS's orange jumpsuits, clean and bright as tangerines. They held their respirator and hardhat in the crook of their arms.

"It's time, *pops*."

There was a note of promise in the man's voice, as if he was the impatient bearer of such grand things and addressing Glen as his father was mere formality.

"Where are you taking me?" Glen's voice shook with anticipation.

"To the center of course." The woman removed a sheet of paper from a folder Glen hadn't previously noticed. Placing it on the nightstand, she handed him a pen.

"Sign it."

Glen's son was born small and jaundiced, his daughter loud and vivacious. He felt the ache of years and the stress of every ailment. That dread of becoming useless when his son grew taller than him and his daughter no longer laughed at his jokes. That inevitable decline into irrelevance never diminished as he grew older. Every passing year reduced his worth on this planet that much more. Parents want nothing more than to die before their children, but the fear that there might be an afterlife spent yearning for loved ones to join them was too painful to contemplate.

Maybe it was time to forget everything. He took the pen.

He tried to sign, but the tip of the pen pressed against the page with so much pressure a pool of darkness spread like a dilated pupil. He didn't know how to spell his name.

Glen suddenly remembered his children's names.

"Candace."

"Alex."

Glen punctuated each name by pointing at them with the pen. They both appeared saddened by the recognition.

Glen kissed his daughter on the forehead. He embraced his son. He told them how much he loved them, how happy he was that they'd become such wonderful people.

"I remember you," Glen said.

"Let's go. SPARAGMOS is waiting," Candace replied angrily. Alex held Glen's wrist with more force than was necessary.

Candace swiftly jabbed a needle into Glen's arm. Casually dropping the emptied syringe to the floor, it broke into equally proportioned slices of glass.

Glen felt no pain, just the pressure of his son's grip. A relaxing warmth loosened his muscles. The pen fell from numb fingers. He looked at the document on the nightstand,

...able to make choices about my care before my mental facilities are no longer sufficient.

"I am so proud of you both." His vision blurred, legs weakened.

Glen used to write everything in his notebook. Dementia couldn't win as long as he kept writing everything down. As long as he kept a record. Someone was singing on the radio, but he didn't recognize the words.

Glen's bare feet slid across the filthy floor as Candace and Alex roughly dragged him away. Taking one last look at his home he wondered how much more he might remember if they'd only let him stay here a bit longer. Just one more day. Let him piece together more of the maze before disposing of him.

But there was no longer any need to remember. SPARAGMOS would take care of everything. Candace and Alex would transport their new specimen to the cellar where researchers ritually separated memory from skin, dissected sorrow from hope. In that sterile lab gleaming scalpels split dreams from truth, hollowed out old men and discarded their mutilated husks into piles to be disposed of later. Glen had navigated the maze, and his reward would be the balm of nonexistence.

Nearing the front doorway, he didn't bother to request they grab his journal on the table. He was more than happy to leave those memories behind with all the other hoarded trash.

QUEER WOMAN SURGEON

m I pretty?

Carrie yanked her headphones off and peered into the shadowy corner of the library. She expected to see a woman's corpse swoop towards her, a surgical mask hiding a lower jaw dangling from slit flaps of cheek skin.

There was nothing in the dark of course. Ambient noise in the building, misinterpreted as a voice. Carrie was on edge, experiencing auditory hallucinations from lack of sleep. Ghosts weren't real.

All supernatural things aside, it was best to be vigilant; assaults against women on campus had been reported recently, and Carrie had no intention of being a victim. She pressed the cassette recorder's STOP button.

The third floor of the Cal State Fullerton library retained a recently renovated smell, the dusty scent of drywall and acetic traces of new paint. The eerie sounds and heavy shadows felt incongruous in such a pristine setting—the rustling better suited to a haunted library stacked with moldering books; the darkness the ghosts of cobwebbed librarians shushing the living. Carrie laughed quietly at the notion, her voice echoing slightly in the unpopulated building.

There wasn't time to pause at every creak and rasp of the library's architecture cooling down after an 89-degree winter day—she'd a dissertation to fine-tune. Poring over her paper for 9-hours straight had the rational portions of her brain focusing on ethnographic minutiae, while the irrational had her expecting a visit from Kuchisake-onna, literally mouth (*kuchi*), lacerate (*saku*), woman (*onna*), or more simply, the Slit Mouthed Woman. Starting at every little distraction and hearing Kuchisake-onna's *am I pretty?* was her body's way of warning her that she was pushing herself too hard.

The Slit Mouthed Woman haunted Carrie's every waking and sleeping moment ever since discussing the urban legend with her thesis advisor. Fortunately, she was satisfied with the way *A Cross Cultural Ontography of Women Yūrei in North America* was coming along. A year immersed in Yanagita Kunio, Inoue Enryō, and *mononoke* had her looking at the world through spirit haunted eyes. She'd a comprehensive list of the various versions of the Split-Mouth myth, though the details varied in subtle ways.

On December 1978, in the city of Gifu, a woman wearing a surgical mask was reportedly stalking children. Rumors spread, successive versions transformed the mysterious woman from child snatcher to ghost, her beauty marred by a jealous lover, split from lips to ears, or the disfigured victim of botched cosmetic surgery. So was born Kuchisake-onna, an avenging spirit who'd ask *watashi kerei?* (am I pretty?), then mutilate the victim no matter their answer. Between December '78 and early '79 the urban legend spread across Japan from exposure in magazines, newspapers, TV, and word of mouth. Every version of the story emphasized her savaged mouth, the surgical mask, and that enigmatic question.

In the Ibaraki Prefecture, children were warned to avoid any women wearing surgical masks; in the Fukushima and Kanagawa Prefectures, the frequency of police patrols was increased. But *A Cross Cultural Ontography of Women Yūrei in North America* analyzed the cross-pollination of this particular piece of Japanese folklore to claims of sightings of the Slit Mouthed Woman *outside* Japan.

There were many instances of cultural universals, or at the very least cultural commonalities—the similarity of flood narratives between many peoples was an uncontroversial consequence of the importance of water to all civilizations. But the recorded claims of encounters with Kuchisake-onna in North America were more difficult to explain.

Carrie looked over her notes.

...several cultures emphasize sacrificial deities, a motif for agricultural societies, reflecting their reliance on the death and resurrection of crops.

Sleep paralysis is another example. Every culture has a version of a ghost that visits in the middle of the night, to immobilize their victim: the Japanese tradition of kanashibari, *literally "to immobilize as if bound with metal chains", is one such manifestation. Sleep paralysis is culturally manifested as the Incubus or the Old Hag in European traditions, beautifully rendered in Fuseli's "The Nightmare". In Thailand, a tradition of* khmaoch sângkât *exists where a ghost holds the sleeper down. Our shared biology and cultural standards necessitate a common narrative, though the details vary.*

Carrie had compiled several hours of recorded interviews over the last four months, but had whittled them down to a dozen of the most relevant and interesting. It'd been nearly a year since she'd corresponded with Harry Roth, director of the Eastern California Museum in Independence California, near the Manzanar camp, for potential interview candidates who might have some experience with yōkai—anomalous entities confined to Japan, and yūrei, beings which haunted far flung regions beyond Japanese folkways. How this strange slash-mouthed apparition was diffused to regions outside of Japan was the question she wished to examine in her report. Supernatural experiences were produced by cultural influences, or cultural sources, but the Slit Mouthed Woman had visited several witnesses outside any specific tradition. She'd invaded a cultural void as it were.

Carrie loved monsters, Yōkaigaku, anthropology, and minzokugaku. A people were best described by their monsters, in the complexities of their hauntings and strangeness. The weird gave substance to a culture as much, if not more so, than any faith or language. She figured if any cultural awareness of Kuchisake-onna was to be studied, the potential to ferret out stories connected to the Japanese internment camps was a good place to start. There'd been many responses, but this week she'd focused on Karl Simmons and May Wakashima—two interviews which held fascinating potential. She sighed, shook her head. She could've written about the folklore of any other culture, but no, it had to be Japanese. Christ, she was as far from a racist stereotype as she could imagine—terrible at math and computers, and she'd no interest in manga or whatever bullshit people expected her to know about. Born in Hawaii, her parents were third generation and Carrie had picked up very little Japanese in her childhood, and less awareness of her family history. Her father saw to that.

There was something of a stereotype there; her father was a renowned ophthalmologist who'd expected a medical career from Carrie as well. When she'd refused and started racking up college credits for a B.A in anthropology, her father didn't speak to her for an entire semester. He'd always been stern, but she'd actually feared his anger at times, anticipating a confrontation that thankfully had yet to explode.

What was the Japanese proverb? The things Japanese fear the most? *Jishin, kaminari, kaji, oyaji.*

Earthquakes, thunder, fire, and fathers.

She glanced at her watch. It was already 10:26. The library's Apple II Plus monitor screen glowed a dull green, the disk drive warm from so many hours of use. She sipped her flavorless instant coffee. The wide window facing the main campus was pitch black. She heard footsteps in the hall, though she'd been assured by Amber, the Head Librarian, she'd free reign of the place. Nobody else was supposed to have access to the building at this time of night. The library doors swung open.

Carrie slapped her palm against the table. "Holy shit, Joshua. You scared me half to death."

Joshua smiled apologetically, pushed a mop bucket ahead of him through the doorway. He pulled his L.A. Raiders cap off, ran a hand through thinning hair, tugged the cap back over his scalp.

"Sorry, Carrie. Didn't know you'd be pulling another all-nighter."

"I'm nearing the finish line. If this paper doesn't kill me, it won't be for lack of trying."

"You mind if I clean up in here? I'll be quick."

"Please, don't let me get in your way. Pretend I'm not even here."

Joshua did a perfunctory mop of the room, emptied the trash cans, then said good night to Carrie before leaving. She felt slightly relieved when he left; it was difficult to concentrate with someone else in the room.

But there was an underlying anxiety as well. It felt as if the campus had been evacuated and Carrie was the only one who hadn't been notified. The building was a lonely, foreboding place, even though it was Friday night, the dorms active, and the congested Orange Freeway noisy as ever just East of campus. She felt oddly abandoned in the middle of a bustling urban landscape. She was tired of feeling afraid all the time.

Yanagita Kunio believed that yōkai were fallen deities who were no longer worshipped, condemned to wander the confines of Japan in their various manifestations as ghosts, monsters, goblins, shape-changers, demons, oni (devils or ogres) or all manner of supernatural entities. While yōkai were limited to Japan, yūrei could appear anywhere in the world, including North America.
Anywhere...

Carrie looked over her notes, turned her attention to a small box of loose cassette tapes. She found the one with the label she was looking for: BRONZEVILLE KARL.

This was an odd find. Karl Simmons wasn't Asian, or even associated with any Japanese camps, but he'd contacted the university after seeing the anthropology department's inquiry ad in the *Daily Titan* paper. Karl claimed he'd caught wind of "some Oriental ghost lady talk," and he wanted to share an anecdote.

Karl had been cagey at first, but reluctantly agreed to an hour-long phone call describing his life in Los Angeles, and why his experience might be relevant to Carrie's search for people who'd experienced something anomalous in relation to yūrei. He'd rambled on about the Black Dahlia murder and mafia hits, but had a compelling story that tentatively connected all of it to Carrie's thesis on the Slit Mouth Woman. Not only was Karl's experience with her geographically incongruous, it also occurred more than 30 years before the legend even appeared in Japan.

She adjusted her headphones, pressed PLAY on the cassette recorder.

She began typing:

BRONZEVILLE KARL TRANSCRIPT

(This is an interview with Karl [K] [last name omitted for anonymity] by Carrie Deguchi [CD] for the California State University, Fullerton, Anthropology Department on August 3, 1983. The interview was conducted by phone to protect the interviewee's privacy. Karl has given consent for the following unedited exchange on the stipulation his identity and location be kept secret).

CD: Thank you for allowing me to ask some questions. Can you tell me your story?

K: My story? Revenge. All stories are about revenge. What else is there?

CD: As mentioned before this recording, I'm researching the cultural significance of *yokai* independent of Japanese cultures. I'm interested specifically in January 15, 1947. Would you mind elaborating on what you saw?

K: Saw a goddamn demon.

CD: In our preliminary phone discussion you described her as a "puppet-jawed lady". Could you elaborate?

K: Yeah. I could. But that's enough for now.

CD: May I ask why?

K: No. Well, yeah. I'm still not sure about the whole thing. That was, what, damn near 35 years ago? Shit, more than that. Not old enough to drink back then, and my memory ain't wine, so not much has improved with age.

CD: You were 14?

K: Sounds about right.

CD: How would you define the sighting of the Slit Mouthed Woman? Not to lead you, but is the memory frightening? Sad? Angry?

K: It's not an easy thing to talk about.

CD: Ok. Let's set up your background then and come back to this. You mentioned your father was white, your mother black. I imagine this incited talk back then.

K: Well, it wasn't a walk in the park. It was never really spoken about because it was illegal for them to marry each other at the time, but mama passed for white until my daddy died. Never felt completely at home in either community. But my father wasn't a good man, so that helped clarify things for me. Didn't feel accepted by nobody, but I sure as hell never received a scrap of positive from white folks.

CD: You lived in Los Angeles, near the area that was

Little Tokyo as a child?

K: That's right. With my parents and two sisters. I was the oldest. We moved from Connecticut to Lincoln Heights when I was a boy. Daddy worked in Little Tokyo.

CD: This would be '43? When the area was renamed Bronzeville.

K: Yeah. Japs got kicked out of the North end of Central Avenue. Black folks moved in. Mainly poor families from the Deep South, looking for work in the defense industry. Little Tokyo was a ghost town after they'd booted everyone out, so white landlords rented the empty spaces to blacks looking for a new home. Bastards sold the Jap owned businesses to the new tenants. Area was renamed Bronzeville. All kinds a businesses popped up. There was the Cobra Room, Shepp's Playhouse, the Cherryland Cocktail Lounge. Scatman Crothers and Charlie Parker played at all these places. All sorts of culture and clubs and music then. My daddy worked 'em all.

You see white folks are predictable; they're gonna boot black, brown and yellow people out, then exploit those that move in afterwards. Lot of angry citizens after Pearl Harbor, so I wasn't surprised when Roosevelt sent the Orientals packin'. But black folks are resilient. Always had the short end of the stick, so we know our way around that stick and manage to survive no matter what they throw at us. Japs were the same way. Pushed around and treated like dogs, but never let that shit hold them back.

CD: What did your parents do in Bronzeville as far as occupations?

K: Mom was a stay at home sort. Daddy was a gangster [coughs].

CD: The mafia?

K: In the mafia back in Cleveland too. Joined the Siegel gang when we moved to L.A. Bronzeville got crowded right quick. Couldn't spread out to nearby neighborhoods on account of segregation, so they had ten, twenty people living in stores and tiny apartments meant for a family of four. Crime was bad. Pack too many sardines into one can and somethin' is gonna give. So, daddy worked for Siegel's crew, Murder, Inc. He let me tag along a few times. Take your kid to work day kinda shit. I even saw Mickey Cohen once.

CD: What did he do for Siegel?

K: Busted heads. They called my daddy the "Glacier". Not because he was big or cold or any bullshit like that, but he was slow. Not dumb, but methodical, calculated. Patient, like a slow moving glacier, I guess. Meticulous is the word. Real clean freak. Manicured his nails. Neat and tidy. Always dressed to the minute. Like I said, he worked the clubs and collected rents.

He thought things through, really careful with what he said. Had a reputation for collecting loans just by patiently explaining why it was in their best interest to pay up. No need to threaten—don't get me wrong, cracked more than his fair share of skulls, but he was usually more interested in tellin' it like it is, and how things was gonna be.

He had a meanness in him. Above and beyond slappin' around skinflints.

CD: How so?

K: Hated women. Thought they were there for him to callous his knuckles on. Liked black women enough to marry Mom, but not enough to treat her decently. He was a brute. Terrorized the whole family. I was happy as I'd ever been when he died.

CD: May I ask...?

K: Cancer. 1960. Not important enough to remember the exact date.

CD: I'm sorry.

K: Don't be. I ain't. I think he had somethin' to do with that Black Dahlia murder. Slit that bitch in two.

Carrie hit STOP. The cassette squeaked. It was slow going wading through these racist, misogynistic asshole's anecdotes. The recent influx of Indochinese refugees after the Vietnam war had contributed to a protectionist attitude and a virulent renewed wave of racism as evident in Karl's rants. Maybe she'd edit the slurs out before submission. Or she could always keep it as is and leave no doubt as to Karl's opinion of woman and Asians. She'd deal with that on the final draft.

This creep certainly had daddy issues.
Earthquakes, thunder, fire, and fathers.
She hit PLAY.

CD: Why do you think that? *[born Elizabeth Short, dubbed the Black Dahlia by the press, her body was found mutilated in a Los Angeles field on January 15, 1947. The murder remains unsolved to this day]*

K: He hurt girls. He really thought the Lord created him to go around beatin' up women. I could tell he was always holding back, like if he had his way, he'd drop the whole civilized man act and toss it aside like an old jacket.

Long story short, Siegel had daddy hurt some teenage Oriental kid. The kid's father asked Siegel's crew to protect his barbershop business while he was at Jap camp. You know, board things up, keep everything from being looted so he could come right back to work after his Tule Lake stint was done. Oriental assets had all been seized. Nothing to do but make nice with the mob. Pay them. Get protected. Same ol' song and dance.

Turns out this Jap wise guy enlists in the 442nd Infantry Regimental Combat Team. That was the only way for an Oriental to avoid being interned, though his family was still sent away. So, this guy doesn't pay one cent to the mob, and just abandons his shop. I guess he thought his family would be safe in camps, and he'd be far enough away the mob wasn't gonna do anything to get him—so what if he reneged?

But they found his family. Tracked the girl down to the Santa Anita temporary assembly center— that's what they called them. Kind of a layover until they got sent to Manzanar or somewhere else. Shacked 'em up in horse stalls. Government cleared out the stalls and hosed everything down, but they were small spaces that still stank of horse piss.

Families took to covering their mouths with cloth or surgical masks to keep from breathing the diseased air. Mob sent my daddy to hurt the little girl at Santa Anita.

CD: A mafia hit?

K: Not kill. Just scare. This wasn't a situation where he could talk someone into anything. He was there to hurt. That was that. So he cut her mouth open real wide. From lips to ears so she was always grinnin'. A fuckin' puppet mouth. Just like that Black Dahlia cooze. Leerin' even in death.

CD: What does the Black Dahlia murder have to do with—

K: Let me finish. I learned all this years after the fact. Like I said, daddy died of throat cancer in '60, and mama told me all she knew about his criminal career after that. I don't know what happened to the Oriental girl he sliced, but I heard she survived. Mom said daddy told her the girl wore a mask after he slit her. Like I said, those Santa Anita stalls were so shitty people took to wearing cloths over their mouths to keep out the smell. So, this girl took to wearing a mask after she was cut up too, to hide her fucked up face.

CD: You think he—

K: Not done yet. I'm not one of those true crime perverts, but I read that there were several men and women murdered in the Kingsbury Run district in Cleveland in the mid-30s. We lived there at that time. The killings stopped in 1938. We moved to L.A. in '39. But the way they were mutilated in Cleveland, well, makes me wonder what the old man had been up to back there. So yeah, the way the Black Dahlia was cut, mouth carved into a smile and all, made me think of dear old dad.

CD: Now are you ok with talking about what you saw on January 15, 1947?

K: Yeah. I am now. Five in the morning. Deliverin' newspapers. I was the first to see it. Before the crowd gathered. I knew it was a body.

CD: Elizabeth Short?

K: Uh huh. The Black Dahlia herself. I didn't know what to do. Didn't know what to think. Never seen a naked woman outside a magazine before.

I stood at the edge of the empty lot, the field was dry grass. At first, I thought it was a mannequin someone had dumped in the field. But as I got close, I saw she wasn't hard plastic.

Something about the way stiff grass poked against her skin was too real. All soft and the way the sun fell on her skin was strange.

So pale, scrubbed clean, hair like an oil slick in the morning light. Like a printer error where the ink runs out and the words trail away into pale nothingness. A drawing where the artist has left everything in except for the figure in the center, erased so perfectly all you see is the outline and everything inside is just whited out. She was cut in half. So clean. Washed, hair shampooed. Cleaned.

My vision swam. My mouth opened and closed like a dying fish. The sky was hot as if it was yawning breath. That corpse... Like someone had put a wig on a papier-mâché dummy and left it to dry in the morning sun. Too white, glaring.

Then I saw what someone'd done to her mouth. I knew then my daddy killed her. That crime scene was a sacred site. A terrible ritual had gone down there. All I could think about was that kid my dad sliced. Like this corpse was all the damaged, brutalized women he'd hurt, and I was to bear witness.

CD: In our preliminary discussion, you mentioned the Slit Mouthed Woman encounter occurred that night.

K: I saw her outside. In front of my house.

CD: Go on.

K: I'd gone to bed, woke up on the sidewalk.

I used to sleepwalk then, so I thought that's what was goin' on. It was a bright night, starry skies.

I saw this woman. Floating in the air, not too high up, but just out of reach. At first, I thought it was the Black Dahlia. But it wasn't.

CD: It was *her?*

K: She had long black hair that covered her face, so I didn't know at first. Could a been anyone. Maybe every woman I ever thought about.

CD: Did you think at the time it might have been the girl your father hurt?

K: Maybe. A wind yanked her long black hair around, but it wasn't windy. Some old dry newspapers in the gutters didn't move, and I couldn't feel any air. None at all. Hard to even breathe 'cause it was so warm. But she floated there. Like something dunked in water and the current slowly moved it in a circle until you just know it's gonna face you and you sure as hell don't want that.

But she did.

CD: What did she look like?

K: She pulled her surgical mask off and I saw her wide open, rotten mouth.

CD: Did she say anything?

K: She said, "Am I pretty?"

CD: Could it have been a dream?

K: I don't think so. Does it matter if it was?

Carrie hit STOP. Karl's eloquence in describing the incident bothered her. It was as if he'd memorized a beautiful poem, a portion of a song that moved him in some way and reiterated it in an uncharacteristically loquacious manner. But it was all there—the torn mouth, the surgical mask, the infamous question. A menacing air pervaded the room, a threatening sense that she'd transgressed some border into unexplored regions.

It was strange how Karl had seen something from Japanese folklore independent of any knowledge of what he'd experienced. Maybe he'd picked up the urban legend by just being in the Little Tokyo area, and then heard about the University looking for contributions from people who had stories about yokei. It wasn't impossible for Karl to have researched Kuchisake-onna and pranked the University with his interview. Stranger things had happened. But Kuchisake-onna was quite specific in springing from Japan in 1978, and not particularly inductive to a broad application, culturally speaking.

Or was she? Perhaps the answer was inexorably linked to patriarchal practices. Female monsters dominated many culture's folklore, and nowhere was it more apparent than in Japan with Yuki-onna (Snow Woman), ubume (Birthing Woman), and Yomotsu- shikome (ugly woman of the other world). Men brutalizing women was so widespread, maybe Kuchisake-onna's disfigurement was simply one of many stories reflecting this. Every passive-aggressive *you'd look pretty if you smiled*, every fake display of affection or kindness demanded of her. Every battered, assaulted, or murdered soul. Maybe the only sane response was a bloodied, unhinged smile in the face of the world's unrelenting violence.

Japan in the 50s and 60s brought social transition and
upheaval with unprecedented economic growth, mass migration to

city centers, and depopulation of rural communities. A movement in the '70s to "rediscover Japan", was implemented. Japan National Railway sponsored a "Discover Japan" campaign, in a plea to rediscover the abandoned countryside and the mysteries it hid. A return to a rural life and all its joys and mysteries of their furosato (old home) roots. It's no coincidence the Slit Mouthed Woman appeared just as urban ethnographies were being written, and the cityscapes offered folkloric studies. The very concrete apartments and streets were ripe for anthropological studies and the specters lurking within their environs.

Carrie set aside her notes. Contemplating it all left her feeling unsettled and exhausted. She removed the cassette labeled BRONZEVILLE KARL and replaced it with one titled MANZANAR WAKASHIMA.

This interview was gold. The only concern Carrie had was to keep her references to the camps as "concentration camps" and not "internment". It was a controversial use of the word, but accurate as "concentration camp" predated Hitler and the Russian Gulags. She was confident in the accuracy of calling the forced relocation of Japanese citizens into concentration camps. To hell with the racist revisionists that claimed otherwise.

She hit PLAY and began typing:

MANZANAR MAY TRANSCRIPT

(This is an interview with May Wakashima [MW] by Carrie Deguchi [CD] for the California State University, Fullerton, Anthropology Department on June 12, 1983, at her home in North Hollywood. Mrs. Wakashima was contacted by the university and she gave her consent for the following unedited exchange).

CD: There's a lot to get into about the concentration camp and sighting, but first, do you mind telling me where and when you were born?

MW: Los Angeles County Hospital, May 12th, 1932.

CD: Would you mind telling me what happened on Sunday, December 6, 1942?

MW: I was visited by the Split Mouth Woman.

CD: As we discussed before I started recording, I'm researching the cultural significance of *Kuchisake-onna* independent of Japanese cultures, and before her first reported sighting in 1978. But there's a lot of ground to cover—let's get back to that in a moment. May I ask when you were interred in Manzanar?

MW: Oh, we arrived there on the 10th of April, 1942.

CD: How long were you there?

MW: Just over two years? That sounds right.

CD: Did being Nisei make the relocation that much more surprising?

MW: Oh, definitely. We felt raw about that. It was a shock to say the least. I was born in California! We never showed any loyalty to Japan or anywhere else besides the U.S. I didn't know Emperor Hirohito from Tom Mix! It didn't make any sense.

CD: Where were your parents from?

MW: They emigrated from Katori. Made it into the

U.S. just before the Johnson-Reed Act was passed. They'd farming experience, so they worked the strawberry fields in the San Fernando Valley before saving up to buy a small house and vegetable shop on Alameda not long before I was born. I say "shop", but it was really little more than a stand. [laughs] I have many fond memories of going to work with my father and watching all the interesting people walk by. It seemed to me that my dad was friends with everyone. I miss him.

CD: Did your parents have any interest in the occult or the supernatural?

MW: Not that I can think of. They were quiet, hardworking farmers. I don't remember them being superstitious or religious or anything like that. Nominal Buddhists at best. Dad read novels all the time. Crime detective books. Mom loved languages. She spoke English, French, and Spanish fluently. She tried to pass it along to me, but I never had a head for learning new languages. They burned most of their books before we were interned. Rumor was the FBI came to your home and found any Japanese language items you could be taken away immediately, and maybe even executed. There was so much fear. We had no idea what kind of future was waiting for us, if any.

CD: Was there anything in their background that would suggest an interest in Japanese folklore, traditional ghost stories and the like?

MW: No. They never spoke about ghosts or anything like that. Level-headed boring farmers. [laughs] They didn't really emphasize our Japanese heritage. I think they wanted us to be as American as possible. We spoke Japanese at home, but rarely in public. And we never discussed folk tales or anything spooky that I recall.

CD: Would you be opposed to describing the day your family was relocated?

MW: Not at all.

I remember our neighbor Mr. Follett. He was an attorney, bankruptcy law, I think. He kept insisting the government couldn't do what they were doing. But after Order 9066 was the law of the land, my father reported to a designated civil control station. We were registered. Labeled. And within three weeks we were evicted. Father even turned in our radio to the police department. I never understood that until someone told me the government didn't want the Japanese to hear any coded spy message broadcasts.

My father never came across as worried by any of this, though I knew the 8 p.m. curfew was the final straw for him. It meant his late-night walks through the neighborhood were over. That was a travesty! [laughs]

The Folletts offered to hold all of our furniture and keepsakes, to put them in storage for us. Some friends had stored their items at the Hompa Hongwanji Buddhist Temple on 1st and Central, but my parents held out until the last minute. I think they couldn't believe it was going to happen, so they kept putting things off.

They sold a lot of our possessions for a fraction of what they were worth, but the Folletts held onto the rest for us so we could pick up where we left off when all this ended. My father sold our home to the government. Received less than half of what it was worth. But he didn't want to get nothing.

When we were driven away by the bus Mr. Follett shouted "*Itsuka mata omemoji no hi made!*" after us. I saw that mother was crying.

CD: What did that mean?

MW: "Until we meet again."

CD: So, there was some support in the community?

MW: Not as much as you'd hope.

CD: What then?

MW: We were tagged and numbered, given a family number. Then a train took us North. There were armed guards on the train. They had bayonets on their rifles. The guard nearest us was a young man named Javier. He kept saying that this wasn't right, and he couldn't believe what his country was doing to us. He was so apologetic I felt sorry for him. Once we were in Bishop, we were transferred to a bus that drove the rest of the way to Manzanar.

CD: What were your first impressions on arriving at Manzanar?

MW: I thought we'd made a wrong turn! [laughs] It was desert as far as the eye could see. Awe inspiring, but terrifying. I was an L.A. girl! All I knew was Leimert Park, freeways, Red Cars. This was something else to a 10-year old girl. I might as well have been on the surface of another planet. To the West were the Sierra Nevadas, nothing but boulders and sand until the land rose into these huge mountains. The Inyo were East, craggy and topped with snow. Desolate but beautiful, you know?

CD: You said you were bussed to Manzanar—was that common or did some people drive themselves?

MW: There were rows of cars parked outside the camp. Such a strange thing. Must've been two miles of cars. I later learned they were all vehicles families had driven in to report to Manzanar, and they were parked and lined up to be sold. A local appraiser took advantage of them since they had to accept whatever was offered.

It was the saddest place. It felt like we were being dumped off in a ghost town behind barbed wire fence. But we were the living and the ghosts were MPs with rifles.

CD: What were the accommodations like? I'm sorry.

That sounds insensitive—how were the barracks and housing in general?

MW: [jovially] Not at all! They weren't really homes to us. The entrance had two stone sentry houses with military police. The jail was just to the right. There were towers at the four-corners of the camp. There were rows of barracks, a first-aid shack with stacks of lumber and saw tables next to it. Many of the barracks weren't finished being built yet.

We moved into a small cubicle. It was very cramped. There was just a pot-bellied stove in the middle, and one metal bed with no mattress. A guard gave us burlap sacks and told us where we could get some hay to stuff them with to make mattresses.

CD: What was day to day life like for a 10-year-old girl?

MW: Miserable. 100 degrees during the day, as high as 116 at times. And cold at night. Dust storms came through all the time, so bad you couldn't see your feet on the ground. I went to school every day. Played a lot of softball. All we had to eat in the first few months were government supplied foods like beans, pasta, and bread—so much starch. No vegetables or fruit at all. I got really sick so often, and medicine was scarce, so my mother always had some rice water on hand to help with digestion problems. I dreamt about eating persimmons, dates and strawberries. I'd wake up with saliva all over my cheeks. I think our diet was the reason my father got stomach cancer years later.

I could tell my mother was depressed, but she was always there for me. She showed me how wearing geta sandals made it easier to walk in the dust. I felt so rebellious! Here I was being so Japanese! [laughs] We practiced softball together, and I loved working in the gardens with her. Other families even raised chickens and pigs. I made new friends. Kids can fit in anywhere no matter the circumstances.

CD: So, your mother was a survivor also. How did your father handle it?

MW: He kept his sense of humor. I remember him reading an old issue of LIFE, a few months old at the time anyway, and there was an article on how to tell the difference between Japanese and Chinese, because, well, you know, we were barbarians apparently. The Japanese were brutish and evil; the Chinese benevolent and less likely to be traitors. My dad showed me the pictures of two men in the magazine, diagrammed to show the different features with helpful hints on how to spot a Nippon traitor. He pointed at the page and said, "I don't know about this sinister looking fellow, but I think I'm a regular Clark Gable." [laughs]

CD: Did your mother or father ever mention the Split Mouth Woman? Or did others at the camp?

MW: Not directly. A group of men would slip through the fence and make their way to the Sierra creeks to fish. There was a tree-lined stream on the Sierra Nevada's eastern slope. And on George Creek, and Shepherd Creek further north. The waters were stocked by the Department of Fish and Game.

One of the regular fishermen was Jon Okamoto. Strange young man. A Kibei I believe. Bad news. He was always going on about the Emperor and spreading pro-Japan propaganda. He was with the Black Dragon Society. Anyway, he said he saw a woman out there at night when he was fishing by himself.

CD: Did he elaborate?

MW: My father once asked if he knew who the woman might be. Mr. Okamoto just said, "a Queer Woman Surgeon."

CD: What do you think he meant by that?

MW: No idea. I didn't know what *queer* meant then, like lesbian or something I suppose. It didn't make sense to me. But like I said, Mr. Okamoto was a troublemaker. A No-No rebel. We kind of laughed at his response. Did he mean a woman wearing a surgical mask? I thought he'd seen a nurse walking around in the desert at night!

CD: Did he happen to mention whether she said anything to him?

MW: He did actually. I overheard him tell some of his fishing buddies that she asked him if he thought she was pretty. They all laughed. He was crazy. He told tall tales. Ghost stories. It was Paiute country, so there were all sorts of rumors about Indian ghosts. But woman ghosts wearing hospital masks was a little crazy, even for that place. But now I think I know who he meant.

CD: Do you know what happened to Mr. Okamoto after the camp was closed in November, 1945?

MW: Oh, he was gone long before that.

CD: Gone?

MW: Yes. He disappeared on one of his overnight fishing trips. Headed out on his own and was never heard from again. I thought he'd been relocated to Tule Lake—that's where the troublemakers were sent. But I later heard they found his bamboo fishing pole, but nothing else. Probably got turned around and confused out there. Miles of desert to get lost in.

CD: Are you ready to talk about the sighting?

MW: I think so.

CD: No hurry. And only if you feel comfortable.

MW: It was the first week of December, a Sunday. I remember going to church that morning. The night before there was a fight between the Japanese American Group... Oh, I forget the name.

CD: The Japanese American Citizens League.

MW: Yes. Fred Tayama was their leader. The head of the Kitchen Worker's Union was Mr. Ueno. He was arrested and jailed for beating Fred up, and locked up in Independence. The two groups had been fighting like cats and dogs for a while. So, the next day, Sunday, I saw hundreds of people in the camp gathered in support of Mr. Ueno. Somehow, they negotiated bringing him back to Manzanar. They held him in the camp jail.

It was Sunday evening. I was helping finish the laundry before the wind got worse. It was terribly windy and only getting worse. Protesters surrounded the camp jail. They demanded Mr. Ueno's release. They had knives, hatchets, and rocks in their hands. It continued like that for hours, late into the night. Military police were ready to shoot at the drop of a hat. One of the MPs kept shouting "Hold your ground men! Remember Pearl Harbor!"

My parents told me to stay away from there. To come back into the barracks and let this all blow over. But I disobeyed them. I lied and said I'd left a shirt on the laundry line. But I ran along the fence until I was near the jail. It was so dark, I had to carefully feel my way along and try not to cut myself on the barbed wire.

Someone out there in the desert called my name.

CD: On the other side of the fence? Outside the camp?

MW: Yes. Somewhere out there.

CD: The Split Mouth Woman?

MW: Yes. But people started shouting and I heard...
Everyone was shouting. The crowd threatened the
MPs, or someone said the wrong thing or—I don't
know. I don't—

The audio warbled, stretched May Wakashima's voice into a deep haunting drawl that hissed like molten whispers in Carrie's ears. She quickly pressed STOP.

Oh shit! Please don't be ruined!

She opened the tape recorder and removed the cassette. A short loop of tape dangled like a curled tongue.

"No no no no!"

Panicked, Carrie poked her pencil into the reel and twisted to retract and tighten the loose tape. The strip looked smooth and undamaged, so she hoped her minor surgery had set things right. She popped the cassette back in, hit PLAY.

But there was only several minutes of crackles and hisses. Her heart sank the longer she listened.

I've lost the audio. I'm beyond screwed.

She was about to hit STOP again when she heard raised voices in the background. She lifted a headphone to make sure the sound wasn't coming from outside. It was clearly on the tape. The voices were faint but angry, something in their cadence suggesting they were screaming in Japanese.

Gunshots rang out.

Carrie jerked in her seat, dropped the pencil in surprise. The noise was definitely on the audio, but she had no idea how any of this had been recorded.

Am I pretty?

She slammed the STOP button down, hit rewind, then PLAY. But there was nothing. Just the sibilant buzz of damaged audio tape.

She rewound the cassette to where the interview had been cut off, and played it again. Nothing. White noise after that point. No shouting in Japanese, gunshots, or spectral *am I pretty?*

The tape was ruined. Carrie slid it away from her in anger. She was hearing things again.

Maybe she could remember enough of the interview to scavenge for her dissertation somehow. Maybe she could get ahold of May Wakashima and interview her again. Maybe...

Carrie pinched the bridge of her nose with thumb and forefinger, closed her eyes, gently massaged until her vision was filled with a warm soothing vacancy. She needed a change of pace. Something to break the stress. Something to tamp down her frustration.

Kuchisake-onna's face is the disfigured environment, the mutilation of woman, their bodies expendable mannequins to inflict societal rage and loathing against. The surgeon's mask not only "gussies" up the hideous truth, but portends something ominous, the barely restrained rage and frustration beneath her surface. Her mask represents an indignant political response, an uprising against social patriarchal norms instigated by centuries of oppression.

Protesters wore similar masks over their mouths while lashing out against the U.S.-Japan Security Treaty in 1960 and 1970. The Ūman Ribu (woman's liberation) movement, public protests from Chūpiren (an organization devoted to women's contraceptive rights) and opposition to the expansion of the Narita International Airport in May of 1977 resulted in masked demonstrators clashing with riot police. Four hundred were injured, and one person died. A masked and slashed Kuchisake-onna is merely every woman attempting to assert their basic human rights against their oppressors, and the revelation of what they're saying on removing said masks invokes antagonism.

Carrie realized she'd have to leave soon. It was so late, and she'd no reason to stay any longer in this empty building now that her interview transcript was in limbo. But a lingering hesitation kept her here. Prevented her from leaving the library. Something wasn't right.

A clatter in the hallway.

It must be Joshua. He probably hadn't finished yet and accidentally dropped his mop or broom. She removed her headphones, left the table, and opened the library door a crack to peek into the hall.

There was nobody there. Thoughts of assaults on campus ran through her head. She returned to the table.

What if she wasn't alone? What if she stepped back into the hallway and somebody was there, waiting to confront her? What if she made it to the exit doors, only to see someone smiling at her?

What if once outside, the night split into the jagged grin of a vengeful universe?

It made sense to be cautious about violence from men, but spirits and monsters weren't real. It wasn't a challenge to trace the psychological and socio-political influences on the Slit Mouthed Woman's appearance in times of strife—particularly in tragedies replete with racism as that which resulted in thousands of Japanese citizens being corralled into concentration camps. Class conflict, and times of turmoil agitates the public imagination, and the public in turn conjures demons, apparitions, and malevolent entities into stories they insist are true.

Even so, the library no longer felt like a safe haven. The world no longer felt rational, no more a puzzle to be solved in the gathering of fragments and pieces. She'd overstepped unseen boundaries to upset an unnatural *idea* that now insisted on visiting her. Her explorations yielded answers that made the world that much less explicable. She put her headphones back on.

The cassette began playing though Carrie hadn't touched the PLAY button. Miraculously, the tape was working. But May Wakashima sounded as if she were in a trance, whispering from deep underground, and Carrie's voice was wobbly and distant. She didn't remember this part of the interview at all. She wasn't sure if she'd fallen asleep and was dreaming. She could almost smell the hot, dusty scent of the desert wind.

MW: [faint] I stared into the darkness of the desert. The rows of barbed wire were spaced wide enough for me to easily step through, but the desert was no place for children to wander late at night. This land was mysterious, terrifying and cruel. The night wind splintered air into dark shards, spread the cold like razor honed crystals. Several men shouted in Japanese.

A woman drifted by, her feet scarcely touched the sand. She moved with the grace of a wind born tumbleweed, with no destination or intent. I thought of the misconception that tumbleweeds were sagebrush, when they're actually mustard plants. It was a distracted and silly thought.

The ghostly woman was weightless. Something exhaled by ancient and inscrutable forces. She floated into the distance.

Just before the phantom was absorbed by the desert night, she looked over her shoulder. Her mouth fell open into a dark chasm. A melodious voice poured out of the hole. She said,

Sabaku de ai mashou.

CD: ...let's meet...?

MW: Come meet me in the desert.

I didn't say a word. The desert was too vast, too old for anything I said to cross such a distance to the woman. Her lower body was absent, as if waist deep in ink, shimmering in and out of view like a corroded coin under rippling water at the bottom of a well.

Then she vanished. I peered into the blackness, trying to locate her. I shouted "Where are you? It's too dark. I can't see you!"

She replied from the dark, *Watashi kerei?*

CD: That means "am I pretty?"

MW: Yes. Gun shots rang out. I wondered why people were screaming. I later learned that the MPs had fired into the unarmed crowd. I didn't know until a few days later that a boy, Ito James, was shot and killed.

I didn't want to talk to the woman anymore. I wanted to go back home to L.A. with my parents, return to the way life was before we were taken away and brought to this camp where we didn't belong. I could only look at the Alabama Hills' silhouette rolling and bare, smooth and lifeless as the dead sky.

Years later, when we got back to Los Angeles, we found that Mr. Follett had sold off all of our items he'd promised to hold and put his home up for sale, then moved away. We never found out where. Never got our things back.

But Kuchisake-onna spoke to me one more time before she disappeared completely that night in Manzanar.

CD: What did she say?

MW: *Watashi wa suna no naka de matsu.*

CD: I'm sorry, my Japanese is rusty...

MW: "I'm under the sand."

Carrie sat watching the tape reel spin. She listened to it squeak *pretty? pretty? pretty?* on every rotation, fearing that it would never end.

The Immeasurable
Corpse of Nature

Taphonomy of Child-Sized Remains: a Study of Piglet Decomposition Rates

L. Caroline Jantz Ph.D., Mina Fawn M.S.

Mina Fawn, M.S.

Department of Anthropology

1218 University of Oregon

Eugene, OR 97403

mfawn@uoregon.edu

The identification of infant and children's remains has been greatly improved by new methodologies in forensic odontology and skeletal aging techniques. Recent procedures and technological advances offer as much as an 83% success rate in classifying skeletal samples (Aggrawai 2008: 456). Despite this progress, and the importance of precise postmortem interval (PMI) determination for medicolegal cases, a comprehensive curation of literature on taphonomic processes of juvenile remains has yet to be compiled.

Definitive studies on decomposition rates of infants have been elusive given the lack of donated bodies to anthropology departments, given the obvious cultural reservations of utilizing children's bodies for scientific inquiries (see Tantoco and Moody-Jurado 2002). To circumnavigate this, juvenile *Sus scrofa domesticus* were used as test subjects in this study.

Dr. Karen Solberg's decay-ravaged head floated through space. When she sang, a stew of maggots and stars poured from her livor mortis colored mouth. When she wept from eyeless sockets, flesh sloughed off beneath the trail of scalding acid tears.

Mina kneeled helpless on the Earth's surface and watched the deteriorating Solberg-planetoid spread blight across the sky. The ground beneath her softened into the consistency of menstrual blood. A baby screamed. It was at that moment Mina realized the stars falling from Dr. Solberg's ruin of a mouth were actually broken teeth.

Mina woke with the sour taste of gastric juices on her tongue. The plane vibrated violently as it lifted off the runway. An infant a few rows behind wailed in distress. She could smell the sour tang of the screaming thing's breath.

Surprised she'd fallen asleep already, she removed her earbuds and turned the soothing, ambient music on her phone off. Adrenaline and anxiety were a potent mix. She'd never been comfortable flying. Now wide-awake, she stared out the plane's window.

Yesterday, Mina had been elbow-deep in putrid swine meat when her phone vibrated. She'd been working with her students, documenting the temperature variations of fly larvae infested pig flesh at the body farm. Well into their third trial, the evidence was slowly but surely demonstrating that human decomposition was far more variable than swine decay rates had initially led them to believe. The recent findings didn't invalidate the previous studies but had raised questions as to whether continuing in this manner would be a waste of time; pigs were simply not adequate stand-ins for humans when it came to analyzing decay. She'd removed her gloves and answered her phone.

The call had been from Dr. Genet. As a graduate student, Mina worked under Genet in Rwanda. In '96, Mina had been chosen by the United Nations International Criminal Tribunal on Dr. Genet's referral to accompany a group of pathologists, archaeologists, and fellow anthropologists to examine a mass gravesite in Kibuye. The country was reeling from the aftermath of the Hutu nationalist's genocidal campaign against the Tutsi. An estimated 800,000 people slaughtered, 2 million refugees forced to flee their homeland, and the international community had simply looked the other way.

Mina had long wanted to report to Dr. Genet again, but the intervening years had never offered an opportunity to do so. They'd briefly exchanged pleasantries on the phone before Genet asked Mina to join the Disaster Mortuary Operational Response Team on a case in Northern Oregon. She gave the details in her Amharic accent, just as comforting to Mina as it had been years ago.

A cult calling themselves The Ones Who Walk Away had done the unthinkable and ended their lives on an isolated compound called Omelas Farm.

Dozens of badly decomposed remains required sorting, cataloguing and identification. Many more were expected to be found—the cult had an estimated 249 members who'd taken residence on the Farm, and more potential survivors off-site. If the membership roster was even close to accurate, it looked as if this was going to be the biggest cult mass suicide since The Order of the Solar Temple in '94. There were a staggering number of bodies to identify.

Mina had immediately accepted Genet's offer to join DMORT on this investigation. Genet's assistant at the Oregon Office of the Medical Investigator e-mailed the paperwork details and flight information over so Mina could be in Portland first thing the following day. With that, after the thank yous and promises to catch up on old times, they'd ended the call. Clearing her teaching itinerary, Mina collected her DMORT carry-on bag containing enough personal belongings to last about two-weeks.

Now that the plane was in the air and her destination over two hours away with a brief layover, Mina searched online for everything she could find on The Ones Who Walk Away, as if cramming for a test. Their site hadn't been updated since 1997, and the obsolete web design had given her a headache. They were a radical environmentalist compound founded by Dr. Karen Solberg, a biologist inspired by the writings of James Lovelock and Lynn Margulis. Solberg was interested in symbiotic participation between species, even entire environments, as opposed to the Darwinian emphasis on competition. Her papers on abiogenesis were renowned, and still referenced as exemplars of origin-of-life studies nearly 50 years later.

On founding her collective in 1974, Solberg had first named them The Borborites. The obscure moniker was later interpreted as offensive to some members, so, in 1976, she officially changed it to The Ones Who Walk Away after an Ursula K. LeGuin story she was reportedly obsessed with.

That same year, Solberg purchased 52-acres of land and turned it into a working ranch and farm. Her people planted crops, bred livestock, dug a system of wells, and transformed the property into a self-sustaining community. They built 67 modest prefabricated homes, and a large auditorium for lectures and community events. Dr. Solberg even had a state-of-the-art laboratory for her continuing research. All of this was powered by solar energy and generators designed by some of the top minds that flocked to Solberg's utopian compound.

Solberg had once expounded on her Farm in a rare interview with the journal *Anima Mundi*. According to her, it was an experiment in cultural, scientific, and biological autopoiesis. The Farm was to be a self-regulated machine, a system that reproduced itself without any biological processes, thus avoiding any questions about exposing beings to suffering. Her intent was to create something more complex than the sum of its parts.

Apparently, the parts hadn't meshed too well, Mina thought.

Solberg had more than her share of controversies, even before founding the cult. Her interpretation of the Gaia theory was unusual. She'd emphasized that it was something beyond the holistic interaction of organic and inorganic to create self-regulating systems, and ultimately, emergent properties that made conditions for life optimal on Earth. She opined that the planet was a distinct organism, and humans were slaughtering this world as they heralded in the End of Times with the Anthropocene. This view wasn't particularly contentious, but Solberg insisted the planet was an individual consciousness capable of communication.

While Lovelock's critics dismissed his Gaia theory as poetic metaphors with the potential to become a protoscience dependent on further research, Solberg's detractors accused her of being a crackpot, her theories as deranged fantasies. The misogynistic attitudes were obvious, though it didn't help that Solberg also emphatically defended other strange ideas outside her expertise, most notably James McConnell's experiments on RNA memory transfer. McConnell's claim that he'd demonstrated this through experiments utilizing planarians to cannibalize other planarians and passing on the memory of a conditioned response remained unsubstantiated at best.

The Ones Who Walk Away were strict anti-natalists, arguing procreation was harmful, and human proliferation had a long demonstrated negative impact on the environment. The mere act of creating new life was selfish and cruel; subjecting a sentient being to any potential for harm or misery was inherently immoral.

Mina was surprised to read the cult experienced a brief upsurge in membership in the late 90s, after a flurry of news reports raised questions about potentially dangerous groups in the weeks following the Heaven's Gate suicide. She was also startled to discover a surprising number of academics and scientists had joined The Ones Who Walk Away. A disproportionate number were biologists, neurologists, and neurophilosophers or in a related sub-discipline. Rumor had it Patricia Churchland spent some time at the Farm under confidence in early '80, though she never substantiated the visit, and Dr. Solberg was silent on the matter as well.

A former member who'd defected in the early 80s published a scathing critique of the group in his 2002 memoir, *Anti-Natalism: The Untenable Faith*. Mina quickly bought an e-copy of the book and skipped around to the chapters that sounded the most interesting.

The author accused Solberg of trying to "communicate and reconcile with Nature," critical of her attempts to "introduce a hybrid to reach out and make amends with the Earth." Mina had no idea what that entailed, and neither did the writer apparently; his brief chapter on Solberg's ideology neglected to elaborate on what any of this meant.

The book's sensational claims combined with the increasingly apparent environmental disaster humanity faced meant it managed to sneak onto the New York Times bestseller list for one week in the summer of 2003.

Mina looked away from her laptop and rubbed the fatigue from her eyes. Just three days ago, a concerned feed and tack owner had driven out to Omelas Farm after unsuccessfully trying to contact their buyer to let them know their large order of fertilizer and soil acidifier had arrived. On discovering the gruesome scene of corpses dumped in a sewage-filled ditch, he immediately called the police.

Mina opened a website tab that displayed a scanned image of one of Solberg's philosophical tracts:

```
Let our species die out. Let it all cease
to be. Parenthood is sadism; reproduction is
offensive.

You exist only to make babies. You live only
to add fodder to the machinery of cruelty. You
breathe only to feed the gaping maw of brutality.

Pregnancy is oncogenesis. A molecular
reprogramming of cells to proliferate no matter
what harm befalls all other life on this planet. Our
original sin is the sin of wanton birth. Humanity
```

is a collection of cells reproducing other cells,
cancers building on cancers.

Time to end the cycle of perpetual breeding.

Mina looked out the plane's window to see a dark sheet of clouds roiling beneath the plane like an angry ocean. The weird planet-head dream faded into the farthest recesses of her memory. The cabin's recycled air was unpleasantly greasy. She could taste the breath of so many strangers, their sickening molecules slipping into her mouth, over her tongue, into her nostrils, down her throat into her lungs, polluting her insides with foreign particles. She stifled her gag reflex. Willing herself to ignore the tainted cabin air, she concentrated on what might be waiting for her at Omelas Farm.

She was eager to dive into the work. Ever since she'd started teaching at UCSB, countless bone bits had been brought to her attention by hikers and weekend campers hoping they'd stumbled across a gruesome trophy or fodder for the next big true crime podcast.

But all too often what was thought to be human hand bones on professional examination proved to be skinned bear paws. How many battered, empty tortoise shells had been misidentified as craniums, or sheep ribs offered up as human remnants? There was something comforting about the never-ending assembly line of grisly souvenirs brought to her office, because they also offered a sense of normalcy. A respite from identifying the corpses of savaged human bodies.

But she was embarking into what was sure to be a parade of repulsive sights and heartbreaking discoveries at the Farm. It was always a balancing act— Mina found the science and processes involved in studying human remains fascinating, exhilarating even, but exposure to tragedies and the depths of depravity humanity was capable of had grown harrowing over time. The faces of babies who'd been beaten so badly they'd lost an eye, or finding different levels of healing in a dead child's rib fractures marking their history of abuse like tree rings never ceased to weigh on her.

But she was professional. Calm. Rational. She didn't care what the head medical examiner would have waiting for her; she'd be happy if they put her to work distinguishing commingled remains from animal and plant matter. She'd profound respect and admiration for Dr. Genet, and the chance to work once more with the woman who'd essentially started her career was a rare opportunity. It'd be a breath of fresh air to visit Oregon, where, time permitting, she might even swing by her old alma mater, the U of O.

She'd do what she had to do. This was all she ever asked of herself.

The flight from LAX to SFO, where she had a quick layover, then on to PDX, wouldn't take long. Mina pulled down the window blind and thought about the cases she'd worked previously. Years ago, after her experience in Rwanda, she'd assisted DMORT in recovering scattered remains and extant bodies illegally disposed in the woods behind an operational crematorium in rural Georgia. Over 300 cadavers had been recovered on that case. The gruesome story made national news, and Mina's participation garnered a few articles that focused on her efforts specifically and mentioned her work in Rwanda as well. Summer of 2005 she'd flown to Baton Rouge in anticipation of the body count expected from Hurricane Katrina. A gathering of dozens of pathologists, coroners, and medical examiners had shacked up in a temporary morgue arranged inside an abandoned brick warehouse that housed lepers a century before. While the vast majority of the Katrina dead had been elderly, Mina's participation was invaluable in identifying several damaged infant and adolescent corpses.

Following Katrina, she was contacted by various agencies to look into cases that challenged the authorities. As most states don't have a forensic anthropologist on payroll, Mina was the go-to consultant all over the country, at the top of every medical examiner's contact list. Heralded as a rising star anthropologist, she was brilliant, and years ahead of her colleagues. Even her peer reviewed papers on human and pig decomposition rates were quoted in various news reports.

But she felt she'd never been good enough. The media played up her Korean heritage and adoption by a devout white American couple in 1977. Her history played neatly into the press' narrative of a foreign-born underdog attaining success in the U.S. despite coming from humble roots, of dreams being fulfilled through the altruism of a loving Christian husband and wife. Mina found the coverage more condescending than not, not to mention racist and classist, but she'd always done her best to present herself, her adoptive parents, and her career in the best possible light. She knew she was fortunate, privileged even, which made her cynicism and second-guessing her every action that much more difficult to reconcile.

Though her adoptive parents had been mindful of Mina learning about where she'd come from, exposing her to Korean culture and her native language, she'd never been particularly interested in finding her birth parents. They hadn't cared enough to keep her around—why bother retaining any emotional investment in their lives?

All she had left of her past was a slim folder the Korean adoption agency had given her adoptive parents. The folder held a cursory medical report that simply made note of her live birth and real name, Kim Mi-nah. The file's tab was marked with her case number and birthdate:

#K76-2147

1976-3-22

Not counting Missy Asuncion in high school, there'd been two relationships she'd considered serious until her partners decided otherwise. Her twenties had been spent studying and working abroad to patch together the remnants of the dead to find some closure for their families. Her thirties were a blur of honing and fine-tuning her vocation. She thought herself unattractive, her features blunt and odd, deformed even. She was certain her previous lovers had long forgotten about her. No matter how much good she did it always fell short of relevance. Mina was 44 years old.

A folder with her birth details. That's all she had left from the beginning of her life.

Maybe that was why she chose to pursue a career in forensic anthropology. Maybe that vestige of her past was something of an inspiration. She'd been driven early on to piece together fragments of dead histories in an attempt to find a semblance of meaning to it all. If she herself had no meaning, she'd have to create some in others.

After the plane landed in Portland, she picked up her state-supplied rental and drove the three hours to the little town of Moss Creek in Clatsop County. The drive was quiet and uneventful, though the darkening sky seemed a cliché given her destination. She navigated carefully, not accustomed to the rainy Pacific Northwest weather.

Moss Creek was less than a mile outside of Omelas Farm. The town had one bar, two small convenience stores, "Hay Stack" and "Hay Bale"; a feed and tack provider named Mister Pitchforks; a lone mechanic whose sign had been erased by years of neglect but looked like it might be Jaunty Jacks; and the Harvest Hotel. Most of the buildings needed major repairs. The homes were tucked further back in the woods, though a handful managed to remain intact on the outskirts. These small ramshackle houses looked like debris broken off from the larger, older homes on the mountainside, slipped free from their place of origin to slide down closer to town.

The WELCOME TO MOSS CREEK sign boasted a population of 1,306. Mina suspected that number was nowhere near accurate. The place was quaint, though a menacing aspect made her uneasy on first driving down its one paved road. A stretch of blacktop full of holes, it functioned as a sort of main thoroughfare for the handful of businesses on display.

She checked into the Harvest Hotel. The rest of the DMORT crew were staying in nearby Clatter Creek, a slightly larger town East of the Farm. She'd no idea why she was the only one housed in Moss Creek, while the others were elsewhere. Maybe she'd been added to the DMORT team later than her peers and Clatter Creek had no hotel vacancies? This was what the state had provided her. She'd take what was offered and work with what she had. Regardless the situation, Mina wanted to get settled into the room that would be her home for the near future.

The hotel was dank and silent, a rundown place with no other obvious guests. Liquids sloshed inside pipes hidden behind thin drywall. The incessant *plink plink* of dripping fluids played in the background like a soundtrack. The faucets ran cold and took too long to warm up. The water tasted off.

Someone had left the TV on in her room. The volume was muted. A strangely familiar black and white horror film played on whatever channel the previous guest had chosen. Scenes of people eating survivors, wet open mouths of screaming prey, bones protruding from moist orifices. Mina barely registered the blur of motion, a moving smudge of gray on the screen like a gathering of fungus gnats.

The smell of Lysol reached her from the bathroom, a disinfectant ploy to disguise oily fingerprints left behind from previous guests, their residue remaining on the plastic toilet seat and faucet handles. Invisible smears of ejaculate and sticky genital sweat, poorly wiped asses, cells clinging like beads of disease to careless fingertips, casually wiped across inadequately bleached towels. Hands brushed against an unwashed shower curtain, gripped door handles that hadn't been cleaned since the place opened decades ago. The bed sheets were coarse and smelled artificial, of floral chemicals and synthetic air fresheners.

She hadn't expected a luxury vacation, but the DMORT planning here seemed a bit hodgepodge, even this early in the game. It felt backwards given the seriousness and importance of the investigation. Then again, out here in the boonies, coroners were elected to office, and most had no medical training, so autopsies were farmed out to local doctors. Like most areas in the U.S., this region relied on a coroner system where practitioners operated independently of other counties. A background in forensic anthropology was all but unheard of, so those with the requisite skills to investigate medicolegal emergencies were shipped in to offer their expertise. Maybe some leeway on the lack of professionalism was warranted given how much had to be dealt with on such limited resources out here.

She closed the bathroom door, hoping that'd tone down the imitation flowery stink. She lit a cigarette, sat on the bed and stared at the TV.

Something had grown inside Mina over the years. A dark angry mass, malignant in its despair. Numbed by every naked mutilated corpse found in a dumpster, every burnt child's body adhered to a crib's plastic mattress cover, skull betraying telltale signs of parental violence. It forced her to retreat deeper into her work. Babies shot full of heroin to silence their incessant bawling. Humanity fished from septic graves, disintegrating into sludge, mangled ruins of once vital human monuments. Bodies breaking down into that from which they came. Mud. Excrement. Waste matter.

Shit and spit and piss was all that held life together. Mina was proficient at taking it all apart to finalize their stories. This is what she did. This is what she would do until she grew too old to be of any use. Mute corpses. Silent bones. Her life could be mapped out in lengths of quiet, calm horrors.

She remembered one investigation where a child's body had been recovered from the burnt-out remains of a house. The 10-month old suffered multiple stab wounds by a hypodermic needle, then set on fire. The detectives also found a 7-year-old's corpse in a hallway the fire hadn't reached before the blaze had been doused. The girl's skirt had been hiked up high, panties wound around her ankles like impromptu cuffs. Her lower body, from the waist down, was black with blood, a dark pool spread beneath her buttocks. Her face was turned to the ceiling as if wondering why God allowed this to happen.

Mina stole the bindle of heroin clenched in the girl's hand before any of the EMTs on the scene could notice.

The world reveled in harming innocent people. It had already damaged a substantial portion of Mina's soul. She needed a respite. She'd told herself the heroin would have just been confiscated, lost in the red tape of police bureaucracy—if not stolen by them in the first place. She'd deserved the drugs more than them.

Experimenting with narcotics in college had helped her get through the tougher times. She used, but her relationship with heroin was methodical, meticulously controlled. She shot dope responsibly, had no doubts her will and strength meant she was in complete charge. She wasn't some lowlife junkie.

The dope fortified the wall between what he'd seen and how she managed to go about living day by day. She'd an idea of what to expect when pursuing her education and subsequent career, but the reality had become uglier than she'd prepared herself for.

At her first autopsy in college, on shucking the gray flaps of an old man's skin from his clavicle, she felt a religious epiphany. The man's donated body supine on the stainless-steel gurney was a religious artifact, abandoned and committed to the reliquary of the university. A holy antiseptic Church, its lifeless flock stretched out on stainless steel pews.

Bloodless, the cleanly sliced flesh was thick and heavy, muscles dry and gray. The assignment had been for Mina and her lab partner to remove the internal organs, then place them back in their original positions. Physical building blocks, sterile, dull and useless in death. No hint of animation, of anything suggesting this was once a living thing.

A geriatric's lifetime of love and joy, of hopes and dreams, had been relegated to a flabby corpse on a cold table surrounded by gawking students torn between solemn respect and embarrassment at viewing a corpse with his legs spread wide. A sad mechanism wrapped in skin and hair. A contrivance that had once been draped in clothes, propped up to stare out across the pastures of his life like some magnificent scarecrow tricked into thinking it'd been born with a purpose.

Still tired, Mina dropped her bag onto the floor next to the hotel bed. She rose from the lumpy mattress and turned the TV off. Glancing at her phone, she saw the reminder that she was scheduled to be at Omelas Farm in two hours to meet with Dr. Genet. Enough time to decompress with a quick nap. She dropped her cigarette into a plastic cup half-filled with water, flopped onto the bed, and quickly fell asleep.

She was on the moon.

Surrounded by mountains of the dead, a mass of maggoty activity warmed the putrid pillow of flesh beneath her body. Burlap sack complexions floated in space, faces bulged with corruption. Eyes protruded with such intensity they burst out of their sockets.

Before Mina woke up, she realized she wasn't on the moon. She was on a massive decapitated human head.

❋

(cont.)

A child's body has unique properties compared to adolescents and adults: greater surface-to-volume ratios, higher composition of fat, and bones with greater mineral content (Toth 1997: 216-226). As a consequence, immature bodies may degrade and skeletonize in as few as 7 days , depending on environmental factors (Miyake 2000 : 256). Recovering diminutive remains, particularly small bones and baby teeth, are also exceptionally difficult given the inevitable impact of scavengers .

To alleviate these challenges, we found that piglets make an effective surrogate infant corpse : both possess analogous fat deposits, comparable organ anatomy, and similar skin depths . For this paper's research, ten piglet carcasses were purchased, each weighing between 8 and 9kg, accurately representing the average weight of a 6-12-month-old child (CDC Growth Charts for the United States : Methods and Development, 2010).

❋

Mina drove slowly on the way to Omelas Farm. The sun was setting. Dark clouds still filled the sky, though the landscape had yet to be subsumed by darkness. Each field had at least one scarecrow keeping guard, even if the land grew nothing but weeds. Mina was mystified as to why some land was dead and bare, while other plots were vibrant with emerald swathes of grass and snakeroot. There was a pleasant loneliness here. The romanticism of rural life in the quiet and pristine air. It was an invigorating beauty.

But Mina also found something ominous about the woods. The Red and Big-leaf maple trees grew thick on the mountainside, impenetrable by vehicle, hiding so many secrets. Perhaps even more bodies waiting to be discovered, stuffed inside rotten logs, or interred beneath the mossy forest floor.

The two-mile dirt road leading to Omelas Farm was slippery with mud. Lined with blackberry bushes that grew thick during the summer, now withered and free of berries, their thorns scraped the side of Mina's rental. She saw the media presence had been confined to the outskirts of the property where police had set up crowd control barriers. Only authorized investigators were allowed direct access to the Farm itself.

A tall, lanky officer scrutinized Mina's ID and compared it to a database on his rugged tablet. He waved her through. His movements were curt, artificial in their sparseness. His gangly limbs looked like a cheap Halloween costume to Mina. This made her uneasy for reasons she couldn't explain. Every little abnormality was magnified to grotesque proportions in her brain. She was anxious about what she'd gotten herself into.

She parked the rental. Herds of people milled back and forth. Pathologists and law enforcement spoke in reverent tones. She walked to the three-sided tent where DMORT was headquartered. Three refrigerated diesel-powered trailers had been set up nearby. The furthest from the DMORT tent had four guards outside the closed entrance. Each held a Colt M4 carbine. Mina stared at them, incredulous as to why they were necessary. She'd worked many a disaster site, even on cases necessitating armed security at the coroner's office in anticipation of the victim's family retaliating, but nothing like this. The guards stood at ease. They leaned close to each other, chatted in hushed tones. They seemed well practiced in intimidation; even their quiet banter came across as gruff and threatening. Did they expect violence from any cult survivors still lurking in the woods?

The guarded trailer emanated something unusual. A temperature differential. A vibration that made Mina's teeth ache. A shuddering abnormality.

She entered the DMORT tent. The space was large but packed with busy investigators. The crowd passed file folders back and forth, listened intently to their phones or scrutinized their tablets as new information came through. Mina walked past cardboard boxes and glanced at the open ones. They contained surgical gloves and gowns, paper towels, office supplies, toiletries and socks—in case any workers were stuck in here for days on end. On her previous assignments, teams of four worked in tandem so one person could take a break without slowing down the identification process. They typically followed a 12- hour, 7-7 shift, if possible, rotating fresh forensic examiners on and off site every two weeks, for however long it took to wrap things up. Mina had been through it all before.

The cots at the back of the tent looked less than inviting, though exhausted examiners hoping to catch up on naps they'd most certainly be deprived of were unlikely to complain. Large upside-down wooden barrels functioned as makeshift tables. Several laptops and phones were charging on the surface of the one closest to her. A half-circle of folding chairs were arranged around it, one of which was occupied by a young woman Mina assumed to be a pathologist. Dr. Genet was speaking with the seated woman. On noticing Mina's approach, Genet turned to her. "Mina Fawn! So good to see you. What has it been? 15 years now?"

"Over 20, I think."

Exhaustion cast deep shadows across Dr. Genet's face. As resilient and experienced as she was, the mass suicide had clearly shaken her. She spoke slowly, to prevent the relentless disorientation of fatigue from warping her speech.

"Holy mother, time flies. My old brain can't keep up. I suppose we've both been busy."

"No rest for the wicked."

"Wouldn't dream of it." Genet turned towards the woman seated at the table, "Speaking of wicked: this is Daria Folberg, one of many faces you'll become familiar with."

Daria stood, gave a sheepish wave with a bandaged hand, "Pleasure to meet you."

"Likewise." Mina's gaze settled on the wounded hand.

Daria sat down, rubbed the wrapping, "Oh, *this*. Cut myself on something. I think that scarecrow had a piece of glass or sharp metal jammed inside its mouth."

"Oh. A scarecrow." Mina said, unable to think of any other response.

"It's nothing. No stitches. I'm just taking a break after getting patched up before I dive back into the mix." Daria said nonchalantly.

Mina wanted to ask why she'd been rooting around inside a scarecrow's mouth but decided to let it go. She could smell faint traces of apple cider in the wood of the old barrel. She expected unpleasant body odors in this cluster of stressed out, hardworking humanity in such a confined space, but there was an underlying stench of wet straw beneath everything, of rotten gourds and mold.

Dr. Genet touched Mina's shoulder and gestured towards a suspended clipboard. A wire stretched from one chair to another, running through the hole of the metal clip. A sheet was attached to the board. "Go ahead and sign in if you please, Mina. It's old fashioned, but I'm a pen and paper gal myself."

Mina smiled politely at Genet's self-deprecation. She checked her phone, wrote the time and her name down. Genet's breath was unsettlingly strong. Mina found the smell strangely reminiscent of wet dirt.

Genet handed her a lanyard attached to a plastic badge. MINA FAWN was printed at the bottom, NDMS and the DMORT logo across the top.

"Let me give you an idea of what we're looking at," Dr. Genet said as she made her way to the tent's exit. "We'll conduct a walk-through. Document the scene. Take some photos and video if you feel the need to do so."

Outside, Dr. Genet continued, "You've seen the reefers parked here," she nodded towards the refrigerated units. "The remains are stored inside this one."

Mina knew this was where bodies were cleaned, then decontaminated with a chlorine solution, numbered, assigned a folder, and processed.

"And this other one, well, this'll be your new office for a while." Genet opened the unit's door for Mina.

The interior was chilled with a state of the art Mortuary Enhanced Remains Cooling system. A frenzy of activity, a few pathologists glanced their way as they entered, then quickly resumed working. It was controlled chaos. Pathologists hunched over computers, poring over data to corroborate IDs. Someone shouted *I have a torso here!* Another voice yelled back in response, *Two female legs in this bag! Both lefties!*

A massive Disaster Portable Morgue Unit, the 650 square foot space had a wet laboratory, microscopy and photography stations, and the latest osteometric equipment. The large room held six autopsy trays supported by sawhorses. Beside each was a stainless-steel cart, shiny and pristine. Latex gloves, plastic bags of various sizes, scissors, knives, and Stryker bone saws were neatly arranged on each.

Plastic containers stacked at the DPMU's entrance held body parts, each carefully labeled with a control number and location, written in pencil, so as to minimize any chance of smudging important data.

"The unit next too this one is where personnel bring in remains to be photographed, x-rayed, and the preliminary identification based on hair color, skin color, clothing—you know the drill." Dr. Genet pointed to a pile of body bags. "Extant remains are slated for autopsy from the forensic pathologist. Dr. Mullins is in charge of that."

Mina recognized the setup: here, personal items were inventoried, then stored in containers. Fingerprints would be taken if the body wasn't too soft or damaged.

Dr. Genet continued, "If not extant, triage sorts the bits and pieces over in the other trailer. That one has the dental exam station. Dental teams of three or four can work simultaneously. If need be, we could process over a hundred bodies a day. We're taking our time though, being extra thorough, due to the sensitivity of all that's going on. Mitochondrial DNA tests are prepared in this..."

Genet stopped, looked at Mina with an apologetic frown. "I am so sorry, Mina. Here I am going on and on. This is *not* your first rodeo. I tell you, my memory is not what it used to be."

"No worries at all. I do have a question though—what about that trailer with the armed guards?"

"Authorized personnel only. I wasn't allowed a peek inside."

"Any idea why?"

"None. This way."

Genet's terse response left Mina on edge, but she pushed any apprehension aside and followed her towards the pasture.

The ground was soppy and tender as a blister. In the distance, a cadaverous scarecrow leaned at an odd angle. It was impaled on a creosote coated wooden pole, like a mythological resurrected deity. Figures moved around with purpose,

CID and pathologists on the hunt for more corpses. Human Recovery Dogs paced low to the ground, sniffing out the stench of death.

Dr. Genet raised a chin towards a structure in the distance. "There's the barn house. Fifty stalls, equestrian arena, chickens, cattle, all kinds of animals. All dead now. Starved to death. They let things go awhile back it seems.

"Their living quarters are all lined up over there. Solberg's laboratory is that one-story building closer to the forest. Lots of Feds turning everything over inside right now. You'll find the County Deputy Medical Investigator in there at this very moment. Deputy Maurice. Nice man, a bit stressed out at the moment. For obvious reasons."

They walked out further onto the field. The floodlights powered by the crime van's generator etched a stark silhouette of the scarecrow across the landscape like a paralyzed shadow puppet. Mina's boots sank into the muck with flatulent sounds. Her gaze swept the ground, instincts kicking in, examining the soil for any suggestive disturbances. Swollen patches of earth teased a potential gravesite; oddly clustered configurations of plant-life might mean a bounty of nitrogen below. Reflex observations. All too familiar.

They approached a furrow in the ground, deep enough for Mina to stand in and require help getting out. The trench ran for about 200 feet. Dark liquid glistened inside. Black bits in the stagnant waters reflected from the floodlight's glare like obsidian particles.

Dr. Genet stopped well before the lip of the trench. "Most of the corpses were found here. Just thrown in and left to rot. Or killed here. Scavengers dragged bits everywhere."

Mina nodded somberly. It was difficult to take in the entire scene.

"The cultists committed mass suicide in batches over the last month. Some of the bodies were found buried even deeper down in there; others in shallow graves nearby, a few left to the elements. The vic's wounds are varied: close range gunshots to the temple, skulls crushed by blunt force, strangulation, a few with slit throats."

Mina glanced to the sky, expecting rain. "Whatever happened to the days of peaceful mass poisonings?"

Dr. Genet laughed at the morbid joke. Gallows humor was part and parcel of their discipline. "Shame on them for making our job that much more difficult."

They'd all died outside, beneath the stars or sun, presumably to encourage nature to disperse the remains and hasten their return to the earth. Several burst clay pipes were visible above the ground. Rudimentary plumbing that'd failed long ago. A sluggish thick stream of sewage ran into the trench. Human waste covered everything, exacerbating decomposition, breaking down tissues into spoiled refuse.

Mina noticed that failed crops littered the ground like treasures crumbling to ruin. Blackened heads of lettuce and desiccated zucchini protruded from the soil as if impersonating fat, wrinkly worms. Gourds collapsed on themselves, bacteria devouring their insides, weakening vegetable walls. Solberg's property covered a vast area, but everything was now a sprawling landscape of mud and excrement and decay, both plant and human.

Mina looked out over the expanse of manure and waste. "I can't understand how anyone would do this. The Ones Who Walk Away had some strange beliefs, but some reasonable ones too. I'm no apologist, but some of their environmental talking points made sense. But this... I can't..."

Dr. Genet spoke quietly. "You've read their literature?"

"A few of Dr. Solberg's papers. Their website. Some articles. Bits of that one biography. And what's in the news of course."

Dr. Genet clapped her hands as if she were preparing for a long lecture. "They wanted to be a self-sufficient community, living alongside nature. Living off the grid. I'm not sure the Farm lived up to such grand ideals."

Mina made a sound of acknowledgement in the back of her throat. Genet took this as incentive to go on.

"Humanity had distanced themselves so much from the natural world, the destruction of the planet was always happening to the *other*, never a consequence for us. Dr. Karen Solberg saw herself as an ambassador between our species and *Nature*. That's capital 'N' Nature I'm talking about. An intermediary, someone who could make contact with Gaia to make amends, to reach a common ground, no pun intended. And if humans themselves were incapable of speaking the language of Nature, Dr. Solberg was determined to create something that could."

"So, she created The Ones Who Walk Away to help with this *communicating?*" Mina emphasized the last word as if it were a poor choice.

"I believe so. What I can gather is that they believed consciousness is an aberration, something unnatural. Souls are unique to humanity and mark us as *different*. Souls, a mind, whatever—it all makes us too deformed to fit into the natural world. Minds remove us from fitting in. To Dr. Solberg, well, that was a sin. She had to correct that flaw. So, she reached out to the only other thing she thought might have a mind as big as ours. Mother Nature herself."

Mina rubbed a temple with thumb and forefinger. "I can see where they're coming from. The anti-natalist stuff. A mind allows us to question our mortality. It lets us see how existing is suffering, so bringing new minds into this world is a guarantee that more lives are going to feel pain. Life fucks up everything."

Dr. Genet's eyes widened at the profanity, but she responded in a mock pedantic tone. "Now Mina, none of this makes much sense to me—humans *are* clearly part of this world. Of course, Nature is responsible for our predicament, our pain and longing for non-existence. Natural selection shaped our brains in such a way we have to run these agonizing questions over and over in our heads until we go mad or allow ourselves to be distracted by other things. Important things. Like TV and fast food."

Mina gave an amused expression. "I'll take distractions over going nuts any day."

Dogs barked in the distance, but Dr. Genet didn't seem to notice. "Here's how I see it, Mina: by condemning a mind that experiences suffering, by saying consciousness is terrible and unnatural, they appeal to a kind of nihilistic anthropocentrism. Anti-natalism is misanthropic *and* anthropocentric. It's a philosophy of—I'm not sure how to put it— solipsism? That's it. Solipsistic epistemology."

Mina had crammed as much information on Solberg's followers as she could before flying out here, but she still only knew the basics. Dr. Genet came across as a seasoned expert on the cult. When did she have the time to study and learn all of this?

The barking drew closer. A short, heavyset man ran behind two HRD canines bolting across the field, their leashes stretched taut. The hounds made a beeline for the scarecrow. Mina and Genet paused to watch the dogs excitedly howl and leap into the air before the weathered effigy.

"It's always the fanatics that cause the most harm." Mina said without looking away from the strange scene.

"Human beings are quite good at making up reasons for destroying others, hiding their justifications behind politics and philosophy and religion. My philosophy comes from seeing far more than I care to think about when it comes to genocide."

Mina didn't respond but watched the dogs frantically bay at the scarecrow. Their handler shouted something, but he was too far away and the dogs too loud to hear what was being said. The two anthropologists jogged over to see what the dogs had found.

The scarecrow was taller than it appeared to be from a distance. It wasn't lashed to the post in the typical cruciform pose, but clenched into a fetal posture, arms pulled to its chest, knees drawn to its stomach. The pugilist's position burn victims curl into at death.

A stained burlap sack with what appeared to be melted buttons for eyes did its best to pass for a head. The lumpy mass was soot covered, disproportionately large compared to the thin frame, sagging under its own weight. Straws of rotten hay poked out of a tear in the old panty hose neck.

Its shirt and pants were patchy from fire damage. A bulbous root vegetable dangled from the torn crotch of the old slacks, the cloth having rotted away long ago, zipper presumably lost beneath years of dirt. Rodents had gnawed holes into the vegetable phallus. The crass fertility offering must have been recently placed; though furred with black mold, it didn't look burnt like the rest of it. The whole thing stank of stale smoke.

"What the hell was wrong with these people." The HRD handler said with disgust. He spat a wad of phlegm onto the ground.

The dogs had dug up large mounds of dirt surrounding the pole before the handler managed to restrain them. Without the soil support, the scarecrow leaned so low its face was level with Mina's.

The mouth was a jagged slit, as if hastily slashed by a dull blade. Burlap sack fibers dangled from the opening. Mina thought it looked like an unkempt old man. There was an unsettling puffy aspect to the mouth, as if fluids had built up inside due to a healing injury. She thought of a stubborn geriatric hiding something in their mouth, pills they didn't want to swallow. There was definitely something in there.

Beneath its feet, in the hole created by the HRD dogs, were piles of gray, rotting meat. Mina had the discomfiting thought it'd been planted to encourage the scarecrow's growth.

"Holy shit. Is that human? You think it's human?" The handler's voice was panicky. The dogs started to howl again.

"No, I don't think so." Mina said. "The pathologists will be happy about that." A post-grad mantra reflexively ran through her head, *Freshly dead—call a pathologist. Rotten, charred, or skeletonized—call an anthropologist.*

She slipped on some latex gloves, then reached into the depression and picked up a slab of tissue. Moving more pieces aside, she uncovered hunks of flesh, steaks, and links. A mass of meat was exposed. Mina shoved the pile with both hands to reveal an entire hog's head.

The handler let out a whistle. "Thank Christ. These dogs are trained to ignore the scent of living things or other animals. Except pigs. They go ape-shit over pigs."

Mina stood, rolled her soiled gloves to her fingertips to avoid touching their exterior as she removed them. "Never expected anything like this."

"You've forgotten all about Kibuye already? Going down into that mineshaft full of bodies? By yourself if I remember correctly." Dr. Genet said.

Mina shook her head. "No. That's not something I'll ever forget."

"Remember when you tore the jaw off of that corpse to make it easier to read the dentition in the dark down there?"

"It was also the only way to get the Bicondylar Breadth, HMF, and—"

"Then you can expect this, and worse."

Genet turned her attention back to the deposits of meat. The handler struggled to keep his dogs under check as he waved a pair of Federal investigators over to the scene. He jabbed an index finger frantically at the scarecrow as if it were an immediate threat.

Mina had to act quickly. She forced her fingers into the scarecrow's swollen mouth. The opening tore into a wide grin. Inside, mushy gourd meat slopped over her hands, unnervingly warm, like compost generating its own heat. Maggots squirmed against her skin— a sensation she was all too familiar with. She wished she'd kept her gloves on.

Maneuvering her fingers against the inside of the plump cheek, she felt something the size of a pencil eraser. Hard, firmly planted. She glanced to her side—Dr. Genet was still engrossed with the mystery of the unearthed meat. The HRD handler was deep in conversation with the two agents.

Mina gripped the foreign object between thumb and forefinger and pulled with all her might. It was embedded deep inside, but after the second firm tug it wrenched free. A scattering of maggots fell out as she removed her hand. She brushed them off her arm, glanced back to make sure nobody was paying attention. Certain they hadn't noticed, she held the item up against the glare from the floodlights.

It was a lateral incisor. Mina's first thought was that the cult had planted dog teeth inside the scarecrow. Though canine carnassial teeth were easily mistaken as human she knew better; this was clearly not a dog's tooth. Thin wisps of skin were still attached to the root. The lateral incisor's layer of cementum, the connective tissue that binds its roots to the gums, hadn't rotted away yet.

This couldn't be. She'd misinterpreted something. Didn't have enough evidence to even guess what was going on here. The tooth had clearly erupted from the seeping dead vegetation of the scarecrow's head. Mina wasn't sure why, but she decided not to mention her find to anybody else. Confident nobody was aware of her discovery, she slipped the tooth into a pocket.

The two agents turned away from the HRD handler to approach Mina and Genet. They requested they leave the scene since the area needed to be secured.

The anthropologists retreated back to the DMORT tent. Dr. Genet gave a brief orientation to some other recent arrivals, and Mina quickly finished the remaining DMORT online paperwork before heading to the DPMU trailer to get started. On stepping inside, an escort immediately handed her a bag of badly decomposed cadaver parts before recording the information in the Victim Processing Records.

Later that evening, after Mina was well into her shift IDing bodies, Dr. Genet gave her the news. Preliminary lab tests run on the meat cache revealed that, as suspected, all of it was pork of some variety.

Mina thought about the tooth hidden in her pocket. She thought of Cadmus sowing dragon teeth, and the life that sprang from the ground like corrupt seeds.

She could make it through this without any drugs. She was strong. Even so, she couldn't help but wonder where she'd be able to buy some heroin in Moss Creek.

Mina shivered in the autumn air. She needed a drink after the 12-hour shift at the Farm. She was too riled up to stay in the hotel room. It had been good to work with Dr. Genet again, cathartic to plunge into the job as aggressively as she had. But the effort had beaten her down already. The scarecrows, buried meat, cadavers oozing with filth and bacteria, the weird tooth she'd dug out of the mouth—she was exhausted from the horrors. Digging through oatmeal-soft infant corpses, their ulna as small as wooden matchsticks, toe cartilage as fine as little grains of rice, could never be anything but tragic. It was all a nightmare that felt less real than her previous investigations. Day one and she'd already started to regret her decision to join the team. She'd been through it all before, but this one was far grimmer than she'd imagined it could be.

After her long day was done, she'd driven back to the seedy hotel, then walked into town to Old Joe Croaker's bar where she'd proceeded to drink herself into apathy. On the short stroll over, she'd counted five scarecrows total: three planted at the side of the road, another further back in the fields, and one high up in a Bigleaf Maple tree. The bright yellow leaves had nearly camouflaged the oddly plump scarecrow in its dingy ochre overalls and blond straw explosion of a head. But it was there. Beaming with a fake stitched grin at any who walked beneath its dangling feet.

She stepped outside Old Joe Croaker's to light up a cigarette. Someone turned on the TV inside, its audio hissing with static. She glanced back, saw three patrons still at the bar drinking, transfixed by what was playing on the set attached above the multi-colored bottles. The bartender's head leaned to the side, her gaze locked onto the screen. They were watching an old cannibal film, something exploitative and violent that would've played at the discount drive-in when Mina was a kid. Maybe it was the same film that was on her TV in the hotel when she'd first arrived.

The jittery scene of an obese man in a stained leather apron was reflected against the blank window of a store on the other side of the street. In the reflection, the fat man raised a tumor shiny with pus to his mouth. His fellow cannibals celebrated by waving red gobbets above their heads. They were all naked and slick with sweat. Rolls of neck blubber glistened. Their distended bellies jiggled in an obscene display of gluttony.

Near the bar's entrance, hidden in the shadows so Mina hadn't noticed her until now, a woman stood beneath the establishment's canopy. Her thin body was silhouetted against the piss-colored light leaking from a malfunctioning **OPEN** sign. A cigarette etched trails in the dark. Her head was at such an angle Mina could tell she was watching the movie as well.

"This part is so fucking gross." The woman said, her voice indicating she was quite young.

"I think I saw it once. Many years ago. Don't remember the name." Mina replied.

"It's called *Unholy Appetite*. Ancient horror film, like the 80s ancient." The hand holding the cigarette paused. An acne pocked face lowered. Lips touched the tan filter. She inhaled, her features illuminated. Mina could see her freshly shaved Chelsea cut. The width of her forehead and upper lip reminded her of someone she'd once known, but she couldn't quite remember a name. She looked far too young to have been allowed in the bar. No older than 14. Mina waved an unlit cigarette in silent communication at she-who-looked-familiar. She didn't notice.

Mina waved again, more emphatically this time. The girl tore her attention from the movie, stretched a thin arm spotted with tiny, scabby craters towards her. Her nails had been bitten short, cuticles inflamed and red. **88** and **14** were tattooed across the knuckles of her right hand.

A lighter sputtered, ignited. Mina took advantage of the offered flame. "What's your name?" the girl asked.

"Mina Fawn. Good to meet you..." she raised an eyebrow to indicate it was a question.

"Amber."

In the distance, further up the road, Mina saw a scarecrow she hadn't noticed. They were everywhere in these parts, but this one startled her. It couldn't have just sprouted from the ground.

"You with the cops looking into that suicide cult?" Amber asked.

Not a suicide cult, an anti-natalist human extinction environmentalist movement, Mina silently corrected Amber. The Medical Examiner had insisted that none of them were to talk about what they'd found on the Farm so far. Not to the media, no family members, and certainly no strangers outside of bars. "I suppose I am involved. But I'm no cop."

"FBI?"

Mina could smell the girl now. Alcohol, salt, nicotine, the sour tang of dried vomit.

"No. And not a reporter either."

The scarecrow up the road started to move.

Probably just a tipsy resident clumsily making their way home after a night out. She was jumping at the sight of rednecks and hill Bettys.

"New people around. Figure it's the media and Feds, 'cause they were up at Omelas Farm." Amber spewed smoke in the direction of the Farm.

"Omelas Farm." Mina repeated without elaborating.

Mina watched the figure stumble along the road. A trick of the dim light strained through an overcast sky made it appear as if the drunk was painfully thin. They were wearing a wide-brimmed hat, like something a farmer would put on in the field for protection from the sun.

"Heard they even found kids. Imagine that. Killing babies." Amber said.

Mina had imagined this and worse. Lived this and worse. "Where'd you hear that?"

Amber shrugged.

Mina didn't understand why an anti-natalist cult would include kids. She didn't understand why *anyone* would have kids, no matter what strange faith they'd dedicated their lives to.

As awful as it was to even contemplate, there *was* something to be said for those who wanted to put a loved one out of their misery. How many mothers have looked their children in the eyes as they strangled them in hopes of ending any chance of pain? How many fathers have held their dying child after cracking the back of their head open with a hammer? How many were certain theirs wasn't a violent act, but of kindness, a loving gesture to escape this malignant existence? All of this was immoral of course; killing wasn't the answer. The only certain answer was to never have kids.

It wasn't a difficult decision for Mina. Motherhood was an alien concept. She couldn't imagine living with the perpetual anxiety of caring for one of her own, every waking moment spent agonizing about their well-being. A lifetime of fearing that cancerous cells were mutating in their little bodies; constantly worried that every outing, every sleepover, every trip to the store increased the chances they'd suffer an injury, an assault, abduction or rape.

How could parents stomach the possibility that someone they loved so much could be damaged or taken away forever? Best to avoid the risk in its entirety. Birth was immoral. A callous display of selfishness and cruelty dictated by a genetic program.

Amber broke the silence. "I grew up here."

Mina took a satisfying drag on her cigarette. "Pretty area. Could've grown up somewhere worse."

"Where's that?"

"What?"

"Where's a worse place?"

Mina took a moment to flick ash into the night. "You know. Rough places."

"I know rough."

Mina didn't respond. Amber continued anyway. "Dad raised me after mom died. He was rough."

"Moss Creek seems quaint. Really pretty." Mina said, hoping to steer things away from further awkwardness.

"I got the good blood." Amber said.

Forehead wrinkled in consternation, Mina asked, "What do you mean?"

"I got the blood of white heritage. Strong blood, my daddy says."

Mina shook her head, dropped the cigarette butt onto the ground. It was just her luck to meet up with a white trash supremacist. And a child at that. She changed the subject.

"What do you know about Omelas Farm?"

Amber sounded disinterested. "Environmentalist weirdoes. Worshipped nature or some shit. I used to go up there. They had a good farmer's market. We'd get corn, and tomatoes. When I was little."

"How many months ago was that?" Mina's joke didn't elicit a reaction.

Amber raised her face to the sky. Her voice became dreamy, far away.

"My grandparents used to take me to the Farm every October when I was a little kid. I wanted the perfect Halloween pumpkin, and they always had one. Of course, there were markets near us in the city selling Halloween shit for the season, but the long drive, along these gravel roads that turned to dirt before ending at the farm, was worth it."

She paused, lowered her gaze towards the dark mountains. Her voice slipped down somewhere faint and wistful, as if channeling someone far more mature and nostalgic than she could ever be,

"The Autumn countryside was beautiful, the grasses a bright green. Ponds were mirrors reflecting forests. Leaves so scarlet and orange I thought the treetops were on fire.

"There were scarecrows everywhere. Up and down the road, deep back into the dark forest where you could only catch a glimpse of their sackcloth heads from the car window. Scarecrows have always been here. Part of the town's culture. Old roots.

"Omelas Farm had a petting zoo back then. With goats and rabbits and horses. There was a corn maze. Jack-o'-lanterns carved from pumpkins and squash and corn, messed up Halloween faces cut into them. A tractor ride through the fields, past all these creepy looking scarecrows dressed as hobos and clowns and cowboys.

"The scarecrows bothered me. They looked like dirty old men. All beat the fuck up. I could smell them. Like bad breath, or something that crawled under the porch and died down there during the summer.

"They had teeth. Grandma used to joke and say they had my grandpa's dentures. I didn't think it was funny then."

Mina looked Amber up and down, from buzz cut scalp to white-laced Doc Martens. She studied Amber's arms, the damaged veins, the map of abuse.

"Can you hook me up?" Mina asked.

Amber snapped out of her reverie. She hesitated, not sure she'd heard Mina correctly. "You fuckin' serious?"

"Very fuckin' serious."

"Didn't know Feds were addicts."

"I'm not a Fed."

"You sure?"

"Yes. I'm also not an addict."

"Sure. Crank? Mud?"

"The second one." Mina said, handing her a 20-dollar bill.

Amber looked over the money as if it were foreign currency, but quickly decided it was good. "Sure you're not a cop?"

"Positive."

"I'll be back."

Amber walked away at a brisk pace. She circled around Old Joe Croaker's, then entered through a back door behind the building. A few moments passed before Mina could see Amber speaking with the bartender. Mina looked up the street while she waited.

The drunk was gone. There was nobody on the path.

(cont.)

Piglet specimens were washed in soaps typically utilized for infants (Johnson's Baby Shampoo). The carcasses were dressed in children's clothing, each wrapped in an identical 4 x 3ft purple cotton blanket, since blankets are commonly employed to hide a body in child homicide cases (Koph 2007).

The carcasses were buried in shallow graves at various isolated wooded locations; the depth (approx. 10-inches), temperature(s), soil matrix, and geographies carefully recorded. The aerobic decomposition processes of the piglets were systematically tracked over a 12-month duration. As hypothesized, scavengers and insects, specifically Phormia regina and Lucilia illustris, favored soft tissues. As previous studies have attested, open wounds, anus, eyes, mouth, ears, and genitals were the first to show decomposition damage (see Hogue 2000: 134-205).

Mina held the child's head beneath the running faucet.

I won't hurt you.

She used a soft toothbrush to scrub the decayed skull. Chemical-macerated skin slid from butter-yellow bone. Water streamed steadily. Foul smelling liquid thin as diarrhea snaked down the stainless-steel sink drain. Mina's breath was unpleasantly warm and sticky every time she exhaled against her surgical mask.

Her hands were ice cold inside thin rubber gloves. Tyvek suit clammy against her arms, cadaver fluids trailed down the polyethylene surface in rivulets. She touched the child's head as if it were a hollow egg. Hairline cracks attested to its rare and delicate nature. Its mass was minimal, yet substantial in her palms. A weight that spoke of lost love, lost potential.

I won't hurt you.

A container next to her elbow brimmed with water-diluted Greased Lightning. The soap was degreasing a child's scapula. Though maceration techniques varied, and some forensic scientists used boiling liquid to remove rotten flesh and muscle, Mina preferred Greased Lightning. The detergent broke down any remaining tissue, scoured bodies free of meat, provided an unobstructed view of bone for meticulous observation.

All of the remains so far had been found without a head. And when heads had been found, the rest of the body was absent. Puzzle pieces. Segments. Fragments of humanity.

Fragments of a god that has committed suicide.

What was that from? Mina thought it might be Mainländer. Or was it Cioran? Philosophy had never been her strong suit. Apparently, it was Dr. Genet's though. She'd ask her later.

Two days in and Mina had been unable to reconstruct the entirety of any one corpse. The children's heads didn't belong with the bodies; the baby bodies didn't match the heads. She couldn't fathom why. Scavenger activity was certainly a factor, but she'd never seen anything so *thorough.*

Statistically speaking, she should have been able to connect at least one head with its body by now. It was odd, a seemingly intentional confusion of the scene of the crime, like an intelligence had gone out of its way to obscure the aftermath of these children's deaths. Despite the disinfectant sprays and cool interior, the stink of fetid human flesh was thick in the mobile morgue. A tree branch bobbed in the increasing wind, tapped a mysterious tune against the roof.

She held the reason she'd never have a baby in her hands. Some women acted as if they were hardwired to coddle a newborn, to calm shrieking infants with kisses and soft words. Too many in Mina's life dedicated every precious moment they had on this planet to raising children. Mina had no interest in that. Children were not in her future.

She glanced over a shoulder. Why hadn't she noticed how rusty the faucets were? How warped the autopsy trays appeared to be? The trailer was brand new—how could this be? The pathologists' greasy skin, trickles of unctuous sweat on brows, sagging bags under eyes, puffy and purple with blood—how drained everyone looked as they went about their tasks. How could she possibly have failed to notice any of this before?

Was the guarded trailer this run down? Mina didn't like to obsess on that thought. She watched her co-workers, their expressions rigid with concentration as the shrill whine of bone saws filled the air. The disorder of people yelling, trying to get someone's attention as they were handed another folder with information inside that should match each new bag of jumbled human scraps introduced. A radio played the Carter Family song, "Will You Miss Me When I'm Gone?". The tune was muffled by the frenetic activity.

I'm somewhere else.

The air reeled around Mina's head. A suffocating panic. She steadied her breathing to keep from hyperventilating and tasting the foul air. A rich, organic scummy layer like cold fat permeated the unit's interior.

She shouldn't be here. She inhaled.

Warm water and detergent.

She was still in the mobile unit, surrounded by rotting corpses and the hustle and bustle of DMORT professionals at work. She'd only imagined the rusty sinks. The odor of decomposition stayed with her always. She fell asleep with corruption in her nose and mouth. Every night.

Every night.

The small mastoid process, mental eminence, and thin bone density meant this was likely a young girl's skull. Skull sutures, vault closure. A child. Large aviator eyeglass-sized sockets and pronounced nasal region. Likely European ancestry. Applying the Buikstra-Ubelaker standard, Mina assigned numeric values to the 17 suture sites. Her estimate meant they were in the 6 to 8 years of age range, but she had to make an informed assumption absent the entirety of the child's skeleton. Running the skull's measurements through

FORDISC would further clarify the details. Later, she'd enter the data into her laptop and submit the information.

The skull was nothing, a trivial thing, hollow in Mina's grip.

A child.

Where had the rest of her body disappeared to?

Mina had yet to see anybody enter or leave the off-limits trailer. She stood on the outskirts of the pasture, the heavily guarded trailer behind her like a looming beast feigning sleep. Investigators roamed around the field, their flashlight beams skimming across the ground like luminous skipping stones. She wanted to take a moment to collect her thoughts before driving back to the hotel. A minute to mull over what could have happened to the child's body.

I am deformed.

This came out of nowhere, simmered in her head angrily. She'd never felt more satisfied or accomplished than when she was scrutinizing bones. Sussing out the history of the muscle and flesh built upon that osteological foundation was what she lived for. This is what brought her something nearing contentment—the intimate details of a wasted life etched out in their remains like a secret language spoken in biological scrimshaw. But even that had become something to dread as of late. Her soul was battered, any hope of joy fading like breath on a mirror.

Movement caught her eye. The sun had set long ago, but the heap of hay bales where thick grass met mossy forest floor stood out. It looked like a fort, something a child had stacked up to play on and in. The interior was so black there must have been something crouched inside, blocking the spillover glare from a Remote Area Light unit. A dark shape contrasted against the gray, rotten hay, nestled in its domicile.

What kind of animal could be living in there? Mina didn't like to acknowledge that the fort looked big enough for something grotesquely tall to stretch out within. The two objects jutting out of the opening were most certainly abandoned pitchforks and not spindly limbs.

"Mina?"

Startled, she turned abruptly. Daria had walked up to her without making a sound. The pathologist's expression was beleaguered, eyes wide and frantic like a stunned doe.

"Got a minute?" Daria asked.

"I was about to call it a day."

"Same here. It'll just be a minute." Daria looked nervous.

"Go ahead." Mina tried to sound interested, though she wanted to be anywhere else but at the Farm.

"The FBI is afraid there's something really wrong here. I mean more wrong than a fucking mass suicide."

Mina almost confessed about the tooth she still had on her person but thought better of it. What did it prove? What did it even suggest? Let Daria divulge what was bothering her. Maybe she had information that would help her decide her next move.

"More wrong?"

Daria's speech sped up, her hands trembled as she held them before her. "Yeah, *more wrong*. It's not something I can really put my finger on. Nothing I can describe or make sense of. "

Mina was growing impatient but thought of the weird tooth again.

"Give it a try."

"There's something in Dr. Solberg's lab."

"Like what?"

"Scientific equipment, a fully working lab." Daria looked over a shoulder.

"That's no secret. Dr. Genet mentioned the same thing to me when she was giving the grand tour."

"Did she tell you Solberg left handwritten notes behind? Did she mention that Solberg was also too paranoid to trust a computer?"

"That's news to me."

"Hand-drawn formulas, blueprints, engineering stuff. It looked like designs for something organic. Biomolecules, but unnatural. Along the lines of mycoplasma laboratorium, but plastic cells." Daria spoke low, as if afraid someone was listening in.

Mina shrugged. "She was a biologist. She'd written dozens of papers on origin of life stuff. It was kind of what she was known for."

"This is different. They were synthetic bioreactors, something along those lines. It looked wrong. They were *deformed* cells."

"Deformed?"

"Hybrids. Intermediate forms. I'm no biologist, but..." Daria's voice trailed off. She lowered her gaze to the ground.

Why was Daria confiding in her? This was all too conspiratorial, too weird to be anything real. A bunch of suicidal fanatics followed through on their calling and Mina had been called in to help clean up and make sure next of kin could be notified. Their loved ones had been involved in a fucked-up cult, and DMORT was there to smooth everything over until another tragedy inevitably came along.

Mina looked out across the field. Daria had clearly been investigating the underbelly of whatever was going on here, so she might be the only one who could answer her question.

"Daria, why does that mobile lab have guards with that kind of firepower? What are they hiding?"

Daria began to make strange sounds, low and deep. Not crying, but a strangled panicky wheezing. Mina was transfixed by a translucent string of mucous that ran from her upper lip to cheek. She wasn't comfortable with people expressing their emotions in such a raw, uninhibited manner, so she waited patiently for Daria to regain her composure.

When Daria recovered from her panic attack, she said, "Nobody will tell you, Mina, and I won't say how I found out. It doesn't matter since I don't understand exactly what's going on."

"What is it, Daria?"

"They haven't found Dr. Solberg's body yet. There are rumors she's still out there somewhere."

"Do you mean alive? Or that her corpse is somewhere on the Farm?"

Daria started laughing. A hysterical, desperate laugh.

"Both."

"You're not making any goddamn sense, Daria. What's in the trailer?"

"They found something wrong with the scarecrows."

Deformed.

Outside Old Joe Croaker's bar, Mina thought about what Daria had told her. Solberg was dead. They'd find her soon enough. What did Daria mean by saying the scarecrows were *wrong?* No bodies had been found in any of them, and as far as she knew, the lateral incisor safe in her pocket was the only anomaly discovered.

That trailer held the answer. She was certain of this.

Amber stood at her side, a cigarette hanging from her lips.

"You're an anthropologist, right? You study African tribes, cannibalism, shit like that?" Amber looked to Mina expectantly.

Mina clenched her jaw in annoyance. "I'm not going to bother explaining just how racist that is, and I'm not-"

"You're smart," Amber interrupted, "probably know all about this cult. Explain it to me. What they believed in."

Mina had to be back at Omelas Farm by 7 a.m. She was too tired and stressed to deal with this pathetic girl. They weren't friends. She was a drug contact. Nothing more. She closed her eyes, thought about her bed in the shitty hotel. But Old Joe Croaker's was open until 2 a.m., and she meant to take advantage of the town's flexible liquor laws and the one reliable heroin contact she had in this redneck town.

"It's complicated," Mina said.

Amber nodded, spoke softly, "My mom was one of the people who killed themselves at the Farm."

"I'm sorry. Why didn't you mention this before?"

Amber looked away from Mina, her voice wavered with emotion,

"Because she will be more useful in death than I could ever be in life."

"Who told you that?"

"She did. In a dream."

Mina wondered if her own parents were still alive somewhere in Korea. If so, did they ever think of their daughter? Or was she a memory lost to decay? She couldn't feign sorrow, couldn't pretend to care about Amber or her parents. Everything was transitional. The world was amorphous. Everyone changed depending on their own selfish desires. Nothing you do in childhood has any reverberations. But bones were a permanent reminder of what you were. This brought Mina a sliver of contentment.

"A dream?" Mina asked after the long silence.

"I dreamt my mother's head was floating through space. She sang to me."

Mina inadvertently gasped, but it was quiet enough to disguise by clearing her throat.

Amber looked to the sky. "Oh God, we're all wearing clay masks," she whispered.

Mina had no idea what she was talking about. She said nothing but handed Amber two tens in exchange for the heroin. Amber tearfully gave her the bindle. She said something as Mina began the short walk back to the hotel, but she didn't hear what it was.

Mina's clay mask stiffened.

That couldn't be right.

A leaky faucet dripped. The sound was slushy and sickening, yet strangely piercing. One of the pathologists made a ghoulish joke to break the tension,

How much burnt skin can you stuff into a trash bag?

Mina stood at her station, pushed thumbs against the skull's smooth supraorbital ridge. Dead flesh slipped away.

I don't know, but if you find out, notify their parents.

She didn't get it. It wasn't even a real joke.

Probably heard it incorrectly. She didn't understand why a few of the others were laughing. It was not funny.

She rolled a flap of gray skin away with a gloved thumb. Pliable tissue peeled. A sensual act. A subversive thrill tingled through her.

Dr. Genet was still talking about The Ones Who Walk Away's philosophy, as if their conversation in the field had never stopped. Mina had no sense of continuity, no anchor on when this discussion had actually started. It may have been moments ago. It may have been days before.

"It's all about avoiding suffering. It's impossible to define what is and what isn't an acceptable degree of suffering. Without establishing that foundation the argument collapses. Anti-natalism is the philosophy of the privileged. How much inconvenience can I experience before I can justify condemning it as suffering? Being born without limbs and in constant pain? Burning your lips on a hot cappuccino?"

Laughter.

Caresses sloughed off decay and ruined skin. Sticky fat clumped into globules, rolled away under Mina's fingertips. A tender touch, a toothbrush across cheese-soft flesh revealed more of the damaged skull. A blemish of damage ran across the Metopic suture like jagged faults across a pale plain.

The outer bone table and diploë was intact, but a nickel-sized bone plug of the inner table had been knocked loose. The child had been killed by a blunt force impact to the parietal foramen.

A broom handle's tip. Maybe a ball-peen hammer. There were many options available to inflict damage.

A map of abuse.

A world of violence beneath a placid facade.

"Or maybe even not knowing who your real mother is?"

Had Dr. Genet actually said that? Or was Mina hearing things?

Somebody laughed, a shrill, deranged sound.

She focused on the skull in her hands. Putrid soil clumped against the occipital orb loosened, trickled through the pitted bone.

"*Mortui Vivos Docent*, right Mina?" Dr. Genet gave an enthusiastic thumbs up.

Mina hesitated, nodded because she had no idea what that meant. "What's wrong with the scarecrows?" she said quietly.

But Dr. Genet didn't hear her.

"Shift is up, Mina. We need you to be roaring to go first thing tomorrow morning. Go back to your room. Get a few winks."

Roaring to go. What did that mean? Mina mumbled *what's wrong with the scarecrows*, again, but everybody pretended not to hear her. She closed her eyes and wished she were somewhere else.

She wished she were nowhere.

It's not funny.

A small clot of dirt fell onto her palm. She rubbed it vigorously. The soil dissipated under the water, revealing a tooth that look like a small seashell. She delicately rolled it between thumb and forefinger.

It was a lateral incisor.

Tourniquet tight around her bicep. Wrist veins plump. Mina flagged the sterilized needle, injected. Finished, she sealed the syringe in a biohazard bag taken from the pathology lab, then pressed a warm compress against the injection site to reduce bruising. Her head rested against the pillow.

The drug's crystals transformed into molten caramel once it hit her bloodstream. It coated her muscles with luxuriant filth. Sweet blood sluggish with dope, veins pleasantly gummed up with a contentment surpassing all else. She slumped on the hotel bed, mind drifting to the off-limits trailer.

What were they hiding in there?

Her phone vibrated. It was the head pathologist, Dr. Baker. She instinctively answered, wincing at the reflex.

"Mina? Mina Fawn? Tim Baker here."

"Yes?"

"Sorry to call you. Didn't have time to talk to you earlier so I wanted to get ahold of you ASAP. Got a minute?"

"I just got back to my room." Her voice was thick and syrupy.

"Oh, ok. Would you prefer to call me back when you've time?"

"No. Go ahead."

"Good, good. I saw you CCd me on an e-mail you sent with the craniometric case data folder attached."

"Uh huh, right."

"That data on the remains you were working on, the one you e- mailed to the FDB? The FORDISC info'?"

"Yeah. I gave all my findings and reports to the duty pathologist."

"I'm toggling through the, uh, let's see: Howells measurements, Post-cranial, VCMs. Let's see if I run a query on that..." Dr. Baker hummed an atonal sound, deep in thought. A minute passed before he spoke up.

"I'm confused, Mina. There must be some data corruption. Or a mistake."

"A mistake?"

"The data you sent was for a child."

"That's correct."

"Children's measurements?"

"Yes. I meant to run that query."

"But Mina, there haven't been any children found on Omelas Farm."

The children's corpses were in the guarded trailer.

Mina was as certain of this as she'd been of anything in her life. She'd no idea why they were hiding this from her. What was the purpose? Nobody came or went from that trailer. What was their *plan*? All she was certain of was that she'd chemically macerated a child's remains.

She'd held a young girl's skull in her hands.

At 3 a.m., the drive back to Omelas Farm was quiet and lonely. Her heroin high had peaked, was now subsiding. The car's headlights caught frozen moments of activity in the darkness. Foliage shook from a shape bounding into the woods, tree branches undulated from something that had just dropped to the ground.

Wildlife active at night. Her headlights passed over a scarecrow. The twitchy shadows made it appear as if it struggled against the posts holding it in place.

She dialed Dr. Genet's cell phone but kept getting her voicemail. She didn't leave a message. She'd known more than she'd let on. Mina was certain of this. But she was alone now. She had to accept that she'd always been alone. There was nobody to keep any lost soul company in this life.

The overnight guard allowed her access to the Farm with a cursory glance at her badge. She parked in her assigned spot. There were fewer people around this early in the morning, but any DMORT assignment was a 24/7 operation. She did her best to avoid eye contact with those she encountered.

She moved quickly to the trailer she'd been working in the last few days. Five pathologists were inside, their surgical masks and head coverings obscured their identities. One looked up as Mina entered, then disinterestedly returned to their work.

"Is Dr. Baker around?"

None of them spoke, but they shook their heads in unison as if it were a practiced response.

"Dr. Genet?"

Again, they shared the coordinated headshake.

Mina stepped outside. A stick-thin figure darted from the woods towards the field. She assumed it was a Federal agent. He leaned into his run so far, his upper body appeared far more elongated than was humanly possible.

The night air felt soft in her mouth. Her head was fuzzy, viscid with anxiety and confusion. She heard the nocturnal hum of insects. Fog as pale as congealed fat crept along the ground. Nearing the mysterious third refrigerated unit, she heard its diesel generator humming softly. There were now only two guards at the entrance.

She veered away, made a wide circle towards the back of the trailer. Judging by the violent sound of snapping branches, a deer had been surprised by the skinny agent in the woods.

The units were all windowless, but Mina thought there might be another way inside. She checked the vents, but it was a state-of-the-art refrigerated model built to keep its contents protected, and the outside environment away.

Another person was running around in the woods.

But nobody burst out of the forest. No cops or guards came down on her. Whoever it was out there must have shifted away from the trailers. She looked over the exterior. There was no way she was going to sneak in through an opening, no matter how large. Maybe if she distracted the guards at the front, lured them away for a minute, she could sneak past and...

What was she doing here?

This was ridiculous. She was never going to break into the trailer. She was acting paranoid, delusional.

She suddenly flashed back to Kibuye. Hanging over the mine's narrow entrance, shaft dropping into blackness below. Stench of death wafting upwards. She remembered the little girl whose baby sister's body was down there.

The child stood next to the opening, silent and morose, a heartbreakingly hopeful expression on her face. She didn't understand. A child couldn't comprehend why someone would rape then chop the limbs off of a baby sister no matter how much they begged their captors, or how many *amafarangas* they offered to spare them. There was simply no room in their developing brains to accept such atrocities as commonplace. It took time and experience to become accustomed to just how dismal it was to be alive on this planet.

Mina realized she had dried blood under her fingernails. Her fingertips were black as pitch in the subdued light. *How could this be?* The night was a thick black foam. She looked up. The scattered stars looked like phosphorescent maggots crawling across the gas-burst belly of a decomposing sky.

Something strode out of the woods. It was so tall its upper body swayed unsteadily. Shabbily dressed, its wide brimmed hat blocked the light from the trailer.

Something skipped a beat in Mina's mind, like a cog breaking its teeth. She was so cold. A dizzying nausea suffused her body, rancid as brackish water. A vinegar sting filled her stomach, touched the back of her throat.

An umbilical of veined, gray organs trailed from the thing's abdomen across the forest floor. The mass dragged behind as it took long strides towards her. Conifer needles and leaves stuck to the umbilical's sticky, wet surface.

Coarse hands pressed against Mina's face. They must have been wearing rotten gloves, rough as burlap. Glimpsing the dark forest between its fingers, the trees looked scratched and damaged through Mina's eyes, reminiscent of an old film that hadn't been restored. The branches wiggled madly in the night air, like hairs in the gate.

The thing pressed its entire body against her, its torso pulpy as mulch. Its form degenerated further, loosening into the texture of slop, filling Mina's throat and lungs with mud. Rich and creamy as colostrum, the dirt broth gurgled through her veins. Omelas Farm mud, putrid and life sustaining.

I won't hurt you, the shape said.

(cont.)

As the results demonstrate below, this experiment supports further research employing similar materials and methods, but with a larger sample size. Another benefit of the following study is the volatile organic compound (VOC) scent profile measurements to aid in locating the deceased (see Tejeda 2004).

Additional assessments of the PMI are warranted and could offer an extensive database to create a template of comparison for infant decay calculations. By utilizing piglets as surrogate cadavers, an accurate compilation of children's decomposition rates may be better attained. Further detailed information may aid urban search and rescue (USAR) missions following mass disasters.

Mina dreamt the ground was full of burrows.

Naked cultists wriggled through the tight tunnels. None of them had heads. They writhed in a blind attempt to escape. The passages were foul with the stench of urine. Mud dripped from the slimy walls in gummy clods. When the cultists reached a densely packed patch of dirt, they vomited from their neck holes, then rolled around in the regurgitation to slicken their bare bodies. Their spew loosened the soil, transformed it into a soft stew. They squirmed, bodies frictionless from stomach juices.

Mina could hear their heads crying from the center of the Earth.

One cultist's head broke from the pack and moved upwards. It burst through the effluvium moist soil to the surface. Its mouth opened and closed, gasping for air. Mina recognized Dr. Solberg's face. Her worm-eaten eye sockets shimmered with intensity. The mangled mouth fell open, her words sloppy with mud,

A mass grave is defined as having at least six individuals in it!

Mina woke, her vision cloudy. She blinked, but it was like trying to peer through a grease-obscured window after spitting on it and wiping away the mucous. Everything was a repellent blur.

She knew she was inside the mysterious trailer. This was inevitable. This is where she was meant to be. Her eyesight gradually returned. A dozen body bag occupied gurneys were parked at odd angles, dispersed about the trailer haphazardly. A scarecrow lay on the gurney next to her.

She was holding a human skull. Its weight, brow ridge, and jawline convinced her that it was Amber's.

The skull felt spongy. Tingled with sickness. Vibrated with perversity and filth. It moved in her hands. It was now a 7-year-old girl's skull. It belonged to the child she'd found in the hallway years ago, the one whose baby sister was stabbed to death by a hypodermic needle and set on fire. The one she'd stolen the heroin from.

The walls of the trailer were black from years of filth. Rotten juices festered in small coagulated pools on the floor of the stiflingly hot mobile unit. How had it deteriorated so quickly? The units were as close to sterile as was humanly possible and had only been set up here days ago.

Mina knew that the body bags contained scarecrows.

Her brain was heroin damaged. This wasn't really happening. The skull shifted in her hands.

Suddenly, she thought it might be her own skull. Surprised, she dropped it to the floor with a clatter. It rattled away and vanished into a dark corner.

The scarecrow on the gurney next to her had its torso split open, from lower neck to pubis symphysis. The burlap flaps lay in rotten triangles at its sides, fragrant with corruption. The contours of the expertly performed incision were lined with fungus-black straw. Pale spores rose from moldy growths inside, like pinprick lanterns caught on diseased winds. Mina noticed her own forearms were tacky with blood, hands mottled with decay.

The effigy felt warm. Viscous fluids sloshed inside the torso cavity. Mina prayed it was her trembling hands on the gurney that caused the agitation. There was something deep within.

She reached inside. The scarecrow's biology was comprised of shit, compacted dirt, spoiled plant life. A rudimentary reproductive system.

Leaning further, she pushed into the opening of what she now knew to be a womb. Her fingers touched something sticky with sebaceous gland secretions.

Was her mother an old woman now, sitting in a Dobongsan church wondering why her long lost daughter had never tried to contact her?

Holding her breath, she closed her eyes and saw a massive head drifting through space. The Earth's faults were Squamous sutures. Tectonic plates shifted, temporal bone drifted away from parietal bone. All of life began 4 billion years ago on the surface of a decomposing planet.

She felt such peace at this revelation, such love at the thought, she was now able to accept dying here. For what is the point of anything if not love?

Love is the putrefaction that ruins your darling's lips. Love is clasped hands, heads resting on a friend's shoulder, unrestrained laughter, moonlight on bone.

Are they going to find my skull on Omelas Farm, deep beneath layers of cow patties and human shit and mud? Will they find my remains commingled with the other cult suicide victims?

Something kicked inside the scarecrow. Mina didn't remove her hands.

To see a universe in the gentle symmetry of a loved one's sleepy smile. The grandeur of a loving cosmos in a maggoty grin. The light emanating from behind a dead child's thin eyelids, flickering with the pulse of wonders to come.

That is true beauty.

It made sense now. The universe wasn't apathetic. The universe cared. It just didn't give the kind, benevolent attention we want. This charnel World interacts with us in a bloom of light, in a kiss and a fang, in a song and a whimper. This hateful life is a caress against innocent bloated faces. Nature blunders like a drunk groping a whore in an alley. Her eyes are moonlight reflecting from puddles of piss. But She cares. She cares dearly. Nature saw to it that there are far more bacteria on Earth than stars in the universe. She dearly loves her fungi, viruses, prions, and the glorious symphony of decomposition. These are Her greatest Works. These are Her children. This is what she cares for.

I did not become who I imagined I'd be. I'm a disappointment. I'm deformed.

Nature pretends. Nature deceives. Life's an epidemic. A voracious worm devouring all. Faith is insisting this deterioration will lead to a pious awakening.

But to create something exquisite, something of worth from this cesspool—is there no proportion of suffering that justifies the possibility of happiness? Any degree of agony to make all of this worthwhile?

Omone, I wanted to find you mother, but I never made the effort.

Mina lifted a pig fetus from the scarecrow's odorous womb. The piglet was still draped in a fetid swatch of a pale blue blanket. Tatters dangled from its gas-bloated body. The rest of the blanket dropped inside the scarecrow. Her face felt loose, liquid moving beneath her skin like a hot water bottle whose rubber had worn thin. Blood pooled between skin and bone. Her skull swelled. She thought about Dr. Solberg's head tumbling through space in an eternal ballet of rot.

I am striving for purpose. I am trying to see some worth in being alive, but failing.
I am trying.

All of Creation was suffused with a putrescent, terrible love. A World of failed flesh, and the beauty of dilapidated faces.

A World radiant with wretched loveliness.

I am trying.

The stars secreted milky waste, trailing into space like corpse hair in water. The purulence leaked over Moss Creek, coating it in a contaminated shade.

It was early in the morning. Everyone was at home sleeping in their beds. Children curled against their parents for protection, guests stretched out on couches, or in the front seats of trucks after a drunken argument with a lover.

Far away, in the North Jeolia Province of South Korea, in the city of Namwon, an elderly woman went to bed early. Her husband died long ago. She kept an old, faded Lotte Ghana box on the pillow where he used to lay his head. The open window let the night sky in.

A photo of Mina when she was just days old was tucked inside the Lotte Ghana box. A neatly folded bundle of newborn clothes wrapped around a lock of Mina's baby hair was next to it. A loop of red thread held the tress together.

The lonely old woman slept beneath extinguished stars. Their polluted dying light poisoned her dreams.

I am deformed, the old woman mumbled in her sleep.

Mina's rotten head floated high above the Earth. The dead satellite spun slowly. Pearls of adipocere wax dribbled from the crust of her smiling face and burned on entering the mesosphere.

ABOUT THE AUTHOR

Christopher Slatsky's stories have appeared in *Shadows &
Tall Trees, Year's Best Weird Fiction, Vastarien: A Literary Journal,*
and elsewhere. His debut collection, *Alectryomancer and Other
Weird Tales* (Dunhams Manor Press), was released summer of
2015. He currently resides in Los Angeles.

PUBLICATION CREDITS

"Affirmation of the Spirit: Consciousness, Transformation, and the Fourth World in Film" copyright © 2018, first appeared in *Vastarien* Vol. 1, Issue 1, eds. Matt Cardin and Jon Padgett

"The Anthroparian Integration Technique" copyright © 2017, first appeared in *Walk on the Weird Side*, ed. By Joseph S. Pulver

"The Carcass of the Lion" copyright © 2017, first appeared in *Darker Companions*, eds. Scott David Aniolowski and Joseph S. Pulver

"Devil Gonna Catch You in the Corners" copyright © 2016, first appeared in *Strange Aeons Magazine #20*

"Engines of the Ocean" copyright © 2017, first appeared in *Shadows & Tall Trees #7*, ed. Michael Kelly

"The Figurine" copyright © 2019, first appeared in *Horror for RAICES*, eds. Jennifer Wilson and Robert S. Wilson

"From a People of Strange Language" copyright © 2017, first appeared as a chapbook from Dunhams Manor Press

"The Immeasurable Corpse of Nature" copyright © 2020, original to this collection

"The Numinous in God, Nature, and Horror" copyright © 2018, first appeared in *The Plutonian*, ed. Scott Dwyer

"Palladium at Night" copyright © 2017, first appeared as a chapbook from Dim Shores

"Phantom Airfields" copyright © 2016, first appeared in *Nightscript v. 2*, ed. C.M. Muller

"Professor Cognoscente's Caliginous Charms Carnival" copyright © 2015, first appeared in *Xnoybis #1*, ed. Jordan Krall

"Queer Woman Surgeon" copyright © 2017, first appeared in *Phantasm/Chimera: An Anthology of Strange and Troubling Dreams* as "The Bruised Veil", ed. Scott Dwyer

"SPARAGMOS" copyright © 2017, first appeared in *Looming Low*, eds. Sam Cowan and Justin Steele

"The World is Waiting for the Sunrise" copyright © 2020, original to this collection

Excerpt from "Käthe Kollwitz" in *The Collected Poems of Muriel Rukeyser*, copyright © 2005 by Muriel Rukeyser
Reprinted by permission of ICM Partners

GRIMSCRIBE PRESS

www.ingramcontent.com/pod-product-compliance
Lightning Source LLC
Chambersburg PA
CBHW021229060726

47590CB00005B/1689